The Resurrection of the Gods

The Resurrection of the Gods

Dmitry Merezhkovsky

MINT EDITIONS

The Resurrection of the Gods was first published in 1900.

This edition published by Mint Editions 2021.

ISBN 9781513214719 | E-ISBN 9781513212715

Published by Mint Editions®

minteditionbooks.com

Publishing Director: Jennifer Newens
Design & Production: Rachel Lopez Metzger
Project Manager: Micaela Clark
Translated by: Herbert Trench
Typesetting: Westchester Publishing Services

Contents

Leonardo Da Vinci

"Sentio Rediit Ab Inferis Julianus."
(I feel that Julian has risen again.)

—Petrarch

"We see the encounter of vast contraries: Man-god against God-man—Apollo Belvedere against Christ."

—Dostoievsky

Book I

The White She-Devil—1494

"At Siena was discovered another statue of Venus, to the huge joy of the inhabitants. A great concourse, with much feasting and honour, set it up over the fountain called 'Il Fonte Gaja,' as an adornment. . .

"But great tribulation having come upon the land by reason of the Florentines, there arose one of the council, a citizen, and spake in this wise: 'Fellow-citizens, since the finding of this figure we have had much evil hap, and if we consider how strictly idolatry is prohibited by our faith, what shall we think but that God hath sent us this adversity by reason of sin? I advise that we remove this image from the public square of the city, deface it, break it in pieces, and send it to be buried in the territory of the Florentines.'

*"All agreeing with this opinion, they confirmed it by a decree; and the thing was put into execution, and the statue was buried within our confines." (*Notes of the Florentine sculptor, Lorenzo Ghiberti, XVth. century.*)*

I

In Florence the guild of dyers had their shops hard by the Canonica of Orsanmichele. The houses were disfigured by every sort of shed, outhouse, and projection on crooked wooden supports; tiled roofs leaned so close to each other as almost to shut out the sky, and the street was dark even in the glare of noon. In the doorways below, samples of foreign woollen-stuffs were suspended, sent to Florence to be dyed with litmus-lichen, with madder, or with woad steeped in a corrosive of Tuscan alum. The street was paved roughly, and in the kennel flowed many-coloured streams, oozings from the dye vats. Shields over the portals of the principal shops, or *Fondachi* were blazoned with the arms of the Calimala (so the guild of dyers was named), "on a field gules, an eagle or, upon a ball of wool argent."

Within one of these *Fondachi*, among huge account-books and piles of commercial documents, sat Messer Cipriano Buonaccorsi, a worthy Florentine merchant, and Master of the Noble Guild of the Calimala.

It was a cold March evening, and damp exhaled from the choked and cumbered cellars; the old man was a-cold, and he drew his worn squirrel-mantle tightly round him. A goose-quill was stuck behind his ear, and with omniscient, though weak and myopic eyes, that seemed at once careless and attentive, he conned the parchment leaves of his ponderous ledger; debit to the left, credit to the right; divided by rectangular lines, and annotated in a round, even hand, unadorned by stops, or capitals, or Arabic numerals, which were considered frivolous innovations, impertinent in business-books. On the first page was inscribed in imposing characters; "In the name of our Lord Jesus Christ and the most blessed Virgin Mary, this book is begun in the year of the Lord MCCCCLXXXXIV."

Having corrected an error in the number of bales received in pledge, and satisfied himself as to the latest entries of podded pepper, Mecca ginger, and bundles of cinnamon, Messer Cipriano leaned wearily against the back of his chair, closed his eyes, and meditated upon an epistle he must indite for his emissary at the Wool Fair in Montpellier of France. Just then someone entered, and the old man raising his glance saw his *contadino*, Grillo, who rented from him certain vineyards and fields belonging to his mountain-villa of San Gervaso in the valley of the Mugnone. Grillo did obsequious reverence, tendering a basket of brown eggs, carefully packed, while at his belt clucked two fat chickens, their feet tied and their heads hanging.

"Ah, Grillo!" exclaimed Buonaccorsi, with his customary urbanity, "has the Lord been gracious to you? Meseems, we have the spring season at last."

"Messer Cipriano, to us old men even the spring brings no delight. Our old bones ache worse than before and cry louder for the grave. I have brought your worship eggs and young cockerels for Easter." And he screwed up his greenish eyes, revealing innumerable small creases all round them, the effect of rude acquaintance with wind and sun. Buonaccorsi, having thanked him for the gift, turned to business.

"Well, have you the men ready at the farm? Can we get all done before day-break?"

Grillo sighed prodigiously, and meditated, leaning heavily on his staff. "All is ready, and there are men enough. But I ask you, Messer Cipriano, were it not better we waited a little?"

"Nay, old man, you have said yourself that we must not wait, lest the matter become known."

"True. Yet the thing is terrible. It is sin. And the days now are holydays, days of fasting; and our work is of another sort."

"Well, I will take the sin on my own soul. Fear naught; I will not betray you. Only tell me—shall we find what we seek?"

"Why should we not? We have signs to guide us. Did not our fathers know of the hill behind the mill at the Humid Hollow? And at night there's the Jack o' Lantern over San Giovanni. That means lots of this rubbish all round. I have heard tell that not long ago, when they were digging in the vineyard at Marignola, they drew a whole devil from out the clay."

"A devil? What manner of devil?"

"A bronze one with horns. He had hairy legs—goat's legs—with hoofs. And a face which laughs. And he dances on one leg and snaps his fingers. 'Twas very old; all green and crumbled."

"What did they do with it?"

"They made it into a bell for the new chapel of San Michele."

Messer Cipriano was beside himself. "Grillo, you should have told me of this before!"

"Your worship had gone to Siena."

"You should have sent after me. I would have despatched someone—I would have come myself—I would have grudged no expense—I would have cast ten bells for them in its place. The idiots! To make a Dancing Faun—perhaps a real Scopas—into a bell!"

"Ay, they showed their folly. But, Messer Cipriano, be not wroth. They are punished: for since they hung that new bell the worms have eaten the apples, and the olives have failed. And the tone of the bell is bad."

"How so?"

"That's not for me to say. It hasn't the proper note. It brings no joy to the Christian heart. Somehow it sounds unmeaning. 'Tis what one might expect: one can't get a Christian bell out of a dumb devil. Be it not spoke to anger your worship, but, Messer Cipriano, the good Father is right; of all this filth they dig up, no good is going to come. We must go to work with prudence and defend ourselves with the cross and with prayers; for the Devil is subtle and powerful and the son of a dog, and he creeps in at one ear and out at the other. We were led into temptation even by that stone arm which Zaccheo found at the Hill of the Mill. 'Twas the Evil One tempted us, and we came to harm by it. Lord defend us! 'Tis dreadful even to remember!"

"How got you it, Grillo?"

"The thing happened last autumn on the Eve of Martinmas. We were sitting us down to sup, and the good woman had put the porridge on the table, when my nephew Zaccheo came bursting in from his digging in the field on the Hill of the Mill. 'Master! O master!' he cried, and his face was all drawn and changed, and his teeth chattered. 'The Lord be with you, my son!' says I, and he went on: 'O Lord, master! there's a corpse creeping out from under the pots! Go yourself, master, and see.' So we crossed ourselves and we went. By this time 'twas dark, and the moon was getting up behind the trees. There was the old olive-stump, and beside it where the earth was dug was some shining thing. I stooped, and saw 'twas an arm, very white, and with round dainty fingers, like those of the city ladies. 'Good Lord,' thinks I, 'what sort of devilment is this?' I let down the lantern into the hole, and that arm moved and signalled to me with its finger! That was more than I could bear, and I cried out, and my knees bent under me. But Monna Bonda, my grandame, whom they call a wise woman, and who has all her life in her though she be so old, chided me, saying, 'Fool, what is it you fear? Do not your eyes tell you yon thing is neither of the living nor of the dead, but is a stone?' And she snatched at it and pulled it forth out of the earth. 'Nay, grandame,' I bade her, 'let it be; touch it not; rather let me bury it lest mischief befall us.' 'Not so,' quoth she; 'but take we it to the church, and let the Father exorcise it.' But she deceived me, for she brought it not to the priest, but hid it in the chimney-corner, where in her cot she keeps gear of all sorts—rags, unguents, and herbals, and spells. And when I made insistence, she insisted too and kept it. And from that day 'tis very certain the old beldame hath done cures of great marvel. Is it a toothache? she doth but touch the cheek with the idol and the swelling is gone. She salves fevers, colics, falling sickness. If a cow is in labour and cannot bring forth, Monna Bonda touches her with that same stone hand, and the cow lows, and there's the calf, kicking in the straw. The noise of these wonders has gone abroad, and the old woman has swelled her money-chest. But no good has come of it, for Don Faustino has not allowed me one day's peace. He speaks against me in his preaching, in church before them all. He calls me the son of perdition and the child of the Devil, and he declares he will tell of it to the bishop, and will deny me the Communion. The boys run after me in the street, and point and say, 'There goes Grillo, the sorcerer, and his grandame is a witch, and they have sold themselves to the Evil One.' Even in the night I get no rest. Meseems that stone hand rises up and lies softly on my neck, and then of a sudden takes me by the throat and would strangle me, till I essay to cry out, and cannot. 'Bad jesting, this,' I think to myself. So at last one morning, ere it was light, the old woman having gone forth to pick her herbs, I got up and broke open her cot, and found the thing, and brought it to you. Lotto, the rag-picker, would have given me ten *soldi* for it, and of you I only had eight; but I am ready to sacrifice not only two *soldi*, but even my life for your worship. May the Lord give you His holy benediction, and to Madonna Angelica, and to your sons and your grandsons!"

"It seems, then, by what you tell me, Grillo," said Messer Cipriano thoughtfully, "that we shall have findings on that Hill of the Mill?"

"We are like enough to find," said the old man with a profound sigh; "only we may not tell Don Faustino. If he hear of it he will dress my head without a comb; and he can do your worship a mischief, too, for he can raise the people and not let you finish your work. Well, well—we must pray the Lord to show us mercy! But in the meanwhile, my honoured benefactor, do not abandon me, but say a word for me to the judge."

"What? anent the strip of land the miller would take from you?"

"That is it, master. The miller is a cunning rascal, and he knows how to catch the devil by the tail. I, you see, gave a heifer to the judge; but the miller gave him a lined cow. I fear me the judge will decide for the miller, because the suit is not yet concluded, and already the cow has a fine bull-calf. I pr'ythee, speak for me—father that you are to me. This which we do on the Hill of the Mill, I do only for your kindness. There is no other I would have let bring such a sin upon my conscience."

"Be at ease, Grillo. I will speak for you; the judge is my friend. Now take your steps to the kitchen, and eat and drink. Tonight we will go together to San Gervaso."

The old man, with many reverences, went out, and Messer Cipriano betook himself to his little chamber near the storehouse. It was a museum of marbles and bronzes, hung on walls, arranged on benches. Medals and old coins were assorted on cloth-covered benches; and fragments of statues, not yet pieced together, were waiting in huge cases. Through his trade-agents in many countries he procured antiquities from all classic grounds; from Athens, Smyrna, Halicarnassus, Cyprus, Leucosia, Rhodes, from the remoter Egypt, from the heart of the Levant. The Master of the Guild of the Calimala glanced over his treasures, and then sank into profound consideration of customs-dues on the import of fleeces; and finally composed the letter to his factor at the Wool Fair in Montpellier.

II

Meantime, in the hinder-part of the warehouse, heaped with bales, and lighted only by the glimmer of a lamp before the image of the Madonna, three lads, Dolfo, Antonio, and Giovanni were gossiping together. Dolfo, Messer Buonaccorsi's clerk, a red-haired, snub-nosed, good-natured youth, was entering the number of ells of cloth which Antonio da Vinci, old for his years, with glassy eyes and thin, rough, black locks, was rapidly measuring with the Florentine measure, called a *canna*: Giovanni Boltraffio, a student of painting from Milan, a big boy of nineteen, but shy and awkward, with innocent, sad, grey eyes, and an irresolute expression, was sitting cross-legged on a made-up bale, and listening with all his ears.

"This is what we have come to," cried Antonio excitedly; "digging heathen gods out of the ground!" Then he added, dictating to Dolfo, "of brown Scotch faced-cloth, 32 *braccia*,[1] 6 fingers, 8 nails." Then, having folded the measured piece, he threw it into its place, and raising his finger with the gesture of a menacing prophet, in imitation of Fra Girolamo Savonarola, he cried, "*Gladius Dei super terram cito et velociter!* In the island of Patmos San Giovanni had a vision: he saw the angel lay hold on the dragon, that old serpent, which is the Devil, and bind him a thousand years, and cast him into the bottomless pit, and shut him up, and set a seal upon him, that he should deceive the nations no more till the thousand years should be fulfilled. Today Satan has been released from his prison; today the thousand years are at an end; the false gods, forerunners and followers of Antichrist, are creeping forth from under the seal of the angel back into the world for the temptation of men! Woe to those who live on the earth or on the sea!—Of thin, yellow, Brabant cloth, 17 *braccia*, 4 fingers, 9 nails!"

1. *Braccio*, a measure considerably less than a metre, still in use in Florence.

"How think you, then, Antonio?" asked Giovanni, with alarmed and eager interest; "all these signs bear witness—"

"Ay, ay! You see, the hour has come. Not alone are they digging up the old gods, but they are creating new ones in their likeness. Painters and sculptors alike weary themselves in the service of Moloch—that is, the Devil. They turn the House of God into the temple of Satan; in the sacred pictures, under the guise of martyrs and saints, they paint the gods of uncleanness, and to these the people pray; in place of John the Baptist they give us Bacchus; for the holy Mother of God we get the shameless Venus. The pictures should be burned with fire, and their ashes strewn upon the wind!"

Suppressed fire flashed from the dull, dark eyes of the zealous clerk; and Giovanni, not daring a retort, held his peace. His delicate, childlike eyebrows contracted under the stress of thought. At last, however, he said; "Antonio, they tell me Messer Leonardo, your kinsman, takes scholars into his painting-room. I have long wished—"

Antonio frowned and interrupted him. "If you would lose your soul, Giovanni, then go to Messer Leonardo!"

"What? Why?"

"Though he be my near kinsman, and though he have lived twenty years longer than I, nevertheless in the Scripture it is written: 'From an heretic, after the first and second admonition, turn thou away.' Leonardo is a heretic and an infidel. His mind is darkened by Satanic pride; he seeks to penetrate into the mysteries of nature by steeping himself in mathematics and black magic." Then, raising his eyes to heaven, he repeated from Savonarola's latest discourse; "'The wisdom of this world is foolishness with God. We know them, these learned men; they all go to the house of the devil.'"

"And have you heard, Antonio," persisted Giovanni, still shyly, "that Messer Leonardo is here in Florence? He has even now arrived from Milan."

"For what purpose?"

"The duke has sent him to buy, if possible, pictures from the galleries of the late Lorenzo the Magnificent."

"Well, if he be here, then here he is. 'Tis of no moment to me," said Antonio, turning away; and he proceeded to measure a length of green cloth with his *canna*.

From the church, bells rang out the call to vespers, and Dolfo stretched himself and clapped-to the ledger with an air of relief;

for this day work was over, and the shops and the warehouses were shutting.

Giovanni stepped into the street. A narrow strip of grey sky, faintly tinged with the roseate of evening, showed between the humid roofs: a fine rain fell through the windless air. Suddenly from a window in a neighbouring alley was wafted a song:—

"O vaghe montanine pastorelle
Donde venite si leggiadre e belle?"

(O shepherd-girls so fair,
Say from what mountain air
Light-footed have ye strayed?)

The voice was resonant and young: from the measured beat of the treadle Giovanni guessed at a loom, and at a girl singing as she threw the shuttle. He listened with vague enjoyment, and remembered that the spring had come, and felt his heart swelling with strange emotions of tenderness and melancholy.

"Nanna! Nanna! Where hast thou got to, thou little devil? What hath happened to thine ears? Haste thee! The vermicelli grows cold." After which there was a swift clapping of wooden pattens across the floor, and then silence.

Giovanni stood long, his eyes on the window, the gay song echoing in his ears like the far-off beatings of some shepherd's pipe—

"O vaghe montanine pastorelle—"

Then sighing softly to himself he entered the house of the Master of the Calimala, and mounting the winding stair, with its worm-eaten banisters, he presented himself in the great room, which served as a library, and in which, bending over a desk, was Giorgio Merula, the historiographer of the Court of the Duke of Milan.

III

Merula had come to Florence on a mission from his lord, to purchase rare books from the library of the great Lorenzo. He was lodged in the house of Buonaccorsi, as great an enthusiast as himself for the learning and the arts of the ancients. Journeying to Florence he had fallen into an acquaintance with Giovanni Boltraffio at a road-side inn, and under the pretext that he required an amanuensis, he had brought him in his company to Messer Cipriano's house.

When Boltraffio entered, Merula was in the act of examining with reverent attention a much-worn volume, which had the appearance of a Missal or a Psaltery. He gingerly passed a damp sponge over the parchment—parchment of the most delicate kind, made from the skin of a still-born lamb; here and there he rubbed it with pumice-stone, smoothed it with the blade of a knife and with a polisher; then holding it up to the light, studied it afresh.

"Dainty darlings!" he murmured, sucking in his lips with delight; "come forth to the light of heaven! Ah, how many and how beautiful ye are!"

He raised his bald head from his work and showed a bloated, red-nosed countenance, mobile brows, and eyes small and colourless, but brimming with vivacity; poured wine into a cup beside him on the window-sill, drank it, coughed, and was returning to his work when he caught sight of Giovanni.

"Ha, little monk!" he called out merrily. "You have been lacking to me: 'Where can my little monk be gone?' quoth I. 'Fallen in love, of a surety, with one of the fair maids of Florence.' Fair enough, I warrant you, and falling in love is no sin. Nor have I been wasting my time neither. You never have seen such a pretty piece in your life. Will you have me show her to you? Not I; for you'll be whispering the thing to the four winds! And to think I bought her for a song from a Hebrew rag-vendor! Well, well, I suppose I must show you; you only!" And beckoning mysteriously he whispered, "Come here with you—closer—here!"

And he pointed to a page closely covered with the angular characters of ecclesiastical writing: praises of the Virgin, psalms, prayers, interspersed with huge musical notation. Then he opened the book at another page, and raised it to the light on a level with Giovanni's eyes; the boy noticed that where Merula had scraped away the ecclesiastical writing there emerged other characters—barely distinguishable—not letters, but the ghosts of letters, pallid, attenuated, faint, still lingering impressed upon the parchment.

"See you? See you?" cried Merula, triumphantly; "is it not a darling? Did I not tell you, little brother, 'twas a pretty piece!"

"But what is it?" asked Giovanni, astounded.

"That's what I can't yet tell you. Fragments of an antique anthology; new riches it may be of the Hellenic muse. And, perchance, but for me they would never have come out into God's light—would have been entombed to the end of time under antiphons and psalms of penitence!" And Merula explained to his pupil how some Middle Age, monkish copyist, wishing to use the precious parchment, had expunged, as he thought, the old Pagan writing, and scrawled his pieties over it. As the old man spoke, the sun filled the room with its slowly dying, evening red; in this last radiance the shade of the antique letters, the ghost of the ancient writing, showed itself with redoubled clearness.

"You see! you see!" cried Merula in an ecstasy, "The dead are rising from their age-long sepulchres! It is a hymn to the Olympian gods! Already you can decipher the first lines!"

And translating from the Greek, he read:—

"Glory to the gentle, the richly-crowned Dionysus,
Glory to thee, far-darting Phoebus, silver-bowed, terrible,
God of the flowing curls, slayer of the sons of Niobe—"

And here is a hymn to that Venus, of whom you, little monk, have such a mighty dread:—

"Glory to thee, golden-limbed mother, Aphrodite,
Delight of the gods and of mortals."

But here the verses broke off, hidden under the pious over-writing. Giovanni lowered the book, and at once the traces of the old Greek letters grew faint and confused, sinking into the yellow smoothness of the parchment. Nothing was visible but the clear, black, greasy characters of the monkish scribe, the penitential psalm, and the huge square notes for the chant:—

"Give ear to my prayer, O God, and hide not thyself from my supplication. My heart is sore pained within me, and the terrors of death are fallen upon me."

The roseate reflection faded away, and darkness filled the room. Merula poured wine from the earthen pitcher, drank, and offered it to his companion.

"To my health, boy. *Vinum super omnia bonum diligamus!* You refuse? Well, well! as you will. I will drink for you. But what is ill with you, little monk? You are as green as if you were drowning. Has that bigot of an Antonio been scaring you with his prophesyings? Spit on them, Giovanni, spit on them! A pox upon all these croakings of ill-voiced ravens! Confess now, you have been with Antonio?"

"Ay."

"And of what did he speak?"

"Of Antichrist, and of Messer Leonardo da Vinci."

"So I thought! You have no speech but of Leonardo! Has he bewitched you, simpleton? Hear me now, lad; remove that folly out of your head, and content you as my secretary. I will show you the world; teach you grammar, law; make you an orator and a court poet. There's the road to riches and fame. Painting! what rubbish is that? Seneca called it a trade—no business for a free man. Turn your eyes upon the artists; are they not all ignorant, rude persons—"

"Nay, I have been told Messer Leonardo is a great scholar."

"You tell me news. Where is his Latin, pr'ythee? He confounds Cicero and Quintilian, and has not even a smack of Greek about him. A scholar you call him, do you?"

"But," urged Boltraffio, "he has made wondrous machines; and his studies of the phenomena of nature—"

"Machines! pf—f! Studies of nature! How far is that going to take you? In my *Elegantiæ Linguæ Latinæ* I have culled more than two thousand turns of speech; on my soul, new, and elegance itself. Would you know how much it cost me? But to apply wheels to machinery, and to watch the manner of the flying of birds and the sprouting of the grass in the fields—call you that learning? 'Tis the idleness, the vain toying of babes."

The old man paused: his face had grown stern. Then taking his young friend by the arm, he continued with gravity:—

"Hearken, Giovanni; and what I say to you burn it deep into your mind. Our teachers are the Greeks and the Romans; they have done all that the mind of man can do upon this earth. For us there is nothing left but to follow in their footsteps: is it not written, 'The disciple is not greater than his lord?'" He lifted his wine, and looking straight into Giovanni's eyes with malicious mirth, all his lines and wrinkles dissolving in one broad smile, he added:—

"O youth! youth! I look upon you, little monk, and I envy you. You are a bud blowing in the spring, that is what you are. And you, simpleton, contemn women, and scorn wine, and would make of yourself a hermit and a recluse. For all that, you have a little devil there in your heart; oh, I read you well enough, my friend, through and through to your very soul! Some day that little devil will peep out; it is vain for you to deny it. However glum you may be, there are those who will be merry in your company. See, Giovanni, *carino* you're this parchment—penitential psalms outside, and under them a hymn to Aphrodite!"

"Messer Giorgio," said Giovanni, "it grows dark; were it not well I brought the lights?"

"Why this haste, lad? It pleases me to converse in the twilight, and to recall my lost youth." His tongue had grown stammering and his phrases less perspicuous. "I know," he muttered, "that you are gazing at me, and thinking, 'He is drunk, the old rascal, and talking his folly.' Yet I have that here within me," and he tapped his bald forehead complacently and nodded. "I speak not for boasting," he went on, "but inquire of the scholars whether any have ever surpassed Merula in the elegance of his Latin. Who was it who discovered Martial? Who read the famed inscription on the gate of Tibur? That meant climbing till your head reeled, stones breaking from under your feet, as you clung to a bunch of twigs and thought to fall headlong. Whole days under the blazing sun, just to read and to copy those few ancient letters! And the peasant maids as they passed would cry to each other, 'See yon fat quail up there seeking a nesting place!' And I would answer them with some gallantry, and when they had passed by would set me to my work again. Once, concealed under the ivy and the thorns, where the stones had fallen in ruin, I found these two sole words, '*Gloria Romanorum!*'" And as if listening to the echo of majestic utterance too long silenced, Merula repeated in low, awestruck tones, "'*Gloria Romanorum!*'—Glory of the Romans!"

But then, with an uncertain wave of the hand, he added, "By my troth! 'tis something to remember, even though the past returns no more." And raising his glass, he sang hoarsely the students' drinking-song:—

"Not a single jot miss I,
Not a single drop, Sir!
All my life to the cask I go,
And by the cask I'll stop, Sir.

Wine I love and singing to 't,
And the Latin Graces;
If I drink my throat'll do 't
Better than Horatius.
Vintage spins our brains about
Dum vinum potamus;
Lads, to Bacchus let us shout,
Te Deum laudamus!"

He fell a-coughing and was unable to finish. By this time it was dark, and Giovanni could barely see his master's face. Outside it was still raining, and the swollen and frequent drops plashed noisily in the streaming courtyard below.

"Hear me, little monk," stuttered Merula; "what was it I was saying? My wife is a handsome woman—no—that wasn't it. Have patience. Yes, I have it now. You know the line: '*Tu regere imperio populos, Romane, memento*.' Ah! they were the giants, the lords of the universe!" Here his voice shook, and Giovanni saw tears in his eyes. "I repeat, giants. While today—it is a scandal to speak it! but let us take this duke of ours, Ludovico Il Moro, Duke of Milan. True it is I am paid by him, am writing his history, am a sort of Titus Livius, and am comparing the cowardly hare, the man of straw, to Pompey and to Cæsar; but in my soul, Giovanni, in my soul"—He stopped, and glanced at the door with the suspiciousness of a practised courtier; then bending closer to his companion, he whispered, "In the soul of old Merula the love of liberty is not dead, and will never die. Repeat it not, but I tell you our times are evil, evil as never before. And the men! it sickens me to see them; rotten! mere clods of earth! And they curl up their noses, and think themselves as the ancients. I would fain know what they are so proud of. Hearken; an acquaintance of mine writes to me from Greece, that not many weeks ago in the island of Chios, the convent washer-women as they were beating the linen at dawn, found on the seashore—a god! a real ancient god; a Triton with his fishy-tail, and fins, and scales. The silly fools were affrighted and fled, thinking it the Devil. But when they saw him weak and old, and it would seem sick, lying on his belly on the sand, and warming his green scales in the sun, his hair grey, and his eyes dim as those of a sucking babe, then they took courage, the cowardly wretches! and came around him showering him with Christian prayers, and beat him to death like a dog; he, the ancient deity, last of the mighty gods of the ocean; it might be a scion of Poseidon himself!"

And the old man shook his head sorrowfully, and maudlin tears rolled down his cheeks as he thought of the sea-monster done to death by Christian laundresses. A servant entered bearing a candle, and closed the shutters; with the darkness the pagan phantoms shrank away and vanished. The pair were called to supper, but Merula was so heavy with wine that they had to carry him to bed.

It was long before Boltraffio slept, and as he listened to the peaceful snores of Messer Giorgio, he thought, as usual, of Leonardo da Vinci.

IV

GIOVANNI HAD BEEN SENT TO Florence by his uncle, Oswald Ingrim, the painter on glass (*magister a vitreis*), a German from Grätz, and pupil of Johann Kirchheim, the famous Strasburg master. He was to buy certain transparent and brilliant pigments which could be obtained only in the Tuscan city, and were required by Ingrim for his work in Milan Cathedral. The boy was the natural son of Reinold the lapidary, Oswald's brother, and had got the name of Boltraffio from his Lombard mother, whom Oswald asserted to be a shameless woman and the cause of his brother's ruin. Brought up by his crabbed uncle, Giovanni was a lonely and frightened child, reared on tales of unclean powers, demons, hags, sorcerers, and were-wolves. His special horror was a certain demon which, according to the North Italian tradition, appeared under the form of a woman, and was called the "White She-devil," or the "Mother of the Snowy Eyebrow." Yet even in his earliest infancy, when his uncle would silence his sobs with threats of the *Diavolessa bianca*, the child felt a curiosity mingling with his terror, a shrinking wish that some day he might meet the white one face to face, and behold her countenance with his own eyes.

When the boy was grown, Ingrim handed him over as pupil to Fra Benedetto the sacred painter. This was a kind and simple-minded old man, who taught that the first step in beginning a picture was to invoke God Omnipotent and the beloved Virgin, St. Luke the first Christian painter, and all the saints in Paradise; the second to put on the cloak of charity, fear, patience, and obedience; the last, to temper his colours with yelk of egg, and the juice from young fig-branches mixed with wine, and to prepare his panels of old beechwood by rubbing them with the ashes of bones—if possible the wing bones of capons. His precepts were endless and minute: Giovanni soon learned the contemptuous phrase with which he dismissed the colour known as Dragon's Blood. "Let it lie; 'twill bring you no credit," and Giovanni surmised that the same words had been said by Fra Benedetto's teacher, and by the teacher of his teacher before him. Constant was the smile of quiet pride with which Benedetto initiated his pupil into the secrets of his art. For instance, in the painting of youthful faces the eggs of urban hens were essential: the rural hen laying an egg with a ruddy yelk only suited for the delineation of countenances wrinkled and swarthy. Notwithstanding these subtleties, Fra Benedetto was a painter simple and innocent as a child: he prepared himself for work by fast and vigil; each time he depicted the Crucifixion his face was bathed in tears.

Giovanni loved his master, and had considered him the first of painters; this opinion had however been shaken of late. Fra Benedetto, expounding his one anatomical rule, viz., that the length of a man's body must be reckoned at eight faces and two-thirds, was used to add in the same perfunctory tone in which he spoke of Dragon's Blood; "As for the bodies of women, we will not allude to them, for they have no proportions." This dogma was as much an article of faith with him as these others: that all fish are dark-coloured above and bright below; or that men's ribs are fewer than women's by reason of God's method in the creation of Eve. For an allegorical representation of the elements, he drew a mole to signify earth; a fish, water; a salamander, fire; a chameleon, air; but, supposing the word "chameleon" an augmentative of "camel," the simple monk showed the fluid element as a colossal camel, its jaws gaping alarmingly in its efforts to breathe. Nor were his remaining notions more accurate. Doubts therefore crept into Giovanni's mind, and a mutinous spirit, which Fra Benedetto called "the devil of worldly knowledge." When, shortly before his journey to Florence, the lad chanced to see certain drawings of Leonardo da Vinci's, his doubts grew with such rapidity that he was no longer able to stifle them.

Tonight, here in the Tuscan city, as he lay beside the peacefully-snoring Messer Giorgio, he turned all this over in his mind for the thousandth time; but the more he thought the more puzzled he became. Then he resolved to invoke celestial aid, and full of hope, raising his eyes to the impenetrable darkness of night, he prayed thus:—

"Lord, help me and forsake me not. If Messer Leonardo be truly a godless man, in whose skill lieth temptation and sin, rid me of the thought of him; purge my mind of the memory of his drawings, and deliver me from evil. But if, while pleasing Thee and glorifying Thy name in the noble art of painting, it be yet possible to know all which is hidden from Fra Benedetto, and which I am so fain to learn (such as anatomy, perspective, and the laws of light and shade), then, O God, make strong my will, and lighten my eyes, that I may doubt no more; and permit that Messer Leonardo may receive me into his studio, and that Fra Benedetto may grant me his pardon, and may know that I am in nowise guilty in Thy sight."

After this fervent prayer, Giovanni felt a balsam descend upon his heart: little by little confusion came upon his thoughts; he fancied himself back with his uncle, the glass-worker, and listening to the hissing of the glass as the white-hot steel was plunged into it. He saw the twisting of the leaden ribbons, which form the frames for the several pieces of coloured glass: he heard the voice of Oswald commanding more notches at the edge of the lead for the fixing of the glass; then all vanished: he rolled to his other side and slept.

And a vision came to him, which in after years he often recalled to mind. For he saw himself standing in the gloom of a vast cathedral, and before a many-coloured, Gothic window. On it was depicted the vintage of that mystic vine whereof the Saviour had said, "My Father is the husbandman." The naked body of the Crucified lay in the winepress, blood flowing from His wounds. Popes, cardinals, emperors were receiving it into vats and casks. The Apostles were throwing in grapes; St. Peter was treading them. In the background, prophets and patriarchs were trenching the vineyard and pruning the vines. A waggon was passing, drawn by the lion, the bull, and the eagle, driven by St. Matthew.

Such painted allegories Giovanni had seen in his uncle's workshop; nowhere such colours, dark, yet with the gleam of jewels. Chiefly he marvelled at the crimson of the Saviour's blood. From the depths of the cathedral came the faint echoing of his favourite chant:—

"O fior di castitate,
Odorifero giglio
Con gran suavitate
Sei di color vermiglio."

But the song died away, the window glowed no longer, and the harsh voice of Antonio da Vinci shouted in his ear:—

"Flee! Flee for your life! *She* cometh!"

Nor did he need to inquire who, for he knew the *Diavolessa bianca* was behind him. A waft of icy air; and then a heavy hand, not human, had taken hold at his throat, and was choking him. He seemed to be dying, cried out, and awoke—to see Messer Giorgio standing by his side and dragging away the coverlet.

"Eh! pull yourself from your bed or they will depart without us. Arise! the hour is already past," cried the antiquarian.

"What! Whither?" stammered Giovanni, half-asleep.

"Whither? Can you forget? To the villa of San Gervaso, to dig at the Hill of the Mill."

"I go not thither."

"You go not? What have I waked you for? Why have I bidden them saddle the black mule that the two of us may travel at ease? A truce to this stubbornness. Get up! Get up! Nay, then, a word in your ear, Giovannino: Messer Leonardo will be there."

Giovanni leaped to his feet, and without another word threw on his clothes.

Presently they were in the courtyard, where all was ready for the start. Grillo was running hither and thither advising and directing. At last they set out. Other friends of Cipriano's, and among them Leonardo da Vinci, were to meet them later, by another path to San Gervaso.

V

The rain was over, and the north wind had banished the clouds. Stars scintillated in the moonless heaven, like little wind-blown lamps. Resin-torches flared and fluttered, scattering sparks. The horsemen took their way by the Via Ricasoli, past San Marco and the serrated gate of San Gallo. Here the sentinels argued and swore, but were too sleepy to perceive what was on foot; and presently egress was secured by a good bribe. Outside the gate, the road followed the deep and narrow valley of the Mugnone. After passing several meagre villages, where the streets were even narrower than those in Florence, and the rough stone houses were as tall as fortresses, the party emerged into an olive-grove owned by the *contadini* of San Gervaso. Dismounting at the junction of two roads, they walked to the Hill of the Mill, hard by Messer Cipriano's vineyard. Here men awaited them with spades and mattocks; and here, behind the hill, beyond the marsh known as the Humid Hollow, the villa walls showed shadowy white through the darkness of the trees. Tall cypresses stood up black from the summit of the hill, and down below on the Mugnone was the name-giving watermill.

Grillo signified where, to his thinking, they ought to dig; Merula suggested another place; and Strocco, the gardener, swore they must go lower down, much nearer to the Humid Hollow, because the devils always hide themselves nearest to the slough. Cipriano, however, bade dig where Grillo advised; the spades grated, and soon there was an odour of new-dug earth. Giovanni shuddered, for a bat had brushed his face with its weird pinions; but Merula clapped him on the shoulder, crying, "Fear nothing, little monk! we shall find no devil here. This Grillo is an ass. Thank heaven, it's not the sort of excavation I'm used to. At Rome, in the 45th Olympiad" (Merula scorned the Christian calendar), "in the days of Pope Innocent VIII, diggers from Lombardy, who were working on the Appian Way close to the tomb of Cæcilia Metella, found an ancient sarcophagus with the inscription, 'Julia, daughter of Claudius,' and in it a body clothed in wax—a fair maid of fifteen, with the semblance of one asleep. You would have sworn she breathed: the flush of life was on her cheek. Multitudes flocked to the tomb and refused to leave it; for such was Julia's beauty, as to be incredible to those who had not beheld it. But it ill-suited the Pope that his children should adore a dead heathen, and he caused the body to be interred secretly under the Pincian Hill. Do you take me, lad? That was something like excavating!"

And Merula contemptuously kicked the clods which the diggers were throwing up at his feet. Suddenly all the onlookers started, for a jarring sound had come from one of the spades.

"Bones!" said the gardener; "the ancient burying-place was here."

At this moment the long-drawn howl of a dog was heard from San Gervaso, and Giovanni thought, "We are profaning a grave. May it prove nothing worse!"

"Bones of a horse!" cried Strocco contemptuously, and dragged out a mouldered, long-shaped skull.

"Grillo," said Messer Cipriano anxiously, "were it not better we tried elsewhere?"

"Did I not say so?" cried Merula; and taking two of the workmen with him he began new operations at the base of the hill. Strocco also had detached a party to dig in the Humid Hollow.

Presently excited shouts were heard from Messer Giorgio.

"Hither all ye simpletons! Did not I know where ye should dig?"

All ran to his side; but again the treasure proved naught; the great man's marble fragment was only an ordinary stone. They had all deserted Grillo, who, openly humiliated, was digging alone by the light of a broken lantern.

The wind had fallen and the air grew warmer: out of the Humid Hollow exhaled a mist. The breath of primroses and violets mingled with the dankness of stagnant water. Dawn was in the sky, and the cocks crowed for the second time, signal of the departing of night.

Suddenly from the depths of the pit in which Grillo was concealed there arose a despairing yell.

"Help! Help! I am falling! The ground has given way!"

His lantern was extinguished, and at first nothing could be seen. He was heard struggling and panting, groaning and moaning. Lights were fetched, and disclosed the roof of a subterranean vault broken through by Grillo's weight. Two lads crept into the hole.

"Eh, Grillo! Where are you? Give us your hand! or are you buried alive, poor fool?"

But Grillo seemed to have lost his voice. Heedless of a sprained arm, he dragged himself along, kicking and struggling most strangely. At last he burst into an ecstasy:—

"An idol! An idol! Hasten, Messer Cipriano! 'tis a magnificent idol!"

"Idiot," said Strocco, "you have got the head of another horse."

"I tell you, No! There is but a hand missing. The rest is perfect—feet, head, shoulders!" shouted Grillo beside himself.

Then the labourers descended into the pit, carefully turning over the brickwork ruins. Giovanni, stretched on the ground, looked down into the vault, from which came the chill of a grave, and the mouldy breath of long-covered damp.

Messer Cipriano bade the men stand aside, and Giovanni could see in the profundity between the walls of ancient red brick, a white and naked body which lay like a corpse upon a bier, yet in the flaring of the torchlight seemed rosy and warm with life.

"Venus!" cried Messer Giorgio; "As I live, the Venus of Praxiteles! I cry you honour, friend Cipriano! Not the dukedoms of Milan or Genoa could bring you greater felicity!"

As for Grillo, they dug him out; and though his face was clotted with blood, and his arm had swelled into uselessness, in his old eyes shone the pride of a conqueror.

"Grillo! friend! beloved! benefactor! And I scorned you for a fool: and you—you are the cleverest of men!" cried Messer Giorgio, and falling into his arms he kissed him with deep emotion.

"Once," he continued garrulously, "Filippo Brunelleschi found a Hermes in just such a vault under his own house. Doubtless the pagans, knowing the value of these statues, hid them from the fury of the Christians, who were exterminating the old worship."

Grillo listened, smiling beatifically, inattentive to the pipe of the shepherd and the bleating of sheep. He saw not that the sky shone now with a white and watery brilliance, nor knew that from Florence the belfries were exchanging their morning salutation.

"Gently! gently! To the right there! So! Keep it out from the wall!" cried Messer Cipriano. "Five silver pieces to each, if you can get it out without breakage."

By this time the stars had all disappeared with the exception of the orb of Venus, which still sparkled like a diamond in the glow of day. And slowly, slowly, with her ineffable smile, the goddess herself arose—as once she had risen from the foam of the sea, so now she ascended from her millennial tomb in the darkness of the earth:—

"Glory to thee, golden-limbed Aphrodite,
Delight of the gods and of mortals. . ."

declaimed Merula.

But Giovanni saw her face blanched in the illumination of the white sunlight; and himself paling with terror, the boy murmured, "*La Diavolessa bianca!*"

He rose up and would have fled; but wonder overcame his fear. Not though he had known himself guilty of the mortal sin which is punished with eternal fire, could he have torn his gaze from that chaste and naked body, from that countenance flaming with the effulgence of beauty. Never in the days when Aphrodite was queen of the world had any worshipped her with devouter trembling.

VI

Suddenly from the little church of San Gervaso the bells rang out, and the whole company turned and involuntarily paused in their work, for in the morning stillness the sound seemed irate and menacing.

"Lord have mercy on our souls!" murmured Grillo, putting his hand to his head with a despairing gesture. "Here is Don Faustino, and a multitude with him! They have seen us! Look how they beat their hands and beckon. See, they rush upon us! I am a lost man!"

At this moment arrived those friends of Messer Cipriano's, who had intended to have been present for the excavation, but who had lost their way. Boltraffio threw a glance at them, and, absorbed though he still was in the new-found goddess, his attention was caught on the instant by one of the newcomers. This personage was already inspecting the Venus, with a cold, imperturbable composure, so different from Giovanni's personal agitation, that the lad could not but be struck with astonishment. He continued to gaze at the statue, but his consciousness now was entirely for the man by his side.

"Hearken!" said Messer Cipriano after a few moments' thought, "the villa is not two paces distant, and the doors are strong enough for a siege."

"Yea, verily," cried Grillo; "courage, brothers, we shall save her!" He felt jealous for the image which had cost him so much, and directing the operations himself, he contrived to get it safely transported across the Humid Hollow. Then the statue was borne into the house; but scarcely had it crossed the threshold, when on the hill-top appeared the threatening figure, inflamed countenance and brandished arms of Don Faustino.

The lower part of the villa was at present uninhabited, and its great hall was used as a storehouse for agricultural implements and great jars of olive-oil: in one corner was a mountain of golden straw. Upon this straw, a humble, rustic bed, Aphrodite was delicately laid to rest. But this was no sooner accomplished and the doors barred than the latter were assailed by blows, by shouts, and by curses loud and deep.

"Open! Open!" cried the cracked voice of Don Faustino; "in the name of the true and living God, I bid you open!"

Messer Cipriano mounted the stone inner staircase and surveyed the crowd from a grated window above the hall. Seeing that the assailants were few, he entered into parley, his face wearing his customary smile. But the priest put his fingers in his ears, and vociferously demanded the idol—so he named it—which had been dug out of the ground.

The Master of the Calimala now had recourse to a *ruse de guerre*.

"Beware," he said calmly; "I have summoned the captain of the town guard, and in two hours the horsemen will be on you. I allow none to enter my house by force."

"Break down the door," cried the priest. "God is with us. Fear nothing! Assault!" And snatching an axe from a gentle-faced old peasant beside him, he battered upon the great door with all his strength.

"Don Faustino! Don Faustino!" cried the old man, feebly restraining the furious ecclesiastic, "we are poor folk, and we do not dig up money in our fields. This will be our ruin; they will have us to prison!"

The mention of the redoubtable town guard had struck terror into the rabble; and many were already deserting.

"If it had been on the church-ground, 'twere another matter," muttered some of them.

"The confines established by law—"

"The law? A spider's web, set to catch flies, not hornets. The law does not exist for great folk."

"True for you. And every man is master on his own land."

All this time Giovanni was gazing at the rescued Venus.

The sunshine pouring through a side window seemed waking the tender body to warmth and softness after its long imprisonment in the gloom and the chill of the vault; the golden straw surrounding it shone like an aureole.

Giovanni once more noted the stranger. He was on his knees beside the statue, measuring it with his compasses, his square, and a half-circle made of copper; on his face was the same imperturbable calm; in his cold, blue eyes the same piercing curiosity.

"What is he doing? Who is he?" Giovanni asked himself, almost awestruck, as he watched the quick, bold fingers exploring the limbs of the goddess, the secrets of her beauty, all the subtleties of the marble, too delicate for the apprehension of the eye.

At the gate of the villa the priest was still heard yelling at the melting crowd.

"Stay, rascals! Sellers of Christ! fearful of the town guard, but careless of Antichrist! *Ipse vero Antichristus opes malorum effodiet et exponet*, as said the great preacher St. Anselm of Canterbury. *Effodiet*, hear you?

Antichrist shall dig up the old idols from the earth and again bring them forth to the world."

But none heeded him.

"He is a pestilent fellow, this Don Faustino of ours!" said the prudent miller shaking his head; "his life hangs by a thread, yet see how he storms. For my part, I rejoice they have found the treasure."

"They say the image is of silver."

"Silver? Nay, I saw it myself, and 'tis of marble; naked and shameless."

"Lord forgive us! Are we to soil our hands for such rubbish as that?"

"Whither art going, Zacchello?"

"To the field; to my work."

"God go with you! And I'll to the vineyard."

At this all the fury of the priest was let loose on his parishioners.

"Infidel dogs, abortions of Cain! would you abandon your pastor? Know ye not, spawn of Satan, that did I not pray for you day and night, and beat my breast with weeping and fasting, your whole sinful village would long ere this have been sunk into the earth? But it is ended! I leave you, shaking off the dust from my feet. Cursed be the land! Cursed the corn and the water and the flocks; and your sons and your sons' sons. I am your father, your shepherd no more. I renounce you! Anathema!"

VII

In the restored calm of the villa, where the goddess lay on her golden bed, Giorgio Merula went up to the stranger who was still measuring.

"You are studying the proportions of divinity?" said the scholar patronisingly; "You would reduce beauty to mathematics?"

The other raised his eyes for an instant; then silently, as if he had not heard the question, continued his work. The compasses contracted and expanded, describing geometrical figures; quietly and firmly the stranger put the angle measure to the fair lips of Aphrodite—lips whose smile had struck terror into Giovanni's heart—reckoned the result, and set it in a note-book.

"Pardon my curiosity," insisted Merula, "how many divisions are there?"

"This is a rough measurement," said the unknown, unwillingly; "generally I divide the human face into degrees, minutes, seconds and thirds, each division being the twelfth part of the preceding one."

"Say you so?" cried Merula, "meseems the last subdivision must be less than the finest hair."

"A third," explained the other still grudgingly, "is 1/48823 of the whole face."

Merula lifted his eyebrows with an incredulous smile. "Well, we live and learn. I never thought it were possible to reach such accuracy."

"The more accurate the better," returned his companion.

"Truly it may be so; yet, you know, in Art, in Beauty, all these mathematical calculations—What artist in the glow of enthusiasm, of fiery inspiration, breathed upon by God—"

"Yes, yes," assented the unknown, evidently wearied; "none the less I am anxious to know—"

And stooping he measured the distance from the roots of the hair to the chin.

"To know?" thought Giovanni. "Can one *know* these matters? Folly! Does he not *feel*? understand?"

Merula, anxious to probe the other to the quick, talked on of the ancients, and how they should be imitated. The stranger waited till he had concluded, then said, smiling into his long golden beard:—

"He who can drink from the fountain will not drink from the cup."

"By your leave!" shouted the scholar, "if you call the ancients a cup, whom do you call the fountain?"

"Nature," said the unknown quietly.

And Merula presumptuously and provokingly continuing to prate, he disputed no further, but assented with evasive politeness. Only in his cold eyes weariness and reserve became more manifest. At last Messer Giorgio, having come to the end of his argument, was reduced to silence. Then the other pointed out certain depressions in the marble, which in no light could be detected by the sight, yet were plain to the touch as the hand moved over the smooth surface. "*Moltissime dolcezze*," he called them; and then his eye travelled over the figure, as if in one look he would possess himself of its sum.

"And I who thought he did not feel!" said Giovanni to himself. "Yet if he feels, how can he measure and split it up into numbers? Who is he, Messer Giorgio?" he whispered; "tell me the name of this man?"

"Ha, little monk! is it you?" said Merula turning round; "I had forgot you. Nay, but it is your idol: can it be that you knew him not? It is Messer Leonardo da Vinci."

And the historian presented Giovanni to the Master.

VIII

Through the perfect stillness of early morning in the early spring, when the grass shone emerald between the black olive-roots and the blue iris-flowers were motionless on their slender stems, Giovanni and Leonardo, he on horseback, the lad on foot, returned together to Florence.

"Is this really he?" thought Giovanni, watching him and finding his minutest gesture interesting.

He was over forty. When silent and pensive his small, keen, pale-blue eyes, under overhanging golden eyebrows, seemed cold and piercing; yet when he talked they took an expression of great good nature. The long, fair beard and curling and luxuriant hair gave him an air of majesty. He was tall and powerful in build, yet his face had a subtle charm which was almost feminine, and his thin high voice, though pleasant, was not manly. His hand, reining a restive steed, was very strong, yet it also was delicate, with long, slender fingers like a woman's.

They were nearing the town walls; and the misty morning sun shone upon the dome of the cathedral, and the quaint tower of the Palazzo Vecchio.

"This is my opportunity," thought Boltraffio. "I must tell him I would fain enter his studio as a pupil."

Just then Leonardo checked his horse and fixed his eyes on a young falcon circling slowly and easily in the air above its quarry—some duck or heron in the reeds of the Mugnone's bank. Presently, with a short cry, it dropped headlong, like a stone, swooping down from the height and disappearing behind the trees. Leonardo had followed it with his gaze, not losing a single turn, a movement, a flap of the strong wings; then he took his note-book from his girdle and jotted down the result of his observation.

Boltraffio noticed that he held the pencil in his left hand; and remembered strange tales he had heard of his writing in a mysterious reversed hand only to be read in a mirror, from right to left, as men write in the East. Some said he wrote thus to make an enigma of his wicked heretical opinions about nature and about God.

"Now or never!" Giovanni was saying to himself; but all at once Antonio's harsh words flashed across his mind; "'Go to him if you would lose your soul: he is a sinner and an atheist.'"

Smiling, Leonardo drew his attention to an almond-tree, on the crest of a bare, wind-swept hill, very small, very feeble, very solitary, yet already hopeful and joyous, and decking itself with pale blossoms, which gleamed and glistened against the azure of the sunlit sky.

Boltraffio could not admire it, for his heart was heavy and perplexed. Then Leonardo, as if guessing at his disquietude, spoke gentle words which the young man remembered long afterwards.

"If you wish to be an artist, put away all grief and care from your mind, save that for art itself. Let your soul be as a mirror reflecting all objects, all colours, all movements, but itself remaining ever clear and unmoved."

They passed in through the gates of Florence.

IX

BOLTRAFFIO WENT TO THE CATHEDRAL, where that morning Fra Girolamo Savonarola was to preach. As he entered, the last notes of the organ were dying away under the resounding arches of Santa Maria del Fiore. The throng had filled the church with suffocating heat and with the low rustlings of unceasing small movements. Men, women, and children were separated from each other by drawn curtains. Under the arches, slender and narrow like arrow-heads, deep gloom and mystery reigned as in a sleeping forest. The rays of sunlight, refracted by brilliantly coloured glass, fell in rainbow hues upon the congregation and upon the grey marble of the pillars. The semi-darkness surrounding the altar was broken by the glare of candles. Mass was over and the crowd was awaiting the preacher. All looks were fixed on the wooden pulpit.

Giovanni found a place in the crowd and listened to the whisperings of his neighbours.

"Will he come soon?" was asked impatiently by a carpenter of low stature, with a pale perspiring face and lank hair bound by a fillet.

"God knows!" responded a tinker, big and red-faced, but asthmatic. "He has with him at San Marco a certain little brother named Marufi, with a hunchback and a stammering tongue, and 'tis he chooses the hour for his coming. We waited four hours once, and had thought there would be no preaching, yet in the end he came."

"*Santo Dio Benedetto!* And I have waited since midnight! I am blind for sleep and for want of a crumb in my mouth. I could sit down upon knives!"

"Did I not tell thee, Damiano, 'twas matter of patience? Even now we are so far from the pulpit we shall hear naught."

"Eh! We shall hear well enough. When he falls to at his shouting and his thundering, not the deaf only but the very dead must needs hear."

"They say now, that he prophesies."

"Not yet! Not till he has built Noah's Ark."

"He has built it; to the last plank. Yea, and made a parabolic description thereof. Its length, Faith; its breadth; Charity; its altitude, Hope. Haste, he says, haste to the Ark of Salvation, while the doors stand wide. The day cometh when the doors will be put to, and then many shall weep that they have not repented and have not come in time to enter within. Today he preaches of the Flood, the seventeenth verse of the sixth chapter of the book of Genesis."

"They say he has had another vision, War, Pestilence!"

"The horsedealer in Vallombrosa said that a night or two agone great hosts fought in the sky over the city, and one could hear the clash of swords and the dinting of armour."

"And it is a certainty, good folk, that on the *Nunziata* in the Chiesa dei Servi has been seen a bloody sweat."

"Go to! And tears run nightly from the Madonna on the Rubaconte bridge. Lucia, my aunt, saw it herself!"

"And it means no good, rest assured. The Lord have mercy on us, miserable sinners!"

Meanwhile, among the women, there was a disturbance. An old woman fainted, and when lifted up, still did not recover her senses. The whole multitude indeed was worn by the interminable waiting; the pale carpenter seemed unable to sustain himself longer.

But suddenly a wave stirred the sea of heads, and a whisper ran through the church.

"He is coming!"

"Nay, 'tis not he, 'tis Fra Domenico da Pescia."

"I tell you, yea, 'tis he! He has come."

Giovanni saw a man in the black and white Dominican habit girdled with a rope, who slowly ascended the pulpit-stair and removed his cowl. His face was emaciated and yellow as wax, his lips thick, his nose aquiline, his forehead low. His left hand fell weakly on the desk, his right he raised clutching the crucifix; and silently with burning eyes he looked upon the trembling and expectant crowd. Profound silence reigned, in which each man could hear the beating of his own heart.

The eyes of the monk glowed increasingly, till they were like fiery coals; but he still kept silence, and the strain of waiting became unendurable. It seemed that in another moment the crowd would burst into screams.

Yet the calm became deeper, more awful; till suddenly, rending the silence, came the terrible, lacerating, superhuman cry of the friar:—

"*Ecce ego adduco aquas super terram*, Behold I bring a Flood upon the earth!"

A shudder passed through the crowd, raising the hair from the head. Giovanni paled; he fancied the earth quaking, the cathedral arches about to fall. Beside him the stalwart tinker was shaking like a leaf, his teeth chattering. The head of the feeble carpenter had sunk backward on his shoulders as if he had received a blow, his face was shrivelled, his eyelids closed.

What followed was not a sermon but a delirium, which took hold of these thousands of people and shook them as a storm shakes the withered leaves. Giovanni listened, scarcely understanding. Detached phrases reached his ear:—

"See ye, see how the heavens have already darkened; the sun is purple, like clotted blood. Flee! Hide yourselves! There cometh even now a rain of brimstone and fire; a hail of fiery stones and thunderbolts. *Fuge O Sion quae habitas apud filiam Babylonis!* O Italy, chastisement cometh upon chastisement. After pestilence, war; and hunger after war! Judgment is here, judgment is there! Everywhere there is judgment. Among you the living suffice not to carry the dead. The dead in your houses shall be so many that the grave-diggers shall call to you to throw them out, and shall heap them on carts, yea, to the very necks of the horses, and shall throw them one upon the other and burn them. And then again they shall go through the streets and cry, 'Who has any dead? Who has any dead?' And you will answer them: 'I throw to you my son, I throw to you my brother, I throw to you my husband!' And then they shall go further, and always they shall cry: 'Bring forth your dead! bring forth your dead!' O Florence! O Rome! O Italy! Past is the time of songs and of feasting; ye are sickened unto death. Lord, Thou art witness, that with my words I would have averted this ruin! But I can no more. I have no words more. I can but weep, and run over with my tears. Mercy! Mercy! O merciful Lord! Alas! my poor people! Alas! my Florence!"

He opened his arms, and the last words had sunk to a scarcely audible whisper. They passed over the crowd and died away, like the rustle of wind in the leaves—a sigh of infinite pity.

Pressing his white lips on the crucifix, he knelt and burst into sobs. The sermon was ended. The slow, heavy organ-notes rolled out, persuasive and immense, increasingly solemn and terrible, like the sound of the mighty ocean.

A woman's voice cried "*Misericordia!*"

And thousands of voices answered, calling one to another; and like corn stalks bowing before the wind, the people fell upon their knees, line upon line, wave upon wave, crowding upon, striking against each other, like a flock of sheep panic-struck at the advance of a storm; and the long, agonising wail of penitents upon whom pressed the terror of immediate ruin, rose to Heaven, mingling with the pealing of music, shaking the ground, the marble pillars, and the vaults of the cathedral.

"*Misericordia! Misericordia!*"

Giovanni also sank to his knees, sobbing. The tall tinker rolled against him, breathing hard; the pale carpenter caught his breath and cried like a child, moaning—

"*Misericordia!*"

And Boltraffio remembered his pride, and his love of life, his desire to escape from Fra Benedetto, and to give himself up to the dangerous arts of Messer Leonardo, the enemy of God; he recalled the past fearful night on the Hill of the Mill, the recovered Venus, his sinful enthusiasm for the heathen beauty of the "White She-devil"; stretching forth his hands to heaven, he mingled his voice with that of the despairing crowd, and cried—

"Lord! Lord! have compassion on me! I have sinned before thee. Pardon, and have mercy."

At that moment, raising his face, wet with tears, he saw at his side the tall, upright form of Leonardo da Vinci. The artist, leaning carelessly against a column, held in his right hand his unfailing sketch-book; with his left he was drawing; now and then he glanced at the pulpit as if hoping to see once more the head of the preacher.

A stranger, and surrounded by the terrified crowd, Leonardo maintained a superb composure. In his cool, blue eyes, on his thin lips, tightly compressed like those of a man of minute observation, there was the same aloofness and curiosity with which he had mathematically measured the body of the Aphrodite. At sight of him the tears dried in Giovanni's eyes, and the prayer was silenced upon his lips.

Leaving the church he followed the artist and asked permission to see his sketch. Leonardo demurred, but presently handed the boy his sketch-book. And Giovanni saw a frightful caricature; not Savonarola, but an old and hideous devil in the dress of a monk, like the preacher indeed, but as if disfigured by self-inflicted and torturing penance, his pride and his desires still unsubdued. The lower jaw protruded, wrinkles intersected the cheek, the neck was twisted and black as a mummy's, the bushy, beetling brows, the rabid glance scarce preserved a semblance of humanity. All that was dark, terrible, and superstitious, all which gave Savonarola into the power of the deformed, tongue-tied visionary Marufi, was expressed by Leonardo in this sketch; brought out with neither anger nor pity, but with an imperturbable and impartial clear-sightedness.

And Giovanni remembered his words; "*L'ingegno dell' pittore vuol essere a similitudine dello specchio*. The genius of the painter should be as a mirror, reflecting all objects, and colours, and movements, itself ever transparent and serene."

The pupil of Benedetto raised his eyes to the artist's face, and felt that though threatened by eternal damnation, though he were to find in Messer Leonardo a veritable servant of Antichrist, yet to leave him had become impossible; an irresistible force was drawing him to this man; woe unto him if he failed to penetrate into the very depths of this being and of his art.

X

Two days later, Messer Cipriano having been detained by affairs in Florence, and unable to arrange for the transport of the Venus, Grillo burst in upon him with most unwelcome tidings. Don Faustino, it seemed, had left San Gervaso and betaken himself to San Maurizio, the neighbouring village. Here, having terrified the people with talk of the chastisement of Heaven, he had collected a party by night, besieged the villa, broken in the doors, thrashed Strocco the gardener, who had been left in charge of the statue, and bound him hand and foot. Then the priest had recited over the goddess an ancient prayer called "*Oratio super effigies vasaque in loco antiqua reperta*," in which the servant of the Church asks God to purify all statuary, vessels, and other objects dug out of the ground, and to convert them to the profit of Christian souls, to the glory of the Trinity, "*ut, omni immunditia depulsa, sint fidelibus tuis utenda per Christum dominum nostrum*." Then they broke up the statue of the goddess, cast the fragments into a furnace, made of them a cement, and with it daubed the new-raised wall of the village cemetery.

As he told this tale the old man wept for grief. But the event helped Giovanni Boltraffio to a decision. That very day he presented himself before Messer Leonardo and begged to be received as a pupil. Leonardo accepted him.

A little later, tidings were brought to Florence that Charles VIII, Most Christian King of France, had taken the field with a countless host for the conquering of the Two Sicilies, and probably also of Rome and Florence. Panic spread among the citizens. They perceived that the prophecy of Savonarola was being fulfilled. Punishment was at their door! The sword of the Lord was drawn upon Italy!

Book II

Ecce Deus—Ecce Homo—1494

"Behold the man!"

—St. John xix. 5

"Behold the God!"

(Inscription on the monument of Francesco Sforza.)

I

"If the eagle can sustain himself in the rarest atmosphere, if great ships by sails can float across the waves, why cannot likewise Man, by means of powerful wings, make himself lord of the winds, and rise, the conqueror of space?"

Leonardo found these words in one of his old note-books, written five years earlier with the buoyancy of hope. Opposite was the sketch of a machine; a beam, to which by means of iron rods, were attached wings to be moved by cords and pulleys. Now the apparatus seemed to him clumsy and absurd.

His new machine was like an enormous bat. The body of the wings was formed by five wooden fingers, like a skeleton hand, with many joints and pliant articulations. Tendons and muscles connecting these fingers were formed by strips of tanned leather and laces of raw silk. The wing rose by means of a crank and a moveable piston, and was covered by impermeable taffeta. It resembled the webbed foot of a goose. There were four wings moving in turn like the legs of a horse. Their length was forty *braccia*, their spread, eight. They bent backward for propulsion, and dropped to make the machine rise. A man was to sit in it astride, and with his feet in stirrups was to move the wings by a machinery of cords, blocks, and levers. A great rudder, feathered like the tail of a bird, was to be turned by his head.

But a bird, before the first flap of his wings carries him from the earth, must first raise himself by his feet. The short-legged swift, for instance, if placed upon the ground struggles but cannot fly. Therefore in the machine two cane stilts were indispensable, although their inelegance greatly disturbed the inventor. Perfection could not exist without beauty. He plunged into calculations, hoping to lay his finger on a blunder. Failing, he impatiently drew a pencil across a whole page of figures and wrote on the margin—

"Incorrect"; and presently, "*Satanasso!*" He was enraged.

Then he recommenced; but his calculations became more and more confused, and the scarce perceptible error grew increasingly distinct, as he worked on and on by the light of a flickering candle which offended his eyes.

Then his cat, suddenly waking, leaped on the work-table, stretched himself, humped his back, and began to play with a moth-eaten scarecrow of a stuffed bird dangling from a wooden perch—a contrivance for studying the centre of gravity in the act of flight. The inventor pushed the cat angrily away, nearly knocking him down and causing a plaintive mewing.

"Bless your heart! you may go where you like so long as you don't interfere with me," said Leonardo apologetically, rubbing the smooth, black fur which emitted electric sparks. The cat purred, sat down majestically, doubling his velvet paws under him, and fixing on his master steady green eyes full of self-satisfaction and mystery.

Once more figures, fractions, brackets, equations, cubic and square roots appeared upon the paper. It was the second night he had passed without sleep; for a whole month since his return from Florence he had scarcely set foot outside the house, but had worked unceasingly at the flying-machine.

The branches of a white acacia intruded through an open window, and sometimes cast on the table their tender, odorous blossoms. The moonlight, softened by a mist of clouds, tinted like mother-o'-pearl, flooded the chamber, and mingled with the murky illumination from the tallow candle. The room was choked with machinery and instruments, astronomical, physical, chemical, mechanical, and anatomical. Wheels, levers, springs, screws, chimneys, pistons, arcs, suction-tubes, brass, steel, iron, and glass, like the limbs of half-seen monsters or colossal insects, peered out of the darkness. There was a diving-bell, beside it the dulled crystal of an optical apparatus resembling a great eye; then the skeleton of a horse, a stuffed crocodile, a human abortion preserved in spirit, a pair of boat-shaped shoes for walking on the water, and lastly, the clay head of a child or of an angel, strayed hither from the sculptor's studio, and smiling slyly and mournfully at its surroundings. In the background was a crucible and blacksmith's bellows, and coals lay red upon the ashes of a furnace. Gigantic wings, one still bare, the other already invested with its membrane, were spread out over all the room, dominating the whole from floor to ceiling. And sprawling on the ground, with nodding head, lay a man, Zoroastro, Leonardo's assistant, who had fallen asleep at his post, oil flowing from the blackened brass ladle which he held in his hand. One of the wings touched the chest of the sleeper, and was softly vibrating as he breathed; it seemed alive, and its sharp upper end rustled against the rafters of the ceiling.

In the uncertain light the machine, with this man between its extended and moving wings, was like some stupendous vampire ready to rise and fly.

II

Gardens surrounded Leonardo's house outside Milan—between the fortress and the Convent of Santa Maria delle Grazie—and thence came a fine perfume of fruits and herbs, thyme, and bergamot, and fennel. The moon had set. Swallows under the windows were twittering and preparing to fly, ducks splashed and quacked in the neighbouring pond. The candle was dying in its socket; voices of the pupils were heard from the studio hard by.

The students were two, Giovanni Boltraffio and Andrea Salaino. Giovanni was copying an anatomical figure, and sitting before a contrivance for the study of perspective—a wooden frame with a string network which corresponded with lines traced on the drawing-paper: Salaino was fitting a slab of alabaster to a wooden panel. He was a pretty lad with innocent eyes and fair curls, petted by the Master, who drew his angels from him.

"How think you, Andrea?" asked Boltraffio, "will Messer Leonardo soon finish this machine?"

"God knows!" answered Salaino whistling, and settling the embroidered flaps of his new slippers. "Last year he sat two months at it and nothing resulted but laughter. That crooked bear Zoroastro set himself to fly at all hazards. The master forbade him, but he did it. The fool hung himself all round with a necklace of bullock's bladders, lest he should break anything if he fell; then he mounted the roof, flapped his wings; and true it is he rose, but God wot 'twas the wind carried him, and presently he turned topsy-turvy and fell plump on to a dunghill; by the Lord's mercy 'twas soft and he broke no bones, but the bladders burst with a roar like a cannon, the daws in the belfry fled away for very terror, and there lay the new Icarus kicking the air, on his head in the manure."

Just then the third pupil entered, Cesare da Sesto, a man no longer young; sickly, and splenetic, with malicious but intelligent eyes. He had a sandwich in one hand, wine in the other.

"Peuh! the sour stuff!" he said frowning and spitting, "and the ham, by my troth, is boot-leather—yet one pays two thousand ducats annually for these delicacies!"

"Try the other cask from under the pantry stair."

"I have tried it. Of the two 'tis the worse"; then pointing to Salaino's new plum-coloured and gaily-feathered cap, he added, "Oho! oho! some of us, it seems, get new things. But 'tis the second month since they got any new ham in the kitchen. Of a certainty things are well managed here! We lead dog's lives. Marco vows on the bones of his mother that the master has not one *soldo* left in the bag. He has squandered everything on these cursed wings of his, and begins his sparing by starving us. But I'll teach you where else his money goes. In gifts for his darlings, in medals and velvet caps. Have you no shame, Andrea, to receive alms? Is Messer Leonardo your father or your brother? or are you still a baby?"

"Cesare," interrupted Giovanni, to give a new turn to the discourse, "you made promise to expound me the axioms of perspective. We waste time expecting the master, who is overstudious of his machine—"

"Ay, ay, my friend. We shall all be confounded some day by that machine, devil take it! And if it is not this machine 'tis another. I remember how in the very middle of the *Cenacolo*, the Master, forsooth, must needs break off to invent a new mincing-machine for sausages; and the head of St. James could not get stuck on his shoulders, because Leonardo was dissatisfied with the blades of the cutter. And the best of his Madonnas had to wait in the corner, while he devised a spit for the roasting of sucking-pigs. And what think you of that his other grand discovery, the lye of fowl's-dung for the washing of linen? There is no folly for which Messer Leonardo will not sacrifice his time if he can but get away from his paint-brush"; and Cesare's face puckered itself, and his lips curled in a malicious laugh.

"Why, I pr'ythee, why does God give genius to such men?" he added in a low, trembling voice.

III

LEONARDO WAS STILL AT WORK, bending over his writing-table. A swallow flew in at the window and wheeled about the room, brushing against the ceiling and the walls, till caught by the great bat, its little, living wings fast held by the network of artificial tendons. Cautiously Leonardo rose and delicately freed the prisoner, took it in his hand, kissed the silky black head, and let it fly away. The swallow soared, and was lost in the blue air, screaming its cries of joy.

"How simple, how easy its flight," he thought, as he followed it with disappointed, envious eyes. He threw a contemptuous glance at his machine, the dark skeleton of that tremendous bat.

The man who was lying on the floor suddenly awoke. He was a Florentine, a skilful mechanic and smith, by name Zoroastro, or more shortly, Astro da Paretola. A clumsy giant, with the simple face of a child, always covered with soot and grime, he looked a Cyclops, for he had but one eye, the other having been long ago destroyed by a spark from some blazing metal.

Rubbing his single orb and scratching his shaggy head he cried, "The devil take me for a blockhead! Master, why did you not hinder me from slumbering? I who was so zealously affected, who only thought how to hurry the evening that the morning and the flying might come!"

"You were wise to sleep," said Leonardo, "for the wings have failed."

"What! these also? Nay, master, but I will not make your machine again. Think of the money, the labour we have thrown to the wind! What better can you want? Not to fly, on wings like those, would be impossible! An elephant could rise on them. Pr'ythee, master, let me try! I will prove them over water, and then if I fall I'll come off with no worse than a bathing. I can swim as a fish; I wasn't born to be drowned."

And he clasped his hands supplicatingly. Leonardo, however, shook his head.

"Patience, friend, have yet patience. It will come in its own time, and then—"

"*Then?*" cried the smith, almost in tears. "Why not *now*? Of a surety, master, as true as God is in heaven, I shall fly."

"No, Astro, fly thou wilt not. By a mathematical law—"

"I could have sworn you would say that! To the devil with your mathematical laws, for they upset everything. And to think of the years we have laboured! I am sick to remember it! Every gnat, mosquito, fly, I pray you license—every *muck*-fly, every *dunghill*-fly—has its wings; and men crawl like worms. 'Tis rank injustice! And why should we doubt? There they are, your wings, ready, and beautiful; ready to be blessed of God, and spread, and to be off! And then we shall see what we shall see!"

He paused, seemed to recall something, and continued more calmly:—

"I would tell you a thing, master. This very night I dreamed, nay, but I dreamed—"

"I conceive you! You flew."

"Ay. But how? Hear me. I stood in a chamber, where I know not, and amid a throng. They looked at me and pointed, and then they laughed. And I said to myself, 'cursed spite 'twill be if I fly not.' So I got up and I shook my arms and I rose; I warrant you 'twas hard, as though I would raise a mountain on my back! But 'twas soon lighter, and I rose till my head was in the roof. And they cried aloud, Behold him! he flieth! Ay, and I passed through the window like yon bird, and I circled higher and yet higher, till I touched the sky. And the wind whistled in my ears, and I laughed for very joy. 'Why,' I questioned of myself, 'did I never fly till now? 'Tis mighty easy; and there is no call for any machinery at all.'"

IV

Shouts, oaths, and the quick thump of footsteps interrupted them. The door was flung wide, and a fiery-haired, freckle-faced man, dragging a child of ten by the ear, burst into the chamber. It was Leonardo's pupil, Marco d'Oggione.

"May the Lord send you an ill Easter!" he shouted; "Rascal, I will set my heels upon your throat!"

"What coil is this, Marco?" asked Leonardo.

"I pray you listen, Master. This same young rogue has filched my silver buckles; ten florins each did they cost me! One he has gambled away at his dice; the other I have found in his stocking. I did but pull him by the hair, and now, son of the devil that he is, he hath bitten my finger to the bone."

And he would again have attacked the little lad by his curls had not Leonardo rescued him. Then Marco, who kept the keys of the house, took them from his pouch and flung them on the ground.

"Take them up, sir! I will be warden no longer. I live no longer in the house with rascals and with thieves!"

"Peace, Marco, peace; and leave this babe to me."

The other three now came from the studio, and presently Maturina, the fat cook, squeezed herself into the group, carrying her market basket. Seeing the little sinner, she flung up her hands and gabbled with the monotony of dry peas pouring through a broken bag. Cesare talked also volubly, demanding why this "pagan of a Jacopo" was allowed to stay, for the playing of every malicious and spiteful trick capable of invention; had he not maimed the watch-dog, stoned the nests of the swallows, torn wings from butterflies?

Jacopo had taken refuge with the Master, his pale pretty face quite impassive, his eyes, sinister in their brilliance, turned to Leonardo with mute supplication.

Leonardo would have appeased the tumult, but on his face sat a strange air of perplexity and weakness, not lost upon the contemptuous Cesare.

Presently the noise subsided of itself; and then Leonardo, with his customary calm, called Giovanni and invited him to an inspection of the *Cenacolo*, the Last Supper; his greatest work. Giovanni flushed with pleasure, and they went together.

V

However they paused by the courtyard fountain that Leonardo, after his sleepless night, might refresh himself by bathing his face. The day was cloudy, but windless, and over all things streamed an argent light which seemed to come from under water; days like these pleased the artist best for painting. They were still at the well when the boy Jacopo crept up, bearing in his hands a little case made of bark.

"Messer Leonardo," he murmured, "I have brought it—for you," and cautiously raising the lid he showed a huge imprisoned spider. "I have watched it this three days," he said enthusiastically; "'tis poisonous! And 'tis a terror to see how he devoureth flies!"

His face was radiant now, and catching a fly he gave it to the captive.

The spider seized the victim with its hairy legs, and there was a fight and great buzzing.

"He sucks it! He sucks it!" cried the child in an ecstasy; and Leonardo bent over the struggling creatures to watch.

It seemed to Giovanni that on the two so different faces was the same expression: a hideous pleasure in the horrible.

When the fly had been murdered and devoured the boy closed the little box, and said, "I will put it on your table, Messer Leonardo; you will like to see how he fights with other spiders."

Then he raised supplicating eyes, and went on with quivering lips, "Messere, be not wroth with me. I will go from you. I see that I am a trouble to you; you are good, but those others are evil; as truly am I also—I who understand not pretending, as do they! So be it; I will go very far away, and will live alone. 'Twill be better so. Only do thou pardon me, Master, I pray, I supplicate. Pardon thou me." And great tears shone on the child's long lashes as he went on. "Pardon me, Master Leonardo, and I will leave you the spider for a remembrance of me. Spiders live many years; and I will ask Astro to feed it."

"Whither would you go, poor child? Nay, Marco shall forgive thee; I am not wroth with thee, and truly I will accept thy spider. In the future, little one, seek to live harmlessly."

Jacopo turned his eyes to his Master, and in them was no gratitude, only unbounded astonishment; and Leonardo smiled at him, as if in his great wisdom he understood the child, and knew him one of those innocent in their wrong doing, because by nature formed for evil.

"It grows late, Giovanni; let us go on," said Leonardo; and together they trod the silent street which presently led them between the walls of gardens, vineyards, and orchards, to the convent of Santa Maria delle Grazie.

VI

Boltraffio had for sometime been distressed by the fact that he could no longer pay his master the monthly fee of six florins which had been arranged. His uncle had quarrelled with him, and now refused him further assistance, and Fra Benedetto, who had lent him the means for two months, could do no more.

So this morning Giovanni determined to explain matters to his master. He turned deprecatingly to him, and reddening to the roots of his hair, stammered:—

"Messere, we are at the 14th of the month, and it was agreed I should pay you on the 10th. It irks me to confess it, but I have no more than these three florins. Would you consent to wait? Soon I have hope to get money. Merula has promised me copying."

Leonardo looked at him astonished.

"What speech is this, Giovanni? Are you not ashamed?"

By his disciple's blush, by his confusion, by his patched shoes and threadbare clothes he guessed that Giovanni was very poor. So he frowned, and talked of something else; but presently took occasion to hand the boy a gold piece, saying carelessly, "Lad, go buy me twenty sheets of the blue paper for my drawings, and a parcel of red chalk, and another of badger brushes. Take the money."

"A ducat? to pay a matter of ten *soldi*? I will bring you the surplus."

"By no means. I care not for such trifles. Some day, perchance, you will be able to pay it back. And talk no more to me of money: do you hear?"

He went on at once to remark on the misty outlines of the larch trees along both banks of the straight canal called the Naviglio Grande, which carried the eye into the distance by their long rows.

"Have you observed, Giovanni, that in a light mist the trees show blue, in a thick mist, grey?"

And he talked further of the shadows thrown by the clouds upon the hills, one tone in summer when their trees are in leaf, another in winter when their trees are bare. Then he said abruptly.

"You have thought me a skinflint because on our first coming to terms you saw me note every detail of the bargain in a book. I caught that trick from my good father, Piero, the notary, who knows his way in affairs passing well. But the habit is an idle one for me. I am extreme to mark trifles such as the price of the feather in Salaino's cap; yet thousands of ducats go from me, and I know not whither. For the future, boy, regard not this trick. If thou hast need of money, take it; and be sure I give it to thee as a father gives to a son."

And Leonardo looked at him with a smile so tender, that the pupil's heart was lightened and overflowed with joy. Then again the master talked of trees, and pointing to a misshapen white mulberry, bade his disciple observe that not only every tree but also every leaf has its own figure different from its fellows, even as every son of man has his own face. It seemed to Giovanni that he spoke of trees with no less insight than he had shown in speaking of his needy disciple; as though loving observation of all things living had sharpened his eye to the penetration of a seer and a clairvoyant.

They were now in sight of Santa Maria delle Grazie, the church belonging to the Dominican convent; a brick edifice with a broad dome like a tent—the early work of Bramante. It rose from the plain behind a grove of dark mulberry trees, and seemed rosy and gay against its background of white and rainy clouds.

The pair passed at once into the convent refectory.

VII

IT WAS A LONG BARE hall, whitewashed, and with a roof of wooden rafters. There was a smell of damp, of incense, and of fast-day fare. The Father Superior had his dining-board in the recess by the entrance; on either side were the long narrow tables for the monks. So still was it that the buzz of the flies was audible in the windows, glazed with small, yellow, and dusty panes, and hollowed like the cells of a honeycomb. Now and then voices came from the kitchen with a clatter of iron saucepans.

Opposite the prior's table, at the end of the hall, there rose a scaffolding of wood covered with coarse grey linen; Giovanni divined that behind it was the *magnum opus*, upon which the Master had already laboured for twelve years; the *Cenacolo*, the Last Supper.

Leonardo having ascended the scaffold and opened a wooden case which contained his sketches, cartoons, paints, etc., took a small, well-worn, much-annotated Latin book, and handing it to Giovanni, bade him read the thirteenth chapter of St. John. Then he removed the covering from the fresco.

Giovanni's first impression was that he saw not a painting but a prolongation of the room itself against an actual background of air. Another chamber seemed to have opened out behind the withdrawn curtain; the beams of the ceiling passed on into it, contracting in the distance, and the light of day was blended in the quiet evening light above the hills of Zion, which glowed through the triple window. This second supper-room was little less austere and bare than the convent refectory. Though more solemn, the sacred table, with its cups, plates, knives, and flagons, was like the board at which the monks nightly supped; the cloth with its narrow stripes, its knotted corners, its unsmoothed folds, seemed still damp, as if but just taken from the convent linen room.

Giovanni opened the Gospel and read:—

"Now before the Feast of the Passover, when Jesus knew that his hour was come that he should depart out of this world unto the Father, . . . and supper being ended, the devil having put into the heart of Judas Iscariot, Simon's son, to betray him. . .

"Jesus was troubled in spirit, and testified and said, Verily verily, I say unto you, that one of you shall betray me. Then the disciples looked one on another, doubting of whom he spake. Now there was leaning on Jesus' bosom one of his disciples whom Jesus loved."

Giovanni again raised his eyes to the fresco. The faces of the apostles were so animated that he seemed to hear their speech, to look into the depths of their souls, confounded as they were by the most mysterious, the most terrible of all catastrophes that have ever taken place—the birth of that sin by which God was to die.

Specially was he impressed by Judas, by St. Peter, and St. John. The head of Judas was not yet painted, and the body, bent backward, but dimly outlined. Clutching desperately at the bag with convulsive fingers, he had overturned the salt-cellar, and the salt was spilled. Peter, impetuous in his wrath, was starting up from behind, a knife still in his right hand, his left on the shoulder of John, as if asking the beloved disciple "of whom doth He speak?" With his silver hair, with his splendid resentment, his whole frame showed that fiery zeal, that thirst for great deeds, with which, upon understanding the ineluctable sufferings of his Master he was to cry "Lord, why cannot I follow thee now? I will lay down my life for thy sake!" John, on the contrary, with his long silken tresses, his eyelids lowered as if in the peace of sleep, his folded hands, the long oval of his face—seemed the ideal of calm and heavenly serenity. Alone among the disciples he knew no suffering, no fear, no wrath.

Giovanni saw, and he said to himself, "Here is the true Leonardo! And I had doubted and wellnigh believed the calumnies. The man impious who created that? Nay, who among men is closer to Christ than he?"

The painter, meantime, having completed the face of John with delicate touches of the brush, began the charcoal outline of the head of Jesus. Vainly, however; he had meditated upon that head for ten years, yet still he could not accomplish even the first sketch. Always when confronted by that emptiness where the divine countenance should appear, the artist trembled with mortal anguish and the sense of his own impotence. Throwing the charcoal aside, passing a cloth over the few lines he had lightly traced, he fell into one of those reveries which sometimes lasted for entire hours. Giovanni ventured to approach him, and saw his face as it were aged, severe, wearing the imprint of unremitting tension, of silent despair.

Yet, his eyes falling on those of his pupil, Leonardo said kindly—

"Well, then, *amico mio*, what say you of it?"

"What words have I, Master? It is beautiful, with a beauty beyond aught in this world. None other has so understood that scene! But nay, I will not speak—I cannot."

His voice shook with tears; but presently he added in a low voice, "One thing I would ask. Among such faces, what can be the face of Judas?"

The master, without answering, handed him a paper sketch. It showed a face terrible but not repulsive, not wicked even, but big with infinite grief, with the profound bitterness of great knowledge.

Giovanni compared it with that of St. John. "Yes," he exclaimed awestruck; "it is he! He of whom it is said, Satan entered into him; who perhaps knew more than any of them, but who would not accept the cry, that 'all may be one!' because he desired to be *an one* by himself."

He was interrupted by Cesare da Sesto, who burst into the refectory, followed by a man in the court livery.

"At last! at last!" he cried; "Master, we have sought you in every place! The duchess requires you—on a grave matter."

"Your Worship will have the kindness to come with me to the palace," said the servant.

"What is the cause?"

"A disaster, Messer Leonardo. The water pipes do not work; and this morning when Her Excellence was pleased to get into her bath, and her woman had gone to the adjoining chamber for linen, the tap broke, so that Her Excellence was nearly scalded. She is pleased to be very wroth; and Messer Ambrogio Ferrari, the steward, complains greatly, and saith he hath more than once warned your Worship about these pipes."

"What puerility is this?" replied Leonardo; "can you not see I am at work? Go to Zoroastro. In half an hour he will repair everything."

"Messere, I was told not to return without your Worship."

Leonardo, however, went back to his picture. But when his eye fell on the blank space destined for the Saviour's head, his brows knit with discouragement, and, realising fresh failure, he descended from the easel.

"Well, we will go. You, Giovanni, come for me to the outer courtyard of the castle, Cesare will show you the way; I will expect you by the *Cavallo*."

By this name he spoke of his great equestrian statue of Francesco Sforza.

And to Giovanni's amazement, without another glance at the *Cenacolo*, the Master followed the scullion to mend the pipes of the ducal bath.

"So you can't take your eyes off the thing?" said Cesare mockingly to Boltraffio; "certes, 'tis a wonderful work; at least until one sees through it."

"What is your meaning?"

"Ask me not. I won't spoil your faith. Mayhap in the end you will discover for yourself. Meanwhile, admire."

"Cesare, tell me your thought."

"Good, then. Only be not wroth at the truth. I know all you will find to say and I will not dispute with you. In good sooth, it is wonderful. No master hath so much anatomy, such perspective, such science of chiaroscuro. I challenge it not. All is direct from nature, the face wrinkles, the folds in the cloth, everything. But the living spirit, where is that? the God is absent; and will absent Himself forever. At bottom, in the soul, all is ice and death! Look, Giovanni! use your eyes! See the geometrical regularity; four triangles, two contemplative, two active; and their centre is Christ. Look narrowly. On the right you have perfect goodness in John, perfect badness in Judas, the dividing of good and evil (that is, justice) in Peter. Beside them the active triad, Andrew, James, and Bartholomew. Now turn to the left; another contemplative triangle; the love of Philip, the faith of James, the wisdom of Thomas; then again, activity in another triad. Not inspiration, Giovanni, but geometry; mathematics in the seat of beauty. All calculated, reasoned *ad nauseam*, tested to repulsion, weighed in the balance, measured by the compasses. Under the holy things—contempt."

"Cesare, Cesare!" cried Giovanni with gentle reproof. "How little you know the Master! Why do you hate him?"

"And you think perchance you know him, and therefore you love him?" returned Cesare quickly, turning to his companion with a bitter smile. In his eyes blazed such unextinguishable malice that Giovanni instinctively averted his own.

"You are unjust, Cesare," he resumed after a pause; "the picture is incomplete; the Christ is not yet there."

"And will He be there? Do you expect it? Well, we shall see. Only mark you my words. I say Messer Leonardo will never finish the *Cenacolo*; never paint the Judas, nor the Christ! For, see you, my friend, one may do much by mathematics and by experiments in science; but not everything. More is needed. There is a limit which he, with all his learning, can never pass."

They left the monastery and moved towards the Castello di Porta Giovia. Boltraffio was long silent, then he said:—

"In one point, Cesare, you certainly are in error. The Judas exists already; I have seen it."

"When? Where?"

"Just now—in the convent. He showed me the drawing."

"You?"

Cesare stared, then said slowly, and as if by an effort.

"How was it? Good?"

Giovanni nodded; and Cesare after this kept silence.

VIII

ARRIVED AT THE CASTLE GATES, they crossed the drawbridge to the Torre del Filarete, which looked to the south, and was deeply moated. Here even at noon it was dark; and the air was laden with an undefinable odour of barracks—the smell of stables, straw, and sour bread. Under the resounding arches came echoes of the laughter and curses of the hired foreign soldiery.

Cesare had the pass; but Giovanni was regarded with mistrust, and his name entered in the guard-book. Crossing a second drawbridge, where they submitted to a second examination, they reached the deserted inner court of the castle called the Piazza d'Arme. Straight before them was the stern Torre di Bona; to the right, the entrance to the Corte Ducale; to the left, the Rocchetta, a veritable eagle's nest, the part of the castle most difficult of access. In the centre of the square, surrounded by ill-made wooden fences, which were already moss-grown and weather-stained, rose an unfinished colossal equestrian statue in greenish clay; *Il Cavallo*, the bold achievement of Leonardo da Vinci, no less than twenty *braccia* in altitude. The tremendous horse, dark against the watery sky, was rearing; a fallen warrior was beneath his hoofs; on his back, Francesco Sforza, the great *condottiere*, half-soldier, half brigand, wholly adventurer, who had served with his sword and his blood for money. The son of a peasant, strong as a lion, astute as a fox, he attained by sagacity, by crime, and by great exploits, the summit of power, and died on the throne of the Dukes of Milan. Pale sunshine fell full on the colossal figure, and in the grossness of the double chin, in the rapacity of the fierce and vigilant eye, Giovanni saw the calm of the gorged wild beast. Leonardo himself had inscribed the clay with this distich:—

"Expectant animi molemque futuram
Suscipiunt; fluat aes; vox erit; Ecce Deus."

The last two words were astounding to Giovanni. "Behold the god."

"A god?" he repeated, looking at the colossal clay, at the victim trampled by the violent conqueror. He remembered the quiet convent refectory of "Our Lady of Grace," the hills of Zion, the celestial beauty of St. John, the stillness of the Last Supper: and that God, of whom it was said, "Behold the Man!"

At this moment Leonardo himself appeared.

"Let us hurry," he said; "it seems that the kitchen chimneys are smoking; and if we do not flee they will be calling me back to mend them."

Giovanni could not answer him; he stood downcast and pallid.

"Master," he said presently, "I crave your pardon; but I have thought long, and still I comprehend not how you were able to create the *Cavallo* and the *Cenacolo* at one and the same time."

Leonardo looked at his disciple in quiet surprise.

"Why not?"

"Oh, Messer Leonardo! do you not feel yourself that they are impossible together?"

"No, Giovanni. To my thinking, one helps out the other. My best ideas for the *Cenacolo* come to me when I am working at the Colossus; and in that convent refectory yonder, I love to think upon this monument of Duke Francesco. The works are twins. I began them together, and together I shall finish them."

"Together! Christ, and this man? It is impossible!" And ignorant how to express his thought, yet feeling his heart on fire, he repeated passionately, "It is impossible!"

"And why?" asked the master with his quiet smile.

Giovanni would have tried to reply; but meeting those calm uncomprehending eyes, the words died upon his lips, for Leonardo would not have understood them. So he held his peace and thought within himself.

"Strange! An hour ago, looking at his picture, I fancied that I knew him. And now I find I do not know him at all. Of which of those twain does he say in his heart; 'Behold the god?'"

IX

THAT NIGHT WHEN ALL OTHERS slept, Giovanni, tormented by insomnia, rose and went into the court, where was a stone bench under a tent of vine branches. The court was square, and in its centre was a well; behind the bench was the wall of the house, opposite the stable; to the left a stone wall with a wicket-gate which opened on the street of the Porta Vercellina; to the right the wall of a little garden and a door always locked and leading to a separate building. Here Astro alone was allowed ingress, and here Leonardo was wont to work in complete seclusion.

The night was still and warm, with a thick mist, penetrated by dim moonlight. A low knock sounded on the gate which opened on the road; the shutter of one of the lower windows was opened, and a man peered out, asking:—

"Monna Cassandra?"

"'Tis I. Open!"

Astro came from the house and let her in; a girl clad in white, which the moonlight and the mist changed to a strange green. They parleyed together at the gate; then passed Giovanni without seeing him, where he sat in the deep shadow of the vine branches.

The girl seated herself on the low wall of the well. Her face was an odd one, immobile and placid, like the faces of old statues. She had a low forehead, straight black eyebrows, too small a chin, and eyes of transparent amber. But what chiefly struck Giovanni was her hair, so light, so soft, so crisp, as if possessed of life. Like the Medusa's aureole of serpents, its blackness framed her face, making its paleness paler, its lips more scarlet, its amber eyes more translucent.

"Then you too, Astro, have heard speak of Frate Angelo?" said the girl.

"Yes, Monna Cassandra. They say the Pope hath sent him to extirpate heresy and black magic. And I tell you, merely to hear what is told of the Fathers Inquisitors raises the hair of your skin! God keep us from their claws! Monna Cassandra, be discreet; and, above all, warn your aunt."

"A pretty aunt she is to me!"

"It matters not. Warn that Monna Sidonia with whom you live."

"Then, blacksmith, you suppose us witches?"

"I suppose nothing. Messer Leonardo hath taught me there is no witchcraft; nor can be none, by the law of nature. Messer Leonardo knows everything and believes in nothing."

"Believes in nothing? Not in the devil? Not in God?"

"Jest not! Messer Leonardo is a saint."

"And your flying-machine?" she said contemptuously; "is it ready?"

The smith waved his hand despairingly.

"Ready? We are going to make it all over again!"

"Astro! Astro! You credit this nonsense? These machines are dust cast into the eyes. I wager Messer Leonardo has flown many a time ere now."

"Flown? How?"

"He flies—as I fly."

He surveyed her thoughtfully.

"You fly in dreams, Monna Cassandra."

"You think that is it? Nay, others have seen me fly. Perhaps you know not the tale?"

The smith scratched his head hesitatingly.

"But I forget," she said mockingly; "you are all learned folk here, who believe not in miracles, but in mechanics."

"S'death! Those same mechanics are a weight on my neck. Did you but know—" He spread out his hands appealingly, and continued; "Monna Cassandra; you know my faithfulness. Nor is there temptation to chatter, lest Frate Angelo play eavesdropper. Tell me, then, in all secrecy, tell me of your charity with all the particulars—"

"Tell you what?"

"How you fly."

"Not that, my friend; no. If you know too much you will age too soon."

She paused; then said softly, after a long look straight into his eyes. "What avails it to talk? You must act."

"What is required?" asked Astro in trembling tones, and turning pale.

"You must know a certain word, and you must anoint your skin with a certain unguent."

"Have you this unguent?"
"Yes."
"And you know the word?"
She nodded.
"And then one can fly?"
"Try. You will find my method simpler than your mechanics."
The single eye of the smith blazed with the madness of desire.
"Monna Cassandra, give me your unguent."
She suppressed a laugh.
"You are a simpleton, Astro. Five minutes ago you called magic foolery; now, it seems, you believe in it."
Astro hung his head, convicted, but unrepentant.
"I wish to fly. I care little if I attain by mechanics or by miracles. What I can endure no longer is waiting."
The girl laid her hand on his shoulder.
"I see, I see. Truly, I pity you. It is clear your brain will crack if you don't get to your flying. Good, then; I will give you the drug and I will teach you the word. But you likewise, Astro, you must do what I ask of you."
"I will, Monna Cassandra. I will do anything. Speak." The girl pointed to the wet roof beyond the garden wall.
"Let me enter there."
But Astro frowned and shook his head.
"Nay. I will do whatever you ask, saving only that."
"And why not that?"
"I have promised my master to let none in."
"But you go thither?"
"Yea."
"What is there within?"
"No mystery, Monna Cassandra; nothing of moment. Machines, appliances, books, manuscripts. Certain strange plants, beasts, creeping things. Travellers bring them from distant lands. And there is one tree which has been poisoned."
"What? poisoned?"
"Ay. He has it for experiments; that he may know the effect poison has upon plants."
"Good Astro, tell me all you know of that tree."
"There is naught to tell. Early in the spring season he bored him a hole in its trunk, to the very core; and with a long thin needle he squirted in some venom."

"What strange experiments! And of what sort is the tree?"

"A peach-tree."

"What followed? Was the fruit also poisoned?"

"It will be so when ripe."

"Can you see in the peaches that they are poisoned?"

"No; and that is why he permits no entry, lest someone might eat the fruit and die."

"Have you the key?"

"Ay."

"Good Astro, give it to me!"

"Monna Cassandra! Have I not sworn to him?"

"Give me the key; and I will compass it that tonight you shall fly—this very night. See, this is the drug."

She drew from her bosom a phial which contained a dark liquid; and putting her face close to his, she whispered wheedlingly, "What is it you fear, simpleton? You say there are no mysteries. Well, then, let us go and make sure. The key, Astro, the key!"

"No," he replied, "I will not let you enter; and I care nothing for your secret. Leave me."

"Coward!" cried the girl, fine scorn on her face; "it is possible for you to know the secret, and you dare not hear it! Now I see plainly he is a sorcerer, and he tricks you as he would trick an infant!"

But neither could scorn move him; he turned away his head, listening sullenly. Then Cassandra drew nearer again.

"Well, Astro, so be it. I will not enter. Only do you set the door ajar and let me peep—"

"You will not go in?"

"No; only open and let me just look."

At this he drew forth the key and unlocked the door.

Giovanni, rising softly and drawing nearer, saw a common peach-tree at the far end of the little walled garden; under the dim green moonlight the tree seemed weird and ill-omened.

Standing in the doorway, the girl looked about her with the wide eyes of eager curiosity. Then she took a step forward. The smith held her back; but she freed herself and slipped through his hands like a snake. He again pushed her out, almost overthrowing her. But she recovered her balance easily, and looked him full in the eyes. Her face pale, livid, and contracted with rage, was terrifying; at that moment she truly seemed a witch.

The smith clapped to the door, and without further speech retreated to the house, she following him with her golden eyes. Presently she strode hastily past Giovanni, and through the wicket into the road of the Porta Vercellina. Once more silence reigned, and the mist thickened; all things vanished in it.

Giovanni, left alone, closed his eyes painfully. Before him rose as in a vision the awful tree, the heavy drops on its damp leaves, its poisoned fruits, pallidly illuminated. And he thought of the words:—

"Of every tree of the garden thou mayest freely eat. But of the tree of the knowledge of good and evil thou shalt not eat. For in the day that thou eatest thereof thou shalt surely die."

Book III

The Poisoned Fruits—1494

"And the Serpent said unto the woman, Ye shall not surely die. For God doth know that in the day ye eat thereof, then your eyes shall be opened, and ye shall be as gods, knowing good and evil."

—Gen. iii. 4 and 5

"Faciendo un bucho con un succhiello dentro un albusciello, a chacciandovi arsenicho e risalgallo e sollimato stemperati con acqua arzente, a forza di fare e sua frutti velenosi."

—Leonardo Da Vinci

(Having pierced the heart of a young tree, inject arsenic, a reagent and corrosive sublimate, diluted with alcohol, so as to envenom even the fruit.)

I

Beatrice, the duchess, used every Friday to bathe her hair, and then tincture it with gold, after which she dried it in the sunshine. For her convenience she had caused balustraded "*altane*," or platforms, to be erected on the roof of the splendid ducal villa of the Sforzesca, which stood on the right bank of the Ticino, near the fortress of Vigevano, among the fat pastures and the ever green water-side meadows of the province of Lomellina. Here, then, she sat, patiently supporting the blazing heat at an hour when even husbandmen and their oxen were wont to creep into the shadow. She wore a *schiavinetta*—a loose white silk wrapper without sleeves. On her head was a kind of straw sunshade, or hat, from the opening in the top of which flowed out the broad masses of her gilded and rippling hair. An olive-skinned Circassian slave was moistening the hair with a sponge, fixed on the point of a spindle; and a Tartar, slit-eyed and crooked, was combing it with an ivory comb.

The dye was made in May of the roots of walnut trees, saffron, ox-gall, swallows' lime, ambergris, bears' claws, and the fat of lizards. Close beside the duchess, and watched by herself, an infusion of musk roses and precious spices was simmering in a long-necked retort, upon a tripod over an invisible flame.

Both the waiting-maids were bathed in perspiration; even the duchess's lapdog was ill at ease on this burning *altana*, and, panting and lolling out his tongue, gazed reproachfully at his mistress, nor responded as usual to the provocation of the monkey. The latter was luxuriating in the heat, however, like the negro page, who held the gemmed and jewelled mother-o'-pearl mirror.

Though the Lady Beatrice constantly endeavoured to compose countenance and deportment to the severity becoming her rank, it was hard to believe that she was nineteen, had been married three years, and had borne two children. In the girlish roundness of her dark cheek, in the childish dimple, the slender throat, the chin too plump; in the full lips tightly compressed as if always tempted to pout; in the slight shoulders and flat bosom; in the abrupt boyish movements, she appeared still a schoolgirl, spoiled, wilful, restless and even selfish. Yet prudence and intelligence shone from the steady, dark eyes; and the Venetian ambassador, Marino Sanuto, most astute of statesmen, had written in his private letters to his government that this girl was hard as flint, and gave him far more trouble than did her husband, Il Moro; who indeed showed his wisdom by obeying her about everything.

The dog barked angrily, and up the winding stair which led to the *altana* came laboriously an old woman habited like a widow. In one hand she held a crutch, in the other a rosary; the wrinkles in her face might have given her a reverend aspect, had not the withered mouth smiled hypocritically, and the eyes sparkled with audacious cunning.

"Ugh, ugh! How detestable is old age! I could hardly drag myself hither. May the Lord preserve youth and health to your Excellency," said the old woman, kissing the hem of the *schiavinetta*.

"Well, Monna Sidonia, is it ready?"

The crone drew from her pouch a carefully wrapped, closely-stoppered phial, containing a turbid, whitish liquid,—the milk of a red goat and of an ass, distilled with wild anise, asparagus, and white lilies.

"In good sooth, her Excellency should keep it two little days more in good horse litter. Yet it can be used at once if needful; only first strain it through a filter. Wet with it crumbs of stale bread, and then be pleased to rub your noble countenance for such a period as would take the reciting of three *credos*. In five weeks' time all swarthiness will be removed, and pimples beside."

"Hearken, old woman," said Beatrice; "in this lotion there are again, mayhap, some of the abominable things used in black magic,—snakes' fat, perchance, or plovers' blood; or powdered lizards, fried in a frying-pan; such as there were in that unguent you gave me for withering the hair in my cheek-moles. If it be so, tell me at once."

"Your Excellency should not lend her ear to the calumnies of the malignant. I work honestly, as my conscience dictates; but no one can do without dirt sometimes. The magnificent Madonna Angelica, for example, all last year washed her head with dogs' urine, so as to preserve her hair, which was falling out; and thanked God and me it cured her." Then, bending down to the duchess's ear, she told the latest gossip:—how the young wife of the Master of the Guild of the Salters, the lovely Madonna Filiberta was deceiving her husband with a Spanish cavalier, and diverting herself hugely.

"And doubtless," said Beatrice, jestingly threatening with her finger, "'twas you who brought the poor thing to it, you old bawd!"

"Does your Excellency call her *poor*? Nay, she sings me her thanks every hour. Now she knows the difference between the kiss of a spouse and the kiss of a lover."

"But the sin? Doth not her conscience bite her?"

"Her conscience? Madam, I hold the sin of love the work of nature. And a few drops of holy water can wash the sin away. Madonna Filiberta is but giving her spouse a Roland for his Oliver."

"Is your meaning that likewise the husband—"

"Say it for certain, I do not—but sure it is that all married men harp on one string. There is none of them but would sooner have a single hand than a single wife."

The duchess laughed. "Ah, Monna Sidonia, Monna Sidonia, there's no tripping you! But where do you learn all these things?"

"Believe the word of an old woman; what I tell you is gospel truth. And in matters of conscience I know the difference between a beam and a mote. All fruit gets ripe in its season. If she have not her fill of love when she be young, a woman will fall into such longing when she is old, that she will go straight into the claws of the devil."

"You preach like a doctor of theology."

"Nay, I am unlearned; but I speak from my heart, and I tell your

Excellency that youth comes but once in life; for what the devil—Lord forgive me!—is the use of us women when we are old? Perhaps to throw charcoal on the brazier, and to count the pots and the pans in the kitchen. Not for nothing says the proverb.

'La giovane mangia, la vecchia s'ingozza.'[1]

Beauty without love is like matins without a paternoster."

"What! say that over again!" laughed the duchess.

The old woman, thinking she had now trifled enough, again bent to the lady's ear and whispered. Beatrice ceased to laugh, her face darkened. She dismissed her attendants, excepting the little blackamoor who had no Italian. Around them was only the still and glowing air, which seemed to have paled under the fury of the heat.

"Folly!" answered the duchess; "such chattering is of no moment."

"Signora, I saw with my eyes, I heard with my ears. Others will tell you the like."

"Were there many persons?"

"Ten thousand. The piazza before the Castle of Pavia was thronged."

"What heard you?"

"When Madonna Isabella came forth bearing the little Francesco there was a beating of hands, a waving of caps, and a many who shed tears. '*Viva* Isabella of Aragon,' they cried, '*Viva* Gian Galeazzo and his heir, our true and legitimate lord! Death to the usurpers of his throne!'"

Beatrice frowned. "Those were the very words?"

"Ay; but there was worse."

"Speak—fear nothing."

"They cried—my tongue, *Signora mia*, refuses—but they cried 'Death to the Robbers!'"

Beatrice shivered; mastering herself, however, she asked calmly, "Was there more?"

"Of a truth, I know not how to tell it to your Excellency."

"Haste thee, I would know all."

"Believe me, madam, they said that the most noble duke, Ludovico il Moro, the guardian and the benefactor of Gian Galeazzo, holds his nephew in the fortress of Pavia, and surrounds him with assassins and

1. *Ingozzare*, to swallow; also, to bear an affront meekly.

spies. Then they demanded that the duke himself should come out to them, but Madonna Isabella answered that he lay sick."

And again Monna Sidonia whispered in the duchess's ear.

"But you are distraught, you old hag," cried the lady. "Beware, lest I have you thrown from this roof, so that not even a crow can get your bones together."

The threat did not frighten Monna Sidonia. Beatrice also soon calmed.

"I don't believe a word of it," she said, observing the crone furtively.

"As you please, Excellency," answered the other, shrugging lean shoulders, "but nothing can prevent my words from being true. See you," she continued insinuatingly, "you make a small figure of wax, and you put a swallow's heart in at the right side, at the left its liver, then you pierce it with a needle, uttering charms the while; and he will die of a slow death, nor is there doctor who can save him."

"Silence!" commanded the duchess.

The hag again devoutly kissed the hem of the *schiavinetta*. "Your Grace is my sun. I love you overmuch, 'tis my worst fault." She paused, then added, "It can be done also without witchcraft."

The duchess was silent, but she looked at the woman curiously.

"As I came by the palace garden," resumed Monna Sidonia, dryly, "I saw the gardener collecting fair ripe peaches in a basket, a present doubtless for Messer Gian Galeazzo." Another pause, and she continued, "And likewise in the garden of Messer Leonardo da Vinci, the Florentine, there are fair ripe peaches, but empoisoned."

"Empoisoned?"

"Ay, Monna Cassandra, my niece, saw—" And again she whispered.

The duchess made no answer. By this time her hair was dry, and she rose, threw off the *schiavinetta*, and descended to the apartment known as the wardrobe. Here were three huge presses; the first, large as that in some great sacristy, contained the eighty-four dresses which she had found time to acquire in the three years of her married life; some so stiff with gold and jewels that they could stand on the floor by themselves, others diaphanous, imponderous as the web of a spider. In the second press were riding-dresses, and all furniture for hawking. In the third, essences, waters, washes, unguents, powders for the teeth of white coral and seed-pearls, innumerable vases, retorts, rectified alembics, crucibles, in short, a complete laboratory of female alchemy; precious cedar-wood chests, also, covered with paintings and embroidery. From one of these the waiting-woman drew forth a chemise of the purest whiteness. The room filled with a scent of lavender, oriental iris, and dried Damascus roses.

While she dressed, Beatrice conversed about the trimming of a new gown just received by courier from her sister, Isabella d'Este, the Marchioness of Mantua. The sisters vied with each other in elegance, and Beatrice paid a court spy to keep her informed of all the novelties in the Mantuan wardrobe.

The duchess attired herself in her favourite robe, which, striped with gold satin and green velvet, made her seem taller than she was. The open-work sleeves were tied with bands of grey silk, slashed in the French mode, and showing the white puffings of the undergarment. Her hair was plaited and confined in a gold net and fine gold cord, which was clasped by a scorpion of rubies.

II

SHE WAS IN THE HABIT of spending so long a time at the morning toilette that the duke said he could as quickly have fitted a merchant ship for the Indies. On this occasion, however, hearing a distant sound of horns and the baying of hounds, she remembered that she had ordered a hunt, and consequently hurried. When dressed she paid a passing visit to the chamber of her dwarfs, which, in imitation of the royal playroom of Isabella d'Este, she nicknamed "the Apartment of the Giants." Here everything was arranged for a population of pygmies: chairs, beds, furniture, ladders, even a chapel with a toy altar at which daily service was read by a learned dwarf named Janachi in archiepiscopal robes and mitre. Among the "giants" was always much noise: laughter and weeping, the cries of various and eerie voices from hunchbacks, apes, parrots, idiots, Tartars, buffoons, and other absurd creatures, with whom the youthful duchess sometimes passed whole days playing. Today she looked in merely to inquire after the health of a little negro named Nannino, lately sent from Venice. His skin had been so black, that in the words of his former mistress, "Nothing more exquisite could be desired," but now that he had fallen ill it had become apparent that his hue was not entirely natural, for a coating, black and shining like lacquer, was peeling off and causing great chagrin to Beatrice. However, she loved him in spite of his growing fairness, and hearing with distress that he was likely to die, she gave orders to have him christened as quickly as possible.

Descending the staircase, she met Morgantina, her favourite female fool, who was young, pretty, and so whimsical that she "could rouse even the dead to laughter." She stole and hid booty like a magpie, but if spoken to kindly would confess her crimes, and was simple and innocent as a child. Sometimes, however, she fell into fits of melancholy, wailing for her lost son (who had never existed). This morning she was sitting on the stair hugging her knees and sobbing distractedly. Beatrice patted her on the head.

"Cease, little one, cease," she said, "be good."

The fool, raising her childish blue eyes streaming with tears, made reply, "Oh! oh! oh! they have taken my baby away! And, O Lord, why? What harm had he done?"

Without another word the duchess went down into the courtyard where the huntsmen were awaiting her.

III

Surrounded by outriders, falconers, beaters, equerries, pages, and court-ladies, Beatrice sat her slender dark bay Arab—a superb creature from Gonzaga's stables—like an expert horseman. "A true queen of Amazons," thought her husband proudly, as he came out of the pleached alley before the palace to watch his consort's start.

Behind the duchess rode a falconer in a sumptuous livery, embroidered with gold. A snow-white Cyprus falcon, a gift from the Sultan, its golden hood glittering with emeralds, and little bells attached to its claws, sat on his left hand.

Beatrice was in lively humour; she looked at her husband with a smile, but when he said—

"Be wary! the horse is mettlesome," she signed to her companions and darted off at a gallop, first along the road, then over the open fields, across ditches, hillocks, and trenches. Her retinue fell behind; but Beatrice was attended by a huge wolf-hound, and by her side, on a black Castilian mare, the gayest and boldest of her maidens, rode Madonna Lucrezia Crivelli. The duke was by no means indifferent to this lady, and as he watched her and Beatrice side by side in this mad gallop, it would have perplexed him to say which of the two he admired the more. However, he certainly experienced an invincible anxiety for his young wife, and when she leaped a deep chasm, he closed his eyes and caught his breath. Often he had reproved her for these follies, but had not the heart to forbid them; deficient himself in physical courage, he was proud of the daring of his lady.

The party descended into the ravine and disappeared among the osier thickets of the low banks of the Ticino, the breeding place of ducks, woodcock, and herons.

Then the duke returned to his *studiolo*, where Messer Bartolomeo Calco, his chief secretary, who had charge of the embassies from the foreign courts, was awaiting commands.

IV

Sitting in his high-backed armchair, Ludovico Sforza softly stroked his smooth-shaved chin with a white and well-kept hand. His handsome face wore that expression of perfect candour which is acquired by past masters in political trickery; his high-bridged aquiline nose, and subtly writhen lips recalled his father Francesco, the great *Condottiere*; though if Francesco were, as the poets said, at once lion and fox, Ludovico was merely fox. He was attired in pale blue silk, puffed and embroidered; his smooth hair covered ears and brow like a wig, and a gold chain dangled on his breast; in word and gesture he was uniformly courteous and urbane.

"Have you certain intelligence, Messer Bartolomeo, of the departure of the French army from Lyons?"

"None, your Excellency. Every evening they say 'tomorrow,' every morning they say 'tonight.' The king wastes himself in unwarlike amusements."

"Who is his first favourite?"

"Many names are mentioned, the taste of his Majesty is variable."

"Write to Count Belgioioso that I send him thirty—no—forty or fifty thousand ducats to spend in new donatives, let him spare nothing. We must draw this king out of Lyons by golden chains. And, Bartolomeo—but repeat this not—it were well to send his Majesty the portraits of some of our fairest ladies. By the way, is the letter ready?"

"It is, Signore."

"Show it to me."

Il Moro rubbed his white hands for pleasure. Everytime he contemplated his huge web of policy, he felt an agreeable stirring at heart; he loved the dangerous game. Nor did he blame himself for having summoned the foreigners, the northern barbarians, into

Italy; his enemies had forced him to this extreme measure, chiefly the consort of Gian Galeazzo, Isabella of Aragon, who openly accused him of having usurped the throne of his nephew. Yet it had not been till her father, Alfonso of Naples, had intervened, threatening war and dethronement, that Ludovico had appealed to Charles VIII King of France.

"Inscrutable are thy ways, O Lord!" thought the duke piously, while his secretary searched for the letter in a pile of papers; "the salvation of my kingdom, of Italy, perhaps of all Europe, is in the hands of this abortion of nature, this libertine, this witless boy, whom they name the Most Christian King of France; before whom we, the heirs of the glory of the Sforzas, must crouch, and creep, and play the pander. But such are politics; he who hunts with wolves must howl with them."

He read over the letter, which seemed to him sufficiently well expressed.

"May the Lord bless thy crusading army, O most Christian," so it ran; "the gates of Ausonia stand open to thee. Hesitate not to enter in triumph, a new Hannibal! The peoples of Italy yearn to bow beneath thy gentle yoke, O anointed of the Most High. . ."

So far the duke had read when a humpbacked, bald, old man looked in at the door. Ludovico smiled, but motioned to him to wait. The head vanished, and the door closed again softly; but the secretary saw he had lost his master's attention. Messer Bartolomeo therefore concluded the letter and went out. The duke cautiously stepped to the door on the tips of his toes, and called softly—

"Bernardo! Hist! Bernardo!"

"Here, my lord." And the court poet, Bernardo Bellincioni, advanced with an air of mystery and servility, and he would have fallen on his knees to kiss the duke's hand: the latter, however, restrained him.

"Well? Well?"

"All is right, my lord."

"Is she brought to bed?"

"Last night saw her released from her burden."

"Felicitously? Or shall I send my physician?"

"Nay, the mother is doing perfectly."

"Glory be to God! And the child?"

"Perfect."

"Male or female?"

"A man-child. And with a voice—! Fair hair as his mother's; but the eyes black, burning and quick like those of your Grace. The princely blood shows itself. A little Hercules! Madonna Cecilia is beside herself with joy; and bade me inquire the name that will please your Excellency."

"I have considered that. We will call him Caesar. What think you of that?"

"'Tis a fine name; well mouthing, and ancient. Cesare Sforza! A name meant for a hero."

"Well now—about the husband?"

"The illustrious Count Bergamini is good and courteous as ever."

"Admirable man!" cried the duke.

"Your Excellency will permit me to pronounce him a man of rare virtue. Such men are to seek nowadays. If the gout permit, he would desire to sup with your Worship, to testify to his respect."

The Countess Cecilia of whom they spoke had long been Ludovico's mistress. But Beatrice, his bride, daughter of Ercole d'Este, Duke of Ferrara, having discovered the amour, became furiously jealous; and by threats of return to her paternal home, she induced her lord not only to swear better observance of his conjugal fidelity, but also to bestow Cecilia in wedlock. The husband selected by Ludovico was the ancient and complaisant Count Bergamini.

Bellincioni, taking a small paper from his pocket, presented it to the duke. It was a sonnet in honour of the newly born:—

"Thou weepest, Phoebus! Why this silver rain?
Because this day upon the amazèd skies,
Lo! I have seen a second sun arise,
Before whose splendours all my glories wane."
"This is a tale for laughter!" "Nay, for pain,
Truth suffers no derision from the wise."
"Then tell me more, and still my loud surprise,
That queries whence this newer king shall reign."
"The offspring of a Moor, he makes his nest
In sweet Cecilia's arms—I saw his light
Shine through the brooding feathers of her love;
Now, must I hide me in the cloudy west,
Eclipsed by one more radiant and more bright,
Who shall greater God than Phoebus prove."

The duke bestowed a silver piece upon the poet.

"Bernardo, let it not slip your memory that Saturday is the birthday of the duchess."

Bellincioni hastily fumbled in the folds of his courtly but threadbare raiment, and from some recess therein drew forth a whole sheaf of tumbled papers; and among grandiloquent odes on the death of Madonna Angelina's falcon, and the disorder of Signor Paravicino's dappled Hungarian mare, found the verses required.

"Here be three for my lord to choose from," he said. "I vow by the sacred footprints of Pegasus, you will be content."

In those times sovereigns used their court poets as musical instruments, to serenade not their mistresses only, but also their wives; fashion demanded that between husband and wife at least platonic love should be assumed.

The duke ran through the verses curiously; though he could not himself string two lines together. In the first sonnet he found two lines to his taste, where the husband turns to his wife with these words:—

"Where thy light spittle falls, flowers gem the earth
As dews of spring bring violets to birth."

In the second the poet, comparing Madonna Beatrice with the goddess Diana, asserted that boars and stags felt happiness in falling by the hand of so fair a huntress. The third poem pleased Il Moro better than all the rest. It was put into the mouth of Dante, who prays that God may permit him to return to earth, since there he would once more find his Beatrice in the person of the Duchess of Milan.

"O great Jove!" cried Alighieri, "since thou hast again given her to the earth that she may gladden it with the light of love, permit me also to be with her, and to see him whose felicity she is, and whose life she maketh most proud and glad."

Il Moro graciously slapped the poet on his back, and promised him some scarlet Florentine cloth at ten *soldi* the *braccio* for his winter cloak. Bernardo, by no means satisfied, made many bowings and bendings, and obtained at last the promise of some fox skin linings. He explained that his furs had become by long wear as hairless and transparent as vermicelli drying in the sun.

"Last winter," he continued, "I was so cold that I was ready to burn not only my own staircase but the wooden shoes of St. Francis."

The duke laughed, and promised him firewood, and Bellincioni instantly improvised a laudatory quatrain.

"When to thy servants thou dost promise bread
Like God thou giv'st them heavenly manna,
For which great Phoebus and the choir of nine
Chant, noble Moor, to thee Hosanna."

"You seem in the vein today, Bernardo. Hearken, I require yet another poem."

"Erotic?"

"Ay; and impassioned."

"For the duchess?"

"By no means. But, beware you speak not of this!"

"My lord is pleased to insult me. Have I ever—"

"Not yet."

"I am dumb as any fish," and he blinked his eyes obsequiously and mysteriously. "Impassioned? That I understand. But of what kind? Grateful? Imploring?"

"The last."

The poet drew his brows together with an air of grave solicitude.

"Wedded?"

"A maid."

"Good. But I shall need the name."

"What on earth matters the name?"

"Can't do imploring without the name."

"Madonna Lucrezia.—You have nothing ready?"

"Truly, my lord, I have; but something fresh would please better. Permit me the seclusion of the next apartment; 'twill be the affair of a moment. Already I feel the rhymes crawling in my head."

Just then a page announced "Messer Leonardo da Vinci," and Bellincioni disappeared through one door as Leonardo entered at the other.

V

After the opening salutations the duke and the artist fell to discussing the new canal which was to connect the Sesia and the Ticino, and by a branching network of trenches was to irrigate the meadows and pastures of the Lomellina. Leonardo was superintendent of the excavations for the canal, though he had not the title of Ducal Architect; neither was he called the Court Painter, but only the *Sonatore di lire*, a title which gave him precedence of the court poets like Bellincioni, and had been accorded to him because on arrival in Milan he had presented Sforza with a silver lyre, made by his own hand in the shape of a horse's head.

Having explained his design for the canal, Leonardo requested of the duke that he might be put in possession of the further moneys necessary for the prosecution of the work.

"How much?" asked Ludovico.

"Five hundred and six ducats for every league: in all, fifteen thousand one hundred and eighty-seven."

Ludovico frowned, remembering the fifty thousand he had just devoted to the corruption of French nobles.

"Too much, too much, Messer Leonardo. You would ruin me. It is impossible, unexampled. Why these boundless designs? I might consult Bramante, you know, who is also an expert in construction. He works more cheaply."

Leonardo shrugged his shoulders.

"As you please, my lord. Entrust it to Bramante."

"Nay, be not offended. I have no thought of slighting you." And they fell to bargaining.

"*Va bene, va bene!*" said the duke at last, deferring the conclusion of the agreement; and he took up Leonardo's sketch-book and turned over the unfinished drawings, chiefly architectural and mechanical: the artist, somewhat impatient, had to furnish explanations and commentaries.

On one sheet there was a huge mausoleum, an artificial mountain crowned with a colonnaded temple, its dome pierced like that of the Pantheon; on the next, the exact calculations and the ground-plan for the edifice, with details for the disposition of stairs, cells, corridors; the whole being destined for the reception of five hundred sepulchral urns.

"What is this?" asked the duke; "when and for whom have you designed it?"

"For no one. 'Tis a fantasy."

"Strange fantasy!" commented Ludovico shaking his head; "'tis a cemetery for the gods or the Titans, like a building in a city of dreams."

The next sketch showed the plan for a town with the streets in tiers, one above the other, the upper for the rich, the lower for the poor, for animals, and for refuse; a town to be built in conformity with natural laws; for men without a conscience to be offended by glaring inequality.

"Not so bad!" observed the duke. "You think it would be practicable?"

"Certainly," said Leonardo brightening, "I have long wished your Excellency could be induced to try it, say in one of the suburbs. Five thousand houses would suffice for thirty thousand people; they would be decently divided, whereas now they herd together in dirt and distemper, disseminating the seeds of disease. My plan, Signore, if literally carried out, would provide the finest city in the world."

The duke's laughter checked the enthusiast.

"You are finely crazed, Messer Leonardo. If I gave you the reins you would turn the State topsy-turvy. You do not see that the most submissive of slaves would resent your two-storeyed streets, would spit upon your boasted cleanliness—your pipes and conduits—your finest city in the world, *perdio*; and would flee back to their lousy old towns again, where, as you say, they have a good modicum of filth and distemper, but no insults to their self-respect. Well, and this?" he added, pointing to another drawing.

This proved to be a design for a "house of accommodation," with secret rooms, doors, and passages, so disposed that the visitors should not meet each other.

"Ah! this is admirable!" cried the duke. "I am weary of the robbings and the murderings in these places. Here there would be order and security. I will build at once on your plan." He smiled and added, "Bravo! Bravo! I see nothing is beneath your ingenuity. *A proposito!* I remember once reading of the 'Ear of Dionysius,' a construction at Syracuse, which permitted the tyrant in his palace to hear the speech of his prisoners in the quarry. Think you it were possible to construct an Ear in my palace?"

As he spoke the duke had stammered and blushed a little, but he recovered himself immediately: before such a man as this artist no shame was required. And Leonardo, without trenching on morals, eagerly discussed the acoustics of the notion.

Then Bellincioni reappeared, announcing that his sonnet was ready and passing beautiful; at which Leonardo took flight, having accepted the duke's invitation to supper.

Ludovico requested the poet to read his work. The salamander, so the sonnet ran, lives in the fire, but a lady, of virgin ice, has her dwelling in the lover's fiery heart. The concluding quatrain seemed to the duke surprisingly tender:—

"I sing, poor swan, of my consumèd years,
But singing brings my torture no relief;
Love with his laughter blows the flame of grief,
And mocking cries, 'Extinguish it with tears.'"

VI

WHILE WAITING TILL HIS CONSORT should have returned from the chase, the duke took a walk through his domain. He inspected the stables, built like a Greek temple, with columns, porticos, and doubly-lighted windows; the splendid dairy, where he tasted junkets and new-made cheese; then, passing numberless hay-barns and sheds, came to the farm and the cattle-yards. Here every detail rejoiced his heart; the sound of the milk falling from the udders of his favourite Languedoc cow; the newly-littered sow's motherly gruntings; the smell of honey from the swarming hives. A smile of satisfaction illumined his dark face; truly his home was like a filled goblet! He returned to the house and waited under the gallery. It was towards evening, but not yet the hour of sunset; from the water-meadows of the Ticino came the pungent freshness of the grass. The duke cast his eyes slowly over his estate; pastures, meadows, fields watered by a network of ditches, planted with long rows of apple, and pear, and mulberry trees, trellised with the hanging garlands of the vines. From Mortara to Abbiategrasso and further to the very horizon, where in the creeping twilight the snows of Monte Rosa gleamed with unearthly radiance, the boundless plain of Lombardy flowered like the Paradise of God.

"I thank thee, Lord," said the devout duke raising his eyes heavenward. "I thank Thee for all. What more is there that I could desire of Thee? Once a barren and leafless wilderness stretched on every side, but I and Leonardo have made these canals, watered this land, and now every blade of grass, every ear of corn blesses me as I bless thee, O Lord!"

Then was heard the tongue of the hounds, and the cry of the huntsmen, and above the vines was seen a red lure, a formless object with partridge wings, for bringing back the falcons. Ludovico and his *major domo* went the round of the tables to be sure that all was ready for the evening feast. Presently the duchess made her entry, and then the guests trooped in, among them Leonardo. A grace was recited, and they sat down to table.

The first course consisted of artichokes sent by express from Genoa, fat eels and carp from the Mantua ponds, gift from Isabella d'Este, and a jelly of the breasts of good capons. The company ate with their fingers and with knives, forks being reserved for state occasions. Certain tiny golden ones with crystal prongs were, however, accorded to the ladies at the fruit course. The munificent host assiduously pressed his guests to eat; and as none ever blushed to be hungry, the food and the liquors circulated freely and long.

Lucrezia had her seat beside the duchess, and the admiring eyes of the duke rested on them both. It pleased him that his wife should honour the maiden of his fancy, passing dainties from her own plate to the girl's, and caressing her hand with that expansive and playful tenderness which young women sometimes exhibit towards one another.

The conversation centred in the hunt, and Beatrice told how the sudden burst of a stag from the thicket had almost thrown her from her horse. Much laughter followed when the fool Gioda, the boaster, told of the boar he had slain, singly, and with superhuman boldness and dexterity. The animal was a tame pig, cast in his path designedly, and the carcase was brought in and exhibited. The fool displayed excesses of rage at these aspersions; but his fury and simplicity were equally assumed. He knew a bad jest from a good one.

By degrees the laughter grew louder, and abundant potations reddened all faces; the ladies surreptitiously loosened their stay-laces. The cellarers brought round light Cyprus wine, both red and white, mulled at the fire, and spiced with pistachios, cinnamon, and cloves. When the duke called for wine, his command was passed out from one to the other of the stewards in a solemn chant, as of a church function; a goblet was brought from the buffet, and the chief Seneschal dipped a talisman—an unicorn on a gold chain—into the liquor. If it were poisoned the horn of this animal was to turn black and to shed drops of gore. Similar talismans, of toad's-stone and serpent's-tongue, were put in the salt-cellars. Count Bergamini, Cecilia's husband, had been given the seat of honour, and was especially gay tonight, in spite of age and gout. Pointing to the unicorn, he cried:—

"I fancy not the King of France has such a horn as your most illustrious Excellency!"

"Hee! hee! hee!" crowed Janachi the hunchback, shaking his rattle and clanging the bells of his motley cap, surmounted by ass's ears. "Believe him, nuncle, believe him!"

And the duke good-humouredly threatened the jester with his finger. Now silver trumpets blared to announce the entry of the roasts—boar's head and peacocks. Last came a pasty in the figure of a castle; from its walls sounded a trumpet, and when the crust was cut a dwarf in parrot's plumage sprang out and hopped round the table, till captured and imprisoned in a gilded cage. Thence he screamed out a paternoster.

"Messer," said the duchess to her lord, "to what joyful event must we attribute the unexpected good fare of this feast?"

Il Moro made no answer, but exchanged sly glances with Count Bergamini. Cecilia's husband understood that the celebration was for the new-born Cesare.

They sat over the boar's head for more than an hour, making no economy of time, and remembering the proverb, "At table none groweth old." At the close of the repast, Fra Talpone caused general hilarity. He was a monk of great corpulence, quarrelled for by princes, being renowned for voracity. He had greatly diverted His Holiness the Pope by devouring the third part of a bishop's cassock, cut in pieces, and steeped in vinegar. Now at a signal from the duke a huge platter of "*buzecchio*"—tripe stewed with quinces—was placed before the friar. He sighed, crossed himself, rolled up his sleeves, and consumed it with relish and incredible rapidity.

"If thou had'st dined with Christ when He divided
The loaves and fishes miracle provided,
No morsel had remained a dog to fill,
Whilst thou unsatisfied had'st hungered still,"

sang Bellincioni on the spur of the moment. Roars of laughter broke from the company. Only the face of the lonely and taciturn Leonardo retained its expression of resigned *ennui*.

When the concluding dish of gilded oranges had been served on silver plates, and handed with Malvoisie, then Antonio Camella da Pistoja, a court poet, recited an ode in which the duke was addressed by the Arts and Sciences and Elements in these terms:—

"We were slaves; thou camest, and we are free. *Evviva il Moro*."

VII

After supper the guests adjourned to the garden called "The Paradise"; laid out in geometrical figures with shorn edgings of box, alleys of laurel and myrtle, shaded walks, labyrinths, loggias, and woven arbours. Rugs and silken pillows were thrown on a lawn freshened by a glittering fountain. The ladies and their cavaliers grouped themselves with relaxing ceremony before the little court theatre, and an act of the "*Miles Gloriosus*" of Plautus was performed. It was tedious, but the audience, out of reverence for the ancients, feigned attention. After the comedy the young people played ball, tennis, and blind-man's-buff, running about, laughing and catching each other like children among the luxuriant and fragrant roses and orange-trees, while the elders were at dice, draughts, and chess. Others of the company gathered in a close circle on the steps of the fountain, and told *novelli* after the fashion of the youths and ladies of the *Decameron*.

Then they danced to the tune of the favourite air of "Lorenzo dei Medici":—

"Quant e bella giovinezza
Ma si fugge tuttavia
Chi vuol esser lieto, sia
Di doman non c'è certezza."

(Fair-fleeting Youth must snatch at happiness;
He knows not if tomorrow curse or bless.)

After the dance Madonna Diana, a gentle girl with a pale and lovely face, sang to the low notes of the lute a plaint on unrequited love. As by enchantment the noise and the laughter ceased, and all listened with thoughtful and reminiscent attention. It was long before anyone spoke, and after the ending of the song the hush was broken only by the quiet rustling of the fountain. But presently the voices and the mirth and the music awoke again, and were to be heard till late at night, when the laurels were lighted by fireflies, and in the darkened heaven reigned the new-born moon. And over all the Paradiso floated a soft air, rich with perfume of orange-blossom; and still trembled the notes of the Medicean canzone:—

"Chi vuol esser lieto, sia
Di doman non c'è certezza."

VIII

THE DUKE SAW A GLIMMER of light in one of the four palace towers. It was the lamp of Messer Ambrogio da Rosate, prime astrologer, and a member of the Secret Council, who was observing the conjunction of Mars, Jupiter, and Saturn in the sign of Aquarius, a matter of profound significance for the house of Sforza.

As if pricked in his memory, the duke hastily saluted Madonna Lucrezia, with whom he had been engaged in tender discourse, and entered the palace. He looked at the clock, and having awaited the precise minute and second enjoined by the astrologer, swallowed a rhubarb pill, and consulted a calendar in which he read the following note:—

"*August 5th.*—Eight minutes past ten of the evening, pray heartily on your knees, after folding your hands and raising your eyes to Heaven."

Fearing to be late, and so miss the prescription's efficacy, he hurried to the chapel, unlighted save by a single lamp before a picture. The duke loved the picture; it was by Leonardo, and represented Cecilia, Countess of Bergamini, arrayed like the Madonna, blessing a hundred-petalled rose. He counted eight minutes by the hour-glass, sank on his knees, folded his hands, and recited the *Confiteor*. He prayed long and fervently, his eyes on the picture.

"Mother of God," he murmured, "protect, save, and have mercy on me, on my son Massimiliano, and Cesare, the newly-born. I commend unto thee Beatrice, my consort, and Madonna Cecilia. And likewise Gian Galeazzo, my nephew, for thou see'st my heart, and knowest that I wish no evil to my nephew, though it may be that his death would set free not only my state, but all Italy."

Here he remembered the proof of his right to his throne which he had obtained from the jurisconsult, and which stated that his elder brother (father of Gian Galeazzo) having been born unto Francesco Sforza, the condottiere, before he became Francesco Sforza and Duke of Milan, whereas Ludovico was born unto the said Francesco *after* he had become duke—the younger not the elder was obviously the heir to the ducal dignities of the common father.

At this moment, however, the decision seemed to Ludovico rather ingenious than convincing. He hesitated to put it before the Mother of God, contenting himself thus:—

"If in anything I have sinned or shall sin before thee, O Queen of Heaven, thou knowest that I do so not for myself but for the good of my people and of Italy. Mediate for me with God, and I will glorify thee by the building in splendour of the cathedral in this town of Milan, and of the Certosa at Pavia, and of other glorious monuments."

After his prayer, candle in hand, he went toward his bedchamber, passing through the dark rooms of the sleeping palace. In one of them, however, he encountered Madonna Lucrezia.

"Truly, the god of Love favours me!" he thought.

"Signore!" exclaimed the girl; her voice broke, she would have thrown herself on her knees before him, as she added, "have pity on me, my lord!"

And she told him that her brother Matteo Crivelli, chief of the chamberlains, a man of abandoned life but whom she devotedly loved, had lost at play great sums of the public money.

"Fear not, madonna! I will save your brother."

He was silent for a moment, and added with a deep sigh:—

"And you too, O madonna, will you not be to me less cruel?"

She looked questioningly at him with serene and innocent eyes.

"I do not understand you, signore. What is your meaning?"

Her modesty rendered her yet fairer.

"It means, my sweet," he said, throwing his arm almost roughly round her, "it means—but, Lucrezia, have you not seen that I love you?"

"Loose me! Let me go! What do you, signore! Madonna Beatrice—"

"Shall not know!" said the duke.

"No, my lord, no. She is so good, so generous to me. Leave me, for pity's sake—"

"I will save your brother—do all your desire—be your slave. Only have pity on me."

And half-sincere in his passion and his tears, he murmured in trembling tones those lines of the poet's:—

"I sing, poor swan, of my consumèd years,
But singing brings my torture no relief;
Love with his laughter blows the flame of grief,
And mocking cries, 'Extinguish it with tears.'"

"Let me go! Let me go!" said the girl desperately.

But he bent over her, feeling the freshness of her breath, the perfume of violet and musk, and forcibly kissed her on the lips. For one moment Lucrezia languished in his embrace, then, with a despairing cry, broke from him and fled.

IX

HAVING REACHED THE NUPTIAL APARTMENT, he found the lamp extinguished, and Beatrice already reposing in the huge, mausoleum-like couch on a dais in the middle of the floor under a blue silk baldachin. It was adorned with silver curtains, and a coverlet, costly as the vestment of a priest, of cloth of gold and pearls.

"Bice," he whispered caressingly; "Bice, dost thou sleep?" and he would have saluted her, but she repulsed him.

"Bice—why is this?"

"Leave me in peace; I am fain of sleep."

"But why, dear one, why? If thou knew'st how I adore thee!"

"Yes, yes, I know you adore us all together. Your consort, and Cecilia, and *perdio*! the Muscovy slave-woman, the red-haired fool whom you kissed in the obscurer angle of my wardrobe room!"

"'Twas a jest."

"A jest I care not for."

"Alas, Bice, these many days thou hast been harsh to me! Well, I confess it—I am guilty; 'twas a scurvy jest—a caprice."

"Your caprices, my lord, are many."

She turned towards him angrily. "How is it you have no shame? Why, why these lies? Do I not know you?—read you to the soul? I would not have you think this jealousy; but I will not, hear you, my lord?—I *will not* be one among your lemans."

"I swear to thee, Bice, I have loved none save thee. By my soul's eternal weal, I swear it."

She was silent, surprised less by his words than by the tone in which they were uttered. He was not wholly lying. The more he deceived her the more he felt he loved her, as if passion were inflamed by fear, qualms of conscience, pity, and remorse.

"Pardon, Bice, pardon," he implored; "consider my love for thee—"

She submitted herself; and as he embraced her, invisible in the darkness, he remembered serene and innocent eyes, and a perfume of freshness, of violet and musk; the two loves confused themselves in an exquisite sensation.

"Truly today thou art something like a lover!" she said with inward pride.

"Of a truth, dear one; it is still as it was in our first days—"

"Foolishness!" cried Beatrice laughing; "Fie on this trifling. Rather should'st thou be thinking of deeper matters. It seems as though *his* health were mending."

"Nay, 'tis but few days since Luigi Marliani assured me there was no hope for him," replied the duke; "'tis true we have now a little amendment, but it will not be for long; he is doomed beyond remission."

"Who can tell?" urged Beatrice; "he is over-tended. Of a truth, Ludovico, I marvel at your patience. You bear insults like a sheep. You say 'The power is in our hands,' but were it not better to renounce power at once than to tremble for it night and day like thieves; to lick the dust before that haughty bastard who is the King of France; to be slaves at the mercy of the impudent Alfonso; to weary ourselves in propitiating that perfidious sorceress of Aragon! They say she is pregnant again: a new serpent will come forth from that cursed nest. And to fare thus for our whole lives! Consider, Ludovico, for our whole lives! And you call that having the power in our own hands!"

"But the physicians constantly aver," repeated the duke, "that this malady is incurable; sooner or later—"

"Ay, 'tis later then. For ten years he hath been dying."

There was a silence. Suddenly she threw her beautiful arm round his neck, and drawing herself to him, she whispered in his ear—words which made him shudder.

"Bice! may Christ and His most holy Mother pardon thee! Never—dost heed me?—never again speak to me of that."

"You are afraid, perhaps? Would you wish *me* to try?"

He did not answer, but asked presently:—

"Of what thinkest thou?"

"My lord," she answered, "I am thinking about peaches."

"Ay; I have bidden the gardener send thee of the ripest."

"I care not for them. My thought was of the peaches of Messer Leonardo. Hast thou heard aught of those?"

"What should I have heard?"

"That they be poisoned."

"How poisoned?"

"'Tis true. He hath poisoned them himself, by magic, for his experiments. Monna Sidonia told me; wonderfully beautiful peaches!"

And again they were silent, embracing thus in the stillness and the dark; their thoughts united, each listening to the quickened beat of the other's heart—no further speech needed. At last Il Moro, with almost paternal tenderness, kissed his young wife on the brow, and made the sign of the cross.

"Sleep, dear one," he said, "sleep in peace."

That night the duchess saw in her dreams fair peaches on a platter of gold. She proved one and found it succulent and toothsome; but of a sudden a voice cried unto her:—

"Poison! poison!" and again, "Poison!"

The duke likewise dreamed his dream. And in it he fancied himself walking on the shining lawn beside the fountain. And before him at a little distance he saw three women, white-clad and embracing like fair sisters. And nearing himself, he perceived the one to be Beatrice, and the second Lucrezia, and the third Cecilia. He thanked his God that at last they were friends; but in his heart he blamed them that they had not been friends from the first.

X

THE CLOCK IN THE CASTLE tower struck the hour of midnight, and everywhere was the silence of sleep, saving only on the *altana*, where the duchess was wont to gild her hair; for thither Morgantina, the dwarf, had fled, having escaped from the closet in which she had been confined: there, alone in the darkness, she bewailed the loss of her baby.

"They have slain me my son! And wherefore, O Lord, wherefore? He had done no wrong to anyone; he alone comforted me!"

The night was serene; the air so pure, so transparent, that against the horizon the icy summits of the Alps were visible, like everlasting crystals. The stillness was long perturbed by the mournful cries of the madwoman, like the keening of some bird of evil omen. Suddenly she gave a sigh, raised her eyes to heaven, and was silent.

The stillness of death followed; and the fool smiled at the stars which, far above in the measureless blue of a summer night, were shining upon her—innocently and mysteriously shining.

Book IV

The Witches' Sabbath—1494

"Heaven above—heaven below,
Stars above—stars below,
All which is over man—under him shows;
Glory to him who the riddle readeth!"

—Tabula Smaragdina

I

In an obscure outskirt of Milan, near the Porta Vercellina, the Customs House, and the canal called the Acqua Cantarana, stood an old house, very solitary, and remarkable for the smoke which day and night ascended in large spirals from an immense, winding, and blackened chimney. Here dwelt Monna Sidonia, the wise woman. The upper floor she hired to Messer Galeotto Sacrobosco, an alchemist; and in the lower she lived herself with Cassandra, his niece, the young daughter of Luigi Sacrobosco, a celebrated traveller, who had traversed Greece, the islands of the Archipelago, Syria, Asia Minor, and Egypt, in the quest for specimens of ancient art. He possessed himself of all that came to hand: a Greek marble, or a trifle of amber, a sham inscription from the tomb of Homer, a new tragedy by Euripides, or a peroration by Demosthenes. Some thought him a great man, but others dubbed him an impostor; and not a few believed him crazy. His imagination was so enthralled by pagan recollections that though to the last a good Catholic, he prayed to the Olympian Hermes, and regarded Wednesday (*Mercoledi*) his day, as one singularly propitious for mercantile ventures. No toil, no privations, daunted him in his enterprises. On one occasion, having already put out ten leagues to sea, he returned to copy an inscription of which accident had informed him. Having lost his collection in a shipwreck, his hair turned white with grief. If asked why he so plagued himself and spent his days in such sore labour, he always replied:—

"I desire to raise the dead."

In the little town of Mistra, near the ruins of Lacedæmon, he met a maiden of extraordinary beauty, resembling the statues of Artemis. She was the daughter of a poor and drunken village deacon; Luigi married her and took her to Italy with a new copy of the Iliad, the fragments of a Hecate, and the shreds of an earthenware amphora.

To the pair was born a daughter, whom they called Cassandra, Luigi being at that time impassioned for Æschylean tragedy. The wife died, and the father was off on his wanderings, so the child was left to the care of Demetrius Chalcondylas, a learned Greek from Constantinople who had been brought to Milan by the Sforzas. This old man of seventy, a double-faced, cunning, and secretive person, pretended a vast zeal for the Catholic Church; in his heart, however, like Cardinal Bessarione, and most of the immigrant Greeks, he was a disciple of the last of the masters of the ancient wisdom, Gemistus Pletho, the Replete with Learning, the neoplatonist who had died forty years before at Mistra, where Luigi had become enamoured of his Artemis. This man had been affirmed by his disciples to be a re-incarnation of the illustrious Plato himself; the theologians, on the contrary, maintained that he had revived the anti-Christian heresies of Julian the Apostate, and that he was to be fought not by argument and controversy, but by the Inquisition and the stake. Chiefly they accused him on account of certain words uttered to his disciples three years before his death. He had said; "But a few years after I shall have died, one sole Truth shall reign over all peoples and nations, and men shall unite in the single faith" (*unam eandemque religionem universum orbem esse suscepturam*). Being questioned whether he meant the faith of Christ or of Mahomet, he answered; "Neither the one nor yet the other, but a faith which in naught shall differ from the ancient paganism" (*neutram, inquit, sed a gentilitate non differentem*).

Cassandra was bred by Chalcondylas in strict though feigned Christian piety. Overhearing, however, much neoplatonic talk, and not understanding its philosophical subtleties, the maid wove for herself a fantastic dream of the coming Resurrection of the Gods. On her breast she wore a talisman against fever, a present from her father; it was a gem representing Dionysus as a naked youth, with thyrsus and vine-branch, a rearing panther trying to lick the grapes in his hand. Sometimes, when quite alone, she would hold her amethyst up to the sun and gaze into its purple depths until her head swam, and she saw the god in a vision, living, and ever young and adorable.

Messer Luigi ruined himself at last in his quest for treasures, and died miserably of a putrid fever in a shepherd's hut beside the ruins of a Phoenician temple, which he had himself discovered. Soon after, Galeotto, his brother, who also had wandered for many years in pursuit, not of antiquities but of the philosopher's stone, came to Milan, established himself in the little house by the Vercellina gate, and took his niece to live with him.

She still, however, frequented the house of Chalcondylas, and thither came Giovanni Boltraffio to execute some copying for Messer Giorgio Merula.

Encountering Cassandra again, Giovanni remembered the talk he had overheard between her and Zoroastro about the poisoned tree, and he shuddered. Many told him the maiden was a sorceress, but her charm was not to be resisted, and almost every evening when his work was done he sought her in the lonely cottage by the Vercellina gate. They sat on a hillock together above the dark and silently swift waters of the canal, not far from the sluice gates near the convent of St. Radegonda. A scarce visible path, tangled with elder-bushes, wormwood, and nettles, led to the little hillock; no one ever passed that way, and there the two met and loitered and talked long together.

II

IT WAS A SULTRY EVENING; at rare intervals a gust came flying, raising the white dust and rustling in the leaves. It passed by, leaving the stillness stiller than before. Nothing was heard but the dull, seemingly subterranean growl of distant thunder, and against this low, threatening, and solemn roar, the broken shrillness of a lute and the drunken song of the customs-collector celebrating the Sunday feast in the neighbouring tavern. At times a flash broke across the clouds, and then for a moment the little house with the brick chimney, and the black smoke of the alchemist's furnace, the long lean sacristan fishing from the bank, the straight canal with the rows of larches and willows, the flat-bottomed barges from the Lago Maggiore bringing white marble for the cathedral, and drawn by sorry horses, their loose towing-ropes and the long whips of the drivers dipping in the water—all stood out sharp and clear against the prevailing blackness. All was again wrapped in gloom, save for the alchemist's fire always vividly glowing. It was reflected in the Cantarana, whence came noisome odours of stagnant backwaters, rotting fern-leaves, tar, and decaying wood.

Giovanni and Cassandra were in their accustomed haunt.

"'Tis tedious!" cried the girl, stretching herself wearily and snapping her delicate white fingers behind her head; "everyday the same dull round. Today as yesterday, and tomorrow as today. That same foolish sacristan catching nothing; the same filthy smoke from Messer Galeotto's workshop, where he, too, eternally seeks what he will never find; the same boats towed by the same hateful horses; the same cracked lute! Ah, if it would but change! If the French would come and rid us of Milan! if the sacristan would catch a fish, or my uncle find some gold. *Dio Mio!* what weariness!"

"I know!" cried Giovanni. "I also at times find life so wearisome that I am fain to die. But Fra Benedetto taught me a prayer very prevalent against the demon of discontent. Shall I recite it for you?"

"Nay, Giovanni. It is long since I have been able to pray to your God."

"My God? What god is there but my God? the only God?"

A quick flash, like the lightning of the storm, illumined her face; never had it seemed to him so mystic, so unearthly, so fair. She was silent for a time, passing her hand over the dark aureole of her hair.

"Hearken, friend. It was long ago—yonder—in my native land. I was scarce more than a babe. My father had taken me with him on a journey. We visited the ruins of an ancient temple. They stood high on a promontory; the sea was around us and the screaming gulls; the waves were breaking endlessly on black rocks, sharp as needles, and covered with salt foam, which rose and fell, running off the sharp points of the rocks in a seething stream. He found a half-faded inscription on the fragment of a marble slab. I sat long alone on the temple steps, listening to the sea and breathing in its freshness, mixed with the scent of the sea-herbs. Then I went into the abandoned shrine. The columns were yellow, but scarce crumbled by time, and between them the azure sky seemed dark. There were poppies growing in the crevices between the stones—pink poppies—the poppies of Greece! It was quite still, but for that muffled roar of the waves which filled the temple as if with the voices of prayer. And I fell on my knees and prayed to the god who had once been enshrined there—unknown and now rejected by men. I kissed his marble steps, and I wept and loved him because no one on earth loved him anymore, nor prayed to him—because he was dead.

Never since have I prayed so fervently! And that temple—it was the temple of DIONYSUS!"

"By the love of God, Cassandra, what are you saying? This Dionysus, whom you call God, exists not, nor did exist."

"Did he not?" cried the girl, scornfully; "then why teach the holy fathers, whom you reverence, that the gods, banished in the days of the conquering Jesus, were changed into most potent demons? How could Giorgio da Novara, the great astronomer, learn by exact observation that the conjunction of Jupiter with Saturn produced the teaching of Moses; with Mars, that of the Chaldeans; with Venus, that of Mahomet; with Mercury, that of Christ; and that conjunction with the moon—future for him—would bring the teaching of Antichrist and the Resurrection of the Gods?"

The storm was drawing nearer, the thunder roared louder, the flashes grew ever brighter, heavy clouds were spreading overhead, yet still the broken lute sobbed forth its insistent melody on the threatening air.

"O madonna!" cried Boltraffio clasping his hands, "do you not see that 'tis the devil who is tempting you that he may lure you to the abyss! Eternal curses upon him!"

The girl turned, laid both hands on his shoulders, and said:—

"And does he not tempt you also? Why did you leave your sainted teacher, Benedetto? Why did you enter into the school of the impious Leonardo? What brings you hither unto me? Do you not know I am a witch? Are you not affrighted lest you lose your soul talking here with me?"

"The strength of the Lord defend us!" he stammered, shuddering.

She silently drew near him, fixing him with her wondrous eyes. At that moment the lightning rent the cloud and flashed on her pale face. Was she the goddess who had risen before Giovanni's awestruck gaze from her tomb on the Hill of the Mill?

"'Tis she!" he thought in terror. "She has found me again, the White She-devil!"

He would have risen, but his forces seemed to have left him. He felt the girl's hot breath on his cheek, and listened as she whispered:—

"Will you that I reveal everything to you? Will you fly with me thither where He is? Ah, it is good there! *There* is no weariness; nothing maketh ashamed. There all things are permitted as in Paradise!"

A cold sweat broke out on Giovanni's brow, but curiosity impelled him, and in a low voice he asked:—

"Where?"

"*Al Sabbato!*" she answered with passionate languor, her lips almost touching his cheek.

A peal of thunder, now quite overhead, shook earth and sky, rolling through the air in majestic reverberation, like the laugh of unseen giants. Then slowly it died away into the great silence.

And then rang out the melancholy peaceful sound of the convent bell, the evening Angelus. Giovanni made the sign of the cross.

"It is late," said the girl rising; "I must return homeward. Do you see those torches, there on the road? 'Tis the duke coming to visit Messer Galeotto, who is to show him an interesting experiment with lead. He thinks it can be turned into gold."

True it was, the tramping of hoofs was heard coming from the Porta Vercellina. Cassandra lingered for a moment, then darted through the tangled elder-bushes and disappeared.

III

Messer Galeotto had consumed his whole life in the search for the philosopher's stone. Having finished his medical course at Bologna University, he had entered as *famulus* the service of Count Bernardo Trevisani, renowned as an adept in the occult sciences. Afterwards, for fifteen years, he had sought the transforming mercury in all possible substances; in volatile salts, bismuth, arsenic, human blood, gall, and hair, in animals and plants. In this fashion the six thousand ducats of his patrimony had been dissipated in the smoke which ascended from his chimney. He must needs live on the wealth of others. Money-lenders cast him into prison; he escaped; and for eight years experimented with eggs, destroying some twenty thousand. Next he studied copperas with Maestro Enrico, the papal pronotary, fell ill from the poisonous fumes, lay in bed for fourteen months, and, deserted by everyone, came near dying. Having endured all humiliations and persecutions, starvation, beggary, contempt, and even judicial torture, he wandered as an itinerant artificer through France, Spain, the countries of the Empire, Holland, Greece, Persia, Palestine, Northern Africa. At last, old and worn out, but not yet disillusioned, he returned to Lombardy, where Il Moro promised him the office of court alchemist.

At Milan, in the lonely cottage by the Porta Vercellina, he had set up his laboratory. It was a large chamber, in the middle of which was a clumsy stove of fire-proof earth divided into compartments, and fitted with valves, crucibles and bellows. In one corner of the room was a pile of refuse. The working-table was heaped with every sort of complicated apparatus, cubes, rectifiers, receivers, retorts, funnels, mortars, test-tubes, bottles, baths. A pungent smell was given off by poisonous alkalis and acids. Here the seven gods of Olympus, the seven heavenly planets, a whole occult and mystic universe had its counterpart in metal: the sun in gold, the moon in silver, Venus in brass, Mars, iron, Saturn, lead, Jupiter, tin, and Mercury in quicksilver. Here were substances with barbaric names which struck terror into the profane. Here were wolf's milk, the iron of Achilles, anacardines, asterites (clear-shining stones, having in the midst an image of a full moon), androgyna, and rhaponticum, aristolochia or hart-wort (for giving ease in childbirth); and a priceless drop of the blood of a lion which had cost years to obtain, a gem, red as a ruby, which cures all diseases and blesses with eternal youth.

At his table sat the alchemist, meagre, small, wrinkled as an old mushroom, but still alert and tireless. His head supported on his two hands, Messer Galeotto was gazing intently at a retort, in which with low noise and bubbling was burning oil of Venus, a clear green fluid. The candle that burned by the philosopher's side sent an emerald light through the retort on an ancient parchment folio, a work by the Arab chemist Djabira Abdallah.

Hearing voices and footsteps on the stair, Galeotto rose, threw a glance round the laboratory to make sure all was ready, signed to his silent *famulus* to throw fuel on the furnace, and sallied forth to meet his guests.

IV

THEY WERE A MERRY COMPANY of knights and dames, just risen from supper and Malvoisie. Leonardo was there, and Marliani, the court physician, a man profoundly versed in alchemy. The ladies entered, and the quiet cell of the student was filled with perfumes, with the rustle of silk, with light chatter and laughter like the hum of birds. One damsel overturned a retort with her hanging sleeve, another meddling with a piece of iron slag cut her dainty glove, another spilt the mercury on the table and screamed with delight on seeing the living silver drops.

"And shall we really see Messer Satan in the fire at the moment of the lead's conversion?" asked Madonna Filiberta of her Spanish lover; "is it not a sin to assist at such experiments?"

The alchemist whispered in Leonardo's ear:—

"Believe me, Messere, I hold myself much honoured by your visit." And he warmly clasped his hand, adding before Leonardo could respond:—

"Oh, I know, I know! 'Tis a secret from the crowd; but we understand each other, do we not?"

Then with a smile of great affability he said aloud:—

"With licence from my most illustrious protector, the renowned duke, and of all these loveliest ladies, I will adventure, now to exhibit the divine metamorphosis. Will you all condescend to lend me your honourable attention?"

First he showed his crucible, a melting-pot with thick sides of fire-proof clay; he begged each one to examine it, and tap it, and convince himself there was no concealed deception, while he animadverted on the frauds of pretended philosophers who were wont to have vessels with false bottoms in which gold had been placed, not made. He also craved inspection of the pewter, the fuel, the bellows, and all else, to prove his good faith. Then the lead was chopped into small pieces and consigned to the crucible, which was then put on the hottest place of the furnace. The silent, cross-eyed *famulus*—so pale, corpse-like and surly, that one of the ladies near fainted, believing him the expected Messer Satan—began to work a huge pair of bellows, and the fire quickly leaped into flame. Galeotto meanwhile entertained his visitors with conversation, and awakened general mirth by calling his science of alchemy *casta meretrix*, who had many lovers but deluded them all, offered easy conquest to everybody, but had so far yielded to the embraces of none.

Luigi Marliani, the court physician, a fat, taciturn, gloomy man with a dignified and intelligent face, lost patience with this chatter, and wiping his brow, cried out:—

"Messer Galeotto, methinks 'tis time for business. Your metal is already bubbling."

Galeotto opened a little blue paper packet which contained a bright yellow powder, viscous and sparkling, like highly polished glass. It had a strong smell of burnt sea-salt. This was the momentous tincture, the long-sought, priceless jewel of alchemy, the wonder-working *lapis philosophorum*.

With the point of a knife he detached a speck of the powder no larger than a turnip-seed, wrapped it in a ball of bees-wax, and tossed it into the boiling pewter.

"And what do you consider the strength of that solution?" asked Marliani.

"One to two thousand eight hundred and twenty of the metal to be converted," replied Galeotto. "Naturally my solution is not yet perfected, but shortly, I hope, the figures will be one to a million. Then it will suffice to take of it the weight of a grain of millet, to dissolve it in a barrel of water containing the parings of a hazelnut; and finally, to sprinkle your vines therewith; in result you will have your vintage in May. *Mare tingerem si Mercurius esset.* I would turn the sea into gold had I competency in quicksilver."

Marliani turned away with a shrug. This bombast infuriated him, and he hinted the impossibility of such transformations by arguments supported by Aristotle.

"Have patience, *domine magister*," said Galeotto with a smile; "in a little space I will propound to you such a syllogism as not all your logic can confute."

Therewith he threw a handful of white powder in the fire. Clouds of thick smoke filled the laboratory. Hissing and crackling, up leapt a many-coloured flame, changing like a rainbow from blue to green, from red to yellow. The spectators were alarmed, and Filiberta afterward swore that at the instant the flame was purple, she saw in it the face of the Devil. The alchemist with a long hooked iron raised the lid of the crucible. The metal, white-hot, bubbled and hissed and gurgled. Then the lid was replaced; the bellows soughed and whistled, and when ten minutes later a thin iron rod was dipped into the molten liquid, all saw hanging on its end a yellow drop.

"Ready!" cried the alchemist.

The pot was now removed from the furnace and allowed to cool. Then before the astounded spectators, there fell from it, sparkling and resounding on the earthen floor, a bar of gold. The alchemist pointed dramatically, and exclaimed:—

"*Solve mihi hunc syllogismum!*"

"Unheard of! Incredible! Against all the laws of nature and of logic!" murmured Marliani in stupefaction.

The face of Galeotto was white, his eyes glowed with the fire of inspiration, and looking up to heaven, he cried:—

"*Laudetur Deus in æternum!* Praise God in eternity who deigns to give part of his infinite power unto us, the most abject of his creatures."

The gold was tested with sulphuric acid. It proved to be purer than the finest of Hungary or Arabia. The company pressed about the venerable philosopher, congratulating him, and wringing his hands. Il Moro took him aside.

"You serve me in fidelity and truth, Messer Galeotto?"

"I would I had more lives than one, that I might dedicate them all to your Excellency," replied the alchemist.

"Then, Galeotto, beware lest any of the other princes—"

"*Illustrissimo*, if there be one of them who shall get even a scent of it, have me hanged for a hound." And after a pause he added, bowing very low, "I would pray of your Excellency—"

"What? Again?"

"God is my witness, 'tis for the last time."

"How much?"

"Five thousand ducats."

The duke reflected, reduced the sum by a thousand, and promised. It was now late; Madonna Beatrice might be anxious; the company hastened to take their leave, each one receiving from the alchemist a fragment of the new-made gold. Only Leonardo remained behind.

V

When they were alone Galeotto said to him, "Well, Master, what think you of my experiment?"

"The gold was in the rods," replied Leonardo dryly.

"What rods? What do you mean, Sir?"

"The rods with which you stirred the molten metal. I saw all."

"Did you not yourself examine all my utensils?"

"These rods were not those we examined."

"Not those! Master, permit me—"

"Have I not told you I saw everything?" repeated Leonardo with a smile. "Be not obstinate, Galeotto. The gold was concealed in hollow rods tipped with wood. When the wooden ends were consumed in the molten mass, the gold fell into it."

The old man's legs shook; over his face spread a look at once abject and pathetic. Leonardo touched him on the shoulder.

"Fear not, Messer Galeotto, none shall know. I am no tale-bearer."

The impostor seized his hand feverishly and cried:—

"You will not betray me?"

"No. I wish you no ill. But, Messer Galeotto, why these frauds?"

"Oh, Messer Leonardo," cried the other, and immediately the boundless despair in his eyes was transfigured by a flash of hope, "I swear to you by God, that if I seem to have practised deception, 'tis but for the welfare of the duchy, for the triumph of science, and because my deception shall endure but a brief space. For, Messer Leonardo, truth it is that I have verily found the philosopher's stone. I do not assert that I have it yet in my possession, but I know that it already exists. That is to say, it as good as exists; for I have found the way, and you know that the way is everything. Three or four more experiments, and lo! it is accomplished. What was I to do, Messere? Is not the discovery of so grand a truth justification for so small a deception?"

"Nay, Messer Galeotto," replied Leonardo gravely, "to what purpose would you play with me at blind-man's-buff? You know right well, even as I know, that the transmutation of metals is a baseless dream: that there is no philosopher's stone, nor can be one. Alchemy, necromancy, black magic, all these sciences not founded on mathematics and exact experiment are delusion or deception—flags of charlatans, swelled but by the bellying of the wind, after which runs the gaping herd, applauding it knows not what."

His eyes round and bright with astonishment, the alchemist hung on the lips of the master, and when Leonardo stopped he did not reply. Presently, however, he nodded his head intelligently and winked.

"Ah! ah! Messer Leonardo, but this will not serve. Am I not of the initiated? And do we not all know that thou thyself art the prince of alchemists, the possessor of the most recondite mysteries of nature, the new Hermes Trismegistus, the new Prometheus."

"I?"

"Thou thyself, Master."

"Call you this jesting, Messer Galeotto?"

"Contrariwise. 'Tis you, Messer Leonardo, who would jest. How astute and impenetrable you are! In my time I have seen many who were jealous of their secrets of science, never an one like you."

Leonardo looked at him searchingly; he strove in vain to be angry. He smiled involuntarily.

"Do you seriously believe in these arts?" he asked.

"Do I believe in them? Messere, if God Himself came to me hither at this moment and said to me: 'Galeotto, there is no philosopher's stone,' I should answer him: 'Lord, even as it is true that thou hast created me, so is it true that there is that stone, and that I shall find it.'"

After this Leonardo disputed no more, but listened with interest to the speculations of the alchemist. Presently the talk swerved to the possible assistance of the Devil in the occult sciences; the old man, however, would none of this. He declared the Devil to be the weakest, the most miserable, the most impotent of all the creations of God; he himself had faith only in the human mind, and believed that to science all things were possible.

Then suddenly, without any consciousness of an abrupt transition, and as if playing with some agreeable and diverting recollection, he asked whether Messer Leonardo had frequent apparitions of elemental spirits. And when his interlocutor confessed to never having seen any, Galeotto again refused to believe him; and with relish told how the salamander has a body a finger and a half in length, spotted, thin, and harsh, while the sylphide is blue as the sky, transparent, and ethereal. He spoke also of the nymphs and undines that live in the rivers and the sea; of the gnomes, pygmies, and underground dwarfs; of the durgans and dryads, dwellers in trees, and the rare spirits that inhabit precious stones.

"I cannot convey to you," concluded Galeotto, "how beneficent and exquisite are these genii!"

"Why, then," asked Leonardo, "do they appear only to the elect?"

"Would you have them appear to all? They dread vulgar persons, libertines, materialists, drunkards, and gluttons. They affect the innocent, the childlike, simple ones. They live only where there is no malice nor cunning. Timid and fearful as gazelles they take refuge from human eyes in their native elements."

And a smile of infinite tenderness illuminated the old man's face, as if at the memory of long-ago dreams.

"What a charming old fool!" thought Leonardo, no longer scornful, but ready to simulate participation in any scientific absurdity to please this man, whom now he treated with affectionate consideration, like a child.

They parted as friends; and the moment he was alone the alchemist plunged into new experiments with the oil of Venus.

VI

All this time Monna Sidonia, the mistress of the house, and Cassandra sat before an immense open fireplace in the room below Messer Galeotto's laboratory. Their supper of coarse vegetables was stewing on the hearth, and the old woman with unvarying motion of her wrinkled finger spun the linen thread with her distaff. Cassandra watched her idly, and thought:—

"Always the same thing. Today as yesterday, tomorrow as today. The cricket chirps, the mouse squeaks, the spindle hums. There is a crackling in the dry sticks on the hearth, and I smell turnips and garlic."

Presently the old woman began prating in her usual way; saying that she was not rich, whatever the people might say about her money-pot buried in the vineyard. That was all an idle tale. The truth was, she was ruining herself for Galeotto and his niece. She had too much heart, that was it, or she would never keep them, the two of them hanging on to her neck like a pair of millstones. And of a truth Cassandra was no longer a child, and ought to be thinking of the future; her uncle would die some day or other, and leave her as poor as Job. She might at least get a husband. She might at least accept the hand of the rich horsedealer at Abbiategrasso, who had the folly to run after her. He was not young, but he was a staid, God-fearing man without any bees in his bonnet; had a good business and a mill, and an olive-press. What more did she want?

Cassandra listened in silence; but tedium sat on her like a nightmare; seized her by the throat and suffocated her. She felt an irresistible longing to break out into rebellious weeping and rage.

Monna Sidonia fished in the pot for a succulent turnip, mashed it up with grape-juice, and munched with apparent appetite; but the young girl, submissive though with growing desperation, stretched herself and interlaced her fingers behind her hair. After supper the old woman, like a wearied Fate, nodded over her distaff, and her talk died down into disconnected mumbling. Then Cassandra drew forth her talisman, and the firelight shining through its purple depths, she studied the figure of the naked god, and her heart filled with love for the beautiful Hellenic deities.

She sighed heavily, concealed her amulet, and said diffidently:—

"Monna Sidonia! tonight at Barco di Ferrara and at Benevento there is the gathering. Aunt! good kind aunt! we will not dance. We will go only to see. We will come back at once. I will do whatever you wish; I will even try to get a present out of the horsedealer—only be kind for once. Let us fly! let us fly together—now—at once!"

And the girl's eyes sparkled hungrily. The beldame surveyed her curiously; then her blue and withered lips parted in a smile which displayed her one tusk-like yellow tooth, and her face lit up with a hideous joy.

"Ah, you wish it? Very much, do you? You have caught the taste? Was there ever such a girl? For my part, I am ready to fly every night. But see you here, Cassandra, you take the sin on your own soul. Tonight I wasn't even thinking of it. I'll do it only for your sake, out of my too great goodness of heart."

Without haste the old woman went about the room, shut the shutters, stuffed rags into the chinks, locked all doors, poured water on the fire, lighted a black candle endued with magical properties, and from an iron locker took an earthen vessel containing a pungent ointment. She made show of being deliberate and sensible, but her hands shook as though she were drunk, her sunken eyes were at times turbid, at times they sparkled like coals. Cassandra had dragged the two great troughs used for the kneading of dough into the centre of the room.

Now Monna Sidonia stripped herself, and sitting astride of a broomstick on one of the troughs, she smeared herself with the ointment which she had taken from the locker. A hideous odour filled the room; the medicament, infallible for making witches fly, was composed of poisonous lettuce, hemlock, nightshade, mandragora, poppy, henbane, serpent's blood, and the fat of unchristened children.

Cassandra could not look at the hag's deformity. At the eleventh hour she recoiled.

"What are you about?" grumbled the crone; "are you going to leave me to fly alone? Come—make haste. Take your clothes off."

"All right. But, Monna Sidonia, put the light out. I can't do it in the light."

"Bah! what modesty! Never mind, there'll be no modesty on the mountain."

She blew out the candle, making the sign of the cross with the left hand for the pleasing of the devil, her master.

Then the girl rapidly undressed, knelt in the trough, and smeared herself.

In the darkness the old woman was heard mumbling the senseless disconnected words of an incantation.

"Emen Hetan, Emen Hetan, Palu, Baalberi, Astaroth, help us. Agora, Agora, Patrisa, come and help us!"

Cassandra eagerly snuffed the strong odour of the unguent. Her skin burned; her head swam; delicious thrills ran down her back. Red and green interlacing circles swam before her eyes, she heard the abandoned stridulous voice of Monna Sidonia as if from afar.

"Garr-r! Garr-r-r! Up! Up! Don't knock your head! We fly! We fly!"

VII

Forth from the chimney-top flew Cassandra astride on the soft hide of a black goat. Ravished, panting, with exaltation filling her soul, she screamed like a young swift, plunging for the first time through the blue air.

"Garr-r! Up! Up! We fly! We fly!"

The deformed and withered body of Aunt Sidonia flew beside her on a broomstick; her thin hair streaming in the blast.

"To the north! To the north!" yelled the hag, managing her broomstick like a horse.

Cassandra burst into peals of laughter, remembering poor Messer Leonardo and his cumbrous mechanism.

Now she ascended, and the black clouds rolled together beneath her; now they burned blue in the flashes of jagged lightning. But above the clouds the sky was clear. A full moon shone, huge and round as a millstone, and so near she could touch it with her hand. Affrighted, she guided the goat downwards again, and he plunged with her headlong into the void.

"Devil of a wench, you'll break your neck," screamed Sidonia.

Now they were skimming so close to the ground that they brushed the rustling meadow-grasses; will-o'-the-wisps guided their course past old tree-trunks gleaming with rottenness; while the owl, the bittern, and the goatsucker mourned plaintively among the reeds.

Presently they flew across the summits of the Alps, their icy spars glittering in the moonshine; and again they dropped to the surface of the sea. Cassandra, scooping water in her hand, tossed it in the air, and rejoiced in the sapphire splashes.

Momently their pace increased, and they came up with and distanced fellow-travellers; a sorcerer with long grey hair, in a tub; an ecclesiastic on a muck-rake, red, gorbellied, jovial as Silenus himself; a golden-haired, blue-eyed lass on a broom, a young and red-haired vampire on a grunting porker, and a hundred others.

"Whence come you, little sister?" cried Sidonia, and twenty voices answered her.

"From Candia! From the Isles of Greece! From Valenza! From the Brocken! From Mirandola, Benevento, from the caves and the fjords!"

"Whither go ye?"

"To Biterne! To Biterne! For the marriage of the great goat, the Buck of Biterne. Fly! Fly! Haste to the supper." And they passed over the dreary plain like a cloud of rooks on a whirlwind. The moon shone purple, and against it in the distance gleamed the cross upon a village church. The vampire hurled herself against it, tore away the cross and the great bell, casting them far off into the swamp, where they sank with a despairing clang. The vampire barked like a joyous dog, and the flaxen-headed lass on the cantering broomstick clapped her little hands with glee.

VIII

THE MOON WAS NOW HIDDEN by the clouds. Torches flared with flames of green and blue, and upon the chalky plateau the black shadows of the dancing witches spread and wheeled and interlaced and disentwined.

"Garr-r! Garr-r! 'Tis the Sabbath! 'Tis the Sabbath! From right to left! From right to left!"

They flew and they danced in their endless thousands like the withered and perishing autumn leaves. In their midst sat Hircus Nocturnus, the great he-goat, enthroned upon the mountain.

"Garr-r! Garr-r-r. Praise to the great Becco Notturno! The Buck of Biterne! The Buck of Biterne! Our wars are ended! Rejoice ye and rejoice!"

There was a screeching of pipes made of dead men's bones; the drum, stretched with the skin of the hanged, was beaten with the tail of a wolf. A loathsome stew was boiling in a vast cauldron, not seasoned with salt, for salt is abhorrent to the lord of that place.

Black were-cats were there dancing, lustful and emerald-eyed; slender maidens white as lilies; a shapeless capering incubus, grey as a spider; shuddering nuns; on a low bank, a white-bodied, plump, gigantic witch, with a stupid and good-natured face, was suckling two newly-hatched demons, already greedy and malicious. Three-year-old children, not yet admitted to the revelry, were feeding herds of toads, dressed as cardinals, with the sacred Host in their claws.

Sidonia and Cassandra joined the dance which sucked them in and whirled them away like a howling storm.

"Garr-r-r! from right to left! From right to left!"

Long wet whiskers like those of a walrus swept Cassandra's neck; a thin winding tail tickled her face, she was impudently pinched and bitten, hateful endearments were whispered in her ears. She made no resistance; the wilder the merrier; the more shameless the more intoxicating.

Suddenly petrifaction fell on the assembly; all voices were hushed, all movement was arrested. From the black throne, surrounded by terror, where sat the great Unknown, came a dull hoarse roar, like the growl of an earthquake.

"Receive you my gifts! To the weak, my strength; my pride to the humble; to the poor-spirited, my wisdom; to the afflicted, my joy. Receive my gifts!"

Then an old man of venerable aspect, his grey beard flowing—one of the fathers of the Holy Inquisition, at the same time patriarch of the sorcerers, and celebrant of the Black Mass, chanted in solemn tones:—

"*Sanctificetur nomen tuum per universum mundum et libera nos ab omni malo!* Be in awe, ye faithful ones, and fall prostrate!"

They knelt, falling on their knees with a crash, and as from one voice resounded the Sorcerer's Confession:—

"*Credo in Deum patrem Luciferum, qui creavit coelum et terram. Et in filium suum Beelzebub.*"

When the last sounds had died away, and there was renewed stillness, the same voice of the Unknown, deafening as an earthquake cried:—

"Bring hither my bride—my stainless dove!"

And the old man with the flowing beard inquired:—

"What is the name of thy bride, thy stainless dove?"

"Madonna Cassandra! Madonna Cassandra!" roared the great voice.

Hearing the pronouncement of her name, the girl's blood froze in her veins. Her hair stood erect.

"Madonna Cassandra! Cassandra!" rang the cry from the crowd. "Where hideth she? Where is our sovereign? *Ave Arcisponsa Cassandra!*"

She hid her face and would have fled; but bony fingers, claws, antennæ, and probosces, and the hairy legs of spiders seized her; and dragged her trembling before the throne. The rank odour of a goat, and a chill as of death smote her; she closed her eyes in dread. Then he upon the throne cried; "Come!"

Her head hanging, she saw at her feet a fiery cross gleaming through the darkness. She made a supreme effort, took a step forward, and raised her eyes.

Then a miracle took place.

The goat's skin fell from him as the scales from a sloughing snake; she was face to face with Dionysus the Olympian; thyrsis and vine-branch in his hands, a smile of eternal joy upon his lips, the panther at his feet pawing at the grapes.

And the *Sabbato diabolico* changed into the divine orgies of Bacchus; the witches became Mænads, the monstrous demons were kindly goat-footed Satyrs; the chalk rocks were colonnades of shining marble, lighted by the sun, and between them in the distance was the purple sea. The radiant gods of Hellas, surrounded by an aureole of fire, were gathering in the clouds, and the Satyrs and the Bacchantes, beating their timbrels, cutting their breasts with knives, squeezing the grape-juice into goblets of gold, and mingling it with their blood, danced and circled and sang:—

"Glory to Dionysus! Glory to Dionysus! The gods have risen! Glory to the eternal gods!"

And Bacchus, the ever young, opened his arms to Cassandra. His voice was like thunder, shaking earth and sky as he cried:—

"Come hither my bride! my stainless dove!"

And she sank into the god's embrace.

IX

From the distance sang the morning cry of the cock, and a sharp odour of fog and smoke greeted the nostrils. Slowly through the air came the sound of a bell, and at this sound the mountain was convulsed. Again the Mænads became the monstrous hags, the Satyrs or Fauns were demons, and the beautiful Dionysus resolved once more into the hideous and fetid Hircus Nocturnus.

"Homewards! Fly! Escape!"

"They have stolen my muck-rake!" the gorbellied ecclesiastic roared despairingly.

"Hog! return to me!" screamed the red-haired vampire, shivering and coughing in the mountain damp.

The setting moon once more shone out from behind the clouds, and in the pallid crimson of her light, the frightened witches, swarm after swarm, like unclean flies, streamed away from the mountain.

"Garr-r! Garr-r! Up from the depths! Do not knock your heads. Save yourselves. Fly!"

The Becco Notturno, bleating lamentably, sank through the earth, leaving the rotten and stifling odour of sulphur. And slow and solemn the church bells sounded more triumphantly through the purer air.

X

Cassandra returned to herself in the darkened chamber of the little house by the Porta Vercellina. She was nauseated as if after drunkenness. Her head was like lead; her body broken with weariness.

The bell of St. Radegonda was tolling heavily and monotonously. Outside someone was knocking insistently; someone who had already knocked more than once.

Cassandra listened, and recognised the voice of her suitor, the horsedealer from Abbiategrasso.

"For the Lord's love, open, Monna Sidonia! Monna Cassandra! Nay, then, are ye all gone deaf? I am wet through; would ye have me turn back through this fury of the elements?"

The girl dragged herself to her feet, crept to the shutters, and pulled out the rags with which her aunt had wedged them close. The dull light of a wet day streamed into the room, and fell on the naked crone, still sleeping a deathly sleep on the floor beside the trough, still stained with the unguent, and snoring profoundly.

Cassandra peeped out. The weather was detestable; the rain descending in torrents. Through the network of drops she could see the impatient lover, beside him his little ass, her head dolorously drooping as she leaned against the shafts of the cart, in which a calf, its feet tied together, mooed plaintively, stretching forth its muzzle.

The horsedealer getting no answer knocked louder than ever, and Cassandra waited to see what would happen. At last one of the laboratory windows opened, and the old alchemist looked out, his face sullen, as it generally was in the early morning.

"What's all this noise?" he cried; "have you gone out of your five wits, you old devil? Go to hell with you! Can't you see we're all asleep? Take yourself off!"

"Why insult me thus, Messer Galeotto? I have come on an affair of importance. I bring a present for your exquisite niece—a sucking calf—"

"Go to the devil, blockhead," cried Galeotto, "you and your calf!"

And the shutter was slammed to. The horsedealer stood for a moment dumbfounded; then, recovering himself, he knocked again, violently, as if he would smash the door with his fists.

The donkey's head drooped still lower, the rain pouring in streams off her long ears.

"God! how dull it all is!" murmured Cassandra, closing her eyes. And she thought of the frenzy of the Sabbath, the transformation of the Becco Notturno into Dionysus, the resurrection of the old gods, and she asked herself:—

"Was it reality or dream? In good sooth, 'twas a dream, and this is the reality! After Sunday always there is—just Monday!"

"Open! open!" yelled the horsedealer, hoarse and desperate. And the raindrops plashed monotonously in the miry pools, the calf bleated piteously, and the bell of the neighbouring convent tolled on, with even and melancholy strokes.

Book V

Thy Will Be Done—1494

"O mirabile giustizia di te, Primo Motore, tu non ai voluto mancare a nessuna potenzia l'ordine e qualità de suoi necessari effetti! O Stupenda Necessità."

—Leonardo Da Vinci

(O admirable Justice of Thee, Thou Prime Mover! To no force hast Thou permitted lack of the order and quality of its necessary effects. O Thrice-Marvellous Necessity!)

"Thy Will be done on earth, as it is in heaven."

—Paternoster

I

Corbolo the shoemaker, a citizen of Milan, having returned home one night over merry, received from his wife, as he said, "more blows than would have driven a tired ass from Milan to Rome." The next morning, when his spouse had gone to her neighbour's to fetch the black pudding, Corbolo rooted some concealed coins out of his pouch, left the shop to his apprentice, and went off for a drink, to recover himself.

His hands in the pockets of his threadbare breeches, he sauntered along the narrow street—so narrow that a horseman must needs prick the foot-passengers with his spurs—and sniffed the eternal smell of oil, rotten eggs, sour wine, and mouldy cellars. Whistling a tune, he looked up at the narrow strip of blue sky between the roofs, and at the many-coloured rags and torn garments stretched across the lane on lines that they might be dried in the sun, and solaced himself with his favourite proverb (of which, however, he never took the advice), "*Mala femina, buona femina, vuol bastone.*"

To shorten his road he passed through the cathedral, which was still in process of construction. Here there was noise and bustle as in a market-place. From door to door, notwithstanding the fine of five *soldi* imposed upon intruders, there passed persons carrying wine, baskets, cases, trunks, trays, planks, beams, bundles, some even leading asses and mules. The priests were praying and chanting; lamps burned on the altars, and murmurs came from the Confessional; yet the boys played at leap-frog, the dogs barked and fought, and sturdy beggars jostled each other in the quest for alms. Corbolo stood for a space in the crowd, listening with sly amusement to a dispute between two monks, a Franciscan, and a Domenican, on the comparative claims of St. Francis and St. Catharine to occupy the seat in heaven which had been left vacant by the fall of Lucifer.

Corbolo's eyes blinked as he came out of the cathedral gloom into the strong sunlight of the Piazza dell' Arrengo. This was the liveliest part of Milan, crowded with the booths of small vendors, and so overfilled with packing-cases and rubbish, that foot passengers could hardly make their way. From time immemorial these booths had lumbered the square, and no laws nor penalties could expel them.

"Salad of Valtellina! lemons! oranges! artichokes! asparagus!" cried the vegetable-seller.

The rag-wives babbled and cackled like brood-hens. A donkey, almost concealed under a mountain of grapes, oranges, cauliflowers, fennel, beetroot, tomatoes and onions, brayed in lacerating tones:—

"Hee—ho—Hee—ho." While his driver lustily thumped his shrunken sides, and yelled forth his guttural:—

"Arri—Arri!"

A long string of blind persons with sticks, and guides, chanted a doleful and tedious supplication. A street-dentist, his hat ornamented with a chaplet of teeth, was standing over a man whose head he held between his knees, and with the rapid movements of a juggler, was drawing his teeth with huge pincers. Children were spinning tops under the feet of the pedestrians, and teasing a Jew with offers of a pig's head; Farfanicchio, the leader of the scamps, had let a mouse loose among the market-women. It rushed up the ample petticoats of Barbacchia, the fruit-seller, who jumped up as if she had been scalded, cursing the ragamuffins, and shaking her garments regardless of propriety.

A porter, carrying a pig's carcase, turned round suddenly to see the fun, and terrified the horse of Messer Gabbadeo, the surgeon; it reared and plunged, and overturned a whole pile of kitchenware in the booth beside it; saucepans, frying-pans, skimmers, graters, rolled over with a deafening crash; the horse bolted and carried away the terrified surgeon, his arms round its neck, his great bass voice alternately imploring God and the devil to rescue him. The dogs barked, curious faces were thrust from windows; laughter, cries, curses, whistling, shouting rose on all sides; and the donkeys brayed from every side of the square.

Watching this diverting spectacle, the shoemaker said to himself philosophically:—

"The world would be a good place enough, if it were not for the women, who devour their husbands as rust devours iron."

Then shading his eyes with his hand, he looked up at the vast unfinished pile surrounded with scaffolding. This was the great cathedral, the magnificent temple which Milan was erecting in honour of the Birth of the Virgin. All, small and great, had contributed to the shrine. The queen of Cyprus had sent a precious cloth embroidered with gold. Caterina, the old rag-woman, had laid on the altar of the Virgin her only cloak, worth twenty *soldi*. Corbolo, who from his childhood had watched the progress of the building, saw this morning a new pinnacle, and rejoiced.

All around was heard the tapping of mallets and hammers. The immense blocks of sparkling marble brought from the quarries on the Lago Maggiore were landed on the wharf at Laghetto de Santo Stefano, not far from the Ospedale Maggiore, and were still arriving at the building; cranes creaked and rattled their chains, iron saws grated on the marble, the workmen swarmed around the scaffolding like flies. And daily the great temple was growing, with its countless spires, its belfries and turrets of pure white gleaming against the azure heavens; a perpetual hymn raised by the people of Milan to the glory of Maria Nascente.

II

Corbolo descended by steep stairs from the piazza to a cool arched cellar set with wine casks, of which the master was a German named Tibaldo. The shoemaker greeted the company, and sitting down by his friend Scarabullo the tinman, ordered a flask of wine and hot pastry flavoured with thyme; then he drank a long slow draught, filled his mouth, and said:

"Scarabullo, if you desire wisdom, take unto yourself no wife."

"Why not?" demanded Scarabullo.

"Because, friend, to marry is to thrust your hand into a bag of serpents in order to draw out an eel. Better have the gout than a wedded wife, Scarabullo."

At the table beside them, surrounded by a hungry and credulous crowd, Mascarello, the jolly goldsmith, was singing the praises of a fabulous land, where the vines are hung with sausages, and a goose and a gosling together cost a single penny; where there are mountains of cheese ready grated, and *gnocchi* and macaroni are cooked in the fat of capons and thrown to him who asketh; and *vernaccia*, the best white wine, into which enters not one drop of water, springs from the soil in a natural fountain. A little man named Gorgoglio, a glass-blower, at this moment came running into the tavern: by reason of the king's evil, his eyes were half-shut, like those of a new-born puppy. He was bibulous and a great lover of talk.

"Sirs, sirs!" he cried, raising his hat and wiping his streaming face, "I have seen the Frenchmen!"

"Gorgoglio, you dream. 'Tis impossible they be here yet."

"I' faith, they be here; they are at Pavia. Let me but breathe! 'Tis not weather for running, and I have run the whole course to be first with the news."

"Take my bottle. Drink and recount: of what sort be these French?"

"A bad sort, friends; a very bad sort. Heaven defend us from them! trust not your fingers in their mouths, friends. Choleric, savage infidels, like ferocious brutes; in a word, barbarians. They carry arquebuses eight braccia long, partisans of brass, iron bombards which belch stones; their horses are sea-monsters, shaggy, with docked ears and tails."

"Be they many?"

"Ay, a crowd; they beset the plain as locusts; you can see no end to them. The Lord hath sent them for the chastisement of our sins, this Black Death, these northern devils."

"But why, Gorgoglio, speak thus ill of them?" asked Mascarello; "they come as our friends—our allies."

"Allies! Hold your peace. Look after your pockets, say I, for that kind of ally is worse than an enemy. He'll buy the horn and steal the bullock."

"Rave not, Gorgoglio. Expound simply why you hold these French inimical."

"Because they trample down our crops; because they fell our trees, carry off our beasts, ravish our women. Their king is a baboon; no soul behind his teeth; but he is a great lover of women. He carries a book, pictures of our handsomest women. And they say that, God helping them, they will not leave a maid between Milan and Naples."

"The villains!" cried Scarabullo, thumping with his fist so that the glasses rang.

"And our Moro," continued Gorgoglio, "dances on his hind legs to the sound of the French pipe. And they don't count us to be men, neither. 'You,' they say, making their grimaces, 'you are all thieves and assassins. You have poisoned your rightful duke, you have murdered an innocent boy. For this God punishes you and gives us your land.' And we, friends, are receiving them into our arms and feeding them!"

"These be old wives' tales, Gorgoglio."

"Blind me, cut out my tongue if I speak not the truth! Nor have I told all. Hearken, *signori miei*, to what they have the audacity to say. They say 'We are destined to overcome all the peoples of Italy, to subdue all the seas and the nations of the sea, to destroy the grand Turk, and plant the true cross on the Mount of Olives in Jerusalem; then we will come back to you, and we will execute on you the fury of God. And if you submit not yourselves, your name shall be wiped off from the face of the earth.' That's what they say!"

"'Tis ill news," sighed Mascarello the goldsmith. "Unheard-of news!"

The rest were silent.

Then Fra Timotea, the lean Domenican, who had been disputing in the cathedral with Fra Cipolla about the saints in glory, raised his hands to heaven and said solemnly:—

"Such were the words of Fra Girolamo Savonarola, that great prophet of the Lord. 'Behold,' said he, 'the man cometh who is destined to conquer Italy without drawing the sword from the scabbard. O Florence! O Rome! O Milan! Past is the hour of feasting and of song! Repent ye, repent! The blood of Gian Galeazzo, the blood of Abel which was spilt by Cain, crieth for vengeance before the throne of God.'"

III

At this moment a brace of soldiers came in.

"The French! the French! See!" exclaimed Gorgoglio, nudging his companions.

One of the newcomers was a Gascon; young, tall, and shapely, with a handsome impudent face adorned by red moustachios; a cavalry sergeant named Bonnivart. The other old, fat, bull-necked, red-faced, swollen-eyed, ear-ringed, was a gunner from Picardy named Groguillioche. Both were a little drunk.

"*Sacrement de l'autel!*" said the sergeant slapping the others on the back. "Shall we at last find a mug of good wine in this accursed town? The sour stuff of this Lombardy burns my throat like vinegar." And stretching himself on a bench, and throwing a contemptuous glance at the company, he rapped with his knuckles, and shouted in bad Italian:—

"White wine, dry, your oldest; and brain-sausage for the first course!"

"You are right, comrade," said Groguillioche; "when I think of our wine of Burgundy, of the precious *Beaune* gold as my Lison's hair, my heart bursts with melancholy. Most true is it: 'Like people, like wine.' Let us drink, comrade, to the prosperity of our France."

"Du grand Dieu soit mauldit à outrance
Qui mal vouldroit au royaume de France!"

"What say they?" murmured Scarabullo into Gorgoglio's ear.

"Scurvy talk!" said the latter. "They praise their own wine, and praise not ours."

"Just look at those two French cocks," grumbled the tinman; "my hand itches to be at them."

Meanwhile Tibaldo, the German host, with fat belly on thin legs, and a formidable bunch of keys at his leathern girdle, drew from the cask half *brentas* of wine, and served them to the foreigners in an earthenware jug, looking most suspiciously at his guests. Bonnivart drank his potion at one draught, and found it excellent: none the less, he spat, making a face of disgust. Just then Lotte, Tibaldo's daughter passed by; a slim, flaxen-haired little lass, with kind blue eyes like her father's. The Gascon nudged his comrade, twirled his moustaches seductively, drank, and trolled out a song, to which Groguillioche added a husky chorus:—

"Charles fera si grandes batailles
Qu'il conquerra les Itailles,
En Jerusalem entrera
Et mont Olivet montera."

Presently Lotte passed them again, modestly dropping her eyes, but the sergeant caught her by the waist and tried to pull her to his knee. She pushed him away, broke loose, and fled. He jumped up, caught her and kissed her cheek, his lips still wet with wine. The girl screamed, dropped the pitcher she was carrying, and struck the Frenchman so hard a blow that for a moment he was stunned, at which there was a general laugh.

"Well done, wench!" cried the goldsmith. "By St. Gervaso, I ne'er saw a heartier smack, nor one more seasonably applied."

Groguillioche tried to restrain his companion.

"Let her alone. Don't make a fool of yourself," he said.

But the Gascon was flown with wine, and, laughing with a laugh that was but at one side of his mouth, he cried:—

"That's your way, is it, my beauty? *Ventre bleu!* next time it shall not be on your cheek, but fair on your lips."

Upsetting the table, he sprang after her, captured her, and would have executed his threat, had not the powerful hand of Scarabullo seized him by the throat.

"Ha! son of a dog! Hideous mug of a Frenchman! I'll teach you how to insult the girls of Milan!" and he shook his victim backwards and forwards, nearly choking him.

"*Sacrebleu! Sacrebleu!*" roared Groguillioche infuriated; "hands off, ruffian! *Vive la France! St. Denis et St. George!*" His sword was out, and prompt to be thrust into the tinman's back, but Mascarello, Gorgoglio, Maso, and the rest intervening, tied his hands. Now was utter confusion; tables overset, benches smashed, casks rolling, shards of smashed pitchers under the feet, everywhere pools of wine. Seeing blood, naked swords, and brandished knives, Tibaldo rushed into the street, and, in a voice fit to fill the square, yelled:—

"Assassination! Homicide! The French are sacking the town!"

At once the market bell rang forth and was answered by its brother of the Broletto. The dealers closed their shops. Fruit-sellers and rag-wives ran hither and thither packing their goods.

"San Gervaso and San Protaso! our protecting saints; lend us aid!" cried the fat vegetable-woman with the tremendous voice.

"What is on foot? What is happening? Is it a conflagration?"

"Down! Down with the Frenchmen!"

Farfannichio, the naughty boy, danced with delight, whistling and yelling.

"Down with the Frenchmen! Down with the Frenchmen!"

Guards and soldiers now appeared on the scene, mighty with arquebuses and pikes. They were just in time to rescue Groguillioche and Bonnivart from death at the hands of the mob. Laying hands right and left, they arrested amongst others Corbolo the shoemaker.

His wife, who had run up on sound of the tumult, now wrung her hands piteously, and wailed:—

"For pity's sake, let him go! Have mercy on my poor little husband! I will chastise him at home, and never allow him into a street squabble again. Believe me, Messeri, he is a perfect natural, and not worth the rope you would hang him with."

But Corbolo, hanging his head, fixing his eyes on the ground, and pretending not to hear these intercessions, hid behind the stout person of one of the guards, who seemed to him far less terrible than his spouse.

IV

Right above the scaffolding of the unfinished cathedral, up a narrow stair of rope to one of the slender pinnacles, not far from the principal tower, a certain young mason clomb, bearing a small statue of St. Catharine, to be fixed on the very top of the little spire. Around him rose a perfect forest of pinnacles, sharp-pointed like stalactites; spires, flying arches, stone lacework of unexampled flowers and foliage, prophets, martyrs, and angels, the grinning masks of devils, monstrous birds, sirens, harpies, dragons with scaly wings and gaping mouths, every sort of gargoyle at the terminals of the water-pipes. All was of marble very pure and white, upon which the shadows showed blue as smoke, the whole suggesting a winter wood clothed in sparkling frost. It was quiet, save that the swallows and swifts made joyous cries as they continually circled above and around the building. The hum of the crowd in the square reached the young mason like the low murmur of an ant-hill. At times he fancied organ-notes and prayerful sighs rose from the interior of the temple as from the depth of its stony heart; and then it seemed as if the whole vast edifice breathed and grew and heaved to the sky like the eternal praise of the birth of Mary; like the glad hymn of all ages and of all peoples to the Immaculate Virgin.

Suddenly the hum from the square increased in volume, and an uproar became plain to the ear. The mason paused in his work and looked down. Then his head swam and his eyes grew dim. He felt the edifice rocking under him, and the slender pinnacle towards which he was climbing bent like a reed.

"It is all over!" he said. "I am falling. Lord receive my spirit."

He clung desperately to the rope, closed his eyes, and murmured:—

"Ave Maria, piena di grazia."

Then he felt more at ease. From above swept a breath of cool wind; he recovered himself, collected his strength and climbed higher, listening no longer to the humming of earth, but ascending towards the serene and quiet heaven, saying with great unction:—

"Ave, dolce Maria, di grazia piena."

At this moment, traversing the broad marble roof, came the members of the building committee, Council of the Fabric, architects both native and foreign, summoned by the duke to consult about the Tiburio, the principal tower, which was to rise even higher than the cupola. Among them was Leonardo da Vinci; he had submitted his plan, but the council had rejected it as too daring, too extravagant, and not sufficiently in accord with the traditions of church architecture. The council quarrelled over the matter, and could not arrive at an agreement. Some said the building had been commenced by ignorant people, and that the inner columns were not stable enough to carry the Tiburio and all the lesser towers and pinnacles. According to others the cathedral was like to stand firm till Doomsday.

Leonardo took no part in the dispute, but stood aside, silent and alone. One of the workmen approached and handed him a letter.

"Messere," he said, "it has been brought to Your Magnificence by a messenger from Pavia."

Leonardo read the letter:—

"Leonardo, I need thee. Come to me at once. October 14.

GIAN GALEAZZO, the Duke

The Master excused himself to his fellow-councillors, descended to the square, mounted, and rode off to the Castle of Pavia, a few hours' distant from Milan.

V

IN THE GREAT PARK THE chestnuts, elms, and maples glowed golden and purple under an autumn sun. Slowly, like dead butterflies, the leaves dropped from the branches. There was no bubbling of water in the grass-grown fountains. Asters were withering in neglected flower-beds.

Approaching the castle Leonardo saw a dwarf; it was Gian Galeazzo's old jester, the only servant who had remained faithful to the dying duke. Recognising the painter, he advanced running and leaping.

"How is His Highness?" asked Leonardo.

The dwarf made no reply, only waved his hands with a gesture of despair; Leonardo directed his horse to the principal entrance, but the other stopped him.

"Nay, not by this road," said he, "it hath too many eyes. His Highness prays you to come secretly, for Madonna Isabella would forbid your entry did she know of it. Come by this path."

They entered by a corner tower, then mounted a stair and traversed apartments once magnificent but now gloomy and deserted. The gilded Cordovan leather had been torn from the walls; the throne and its silken canopy was hung with cobwebs; autumn winds had blown yellow leaves through the broken window panes.

"Thieves! ruffians!" muttered the dwarf, pointing out to his companion these marks of desolation. "Believe me, Messere, eyes cannot bear to look on the things done here. I would have fled to the uttermost ends of the earth were it not that my lord hath no one to look to but me, his ancient deformity. This way, I pray you, this way."

Opening a door he introduced Leonardo into a close dark room, heavy with the odour of drugs.

VI

At that moment Gian Galeazzo was being bled: according to the rules of surgery the operation was performed by candle-light, and with closed shutters. The surgeon, or rather the barber, a timid old man, was opening the vein, and his assistant held the brass basin; the physician, a man of grave and impenetrable countenance, wearing spectacles and a hood of dark purple velvet and squirrel's fur, merely watched, for to handle surgical instruments was derogatory to the dignity of a Doctor of Medicine.

"Before night he shall be bled again," said the great man when the arm had been bandaged and the duke was restored to his pillows.

"*Domine magister*," objected the barber respectfully, "were it not wiser to wait? The patient is weakened, and an excessive drain of blood—"

But he stopped short, for the doctor looked at him with freezing irony.

"'Tis time you knew that of the twenty-four pounds of blood in the human body you may let twenty without damage. I have bled sucking babes and seen them recover."

Leonardo listened to this conversation, but reminded himself that to dispute with doctors was vain as to argue with alchemists. He held his peace till the empirics had departed and the dwarf had covered the patient and shaken his pillows. Above the bed hung a little green parrot in a cage; cards and dice strewed the table. On it was also a glass with gold-fish, at the duke's feet slept a little white dog,—all the faithful servant's last attempts at ministering to his master's amusement.

"Has the letter been sent?" asked the sick man, not opening his eyes.

"Excellency, Messer Leonardo has come. We waited, fearing to disturb your Grace's slumber."

A feeble smile illuminated the duke's countenance. He tried to raise himself.

"Master, at last! And I had been fearing you would not come!"

Gian Galeazzo took the artist's hand in his, and a faint colour spread over his beautiful young face:—he was but four-and-twenty. The dwarf left the room to keep guard at the door.

"Friend," began the duke, "you have heard the slander?"

"Which slander, my lord?" asked the painter.

"If you know not which, 'tis that you have heard nothing, and it is not worth the trouble of telling you. Yet no, I will tell you, that we may have our mock at it together. They say—" He paused, looked the artist full in the eyes, and, smiling calmly, completed the phrase; "they say 'tis you have murdered me."

Leonardo thought him delirious, but he repeated:—

"Just that. They say 'tis you have murdered me. Three weeks ago Il Moro and his Beatrice sent me a basket of delectable peaches. But Madonna Isabella says that from the moment I tasted them I have pined away; that in your garden you have a peach-tree which bears poison."

"In very truth," assented Leonardo, "I have such a tree."

"*Amico mio!* can it be possible—"

"Nay; not if the fruit be really that from my garden. I can explain the reason of these rumours. To study the effect of poison upon trees, I inoculated my peach-tree with arsenic, and warned Zoroastro, my disciple, to beware of the fruit. Probably he was over hasty in relating the fact, for as matter of truth the experiment failed and the peaches have proved innocuous."

"I knew it! I knew it!" cried the duke with relief. "No one is guilty of my death. Yet here each one is suspecting the other, and hating and fearing him! If it were but possible to speak openly, as you and I speak to each other at this instant! My uncle is suspected of the deed; but I know him to be a kindly man, though timorous and weak. What interest could he have in my death when I myself am willing to give him my throne? I want nothing; I would gladly have left all these people and lived in retirement and liberty with a few chosen friends. I would have been a monk, or thy pupil, Leonardo. But no one will believe that I do not desire power. Why have they done this evil? *Dio mio!* they have not poisoned me, but they have poisoned themselves, poor blind ones! with the harmless fruit of thy harmless tree. I have grieved over perverse fate which makes me to die young, but now I am calm, I am at ease, Master, as though on a scorching day I had thrown off dusty clothes and cast myself into pure water. I know not how to tell thee, dear friend, but of a surety thou dost comprehend, thou who art thyself—"

Leonardo smiled serenely, and pressed the poor wasted hand, but did not answer.

"I knew that you would understand," continued the invalid with animation. "Do you remember how once you said to me that the study of those eternal laws which govern the vicissitudes of nature conducts men to humility and to great tranquillity of soul? Your phrase struck me even then; but now in sickness, in loneliness—ay, in delirium—how often do I remember thy words, and thyself, and thy countenance, and thy voice, O Master! Sometimes it seems to me that by different ways thou and I have reached the same end: thou by the way of life—I by death."

At this moment the door opened, and the dwarf burst into the room, and announced with agitation:—

"Monna Druda!"

Leonardo would have retired, but the duke detained him, and Gian Galeazzo's old nurse came in bearing a phial of scorpion ointment. It was a precious balsam, made by catching scorpions in the height of summer, when the sun is in Cancer, keeping them for fifty days exposed to the sun, then plunging them alive into hundred-year-old olive oil, mixed with groundsel, mithridates, and snake-root. Nightly the patient must be anointed at the temples, in the armpits, on the belly, round the heart; and then the wise woman swore he would take no ill from spells, from witchcraft, nor eke from poison.

The old nurse, seeing Leonardo seated on the bed, stopped, turned ashy-white, and came nigh dropping her priceless balm.

"*Santa Vergine benedetta!* Defend us!" she murmured. And crossing herself, and mumbling exorcisms and prayers, she ran as fast as her old legs would carry her, to bring Madonna Isabella the terrible tidings.

Monna Druda was entirely convinced that Ludovico the assassin, and Leonardo his accomplice, had brought Gian Galeazzo to his death, if not by poison, at any rate by witchcraft and the evil eye. The duchess Isabella, kneeling in her private chapel before the most sacred image, was praying fervently, when Monna Druda, greatly agitated, rushed in to tell her Leonardo was with the duke. The lady leaped to her feet, and cried, her face scarlet with indignation:—

"It cannot be! Who has allowed him to pass?"

"Nay, Most Illustrious, who can tell how this accursed sorcerer should pass? Have I not been saying to your Excellency—" She was interrupted by a page, who knelt before the lady.

"Most Excellent Madonna, will your ladyship and your ladyship's most illustrious consort deign to receive His Majesty the Most Christian King of France?"

VII

CHARLES VIII WAS LODGED IN the lower floor of the Castle of Pavia, luxuriously prepared for him by Ludovico Il Moro. Reposing after his dinner, he was listening to the reading of a book, absurdly translated out of the Latin into French, and called *Mirabilia urbis Romæ*.

Charles had been a solitary, sickly child, frightened to death by his father. During many weary years, in the Castle of Amboise, he had beguiled his melancholy by the reading of chivalric romances, till his brain, never of the strongest, was completely turned. At twenty years of age he was on the throne; and, his mind full of Lancelot, Tristram, and the other heroes of the Round Table, believed himself destined to rival these legendary persons, and to put into the reality of life what belonged only to books and to dream. The court poets bathed him in an atmosphere of perpetual adulation, calling him the offspring of Mars, the heir of Julius Cæsar, when at the head of a great host he had crossed the Alps, and made his descent into Lombardy, lured by the extravagant hope of conquering Italy and the East, and destroying the heretical Mahometan religion.

Tonight, listening to the description of the wonders of Rome, the King smiled, thinking of the glory to accrue to him from the Eternal City. His thoughts were, however, somewhat confused. He had dined heavily, and was now troubled by stomach-ache and headache, and above all by the recollection of a certain Madonna Lucrezia Crivelli, whose beauty had haunted him for a day and a night.

Charles VIII was low in stature and sufficiently ugly. His chest was narrow, his shoulders crooked, his legs thin as a pair of tongs. His nose was too large, his mouth hung open, his projecting eyes were so short-sighted as to give him a perpetually strained expression; his light hair was scanty, and he had no moustache; his hands and face twitched convulsively, his speech was thick and abrupt, it was said he had six toes, and for this reason had set the court fashion of broad soft shoes of black velvet, rounded at the top to the form of a horse-shoe. This general ungainliness, together with his habitual melancholy and distraction, produced an impression not too ill warranted of natural imbecility.

"Thibaut! Thibaut!" he cried suddenly to his valet, interrupting the reading with his customary abruptness, and stammering with the effort to find his words. "Thibaut! I—somehow think I am thirsty. Eh? Perhaps the heat—Bring me some wine—Thibaut—"

The Cardinal Brissonet, entering, announced that the duke was expecting His Most Christian Majesty.

"Eh—eh? What? The duke? Good; we come immediately. Let me first drink—"

And he stretched his hand for the cup brought by his servant. Brissonet, however, stopped him, and demanded of Thibaut:—

"Is it of our own?"

"No, Monsignore; from the ducal cellar. Our own is consumed."

Brissonet upset the cup.

"Your Majesty will pardon me, but the wines of this place may be unwholesome. Thibaut, send a messenger at once to the camp, and let him fetch a barrel from the field cellar."

"Why—eh? What is this?" asked the King disconcerted.

The cardinal whispered that he feared poison; anything might be expected from men who had done to death their legitimate sovereign; true, nothing suspicious had yet occurred, but prudence never comes amiss.

"Eh? All child's folly!" grumbled Charles, twitching one shoulder: however, he submitted.

The heralds took their places before the king; pages raised over his head the splendid baldachin of blue silk, embroidered with the silver lilies of France; the seneschal threw on his shoulders a scarlet mantle, ermine-bordered, and embroidered with golden bees, and the motto, "*Roi des abeilles n'a pas d'aiguillons*"; the procession traversed gloomy and deserted halls, and took its way to the apartments of the dying man.

Passing the chapel, the king caught sight of the Duchess Isabella at her faldstool. He gallantly removed his cap, stopped, and calling her "dear sister," would have kissed her on the lips, according to the French ceremonial, but the duchess hurried to throw herself at his feet.

"Have compassion on us, most clement lord," she began hurriedly, in set words. "Defend the innocent, O magnanimous knight-errant, and God shall give thee thy reward! Il Moro has robbed us of everything; he has usurped our throne; has given poison to Gian Galeazzo, my husband, legitimate inheritor of the Lords of Milan! In our own house he has surrounded us with spies and assassins. . ."

Charles scarcely understood or even listened.

"Eh? Eh? What?" he asked, stammering and twitching. "No, no, sister. No occasion. . . Rise, rise, I beseech you."

But the unhappy lady knelt on, embracing his knees, weeping, and covering his hands with kisses.

"Ah, Sire, if you also fail me, what remains to me but to take my life?"

This completed the king's embarrassment; puckering his face like a child about to cry, he stuttered:—

"There, there! Good God! 'tis impossible! Brissonet! Brissonet!—I can't. You tell her that—"

Before this lady, who in her humility and her desperation appeared to him sublime as some heroine of antique tragedy, he felt no sentiment of compassion, but only an inane desire to make his escape.

"Most noble lady, calm yourself," said the cardinal, coldly courteous. "His Majesty will do all that is in his power for you and for your consort, Messer Jean Galeas." (So he Gallicised the name.)

The duchess looked at the cardinal; then looked at the king; and as if realising for the first time the sort of being to whom she was making supplication, became silent.

Deformed, pitiful, ridiculous, he stood before her, his mouth gaping, a foolish smile over his whole countenance, his light eyes opened in a senseless stare.

"I, the grand-daughter of Ferdinand of Aragon, at the feet of this abortion!—this idiot!"

She rose, and a flush mounted on her pale cheek.

The king felt it incumbent on him to say something, to end somehow this embarrassing silence. He made a great effort, shrugged his shoulders, blinked, but could get no further than his usual—

"Eh? eh? What?" Then he waved his hand in despair, and relapsed into dumbness. Isabella measured him with her eyes in undissembled scorn, and Charles was abashed and hung his head.

"Brissonet! Brissonet! Let us go! Eh? What?"

The pages threw open the doors, and his progress continued till he had reached the room where Gian Galeazzo lay dying. Here the shutters had been thrown back, and the calm light of the autumn evening fell across the gilded tree-tops and streamed in through the windows.

The king approached the sufferer, and inquired solicitously after his health, calling him "*cousin*," "*mon cousin*." Gian Galeazzo answered with such a gentle smile that the poor king was relieved, and gradually recovered from his confusion.

"May the Lord send victory to the hosts of your Highness," said the duke. "And when you shall be at Jerusalem, at the Holy Sepulchre of Christ, oh, then, pray for the health of my poor soul; for by that time, sire, I—"

"Oh, no! no, brother! Speak not thus," protested Charles, "you shall recover. We must march together against these unclean Turks. Eh? Believe my words. I give you my word—Eh? what?"

Gian Galeazzo shook his head.

"Impossible," he murmured, looking into the king's eyes with his penetrating glance. "And, sire, when I shall be dead, I pray you, abandon not my little Francesco and my unhappy Isabella. They will have none other to look to."

"Good God! Good God!" murmured Charles, overcome by unlooked-for emotion. His lips quivered, their corners drooped, and, as by a sudden light from within, his face shone with an immense kindliness. He bent over the sick man and folded him in his arms.

"Brother! my poor dear brother!" They smiled sadly, like a pair of poor sick children; and kissed each other.

When he had left the room, the king turned to the cardinal.

"Brissonet—Brissonet! We must do something—eh? Defend—protect—This will not do! It cannot be permitted. I am a knight; I must succour the unfortunate. Do you understand?"

"Sire," replied the cardinal, "what is the use? His destiny is to die. We cannot profit him, but we can damn ourselves. Moreover, 'tis Il Moro who is your ally."

"Il Moro is a murderer! that is it; a proper murderer," exclaimed Charles, his eyes sparkling with indignation.

"Is it our business?" asked Brissonet, shrugging his shoulders, with a smile. "Il Moro is neither better nor worse than others. 'Tis political necessity. We are but men, sire."

The cup-bearer now came with a goblet of French wine, which Charles drank thirstily. It refreshed him, and scattered his sad thoughts. With the cup-bearer had entered a messenger from Ludovico, bearing an invitation to supper for the king. Charles declined it: the envoy pressed his suit, but unavailingly. Then the messenger whispered to Thibaut, who in turn whispered to the king.

"Your Highness—Madonna Lucrezia—"

"Eh? what? What Lucrezia?"

"The lady with whom your Majesty danced last night."

"Ah, yes; to be sure. I recall her. Madonna Lucrezia; a pretty little mouthful! Do you hint she would be at supper?"

"Certes, she will be there. And she supplicates your Highness—"

"She supplicates? Eh? What say you, Thibaut? I, forsooth—Well, well, tomorrow we take the field—'tis the last time. Messere, give your master my thanks, and tell him that I—forsooth—"

The King took Thibaut aside.

"Hark you—this Madonna Lucrezia—who is she?"

"Sire, the leman of Il Moro."

"Alas!"

"A single word from your Majesty and all can be accompolished this evening itself, if you will, sire."

"No! no! How? I—his guest?"

"Il Moro will find his pleasure in it. Sire, you understand not this people here!"

"Well then, well! As you will. It is your affair."

"Your Majesty may be at ease. A single word—"

"Speak no more, Thibaut. It mislikes me. Have I not said 'tis your work. I have nothing to say to it. Do what you choose!"

Thibaut bowed and withdrew.

Upon reaching the foot of the stair the king frowned and scratched his head, trying to recall his thoughts.

"Brissonet! Brissonet! What was I saying? Ah yes—to defend—offended innocence. I am sworn knight—"

"Your Majesty must quit these thoughts. They fit not with the present moment. Later, when we shall have returned victorious from Jerusalem—"

"Jerusalem!" echoed the king, and his eyes dilated, and on his lips came a pale, faint, dreamy smile.

"The hand of the Lord leads your Majesty to victory," continued Brissonet; "the finger of God points the way to the army of the cross."

Charles raised his eyes to heaven as if inspired, and repeated, "Finger of God! Finger of God!"

VIII

The young duke died eight days later. Before his death he prayed for an interview with Leonardo, but Isabella refused to permit it, Monna Druda having told her that the bewitched have always an insuperable and fatal wish to see those who have enchanted them. The old woman indefatigably anointed the patient with scorpion ointment, the doctor ordered bloodletting, the barber opened veins. Nevertheless he quietly died.

"Thy will be done," were his last words.

Ludovico had his body taken from Pavia to Milan, and buried him under the shadow of the cathedral.

Nobles and elders of the city assembled at the castle, and Ludovico, after assuring them of the profound grief he suffered at the untimely death of his nephew, made proposal that the child Francesco, Gian Galeazzo's son, should be declared duke. The assembly maintained it were madness to invest an infant with such power. Il Moro himself was implored, in the name of the people, to assume the sceptre. He feigned refusal, but reluctantly yielded to their prayers.

Gold brocade was brought, and the duke put it on; he then rode to the basilica of Sant' Ambrogio surrounded by a crowd of courtiers—

Viva il Moro! Viva il duca!—amid the sounding of trumpets, the firing of cannon, the clashing of bells, and—the silence of the people.

A few days later the most sacred relic in Milan, one of the nails of the True Cross, was solemnly transported to the cathedral. By this function Il Moro hoped to please the populace and to consolidate his power.

IX

THAT NIGHT A CROWD ASSEMBLED before Tibaldo's wine-cellar in the Piazza dell' Arrengo. There were present the tinman Scarabullo, Mascarello the goldsmith, Maso the furrier, Corbolo the shoemaker, and Gorgoglio the glass-blower. Standing on a cask in the middle of the crowd was Fra Timoteo, the Domenican, delivering a sermon.

"Brothers! when Santa Elena had found the life-giving Tree of the Cross and the other instruments of the Lord's Passion, which had been buried by the heathen in the earth under the shrine of Venus, then the Emperor Constantine, taking one of these most holy and awful nails, bade the smiths work it into the bit of his war-horse, that thus the word of the prophet Zechariah might be fulfilled: 'In that day shall there be upon the bells of the horses Holiness unto the Lord.' And this ineffable relic gave him the victory over his enemies and over the adversaries of the Roman Empire." . . . Here Fra Timoteo made a pause, then raising his hands to heaven he cried in a lamentable voice:—"And now, brethren beloved, a great abomination is being committed. Il Moro, the evildoer, the homicide, the usurper, seduceth the people with impious festivals, and would use the most Holy Nail for the support of his trembling throne."

The crowd showed agitation, and low cries were heard.

"And know ye, my brethren, upon whom he hath devolved the construction of the machine for raising the Nail to its place in the cupola above the high altar?"

"To whom?"

"To Leonardo da Vinci, the Florentine."

"Who is this Leonardo?" asked several persons.

"Nay," returned others, "we know him; the poisoner of the young duke!"

"Leonardo the sorcerer! Leonardo the heretic! the infidel!"

Corbolo timidly undertook the defence.

"Friends, I have heard say that Leonardo is a good man, who does ill to none, and is compassionate not only of men but of the meanest animals."

"Speak not foolishly, Corbolo!"

"Hold your tongue. How can a sorcerer be good?"

"My sons! my sons!" declaimed Fra Timoteo, "there shall be a day when men shall praise the great deceiver, him who walketh in darkness, saying of him, 'He is kind, he is just, he is good'; for his face shall be like unto the face of the Christ, and he shall have a voice comforting and pleasant like the voice of a singing woman. And many shall be led astray by his wily kindness. And by the four winds of heaven he shall call together tribes and nations, as a partridge with a deceiving cry calls into her nest the brood of another. Be watchful, O brethren! Behold the angel of darkness, the prince of this world, who is called Antichrist, cometh in human shape. Be watchful, I say, because this Florentine, this Leonardo, is the precursor and the servant of Antichrist."

"'Tis true!" cried Gorgoglio (who, however, had never before even heard of Leonardo); "they say he has sold his soul to the devil, and has signed the covenant with his blood."

"Holy Mother of God, have mercy upon us!" babbled Barbaccia the fruit-woman. "Stamma, the wench at the hangman's who does charing at the prison, told me that this Leonardo (Heaven defend me from speaking his name after dusk) wrests the bodies from the gallows—cuts them up—takes out their bowels—"

"You know not what you speak," said Corbolo; "'tis a matter of science, and called Anatomy."

"They say he has made a contrivance to fly in the air on bird's wings," observed Mascarello the goldsmith.

"Veglias also, that old winged serpent, rebelled against God," commented Fra Timoteo; "Simon Magus also raised himself into the air for flight, but the holy Apostle Saint Paul threw him down."

"He walketh on the water," cried Scarabullo. "He says, 'God walked on the sea and so will I.' Heard you ever so great blasphemy?"

"He goes into a bell, and descends to the bottom of the deep," added Maso.

"Nay, brothers, credit not that!" cried Gorgoglio. "What need hath he of a bell? He transforms himself into a fish and swims; he transforms himself into a bird and doth fly."

"*Ahi!* beloved brothers!" cried Timoteo; "and the nail, the Holy Nail is in the hands of this Leonardo!"

"It shall not be!" shouted Scarabullo, clenching his fists; "Death to us sooner than profanation of our holy things! We will tear the Nail from the hands of the infidel."

"Vengeance for the Holy Nail! Vengeance for our poisoned lord! Burn him! Hang him!"

"Brothers, what do ye?" cried the shoemaker with imploring hands; "the night patrol will pass in a moment, and the captain of justice—"

"To the devil with the captain of justice! Run if you're frightened, Corbolo; run under your wife's petticoat."

And armed with cudgels, staves, poles, and stones, the crowd surged through the streets, shouting and cursing. In front went the monk, bearing the crucifix and chanting the psalm, "Let God arise, let his enemies be scattered! As wax melteth before the fire, so let the wicked perish at the presence of God!"

The torches smoked and flared. In their scarlet light the lonely moon grew pale, and the quiet stars trembled in the heavens.

X

Leonardo in his quiet workshop was occupied with the machine for the elevation of the Holy Nail. Zoroastro was making a casket, all glass and gold, in which the relic was to be displayed. Giovanni Boltraffio was sitting in a dark corner watching the Master.

Gradually, however, Leonardo had forgotten his machine, his thoughts having wandered to theories as to the transmission of force by means of blocks and levers. He had made a complicated calculation in which the mathematical law (the inner principle of reason) had explained to him the mechanical law (the outer principle of nature); two great secrets were thus fused into one still greater secret.

"Man," thought he, "will never invent anything so perfect, as doth Nature, which of necessity so disposeth her laws that every effect is straitly bound up with its cause."

In face of the infinite abyss into which he was directing his penetrating gaze, his soul was filled with that sense of overwhelming wonder which has no likeness to the other sentiments of men. On the margin of the paper, covered with the calculations for the simple machinery required for the elevation of the Holy Nail, he wrote these words which echoed in his heart like a prayer:—

"*O mirabile giustizia di te, Primo Motore! tu non hai voluto mancare a nessuna potenza l'ordine e qualità de suoi necessari effetti!*" (O admirable justice of Thee, Prime Mover! To no force hast Thou permitted lack of the order and quality of its necessary effects!)

But the artist's meditations were interrupted by a furious knocking at the outer door, together with chanting of psalms, and the objurgations and yells of an inflamed rabble. Giovanni and Zoroastro were rushing to see what had happened, when Maturina the cook, with dishevelled hair, burst half dressed into the room, crying:—

"Thieves! Robbers! Murderers! Holy Mother of God have mercy on us!"

"What is it?" asked Leonardo of Marco d'Oggionno, who had also entered, arquebus in hand, and was beginning to shut the shutters.

"I know not exactly. It would seem a crowd of housebreakers, egged on by monks."

"What is their demand?"

"Only their father can understand these sons of the devil! They demand the Holy Nail."

"I have it not. 'Tis in the sacristy in the care of Monsignor Arcimboldi."

"'Tis what I told them. But being mad as dogs in the time of the summer solstice, they hearkened not, but continued to vilify Your Worship as an infidel and a sorcerer, and the poisoner of Gian Galeazzo."

During this colloquy the noise in the street grew apace.

"Open, or we will fire this accursed nest. In one moment, Leonardo, you shall be flayed! Demon! Antichrist!"

"Let God arise, let His enemies be scattered!" chanted Fra Timoteo to the accompaniment of Farfanicchio's stridulous whistle.

Suddenly Jacopo, the wicked little servant, ran in, sprang on the window ledge, opened the shutter, and was going to jump into the courtyard, but Leonardo held him back.

"Whither art going, child?"

"To call the guard. The captain of justice passes at this hour."

"No, no. If they catch you they will kill you without a word spoken."

"They shall not see me. I will get over the wall, through Aunt Trulla's garden, over the green ditch into the backyard. 'Tis as good as done! Likewise it were better they killed me than you, Master."

And glancing back with eyes full of love and daring, the lad leaped from the window, and was off like a flash.

"For once the little devil is some use," said Maturina shaking her head.

A stone came crashing through the window, and shrieking and wringing her hands, the fat woman fled, felt her way down the dark stairs to the cellar, and hid in a wine-cask. Marco hurried upstairs to bar the windows; Giovanni, pale, distressed, but indifferent to the peril, turned a woeful countenance to Leonardo, and fell at his feet.

"O Master, they say—I swear it is not true—nay, I believe it not—but for God's sake tell me yourself—!" and he stopped short, panting with agitation. Leonardo smiled sadly.

"You fear they speak truth that I am a murderer?"

"A word, master! a single word from your own lips!"

"But why, friend? If you can harbour a doubt, you would not believe me."

"Oh, Messer Leonardo, I am in torture. . . A word, a single word!"

Leonardo did not answer immediately; then he said in a shaking voice:—

"You also, Giovanni, with them! You, also, against me!"

Outside the blows were such that the whole house shook. Scarabullo was forcing the door with an axe. Leonardo, hearing the imprecations and the insults of the infuriated crowd, felt his heart contracted with anguish and great solitude. His chin drooped, and his glance fell on the lines just written; "*O mirabile giustizia di te, Primo Motore!*"

He smiled, and with great humility repeated the words of the dying Gian Galeazzo:—

"All is well. Thy will be done on earth, as it is in heaven."

Book VI

The Diary of Giovanni Boltraffio—1494–1495

L'amore di qualunque cosa è figliuolo d'essa cognitione. L'amore à tanto più fervente, quanto la cognitione è più certa.

—Leonardo Da Vinci

(Knowledge of a thing engenders love of it; the more exact the knowledge, the more fervent the love.)

"Be ye wise as serpents and harmless as doves."

—St. Matt. x. 16

Giovanni's Diary

On the 25th of March 1494 I entered myself as a disciple in the studio of Messer Leonardo da Vinci, the Florentine master.

This is the order of his teaching:—perspective; the dimensions and proportions of the human body; drawings from examples by the best masters; drawings from nature.

Today Marco d'Oggionno, my fellow-disciple, has given me a book, taken down entirely from the words of our Master. The book begins thus:—

"The purest joy is given to the body by the light of the sun; to the spirit, by the clear shining of mathematics. That is why the science of Perspective (in which the contemplation of the bright line—*la linia radiosa*—true solace of the eye, goes hand in hand with the clearness of mathematics—true solace of the mind) must be exalted above all other human research and science. May He who said, 'I am the true Light,' lend me His aid that I may know the science of Perspective—the science of His light. I divide this book into three parts: the first, the diminishing, by distance, of the *size of objects*; the second, the diminishing of the *distinctness of the colour*; the third, the diminishing of the *clearness of the outline*."

The Master cares for me like a father. When he learned of my poverty, he refused to take the monthly payment agreed on.

The Master says:—

"When you shall have grasped well your Perspective, and hold in your mind the proportions of the human body, then in your walks abroad notice assiduously the postures and movements of men, how they stand, walk, talk, and quarrel; how they laugh and fight; the manner of their faces when they are doing these things, and the manner of the faces of the bystanders who want to separate the fighters; and the faces of those who look on with apathy. Set all in pencil in a note-book of coloured paper, which you should always have about you. When the booklet is filled, take another; put the first one away and keep it. In no wise destroy nor rub out these sketches; for the movements of the body are so endless that no memory could hold them all. That is why you must look on these rough sketches as your best teachers."

I have made myself such a sketch-book.

Today in the Vicolo dei Pattari, not far from the cathedral, I encountered my uncle, Oswald Ingrim. He told me he renounced me; and accused me of ruining my soul in the house of the heretic and the infidel.

Whenever I am heavy of heart, I have but to look on his face to grow light and gay. How wondrous are his eyes; clear, blue, pale, and cold—cold as ice. The voice, most pleasant and soft. The most cruel, the most obdurate, can by no means resist his persuasiveness. He sits at his work-table, immersed in thoughts, parting and smoothing his golden beard, long and soft as the silk of a maiden. When he talks with anyone, then he partly closes one eye with a merry and kind expression; his glance from under the thick and overhanging eyebrows penetrates the very soul.

He dislikes lively colours, and new and discommoding fashions; nor does he affect perfumes. His linen is of Rhenish stuff, marvellous clean and fine. His black velvet *berretto* carries no plumes nor ornaments. His suiting is of black; but he wears a mantle of dark red which reaches to the knee, and hangs in straight folds, as was the old mode in Florence. His movements are easy and quiet, but notable. He is like no one else.

Shoots excellently with the bow or arbalist, rides, swims, is a master of fence with the small sword. Today I saw him hit the highest point of the cupola of a church with a small thrown coin. Messer Leonardo, by the skill and the strength of his hand, surpassed every competitor.

He is left-handed; but with that same left hand, for all it looks delicate and soft as a woman's, he bends iron fetters and twists the tongue of a brazen bell.

While I was watching him, the child Jacopo ran in laughing and clapping his hands.

"Cripples, Messer Leonardo, monsters! Come your ways into the kitchen, I have brought you such beauties that you shall lick your fingers for joy!"

"Whence came they?"

"From the porch of Sant' Ambrogio. Beggars from Bergamo! I promised you'd give them supper if they'd let themselves be painted."

Leaving the picture of the Virgin unfinished, Leonardo betook him to the kitchen, I following. We found two brothers, very old and swollen with dropsy, great hanging *goîtres* on their throats. With them was the wife of one of them, a withered little old body, whose name Ragnina (little spider) seemed very suitable.

"You see," cried Jacopo triumphantly, "I said you would be pleased! Don't I know exactly what you like?"

Leonardo sat down by the hobgoblin cripples, ordered wine to be brought, served it to them himself, questioned them kindly, told them absurd stories to make them laugh. At first they were restive and suspicious, not understanding why they had been brought in. But when he related an anecdote about a dead Jew, whom his compatriots, to evade the law forbidding the burial of Hebrews within the confines of Bologna, had cut in pieces, pickled, spiced, and sent to Venice where he was eaten by a Florentine Christian, the Little Spider was like to burst with laughter. Soon all three were tipsy, and laughing and talking and making the most horrible faces. I was disgusted and looked away; but

Leonardo watched them with deep and eager curiosity; and when their hideousness had reached its height, took out his sketch-book and drew with the same delighted attention that he had lavished on the smile of the Virgin.

In the evening he showed me a whole collection of caricatures; grotesques not only of men but also of beasts—terrible shapes, like those which haunt sick men in their delirium, the human and the bestial compounded to make one shudder. The muzzle of a porcupine, its quills bristling, its under lip pendent, loose, and thin as a rag, displaying in a human grin two long white teeth like almonds; an old woman, her nose spread and hairy, and scarce bigger than a mole, her lips monstrously thick, like those squat and viscid fungi which grow out of withered trunks.

Cesare da Sesto tells me that sometimes the Master, having met some monstrosity in the street, will follow it for a whole day. Great deformity, he says, is as rare as great beauty; only mediocrity is negligible.

Marco d'Oggionno works like an ox, and carries out all the teacher's rules; the more he tries the less is his success. He is endowed with an invincible constancy. He thinks patience and labour shall possess all things; nor doth he despair of some day becoming a great painter.

He takes also, more than any of us, rare delight in the master's inventions. One of these days he carried his note-book to the Piazza del Broletto, and according to the Master's system he made the required indexed notes of those faces which struck him chiefly in the crowd. But on reaching home he could in no wise translate his notes into a living face. Likewise did he fail in the use of Leonardo's spoon for measuring out colour. His shadows remain thick and unnatural, just as his faces are wooden and devoid of all charm. Marco accounts for this by some small failure in his obedience to the rules. Cesare da Sesto ridicules him.

"This most excellent Marco," he says, "is a martyr in the cause of science. His example shows that all these measures and rules be worth nothing. To know how infants are born does not suffice to beget one. Leonardo deceiveth himself and others; he teaches one thing and performs another. When he paints he follows no rule save that of inspiration; yet he is not content to be a great artist, but would be a man of science also. I fear lest, coursing two hares, he run down neither."

It may be that in this mockery of Cesare's there is a modicum of truth; but no love for the Master. Leonardo hearkens to him, praises his intelligence, and never is wroth with him.

I AM WATCHING HOW HE works at his *Cenacolo*. Betimes, before sunrise, he goes to the convent refectory, and paints till the shadows close in on him, nor does the brush fall from his hands, nor does he remember food and drink. Sometimes he lets whole weeks go by in which he touches not his paints. Sometimes he will stand for two hours on the scaffold before the picture examining it and criticising what he has done. At other times I have known him rush forth in the mid-day heat through the blazing streets, being drawn by some viewless power to the monastery; he will mount his scaffold, do two touches or mayhap three, and rush away at once.

HE IS WORKING AT THE countenance of the Apostle John. Today he should have completed it. Instead he remained at home with the child Jacopo, watching the flight of hornets, wasps, and flies. So absorbed is he in studying the construction of their bodies that 'twould seem on it depended the destiny of the human race. Having perceived that the hind legs of flies serve them as a rudder, he experienced greater pleasure than if he had found the secret of perpetual felicity. He thinks the discovery useful, and like to serve his apparatus for flight. Poor Apostle John!

TODAY THERE IS A NEW distraction, and the flies are abandoned. The Master is working on a design, beautiful and wondrous delicate, which is to form the coat-of-arms of an academy not yet existing outside the brain of the duke. The device is a square containing a crown of cords, geometrically intertwined, in knots without beginning or end. I could not restrain myself, but reminded him of the unfinished apostle. He shrugged his shoulders, and without raising his eyes from the crown of cords, he said through his closed teeth:—

"Patience! time enough! The head of John will not run away!"

I begin to comprehend Cesare's malice!

THE DUKE HAS ENTRUSTED TO him the construction within the palace of hearing-tubes concealed in the thickness of the walls, after the fashion of the Ear of Dionysius. Leonardo began with ardour, but now has cooled and catches at every pretext for laying the work aside. The duke hurries him and is wroth; this morning he summoned him several times to the palace, but the Master is occupied with experiments on vegetables. He has cut away the roots from a pumpkin, leaving but one small shoot, which he assiduously drenches with water. To his great joy the plant has not withered. "The mother," says he, "nourishes well her children." Sixty little oblong pumpkins have formed.

Cesare says Leonardo is the greatest of the libertines. He has written a hundred and twenty volumes on matters of natural science, but all in fragments, in dispersed notes on flying leaves; and he keeps a MS. of over five thousand pages in such disorder that he himself cannot find anything in it.

Coming into my little room, he said; "Giovanni, have you noticed that small rooms dispose the mind to profundity, large ones to breadth? And have you observed how the images of things, seen through the shadow of rain, are clearer than in the sunlight?"

Two days of work on the head of John the Apostle. But, alas! something has been lost through flies, pumpkins, cats, and the ear of Dionysius. He has again failed to complete the head, and now, disgusted with his paint-box, retired into geometry. He says that the odour of the paint nauseates him, and the sight of the brushes. Thus the days pass; at the caprice of chance, and submitting to the will of God, we, as it were, lie in port waiting for a wind. Fortunately he has forgotten the flying-machine or we should starve.

What to others appears perfection is to him teeming with error. He aims at the highest, at the unattainable, at what is forever beyond the reach of the hand of man. Therefore his productions rest incomplete.

Andrea Salaino has fallen sick. The Master nurses him, sits up at night, watches by his pillow; but no one dare speak to him of medicine. Marco d'Oggionno surreptitiously introduced a pill-box, but Leonardo found it, and cast it from the window. Andrea himself desired to be bled, and spoke of a most skilled phlebotomist of his acquaintance; but the Master grew properly indignant, speaking of all doctors with epithets most injurious.

"Heed rather to preserve than to cure your health; and beware of physicians." He added with a smile, good-natured yet malicious, "Every man scrapes up his money only to give it to them, the destroyers of lives."

The Master has taken in hand a treatise on painting; the Lord knows when he will finish it. Latterly he has been much busied (I likewise, helping him) with aerial and line perspective, both in light and shade, and he has given me discourses and fugitive thoughts upon art. I will now write down such as I can remember of the noblest of sciences; and may those into whose hands these pages shall fall, remember in their prayers the soul of the great Florentine master, Leonardo da Vinci, and the soul of Giovanni Boltraffio, his humble disciple.

The Master says "All which is beautiful, even humanly beautiful, dies, except in art." (*Cosa bella mortal passa e non d'arte.*)

"He who despises painting despises the philosophical and refined contemplation of the world. Painting is the grandchild of Nature and the kinswoman of God."

"*Il pittore deve essere universale.* O painter, be thy variety infinite as the phenomena of Nature! Carrying on what God has begun, seek to multiply, not the works of men's hands, but those of the eternal hands of God. Imitate no one; let thy every work be a new phenomenon of Nature."

"For him who is master of the fundamental natural laws; for him who *knows*, it is easy to be universal; because all bodies, whether of men or of beasts, are really formed on the same principles."

"Take heed lest in thee the greed for gold suffocate the love of art; and remember that the conquest of glory excels the glory of conquest. The memory of the rich perishes with them, the memory of the wise endures forever; because science and wisdom are the legitimate children of their father, and money is but his bastard. Love glory, and be not fearful of poverty. Consider how many philosophers have laid down the wealth to which they were born, that they might enrich their souls with virtue, and have lived content in misery."

"Knowledge rejuvenates the soul, and lightens the burden of old age. Therefore gather wisdom, that thou mayest gather sweets for thine age."

"There is a generation of painters who, to hide their meagre knowledge, shelter themselves behind the beauty of gold and azure, and say they give not of their best because of the scanty payment they receive, and that they could surpass any man were they as well rewarded as he. O fools! what hinders them to make something beautiful, and to say, 'This picture is such a price, and this other is less, and this, third least of all; showing that they have work for every price?'"

"Not infrequently the lust for gold brings even the good masters down to the level of craftsmen. Thus my countryman and comrade, Perugino the Florentine, arrived at such rapidity of execution, that once he replied to his wife, who called him to dinner, 'Serve the soup while I paint one more saint!'"

"The artist who has no mistrust of himself will never attain to the supreme heights of art. Well for thee if thy work be higher, ill for thee if it equal, woe to thee if it fall below, thine own estimation! Pitiful is that artificer who, persuaded that he has produced a masterpiece, questions wonderingly how God can have helped him to such purpose."

"Listen with long suffering to the criticisms which men pass on your picture; and weigh their words to see if, perchance, they, faulting it, be in the right. If they be right, correct; if they be wrong, feign deafness; or if they be persons worthy of notice, show them their error. The judgment of an enemy is often nearer the truth than the judgment of a friend; hatred is often profounder than love. The intellect of him who hates, sees and penetrates better than the intellect of him who loves. A true friend is like thyself; but an enemy resembles thee not, and in this is his strength. Hatred throws light. Remember this, and despise not the criticisms of thine enemy."

"Bright colours captivate the vulgar, but the true artist seeks not to please the vulgar, but the elect. His pride and his aim is not in the dazzling by colour, but in the performance of a miracle, namely, that by the play of light and shadow, things which are flat should appear round.

He who neglecting the shadows, sacrifices them to the splendour of tinting, is like the vain babbler who sacrifices significance for sounding and furious words."

"Above all, beware of coarse, sharp outlines. The shadows on a young and delicate body should be neither dead nor stony, but light, evasive, and transparent like air; for the human body is itself transparent, as you can convince yourself by looking through your fingers at the sun. Too brilliant a light gives not good shadows; wherefore be wary of it. Observe the tenderness and charm on the faces of men and women as they pass along the shadowed street between the dark walls of the houses under twilight on clouded days. This is the most perfect light; your shadow, gradually vanishing into the light, will fade like smoke—like a soft music. Remember that between the light and the dark there is something which participates in both; a bright shadow or a dark light. Seek for it, O painter! for therein lies the secret of captivation—of charm."

These words he spoke, and raising his hands as if wishing to imprint the lesson on our memories, he repeated, with indescribable emphasis, "Reject coarse and heavy outlines; confound your shadows in the light, letting them vanish little by little, like smoke; like a tender music."

Cesare, who was listening attentively, raised his eyes and smiled, as if about to dispute; nevertheless he remained silent.

Later, speaking on another topic, Leonardo said:—

"Falsehood is so shameful that even in praising God it dishonours Him. Truth is so excellent that in speaking of the vile it ennobles. Between truth and falsehood there is a difference no less than between light and darkness."

Here Cesare, suddenly struck by an idea, fixed scrutinising eyes on the Master.

"How?" he said. "Yet, Master, have you not told us that between the darkness and the light there exists an intermediary, something which participates in both, and is, as it were, bright shadow and dark light. Then, between truth and lie—but no, 'tis absurd. Master, your metaphor lands me in great temptation! For the painter who, you say, seeks enslaving charm in the compounding of light and shadow, may rightly seek also the twilight between true and false."

At first Leonardo frowned, and seemed indignant that one of his pupils should exhibit such an obsession; then he replied smiling:—

"Tempt me not! Get thee behind me, Satan!"

I had expected a different answer; to my thinking, Cesare's words merited better than an idle jest. In me, at any rate they excited a tumult of strange and tormenting ideas.

Tonight I beheld him, standing in the rain in a close and fetid alley, absorbed in the contemplation of certain spots of dampness on a stone. He stood there a long while, and the urchins in the street nudged each other and mocked him. I asked him what he beheld in the stone.

"Giovanni," he said, "see the splendid monstrous figure! Chimera, with her jaws wide; and beside her an angel with flying hair and airy flight, fleeing from the monster. The caprice of chance has produced a picture worthy of a great artist."

He traced with his finger the outline of the damp spot, and to my amazement I recognised that what he said was true.

"Many," he said, "think this habit of mine an absurdity; but experience has taught me how useful it is for the education of the fancy. I have taken from such things what I wanted, and brought them to completeness. Listen to far-off bells; you can find in their confused clang the very names and words you lack."

For tears the eyebrows contract; for laughter they expand.

The Master goes gladly with those condemned to death, watching in their faces the degrees of their agony and terror; and the very executioners wonder at him, when he makes a study of the last quivering of the muscles.

"Nay, Giovanni, you understand not the man he is!" cried Cesare. "He will lift a worm from the path lest his foot crush it; but if his own mother were a-dying he would watch the contracting of her eyebrows, the wrinkling of her forehead, the drooping of the corners of the mouth."

"Note the expression and the gestures of deaf-mutes."

"When you watch persons, do it without letting them know; so shall their movements, their laughter, and their tears be more natural."

"An artist whose own hands are angular and bony, is apt to depict people with angular and bony hands; for every man likes the faces and the bodies which resemble his own. The ugly painter will choose ugly models, and *vice versâ*. Let not the men and the women whom you paint seem your blood-brothers either in beauty or in deformity. This is a fault which attaches to many Italian artists. In painting there is no error more treacherous. I consider the temptation arises from the fact that the soul makes the body which belongs to it. Of old it shaped and fashioned it in its own likeness; and now when again it is called upon to fashion a new body with brushes and paint, it yearns to reproduce the shape in which it has long had its habitation."

The Master tells us, "'Tis not experience, the mother of all arts and sciences, which deceives men, but imagination, which promises them what experience cannot give. Experience is not to blame, but our own vain and senseless lusts. Experience would have us aim at the possible, and not strive ignorantly for what we can never obtain; lest we become the prey of despair."

When we were alone Cesare repeated these words, and cried as in disgust:—

"Hypocrisy and lies!"

"How has he lied?" asked I.

"Not to aim at the impossible! not to follow the unattainable! Well, it may be someone will believe his words, but 'twill not be I nor you! I have penetrated to his inmost soul."

"And what see you there, Cesare?"

"All his life through, he has done nothing but aim at the impossible, nothing but follow the unattainable! What else is he about in this machine to turn men into birds, in that other to set them in water like fish? And the chimerical monsters he finds in the spots on walls and in the outline of the clouds; and the mystic charm of divine faces seen in angelic visions—whence does he derive all this? From experience? from his diagram of noses, and his ladle for measuring out paint? Why does he deceive himself? Why lie? His mechanical studies are for the performance of a miracle; for raising himself into heaven by flight, for using natural forces to do that which is against Nature. He stretches out towards God or devil, he cares not which, provided 'tis something unexampled, beyond possibility. The less is his faith, the greater is his quenchless curiosity."

These words of Cesare's have filled my soul with anxiety. For several days I have thought them over: I would fain forget them, but I cannot.

Today, however, the Master, as if in answer to my doubts, has said to me:—

"A little knowledge puffs up; great knowledge makes humble. Blasted ears raise proud heads; those full of grain bow down."

"Then," asked Cesare with his accustomed ironic smile, "how happed it that Lucifer, prince of the cherubim, and renowned for wisdom, was moved by wisdom not to humility, but to pride that cast him into hell?"

Leonardo did not answer at once; presently he told us this fable.

"Once a drop of water aspired to reach the sky. Winged by fire, it rose up in fine steam. But mounted on high it met air still finer and very cold, and the fire deserted it. Then it shivered and grew heavy, and, its presumption changing into terror, fell as rain. And cast down from heaven it fell upon the earth, and was drunk up by dryness; and for long time it was shut up in prison underground, and there did penance for its sin."

He added no more, but I thought I understood.

THE LONGER I LIVE WITH him the less I know him. Today he has again been playing like a child. And such strange pranks! Before going to bed I was sitting in my chamber reading my favourite book, *The Little Flowers of Saint Francis*, when suddenly a cry rang through the house from our old woman, the kind and faithful Maturina—

"Fire! Help! Help! Fire!"

I rushed out. An appallingly thick white smoke filled the Master's studio. He was there himself, standing among clouds like some ancient magi, and illumined by unearthly blue flames. His face was merry, and he looked jovially at the pale and terrified Maturina, and at Marco, who had rushed in with two buckets of water, to empty over the drawings and manuscripts strewing the table. Leonardo, however, stopped him, saying it was all a jest. Smoke and flames came from a heated brazier containing a powder of frankincense and resin. I cannot say which took the greater pleasure in the joke, Leonardo or the little scamp, that jackanapes Jacopo. Only a good man could laugh as does Leonardo! I swear it is not true what Cesare says of him! The Master set down in his note-book the effect produced by terror upon Maturina's wrinkles.

He speaks scarce at all of women. Once, however, he said that men maltreat them even as they do their beasts. He ridicules the platonic love which is the fashion; and when a certain youth read to him a peevish sonnet in the manner of Petrarch, he replied in three lines, about Petrarch's loving Laura merely to season his own daily food.

Cesare says that Leonardo has so wasted himself on mechanics and geometry that he has had no time for love of women. But he adds, depend upon it he is no Galahad; he must certainly have embraced a woman at least once, out of mere curiosity.

I should never have talked to Cesare about Leonardo. We seem to watch him like spies, and Cesare finds a malevolent pleasure in detecting new blots in his character. And what does Cesare want with me? Why does he poison my mind?

We now frequently visit a scurvy little tavern by the Cantarana Canal, just beyond the Porta Vercellina. We talk for hours over a half-flagon of sour wine, amid the oaths of boatmen who finger filthy cards and lay plots together for extortion. Today Cesare asked me if I knew that at Florence Leonardo had been accused of immorality. I could not believe my ears, and thought him raving or drunken. Then he told me the story in detail. When Leonardo was twenty-four years of age, and his master, the famous Florentine, Andrea Verrocchio, forty—an anonymous charge against them both was put into one of those round wooden boxes called *tamburi*, which hang on the pillars in the churches, most notably in the Cathedral of Santa Maria del Fiore. In April "the guardians of the night and of monasteries" inquired into the matter, and acquitted the accused on the condition, however, that the charge should be repeated. The fresh accusation was made in June, and they both were finally acquitted. Nothing more was heard of the accusation; but Leonardo soon left Verrocchio and Florence, and came hither to Milan.

"Oh, doubtless, 'tis an abominable calumny," said Cesare with his meaning smile; "though, friend Giovanni, you do not yet know what contradictions nestle in his heart. 'Tis a labyrinth so intricate that even the devil would lose himself therein. He certainly appears chaste, but—"

I had started to my feet, probably pale enough, and cried:—

"How dare you, Cesare?"

"What the devil is the matter with you? Calm yourself. I will say no more. I was a hundred miles from *that* construction—"

"What are you insinuating? Speak out!"

"What folly is this? Why so hot? Is it worth the separating of two such friends as we? Rather let us drink. To your health, sir. *In vino veritas.*"

And we drank and resumed our talk.

But no, no! this suffices! I will forget it; I will abstain from speaking of the Master with this man. Cesare is not his enemy alone, but also mine. He is a bad fellow.

Now I feel nauseated. It is odious to see the hideous delight some men feel when they have thrown mud upon the great.

THE MASTER SAYS: "THY STRENGTH, O painter, is in solitude! When you are alone you belong wholly to yourself (*Se tu sarai solo tu sarai tutto tuo*), but if you have even one companion then you are only half your own; possibly less than half if your friend be indiscreet. If you have many friends, you fall deeper into the same slough. And if you say, 'I will withdraw myself, and practise the contemplation of Nature,' you will not succeed, for you will be lending one ear to the chatterings of your friends, and inasmuch as no man can serve two masters, you will perform ill the duties of a friend, and still worse the observances of art. And if you say, 'I will withdraw beyond the reach of their voices,' then you will be reckoned a madman, and you practically end by being alone."

"But if you must have company, let it be that of the painters and scholars in your studio; all other friendships will be to your detriment. Remember, O painter, that your strength is in solitude!"

Leonardo consorts not with women, because his soul must be absolutely free.

SOMETIMES ANDREA SALAINO COMPLAINS THAT our existence alternates between the monotony of hard work and the tedium of inaction; and he declares that the pupils of other Masters lead a gayer life. He is as fond of fine clothes as a maid, and would like the noise of feastings and merriment and the fire of amorous eyes.

Leonardo today, having overheard the reproaches and laments of his favourite, stroked his long curls affectionately, and said smiling:—

"Be of good cheer, lad. I'll take you to the next feast at the castle. Meantime, shall I tell you a fable?"

Andrea clapped his hands like a child, and threw himself at the Master's feet, all attention. Leonardo began:—

"Once upon a time a large stone, lately washed up by the stream, lay in a retired place high up above the road and surrounded by trees, moss, flowers, and grasses. Looking down on his road he saw a number of stones like himself, and he said, 'What profit have I here among these short-lived plants? I will descend among my kinsmen and live with stones like myself.' Thereupon he rolled himself down to the road, and took a place amongst his brothers. And the wheels of heavy wains ground him, and the hoof of the ass, and the nailed boot of the pedestrian. Then he lifted himself a little, and thought he should breathe more freely; but, lo! became bespattered with mud, and the droppings of animals; and his former fair retreat in the garden of flowers seemed to him a paradise. Thus it is, Andrea, with those who leave their meditation and plunge into city disquiet."

The master permits harm to no living creatures, not even to plants. Zoroastro tells me that from an early age he has abjured meat, and says that the time shall come when all men such as he will be content with a vegetable diet, and will think on the murder of animals as now they think on the murder of men.

Today we passed by a butcher's shop, and he pointed to the dead carcases of calves and oxen and pigs, and said with disgust:—"Truly man is the king of beasts, for his brutality exceeds theirs." And then added sorrowfully; "We live by the death of others. We are burial-places."

God forgive me, I have again been with Cesare to that accursed tavern! We spoke of the Master's compassionateness for animals.

"You refer, Giovanni, to his eating no flesh?"

"It may be so. I know—"

"You know nothing! Messer Leonardo is not moved by goodness, but by the love of singularity."

"What mean you by that?"

He laughed somewhat forcedly.

"Peace. Let us not quarrel. Wait, and I will show you certain of his drawings—i' faith, very interesting drawings."

So upon our return we crept, thief-like, into the Master's studio. Cesare rummaged till he had found a certain concealed sketch-book which he showed to me. My conscience pricked me; nevertheless I looked with interest.

They were drawings of colossal bombards, explosive balls, many-barrelled guns, and such like engines of war, executed with no less delicacy than he lavished on the divine countenances of his Madonnas. Especially do I remember one bomb, half a *braccio* in diameter, called "Fragilità," the construction of which Cesare explained to me. It was cast of bronze, the hollow within being filled with layers of gypsum. Leonardo had written on the margin beside the sketch:—

"Most beautiful bomb. Very useful. After leaving the gun it ignites while one might pronounce an *Ave Maria*."

"*Ave Maria!*" cried Cesare. "How does this use of a Christian prayer please you, my friend? You see the breed of his inventions! And have you heard his definition of war?"

"No."

"'*Pazzia bestialissima*, the most brutal of madnesses.' A pretty definition, methinks, for the inventor of these engines. Here is your holy man who eats no flesh, who lifts a worm from the path lest a boot should tread on it! Both one and the other simultaneously! today a devil, tomorrow a saint. A Janus, with one face toward Christ, the other towards Antichrist. Which is the true Leonardo, which the false! Who can say? And he does it all with a light heart, with a mystic seductive grace. *He is at play.*"

I listened in silence, a chill like the chill of death piercing my heart.

"Eh? What is the matter, friend Giovanni? Quite chapfallen? You take it overmuch to heart. Oh, you'll soon be used to it, just as I am. And now let us go back to the *Tartaruga d'oro*, and sing:—

'Dum vinum potamus
Fratelli cantiamo
A Bacco sià onore!
Te deum laudamus.'"

I said no word, but fled from him.

Today Marco d'Oggionno said to the Master:—

"Messer Leonardo, they accuse us of too scanty church-going, and of work on holy days as on others."

"Let bigots talk at leisure, and heed them not," answered Leonardo. "The study of Nature is well-pleasing to God, and is akin to prayer. Learning the laws of Nature, we magnify the first Inventor, the

Designer of the world; and we learn to love Him, for great love of God results from great knowledge. Who knows little, loves little. If you love the Creator for the favour you expect of Him, and not for His most high goodness and strength, wherein do you excel the dog who licks his master's hand in the hope of dainties? But reflect how that worthy beast, the dog, would adore his master could he comprehend his reason and his soul! Remember, children, love is the daughter of knowledge; and the deeper the knowledge of God the greater the fervency of love. Wherefore in the Scripture it is written, 'Be ye wise as serpents and harmless as doves.'"

"But who," retorted Cesare, "can combine the sweetness of the dove with the cunning of the serpent? To my thinking we must choose between the two."

"Not so," cried Leonardo; "there must be a fusion. I Tell You Perfect Knowledge of The Universe and Perfect Love of God Are One Thing and The Same."

How fain would I return to thy silent and holy cell, O Fra Benedetto! Tell thee all my grief, and fall upon thy breast, that thou mightest pity me and remove from my soul this burden, O beloved father! O gentle shepherd, who dost abide by the word of Christ—"Blessed are the poor in spirit!"

At times the Master's face is so peaceful and innocent, so full of dovelike harmlessness, that I am ready to pardon all, to believe all, to trust him with my very soul. Then of a sudden the subtle lines of his lips take on an expression so incomprehensible, something which so inspires me with fear, that I seem to be looking through the transparency of water into the profundity of the abyss. There is in his soul some impenetrable mystery; and I recall one of his sayings:—

"Very deep rivers flow underground."

The Duke Gian Galeazzo is dead; and they say that Leonardo has been the occasion of his death by means of poisoned fruit. God is my witness, that 'tis not of my own will I lend an ear unto this terrible accusation, and that I would fain reject it out of hand. Yet there stands ever before my eyes that vision of the tree, with its leaves distilling dew, and its fatal fruit maturing in the greenish mist, lit by the moon, pregnant with terror and death. Oh, that I had never seen it!

"'Of every tree of the garden thou mayest freely eat; but of the tree of the knowledge of good and evil thou shalt not eat of it, for in the day that thou eatest thereof thou shalt surely die.'"

Out of the depths I cry unto thee, O Lord! Lord hear my voice; let Thine ears be attentive to the voice of my supplications! Like the thief upon the Cross, I confess Thy name: Remember me, O Lord, when Thou comest into Thy kingdom.

Leonardo has begun to work on the countenance of the Christ.

The Duke has commanded him to construct an engine for raising the Holy Nail. With mathematical accuracy he weighs in a scale the instrument of the Passion of the Saviour, as if it were a fragment of old iron; so many ounces, so many grains. To him it is only a figure among figures; a part among parts of a lifting machine; ropes, wheels, levers, and pulleys.

Says the apostle, "Little children, it is the last time: and as ye have heard that Antichrist shall come, even now are there many antichrists, whereby we know that it is the last time."

Tonight a crowd of people demanding the Holy Nail surrounded our house, crying, "Sorcerer! infidel! poisoner! Antichrist!" Amused, Leonardo listened to the howl of the mob, and when Marco would have discharged his arquebus at them, it was the Master who restrained him.

The Master did not change from his impenetrable serenity, and when I fell at his feet supplicating a word, a single word, to dispel my doubts—and I swear by God I should have believed him—he would not or could not speak.

Little Jacopo, stealing out, evaded the crowd, and having met the guard of the captain of justice, led them to the house: and at the instant when the doors were giving way under the weight and the blows of the crowd, soldiers took them in the rear, and the rioters scattered. Jacopo is wounded, struck on the head by a stone, and like to die.

Today I assisted in the cathedral at the Feast of the most Holy Nail. At the moment recommended by the astrologers it was raised on high. Leonardo's machine acted without a hitch: neither rope nor pulley was visible. Through clouds of incense the round casket with the crystal sides and the golden rays in which the nail was set, rose of itself like the rising sun. 'Twas a triumph of mechanics! The choir sang:—

"Confixa clavis viscera
Tendens manus vestigia
Redemptionis gratia,
Hic immolata est Hostia."

Then the casket was arrested and lodged in a dark niche above the high altar, surrounded by five ever-flaming lamps.

The Archbishop intoned:—

"O Crux benedicta quae sola fuisti digna portare Regem cælorum et Dominum, Alleluia!"

The whole assembled multitude fell on their knees repeating Alleluia!

And the usurper of the throne of Milan, Ludovico the assassin, prostrated himself with the rest, and weeping, raised his hands to the Holy Nail.

After which the populace was glutted with wine, with the flesh of beasts, with five thousand measures of pease, and six hundred weight of salt. Forgetting their murdered lord, they feasted and drank, and cried—"*Viva Il Moro! Viva il Chiodo!*"

Bellincioni has composed some hexameters, in which we learn that by virtue of the ancient nail of iron the age of gold shall be renewed.

After leaving the cathedral the duke came to Leonardo and embraced him; kissing his lips, calling him his Archimedes, and, thanking him for the beautiful machine, he promised to present him with a pure-blooded Barbary mare and two thousand imperial ducats. Then condescendingly tapping him on the shoulder, he said, "Now you'll have time to finish the head of your Christ."

"A DOUBLE-MINDED MAN IS UNSTABLE in all his ways."

I can no longer endure my torment; I perish; I become crazed! My reason loses itself in the duplicity of these thoughts.

Fly, fly, ere it be too late!

I ROSE IN THE NIGHT-TIME, tied up my clothes and my books in a bundle, took a thick stick, felt my way through the darkness to the studio, where I left on the table the thirty florins which I owe for the last six months' teaching—I have sold my mother's emerald ring to do this—and without leave-takings, abandoned Leonardo's house forever.

Fra Benedetto tells me that from the time I left him he has not ceased to pray for me; and he has had a revelation in his sleep that God has brought me back into the true path. He is faring to Florence to visit his sick brother, a Dominican in the monastery of San Marco, where Fra Girolamo Savonarola is prior.

Praise and thanksgiving unto Thee, O Lord! Thou hast brought me out of the shadow of death, from the mouth of the pit. I renounce today the wisdom of this world, upon which is the seal of the dragon with the seven heads, the beast which walketh in darkness, which is Antichrist. I renounce the fruit of the poisonous tree of knowledge, the pride of vain understanding, of that wisdom which is inimical to God, of whom the Devil is the father.

I renounce every aspiration after the enchantments of the world. I renounce all that is not subordinated to Thy glory, Thy will, Thy wisdom, O Christ!

Illumine my soul with Thy light, deliver me from fatal duplicity of thought; make sure my footsteps in Thy paths, and shelter me under the shadow of Thy wings.

My soul, praise the Lord! I will praise the Lord so long as I have my being; I will yet sing praises unto my God.

Two days hence, Fra Benedetto and I go to Florence. I desire, with the blessing of this my second father, to enter as novice in the Convent of San Marco, under the guidance of the holy and elect Fra Girolamo Savonarola.

Here ends the diary of Giovanni Boltraffio.

Book VII

The Bonfire of Vanities—1496

"Dov' è più sentimento, li è più, ne' martiri, gran martire."

—Leonardo Da Vinci

(He who feels most, is the greatest of the martyrs.)

"A double-minded man is unstable in all his ways."

—St. James i. 8

I

More than a year had passed since Giovanni Boltraffio had been received as a novice in the Convent of San Marco.

On a winter's day towards the close of the carnival of 1496, shortly after noon, Fra Girolamo was writing the account of a vision which had lately appeared to him. He had seen two crosses waving above the city of Rome, one black and enveloped in storm, inscribed—"The Cross of the fury of the Lord"; the other of gleaming azure, with the inscription—"The Cross of the Lord's mercy."

February sunshine flooded the narrow cell with its white and naked walls, great black crucifix, and the thick parchment books in antique leather. Now and then from the blue sky came the joyous twitter of the swallows.

Fra Girolamo felt unwonted weariness, and now and then trembled. Laying down his pen, he dropped his head on his hands, closed his eyes, and meditated upon what he had that morning heard about Pope Alexander VI from Fra Paolo, a monk who had been on a secret mission to Rome. Monstrous images like those described in the Apocalypse passed and whirled before the mind of the prior; he saw the blood-stained bull of the shield of the Borgias, reminding him of Apis, the heathen god; the golden calf borne before the pontiff instead of the humble Lamb of God; nightly orgies at the Vatican in the presence of the Holy Father, of his favourite daughter, and of the College of Cardinals; the beautiful Giulia Farnese, mistress of the sexagenarian pope, and the model for contemporary portraits of the saints; his two sons, Cesare the young Cardinal of Valenza, and Giovanni the Duke of Candia, who out of criminal love for Lucrezia their sister, hated each other to the point of fratricide. And haunted by what Fra Paolo had scarcely dared to whisper, the tale of the strange relations between the pope and this Lucrezia his daughter, Girolamo trembled.

"But no, 'tis calumny. It were too great an enormity! God sees that I cannot believe it," he murmured.

But in the depths of his soul he felt that nothing was impossible in that terrible nest of the Borgias, and drops of cold sweat stood out upon his forehead. He had fallen on his knees before the crucifix, when a low knocking was heard at the door of his cell.

"Who is it?"

"It is I, father."

He recognized the voice of his trusty friend, Fra Domenico Buonvicino.

"Ricciardo Becchi, secret legate from the pope, prays for an audience."

"Good. Let him wait. Meanwhile send me Fra Silvestro."

Fra Silvestro Maruffi was epileptic and of weak intellect, but Fra Girolamo, considering him a chosen vessel of the grace of God, both loved and feared him. He interpreted Maruffi's visions according to the precise rules of St. Thomas Aquinas and the Schoolmen, finding by ingenuity, by the arguments of logic, by enthymemes, apophthegms, and syllogisms, prophetical meaning in the vain babble of an idiot. Maruffi showed no respect for his superior, insulted him publicly, and even struck him; offences which Fra Girolamo received with the utmost meekness. So that if the people of Florence were in the hands of Savonarola, Savonarola was in the hands of the half-witted Maruffi.

Having entered, Fra Silvestro sat on the floor and scratched furiously at his red and naked feet, chanting a monotonous song. His face was freckled, with a sharp nose, and a hanging lower lip. His rheumy eyes of a dull green were melancholy.

"Brother," said Savonarola, "the pope has sent me a secret messenger. Tell me, shall I receive him? What should I say? Have you had any voice or vision?"

Maruffi grimaced, barked and grunted. He had great gifts in the imitation of animals.

"Beloved Brother," said Savonarola, "be kind! Speak! My soul faints under the burden of mortal sadness. Pray God that He illuminate thee with His spirit of prophecy."

The other opened wide his mouth and rolled his tongue; his face was strangely contorted; and he burst out angrily:

"Why should you trouble me, you tedious talker, you sheep's-head, you brainless quail? May the rats devour your nose! You have made your bed—lie on it. I am neither prophet nor councillor."

He paused, looked at Savonarola from under his scowling eyebrows, and continued more quietly:—

"Brother, I'm sorry for you! But as for my visions, how know you if they come from God or from the devil?"

Silvestro closed his eyes. His countenance took an expression of repose. Savonarola held his breath in holy expectancy.

Suddenly Maruffi opened his eyes, slowly turned his head like one listening, looked out of the window, and a smile of good nature, peace, almost of intelligence, brightened his face.

"The birds!" he said; "do you hear the birds? To be sure, the grass is springing in the meadows, and the first little yellow flowers! 'Tis enough. It's time to think of God now. Come! let us flee this sinful world; let us flee together to the desert!" And rocking himself, he began to sing in a sweet, lazy voice.

Suddenly he sprang to his feet, ran to Savonarola, seized his hand and cried, choking with excitement:—

"I have seen—I have seen—May the rats devour your nose! You head of an ass—I have seen—"

"Speak, dear brother; speak quickly!"

"Flames! Flames!" cried Maruffi.

"Well? And besides?"

"Flames rising from a stake, and in the midst of the flames a man—"

"Who?"

Nodding his head, and motioning with his hand, Silvestro did not reply at once; then fixing his penetrating eyes on the other, he laughed softly and foolishly, and murmured:—

"Thou!"

Fra Girolamo shuddered, paled, and drew back involuntarily. Maruffi turned away, and shambled out of the cell, singing:—

"Hie we to the smiling woods,
The shy retreat of spring,
Where the streams unsealèd flow,
And the yellow-hammers sing!"

Recovering himself, Fra Girolamo gave orders to admit His Magnificence Ricciardo Becchi.

II

This man, Scriptor of the Papal Court of Chancery, entered Savonarola's cell, rustling a long silk garment shaped like the habit of a monk, but of the modish violet colour, and with hanging embroidered sleeves lined with fox-skin, his whole person emitting a perfume of musk. The studied grace of his movements, his pleasant and intelligent smile, his calm eyes, his dimpled and well-shaven cheek, showed him a master of dignified urbanity. He bent in a courtly reverence, kissed the hand of the Prior of San Marco, and asked his blessing; then entered upon a long speech in Latin beflowered with Ciceronianisms and resounding sententiousness. He began with what in the rules of oratory is called the appeal for goodwill, dilating upon the fame of the Florentine preacher; then he gradually approached the mission entrusted to him. The Holy Father, though righteously angered by Fra Girolamo's refusal to present himself in Rome, nevertheless burning with zeal for the Church's good, for the perfect union of the faithful in Christ, and for the peace of the whole world, declared his fatherly readiness, in the event of Fra Girolamo's repentance, to restore him to favour.

Savonarola raised his eyes and said very quietly:—

"Messere, what think you? do you believe that the Holy Father and our lord has faith in Christ?"

Ricciardo allowed this unseemly question to pass without reply; he continued to dilate on his mission, giving the prior to understand that if he submitted himself, the red hat of a cardinal awaited him in Rome; then, bowing a second time, and touching Savonarola's hand with his lips, he added insinuatingly:—

"One little word, Father Girolamo, one little word, and the red hat is yours."

Savonarola fixed his unflinching eyes on the speaker, and said slowly:—

"And if I refuse to submit, Messere? If I refuse to hold my peace? If the infatuated monk prefer to continue his barkings as the faithful watch-dog of the house of God?"

Raising his eyebrows in a faint grimace, Messer Ricciardo looked at the monk, then turned his eyes to his beautiful almond-shaped nails, and adjusted his priceless rings. Presently he drew slowly from his pocket, unfolded, and handed to the prior a bull of excommunication, to which nothing was lacking but the papal seal. In it Savonarola was called the son of perdition, "the most contemptible of insects" *neauissimus omnipedum*.

"And you are waiting for an answer?" asked the monk quietly, when he had read the document.

The Scriptor assented with a light nod of his head.

Savonarola rose, and flung the bull at the feet of the emissary.

"There," he said, "there is my answer! Return to Rome and tell him who has sent you that I accept his challenge. Minister of Antichrist! We shall see whether he will excommunicate me, or whether it is I who shall drive him out of the pale of the Church!"

The door of the cell was softly opened and showed the head of Fra Domenico who, hearing the sonorous voice, was anxious to know what could be taking place. The monks were massed round the entrance.

Messer Ricciardo, who had cast several furtive glances at the door, now said politely:—

"May I remind you, Fra Girolamo, that I am charged only with a private mission?"

Savonarola moved to the door, and throwing it wide he cried:—"Hear all of ye; for not only to you but to the whole people of Florence I will proclaim the infamous traffic which has been proposed to me, choice between the cardinal's purple and the excommunication of the *Curia Romana*!" Under his low forehead his sunken eyes shone like coals; his ill-shaped lower jaw, trembling with wrath and almost satanic hatred and pride.

"Yea, the hour has come! I will thunder against you, all ye prelates and cardinals of Rome, even as once the holy fathers thundered against the pagans. I will force the key of this unclean house; the Church of God, which you have slain, shall hear my cry: 'Lazarus, come forth!' and shall raise its head and issue from its tomb! What need I your mitres and your cardinal's hats? Give me the red hat of death; the blood-stained crown of martyrdom!"

III

Among the monks who crowded to hear these words of Savonarola was the novice, Giovanni Boltraffio. When the company had dispersed, he too descended by the main staircase of the convent, and sat in his accustomed spot under the portico, where at this hour reigned solitude and calm.

The court was surrounded by the white monastery walls, and in it grew laurels, cypresses, and a thicket of damask roses. Report said that these roses were watered by angels. Fra Girolamo loved to preach amongst them.

The novice opened the Epistle of St. Paul to the Corinthians, and read; "Ye cannot drink the cup of the Lord and the cup of devils; ye cannot be partakers of the Lord's table and of the table of devils."

Then he rose and paced the cloister, recalling his thoughts and emotions during the year he had spent within the walls of San Marco. After the moral torture of the preceding months, he had at first experienced great peace in this retreat among the disciples of Savonarola.

Sometimes Father Girolamo would lead them out beyond the confines of the city. Following a steep path, which seemed to lead to heaven, they climbed the heights of Fiesole, from whence the City of Flowers, surrounded by smiling hills, appeared like some silver vision. The prior would seat himself in a meadow, enamelled with iris, tulips, and violets; the monks reclined in a circle round him, and talked and danced and frolicked like so many children, or played on viols and citherns, like those which the *beato Angelico* placed in the hands of his angels, circling as they sing in the choir of heaven. Fra Girolamo did not preach nor play the master, but talked affectionately and took his part in the games and laughter. And Giovanni, looking at the radiant smile on his countenance, there on the retired Fiesole hill, under the heaven of most pure azure, hearing the vibrating tones of the stringed instruments, and the voices blended in holy song, fancied himself an angel in the paradise of God. Sometimes at dawn Savonarola would walk to the edge of the slope, and look down on his Florence, bathed in the morning mist, even as a mother looks on her sleeping babe, and from below would rise the first clanging of the bells announcing the beginning of day, like the sleepy babble of a half-awakened child.

And on summer nights, when the fireflies moved through the embalmed air like the torches of unseen angels, and the roses exhaled their mystic odour in the convent-yard, Fra Girolamo would tell of the stigmata of St. Francis, of the wounds, perfumed like roses, which her divine love had impressed on the tender body of St. Catharine. The brethren sang:—

"Fac me plagis vulnerari,
Fac me Cruce inebriari,
Ob amorem Filii."

And Giovanni would tremble in the anguished expectation of miracle—the trembling hope that rays of fire, springing from the cup of the Holy Sacrament, would burn his body likewise with the sacred wounds of the Crucified. "*Gesù, Gesù mio, amore!*" he sighed, fainting in voluptuous ecstasy.

Once the prior sent him on a mission to the Villa Carreggi, two miles from Florence, where Lorenzo dei Medici had long sojourned, and at last had died. In one of the deserted saloons, lit by a ghostly light coming through the chinks of the shutters, Giovanni saw a picture of Botticelli's, called "The Birth of Venus."

White as a water-lily, bedewed with the briny freshness of the sea, standing on a pearly shell, the goddess floated over the waves, veiled in the abundant gold of her serpentine tresses, which she gathered in her hand. The fair naked body breathed the enticement of sin; yet was there a strange pathos in the pure childlike lips and the innocent eyes.

Giovanni shuddered; for it seemed to him that the face of the goddess was not new to him; he looked long at it, and remembered that he had already seen that countenance, those ingenuous, dewy eyes, those innocent lips with their tender sadness in another picture by that same Botticelli—a picture of the Mother of God. Inexpressible consternation filled his soul; he averted his eyes and fled from the villa.

Returning to Florence by a narrow lane, he saw at the angle of a cross-way an ancient Rood, and he sank on his knees and prayed for the driving from him of temptation. But at that moment came the trill of a mandoline from the roses behind the wall; a voice cried out, then murmured in a frightened whisper, "No, no—leave me!" and another voice replied, "Beloved! Love!—my love!" and then the mandoline fell, and a kiss was heard.

Giovanni sprang to his feet, reiterating, "*Gesù! Gesù*!" but this time he dared not add "*amore*!"

"Here also is *she*!" he said; "everywhere! in the face of the Madonna, in the words of the holy hymns, in the breath of the roses which crown the crucifix!"

And hiding his face in his hands he fled, as if escaping from an unseen persecution.

Back in the convent, he went to Savonarola and told him all, and the prior exhorted him to fight against the devil by fasting and by prayer; and when the novice sought to explain that this torment was not the temptation of fleshly lust, but the seduction breathing from all the beauty of pagan antiquity, Savonarola, uncomprehending, at first showed astonishment, then told him sternly that he lied in thinking there could be aught in the pagan gods but concupiscence and pride. All beauty was contained in the Christian virtues. And Giovanni, not having found the looked-for comfort, from that day forth was possessed by the demons of restlessness and revolt.

Once Boltraffio heard Fra Girolamo, discoursing on painting, insist that every picture should have some moral utility for men, exciting them to the practice of those ascetic virtues which alone are healthful for the soul. And he added that the Florentines would do a work well-pleasing to God if they should destroy, at the hands of the executioner, all those images which entice to sin.

Then he went on to speak of knowledge:—"That man is a fool," he said "who conceives that by logic and by philosophy the truths of faith can be confirmed. Does a strong light need the help of a weak one? or the divine wisdom that of the human? Which of the apostles and the martyrs studied philosophy and logic? An old woman who can neither read nor write, but who prays fervently before the image of a saint, is nearer to the knowledge of God than all the sages and philosophers of the world. Neither logic nor science will stead them in the day of judgment: Homer and Virgil, Plato and Aristotle, all go to their end in the house of the devil; because, like the sirens, bewitching the ear with magic songs, they draw souls to eternal ruin. Science gives men stones for bread, and, verily, if you look at those who follow the teaching of this world, you will find in them that even their hearts are become as stones."

"Who knows little, loves little. Great love is the daughter of great knowledge!" had said Leonardo da Vinci.

Only now did Giovanni realise the profundity of these words, as he listened to the anathema of the monk against knowledge and art, and remembered the wise reasonings of Leonardo, the calm of his countenance, his cold look, his wise and enchanting smile. Not that he had forgotten the poisoned tree, the Ear, the crane for the Holy Nail, but now he felt that he had not fathomed the depth of his master's soul, had not penetrated into the mysteries of his heart, nor untied the prime knot in which all the threads must meet.

Such were the memories upon which Giovanni looked back at the end of his first convent year. Deep in thought he paced the darkening cloister, till the evening had fallen and the *Ave Maria* rang through the dusk. The monks wended to the chapel, but Giovanni remained outside, reseating himself.

Then with a bitter smile he raised his eyes to the silent heaven, where shone the evening star, the torch of Lucifer, the most beautiful of angels, the bringer of light, son of the morning.

He returned to his cell and slept: towards the dawning he dreamed. And in his dream he was with Monna Cassandra, astride of a black goat, and fleeting through the morning air, "To the Sabbath! to the Sabbath!" cried the witch, turning to him her clear amber eyes; and he knew in her the goddess of earthly love, she with the heavenly sadness in her eyes—the *diavolessa bianca*. The full moon shone on her body. Sweet odours almost overpowered him. His teeth chattered with desire and with fear. "*Amore! Amore!*" she cried and laughed, and the black goat-skin sank beneath them. Away! Away! they careered.

IV

Giovanni was awakened by the sun, by the sound of bells and of childish voices. He dressed hurriedly, and descended into the court where was a great crowd of people, and among them children all dressed in white, and carrying olive-branches and small red crosses. It was "The Sacred Legion of the Child Inquisitors," founded by Savonarola to watch over and reform the purity of morals in the town. Giovanni mixed in the crowd, and listened to their talk.

Then a wave passed over the ranks of the sacred troop; innumerable small hands waved the olive-branches and the red crosses above their heads, acclaiming Savonarola, who was entering, and a chorus of silver voices intoned a psalm in his honour:—

"Lumen ad revelationem gentium et gloriam plebis Israel."

The children made a circle round the Prior, covering him with a rain of violets and anemones, and they knelt before him, kissing his feet. Illumined by a ray of the sun, silently, with a tender smile, the worn-faced Savonarola blessed them.

"Long live Christ, King of Florence! Hallelujah to Christ, the King of Florence. Hail Mary, Blessed Virgin, and our Queen!" shouted the young voices.

The captains gave the order to march, drums beat, flags fluttered, and the sacred troop moved off. For in the Piazza della Signoria was prepared the pyre for the burning of the vanities, and the children were once more to make the circuit of the city to collect "vanities and things under anathema."

V

When the court was clear, Giovanni saw Messer Cipriano Buonaccorsi, Master of the noble Guild of the Calimala, the lover of pagan antiquities, on whose property by the Hill of the Mill the marble figure of the goddess of Love had been found. They greeted each other warmly, and spoke for sometime. From Messer Cipriano Giovanni learned that Leonardo had come from Milan, charged by the duke to purchase such works of art as could escape the Legion of Children. Giorgio Merula was with the painter. Presently Messer Cipriano asked Giovanni to conduct him to Savonarola. The master of the Calimala entered Fra Girolamo's cell, and Giovanni waiting outside heard their talk. Messer Cipriano offered twenty-two thousand gold florins if he might buy all the books, the pictures, the statues, and other treasures which were ordained for the burning. Savonarola refused. Messer Cipriano increased his offer by eight thousand florins. To this the Monk deigned no reply; only his stern and rigid face became yet sterner and more rigid. Buonaccorsi's toothless mouth quivered. He wrapped his fox-skin cloak round his shivering knees; he sighed heavily, and closing his myopic eyes, he said in his quiet voice; "Well, Father Girolamo, I will ruin myself. I will give you all I possess: forty thousand florins."

Savonarola grimly raised his head. "And what were your profit," he asked, "if you ruined yourself?"

"I was born in this city," replied Messer Cipriano. "I love my land; and for no condition in the world can I endure that we, like the barbarian hordes, should destroy the masterpieces of wisdom and of art."

"Would that thou didst love thy heavenly country as thou lovest thine earthly one, my son!" exclaimed the Monk, turning on the old man a look full of admiration; "but be consoled, only things meet for burning shall be burned. What induces to wickedness and vice cannot include anything of beauty, as, indeed, your same wise ancients have said."

"Alas, father!" returned the merchant, eagerly, "are you certain that babes can distinguish so precisely between the evil and the good?"

"Truth and innocency is in the mouth of babes. 'Except ye become as children ye cannot enter into the kingdom of heaven.' Is it not written: 'I will destroy the wisdom of the wise, and will bring to nothing the understanding of the prudent'? Messere, I pray day and night that God may enlighten my babes, so that by His Holy Spirit their minds may be opened to discover all the vanities of science and of art."

"I beseech you to consider—perhaps even a part—"

"You are wasting your breath, messere. My decision is unalterable."

Again Messer Cipriano's old lips moved, but Savonarola heard only one word—"Madness!"

"Madness?" he echoed, his eyes flashing; "and the golden calf of the Borgias offered to the pope in his sacrilegious festivals—is that not madness? And the elevation of the Holy Nail, to the glory of God, by a diabolical machine at the command of an impious assassin and usurper—is that not madness? You dance madly round the golden calf in honour of your God, which is Mammon; let us, then, who are poor in spirit, be mad in honour of our God, who is Christ Jesus the Crucified. You bemock the monks who on the piazza dance around the cross. Wait! There are other spectacles which wait for you. What will you wise men say when I lead not only the monks, but the whole people of Florence, adults as well as children, men and women, to dance around the Cross-Tree of Salvation, as of old David danced before the Ark of the Covenant to the glory of the Most High!"

VI

Leaving the prior's cell, Giovanni Boltraffio turned his steps towards the Piazza della Signoria. In Via Larga he met the sacred troop. The children had stopped a palanquin carried by black slaves, in which reclined a woman gorgeously attired. A lapdog slept on her knee, a parrot and a monkey were on perches by her side, the litter was followed by servants and by guards. She was a courtesan, Lena Griffi, not long come from Venice, one of those whom the most Serene Republic called "*meretrix honesta*," or playfully "Mammola" (little dear); and whose name in the placard, drawn up for the convenience of travellers, was set down in large characters and in a place of honour at the top of the list.

Lolling on her cushions like Cleopatra, or a Queen of Sheba, Lena was reading a love-missive from a youthful bishop. Its postscript was a song ending thus:—

"Listening to thy voice I rise
From this globe towards the skies,
Plato's Sphere of Ecstasies."

The courtesan was meditating on a return sonnet, for she was an accomplished versifier, and used to say that had it depended on herself, she would gladly have passed her whole existence in the *Accademia degli vomini virtuosi*—in the Academy of the Virtuous.

The sacred troop of children encircled the litter. Dolfo, the leader of one of the bands, advanced raising his red cross, and cried; "In the name of Jesus, the King of Florence, and of the Blessed Mary our Queen, we bid you strip off these sinful ornaments, these vanities and anathemata. And if you refuse, may you fall under the malediction of God!"

The dog suddenly awakened began to bark, the monkey chattered, the parrot, flapping its wings, screamed out a verse it had learned from its mistress:—

"Amor che a nullo amato amar perdona!"

Lena was about to bid her attendants rid her of the crowd when her eyes fell on Dolfo, and she beckoned to him.

The boy came, his eyes on the ground.

"Away with these ornaments!" shouted the children. "Away with the vanities and the anathemata."

"Ah, you handsome boy!" said the courtesan softly, disregarding the cries of the crowd. "Mark you, my little Adonis, I would willingly give you all my poor toys, but the matter is they are not mine own!"

Dolfo raised his eyes; and Lena, with a scarcely perceptible smile, nodded as if confirming his secret thoughts, then added caressingly, in her soft Venetian accent; "In the Vicolo de' Bottai, near the Santa Trinità, ask for Lena, the lady from Venice. I'll be expecting you."

Dolfo looked round and saw that his followers had become involved with a party of Savonarola's enemies (called the *Arrabbiati*, the Enraged), and had forgotten the courtesan. It was his duty to bid them fall upon her, but suddenly he felt himself vanquished, and flushed and hung his head.

Lena laughed, showing her white teeth; and behind the sumptuous Cleopatra and Queen of Sheba there shone out the Venetian "Mammola," the saucy street-girl, mischievous and naughty.

The slaves lifted the litter and she pursued her way unmolested, spaniel on lap; the parrot settled down on his perch; only the monkey still grimaced, and tried to snatch the pencil with which the courtesan was beginning verses to the bishop:—

"My love is purer than a seraph's sigh. . ."

Dolfo, meantime, preceding his company, but without his former braggadocio, mounted the stair of the Palazzo dei Medici.

VII

In the dark, silent, and spacious halls of the Medicean palace, where all breathed the solemn grandeur of the past, the children became awestruck. But when the shutters had been flung open, the trumpets had blared, and the drums beat, then the youthful inquisitors scattered themselves through the rooms, shouting and laughing, and singing hymns, and executing the judgment of God on the sins of learning and art, gleefully prying into vanities by the guidance of the Holy Spirit.

Giovanni watched them at work, and noted some who, with frowning foreheads, hands decently folded, and the gravity of judges, paced among the statues of the philosophers and heroes of pagan antiquity. "Pythagoras, Anaximenes, Heraclitus, Plato, Marcus Aurelius, Epictetus," read one of the boys from the Latin inscriptions on the marble bases.

"Epictetus?" said Federici, with the tone of a profound connoisseur, "that is the particular heretic who permitted all pleasures and denied the existence of God. He merits burning; 'tis pity he is marble."

"Never mind," cried the cross-eyed Pippo, "we'll have him in to the feast."

"Nay," interposed Giovanni; "you are confounding Epictetus with Epicurus."

He was too late; down came Pippo's hammer so clean on the philosopher's nose that the boys yelled in admiration.

"Epictetus or Epicurus, it's all one! If it isn't the broth, it's the sippets of bread! They shall all go to the house of the devil," they cried, quoting Fra Girolamo.

However, contention arose before a picture of Botticelli's. Dolfo declared it was the naked Bacchus pierced by the shafts of love, but Federici, whose eye for "anathemata" rivalled Dolfo's, examined the picture attentively and pronounced it a portrait of Stephen the proto-martyr.

The children stood round in perplexity, for the attire and the expression of the figure in nowise suggested a saint.

"Don't you believe him!" cried Dolfo; "'tis Bacchus, the abominable Bacchus!"

"You blasphemer!" shouted Federici, raising his crucifix for weapon, and the two boys fell upon each other with such goodwill that their followers could hardly separate them. The picture was left for future consideration.

Standing in wondering groups, the children rummaged amongst the properties of old carnivals—amongst the horrid masks of satyrs, grapes for bacchantes, bows, amongst quivers, and wings of Eros, the wands of Hermes, the tridents of Poseidon. Finally, drawing them forth amid shouts of laughter, they lighted on the wooden, gilded, cobwebbed thunderbolt of Jupiter Tonans, and the moth-eaten body of the Olympian eagle, with moulted tail, and wires and nails protruding from his perforated crop. A rat jumped out from the dusty golden wig once worn by Aphrodite, girls screamed, jumped on the couches and gathered up their petticoats. The shadows of terrified bats beating against the ceiling seemed the wings of unclean spirits, and a chill of horror and repulsion settled on the children as they touched this heathen lumber, this sepulchral dust of deities.

Dolfo running up announced that there was yet another room, its door guarded by a little, bald, furious, red-nosed, detestable man, who was hurling blasphemy and curses, and would permit no one to pass. The troop filed off to reconnoitre; and Giovanni, following them, found in the janitor his friend the bibliophile, Messer Giorgio Merula.

Dolfo gave the signal for attack; Messer Giorgio stood before the door preparing to defend it with his body. The children fell upon him, rolled him over, beat him with their crosses, searched his pockets till they had found the key, and opened the door. It was a small room with a library of precious books.

"Here, here!" suggested Merula, cunningly, "the books you seek are in this corner. You needn't waste your time over the top shelves. There's nothing there."

But the inquisitors heeded him not. All that came to hand they piled in a vast heap, especially the books in rich bindings. Then they opened the windows and flung the fat folios straight into the street, where carts were being loaded with "vanities." Tibullus, Horace, Ovid, Apuleius, Aristophanes, rare copies, unique editions flew through the air before Merula's very eyes. He rescued one small volume and hid it in his bosom. It was the history of Marcellinus, containing the life of Julian the Apostate. Seeing on the floor a delicately-illuminated manuscript of the tragedies of Sophocles, he snatched it up and made piteous supplication:—

"Children, dear children! spare Sophocles. He is the most innocent of poets. Let him alone! Let him alone!"

And he pressed the precious leaves convulsively to his breast, but finding them tear beneath his too loving hands he burst into sobs and groans, dropped his treasure, and cried in impotent fury:—

"Know, ye sons of dogs, that one line of this inestimable Sophocles is worth all the prophecies put together of your madman, Fra Girolamo."

"Old man, if you don't want to be taken by the heels and thrown after your pagan poets, you'll hold your tongue!" cried the children, dragging him from the library.

Then leaving the palace, they passed by Santa Maria del Fiore, and marched to the Piazza della Signoria.

VIII

In front of the dark and slender tower of the Palazzo Vecchio the pyre stood ready. It was thirty cubits in height, one hundred and twenty in circumference; an octagonal pyramid with at least fifteen steps. On the lowest were the comic masks, dresses, wigs, and other carnival properties; on the next three, profane books from Anacreon and Ovid to the *Decameron*, and the *Morgante Maggiore* of Messer

Luigi Pulci. Above the books were the instruments of female beauty—washes, essences, mirrors, puffs, curling-tongs, hair-pins, nail-nippers. Still higher were lutes and mandolines, cards, chessmen, balls, dice—all the games by means of which men serve the devil. Then came drawings, voluptuous pictures, portraits of light women; lastly, on the summit of the pyramid, the gods, heroes and sages of pagan antiquity, made of wood and of coloured wax. Above the pile, towering higher than anything else, the figure of Satan was enthroned, the lord of all "vanities and things accursed," a monstrous puppet, filled with gunpowder and sulphur, with goat's legs and a hairy skin, like Pan, the ancient god of the woods.

It was evening: the air was cold, but serene and clear, and one by one the stars were beginning their nightly shining. The crowd in the piazza surged and swayed, and pious murmurings filled the air. Hymns went up from Savonarola's followers—*Laudi spirituali*—which retaining the rhymes, the metre, and the air of carnival songs, had been radically changed in words and sense. Giovanni listened, and the incongruity between the lively music and the gloomy words resounded in his ears like some barbarous funeral chant.

"Hope with Faith and Love agrees,
Take three ounces each of these;
Two of tears, and mix them well
On the fire of Fear.
Let them boil for minutes three,
Spice them with Humility,
Adding Grief to make the spell
Of this madness clear;
Lo! my soul, I offer thee
A most sov'ran remedy,
Worthy cure for every ill,
Called by man a madness still."

A man on crutches, paralysed but not old, his face quivering like the wing of a wounded bird, approached Fra Domenico Buonvicino and handed him a parcel.

"What is it," asked the friar; "more drawings?"

"A matter of anatomy. Yesterday I forgot to hand it over, but tonight a voice reproved me: 'Sandro,' it said, 'you have still some "vanities and anathemata" in the loft above your shop.' So I got up and hunted for these drawings of nude bodies."

The monk took the parcel with a good-natured smile.

"We shall light a famous fire, Ser Filippepi!" he said.

The paralytic looked at the pyramid and heaved a profound sigh.

"Lord! Lord! have mercy on us miserable sinners! And to think that but for Fra Girolamo we should be still in our sins! And even now, who knows if we shall save our souls?"

He crossed himself and murmured prayers, fingering his rosary.

"Who is that?" Giovanni asked of Fra Domenico.

"Sandro Botticelli," was the answer, "son of Ser Mariano Filippepi, the tanner."

IX

When at last the curtain of night had fallen upon Florence, a whisper ran through the crowd.

"They come! They come!"

Slowly, silently, without torches, without hymns, the procession advanced. Before the white-robed troop of the child inquisitors was borne the waxen image of the child Jesus, pointing with one hand to his crown of thorns, with the other blessing the people. After the children came monks, the clergy of the whole town, the *gonfalonieri*, the magnificent gentlemen of the Council of Eighty; the cathedral canons, the doctors of theology, the magistrates, the cavaliers, the guards of the Bargello, the heralds and trumpeters. Upon reaching the piazza the procession stood still, and a deathly silence came over the multitude, such as precedes an execution. Then Savonarola mounted the *Ringhiera*, a stone platform before the Palazzo Vecchio, lifted the crucifix, and commanded in sonorous tones:—

"In the name of the Father, the Son, and the Holy Ghost, kindle the flame!"

Four monks approached the pyre with torches, and immediately fire broke out at the four opposing corners. The flames crackled, and a smoke at first grey, then blackening, rose in wreaths to heaven. Trumpets sounded, the monks chanted a canticle in honour of the Lord, and the children sang in chorus:—

"Lumen ad revelationem gentium et gloriam plebis Israel."

The great bell of the Palazzo Vecchio rolled a solemn and majestic sound upon the air, and was answered from all the belfries of the town. The fire rose ever fiercer and more brilliant; and the delicate parchment leaves of the old books curled up and perished. From the lowest step a bunch of false hair rose flaming and floated away, amid the jeers and laughter of the crowd. Among the people were some who prayed, some who wept; others screamed and danced, and waved their arms and kerchiefs and caps; others prophesied.

"Sing, brothers, sing unto the Lord a new song!" shouted a limping shoemaker with wild eyes; "All the world is crumbling! burning, burning to a horrible destruction, even as these vanities in the purifying fire—all—all—all!—Church, laws, governments, powers, arts, learning—one stone shall not be left upon another!—there shall be a new heaven and a new earth; and God shall wipe away all tears from our eyes, and there shall be no more death, neither sorrow nor weeping nor sickness! O Lord Jesus, come! come!"

A young woman, with a thin and suffering face, pregnant, no doubt the wife of some poverty-stricken artisan, fell on her knees, spreading her hands towards the flame, as if in very truth she saw in it a vision of the Christ Himself; then starting up and calling like one possessed, she cried:—

"My Jesus! my Jesus! Come, Lord Jesus! Come!"

X

Among the objects burning at the stake Giovanni could not take his eyes off a picture lighted up but not yet touched by the flame. It was by Leonardo: a shining white Leda, lying on the waves of a mountain-girdled lake, among the low-toned reflections of twilight. A great swan spread his wings over her, bending his long neck, and filling the sky and the earth with his triumphant hymn of love, while Leda watched her twin sons. Giovanni stared at the advance of the flame, his heart beating high in nervous horror.

Just then the monks elevated a sombre cross in the centre of the square, and in honour of the Trinity made themselves into three circles, joining their hands; then testifying to the spiritual joy of the faithful, they danced, first slowly, then faster and faster, till at last they were as a mighty whirlwind, and they sang the while:—

"Ognun gridi com' io grido! Sempre pazzo, pazzo, pazzo!"

"Each and all with me cry out,
Ever madly, madly shout!
All that wise men follow after
Jesu's fools delight in spurning,
Riches, honour, feasting, laughter,
Pomp and pleasure, golden earning—
Unto those things fondly turning
That to wisdom hateful be:
Grief, and pain, and penury.
Christians still may boast of madness—
Never was there greater gladness,
More delightsome solace never
Than for love of Jesu ever
Thus to rage in holy madness."[1]

The heads of the spectators reeled, and their hands and feet were set in motion; suddenly children, men, feeble women joined in the frantic dance. One old and unwieldy monk, like an aged faun, tripped, fell, and was hurt so that the blood flowed; he was flung aside, barely escaping trampling, and the dance rolled on. The fire's crimson and flickering glow lighted convulsed faces: a vast shadow was thrown by the crucifix, the moveless centre of the whirling circles.

"If of wit my mind doth show,
Jesu, in thy courtesie,
Rid it thence and let me know
Ever only phrenesie!
For of all philosophie,
Wisdom, prudence, and the rest,
Loathing such hath me possessed
That I would only ask for madness.

Jesu mine, it doth appear
Wisdom all and man's contriving
In God's sight is folly mere;
All things else but vainest striving,
Saving Thee, Thou fount reviving,

1. Hieronymo Benivieni.

Whence flow out such waters rare,
That who slakes his thirst once there
For love of Thee is seized with madness."

At last the creeping flame had reached the Leda, with its scarlet tongue had licked the pure body, flushed as if living, and grown momentarily yet more mystic and exquisite. Giovanni gazed, shuddering and turning pale, and for him Leda smiled her last smile; then dissolving in the fire, like a cloud in the sunrise, she was lost forever.

And now the flame had attained the huge devil on the apex of the pyramid: its paunch, filled with powder, burst with a tremendous crash. A pillar of fire rose to the sky. The monster tottered on his blazing throne, bowed, fell, and was scattered in a powder of dying embers.

Drums and trumpets sounded. All the bells pealed, the crowd raised a roar of triumph, as though Satan himself had perished in the flames of the holy pile, together with all the falsehood, pain and sins of the whole earth. Giovanni clapped his hands to his temples and would have fled. But a hand was laid upon his shoulder; he turned and looked: beside him stood Leonardo, with his quiet untroubled face. The Master took him by the hand and drew him forth from the crowd.

XI

They moved from the square, pervaded by clouds of stifling smoke, and, lit up by the glow of the dying bonfire, by an obscure lane they took their way to the banks of the Arno. Here all breathed quietness and calm: the stream glided by, gently murmuring: the stars scintillated, coldly brilliant, and the moon bathed the hills in a flood of silver glory.

"Giovanni," said Leonardo, "why did you forsake me?"

The disciple raised his eyes and tried to speak; but his voice died in his throat, his lip trembled, and he burst into tears.

"Master—forgive me!"

"You have done me no wrong."

"I knew not what I did," murmured Boltraffio. "How, O God! how could I have left you?"

He would have told his sufferings, his madness, the anguish of his terrible doubts. But as when at Milan he had stood before the Colossus of Francesco Sforza, he felt that Leonardo would have no comprehension; and in hopeless entreaty he looked into his eyes—eyes clear, calm, and alien as the stars.

As if divining the conflict in his soul, the Master did not question him; he smiled with infinite kindness, and laying his hand on the young head he said:—

"God help you, my poor boy: you know I have ever loved you as my favourite son! Will you come back to me? I will receive you with joy."

Then, scarce audibly, as if speaking to himself, he added:—

"The deeper the sensitiveness, the greater the grief. A martyr among the martyrs!"

From afar came the clash of the bells, the scream of the chant, the cry of the frenzied mob. But Master and pupil were happy.

Book VIII

The Age of Gold—1496–1497

"Tornerà l'età dell' oro
Cantiam tutti: 'Viva il Moro!'"

—Bellincioni

*(The Age of Gold shall brighten as of yore,
And all exulting sing, "Long live the Moor!")*

I

Beatrice d'Este, Duchess of Milan, sat in her boudoir writing a letter to her sister Isabella, wife of the Marchese Francesco Gonzaga, lord of Mantua:—

> "Most excellent madonna and well-beloved Sister, I and *il Signor* Ludovico, my spouse, desire your good health, and that of *il Signor* Francesco, your illustrious consort.
>
> "In obedience to your desire I send you the portrait of Massimiliano, my Son, only I pray you not to conceive of him as of the smallness here indicated. I would send you the precise measurements of how tall he is, but that I am afraid, for the nurse tells me such measurement would impede his growth. He grows *amazingly*. If I see him not for a couple of days, I find him so greatly enlarged that I jump for joy.
>
> "Here at court we have a great grief: the little Fool Nannino hath died. You, my sister, knew him and loved him well; you will therefore comprehend that while I might have replaced any other loss, Nature herself could not fill the void left by Nannino, since in this Being, formed expressly for the delight of princes, she had united the perfection of imbecility with the most entrancing hideousness. Bellincioni has composed a most elegant Elegy, declaring that if Nannino is in Heaven then all paradise must laugh, if he is in hell even Cerberus grinneth. We have buried him, with many

tears, in our family tomb in St. Maria delle Grazie, beside my favourite falcon, and the memorable bitch Puttina. Death shall not wholly separate me from so delightful a possession. I have wept for two entire nights, and Ludovico, my lord, in the hope to console me, has promised me for a Christmas gift a magnificent silver bedside Seat, ornamented with a relief of the fight between the Centaurs and the Lapithæ. Its interior will be of pure gold, very massive, and it hath a Baldachin of velvet, embroidered with our ducal arms. A similar seat has no other prince, neither the Pope, nor the Emperor, nor the grand Turk. It will excel in beauty that one famed by Martial in his epigram. My lord, Ludovico, had wished Leonardo da Vinci to contrive a musical-organ in its Interior, but he hath excused himself on some flimsy pretext, such as the finishing of his Colossus, or his *Cenacolo*. You prayed me, beloved Sister, to lend you this Painter for a time. With pleasure would I accede to your request, and verily not lend but give him to you forever; but my lord, Ludovico, for what reason I cannot say, is exceeding well-disposed toward this man, and would not consent to his removal for all the gold in the world. Be not disappointed overmuch, for verily this Leonardo is occupied to such a degree with alchemy, mechanics, Magic, and other such like follies, that he scarce attends to his painting; secondly, he executes all commissions with a slowness that would lose an Angel his patience; thirdly, he is an infidel.

"Of late we have had a wolf-hunt. They do not permit me to mount on horseback, for I am now advanced in my fifth month; but I watched the hunt from the high platform of a conveyance made expressly for me, in form like a pulpit. I assure you that in this box I was rather tortured than diverted. When the Wolf made his escape into the forest I wept with rage. Had I been upon my horse I swear he should not thus have got away, though I had broken my collar-bone.

"My little sister, do you recall how we used to leap our horses? And how Penthesilea fell in the Ditch and almost destroyed herself? And the boar-hunt at Cusnago? And the tennis? and the angling? What fine times were those!

“Here we amuse ourselves as best we can. We play at cards, and we skate, which is a most pleasing diversion, introduced among us by a Flemish gentleman, for the winter is very severe, and not only the lakes but likewise the rivers are completely frozen. In the park Leonardo hath built out of snow a most elegant Leda embraced by the swan. Pity ’tis that in the spring it will melt!

“And you, delightful sister, how fare you? And has your breed of cats with long hair succeeded well? If you have a male Kitten with tawny hair and blue eyes, I pray you to send him with the young Negress you have promised me; I will give you in exchange my little bitch’s next litter.

“Pray you, do not omit to send the model of the Wrapper of azure satin, with the cross-cut collar and the trimming of sables. I asked for it in my last letter. Pray you, despatch it at once; ’twere best tomorrow at day-break, and by a mounted messenger. And send me also a vessel of your boasted ointment for the king’s evil, and some of that foreign wood for the finger-nails.

“Our astrologer predicts a very hot summer, and War. What saith your prophet? One’s faith jumps always with the astrologer belonging to somebody else.

“I and Ludovico, my lord, commend ourselves to your gracious remembrance, beloved sister, and that of your illustrious consort, the Signor Marchese Francesco.

BEATRICE SFORZA

II

NOTWITHSTANDING THE FRANK TONE OF this letter, it was full of finished policy. Beatrice concealed from her sister her private anxieties and annoyances, for, as matter of fact, peace was very far from reigning between husband and wife. The lady hated Leonardo neither for heresy nor atheism, but because he had painted the portrait of Cecilia Bergamini, the Duchess’s most detested rival. Of late, also, she had suspected an intrigue with one of her ladies, Madonna Lucrezia Crivelli.

At this time Ludovico was at the zenith of his power. Son of Francesco Sforza—that daring mercenary from the Romagna, half soldier, half brigand—he dreamed of making himself lord of an united Italy.

"The Pope," he boasted, "shall be my chaplain, the Emperor my captain, Venice my treasury, and the King of France my courier."

He signed himself "*Ludovicus Maria Sfortia Anglus Dux Mediolani*," deducing his descent from Anglus the Trojan, companion of Æneas. The Colossus, monument to his father Francesco, with the inscription *Ecce Deus*, was designed as a testimony to the divine origin of the Sforzas. For all his external prosperity, however, the Duke was tortured by anxiety and secret fear. He knew himself unloved by the people, and reckoned a usurper. Once in the Piazza dell' Arrengo the people, seeing the widow of Gian Galeazzo with her eldest son, had shouted, "Long live Francesco, our rightful Duke!"

The boy was eight years old, and famed for his intelligence and beauty. Marin Sanuto, the Venetian, wrote of him; "The people desire him for their prince, even as they desire God." Beatrice and her husband had recognised that the death of Gian Galeazzo had not been sufficient to make them lords of Milan, since in this child the shade of his father was rising from the tomb.

There was talk in the city of mysterious portents. At night, above the castle towers, a strange glow had appeared as that of a conflagration. In the palace chambers agonising groans had been heard. It was remembered that when Gian Galeazzo had lain dead it had been impossible to shut his left eye, omen of the imminent death of one of his near kinsmen; the eyelids of the Madonna dell' Albore had quivered; outside the Porta Ticinese an old woman's cow had dropped a double-headed calf. The Duchess herself had seen an apparition in the Sala della Rocchetta, had fainted with terror, and refused to discuss it with anyone, even her husband. She had altogether lost that vivacity and grace which had been so attractive to her spouse, and, filled with the gloomiest prognostications, was awaiting the approaching birth of her child.

III

On a melancholy December evening, while snowflakes were slowly falling on the streets of Milan, Il Moro sat in the little detached apartment of the palace in which he had installed his new love, Madonna Lucrezia Crivelli. The flames from the fire on the open hearth lighted up the polished doors with their inlaid views of the ancient buildings in Rome, the moulded and chequered lacework of the ceiling touched up with gold, the walls covered with Cordovan leather and gold hangings, the tall black chairs and settles, the round table, the novel by Boiardo lying open, the sheets of music, the mother-o'-pearl mandoline, and the crystal goblet of *Balnea aponitana*, a spa water, at that time greatly in fashion. On the wall hung the lady's portrait painted by Leonardo. Caradosso had carved the marble reliefs of the chimney-piece—curled serpents gnawing a vine, and naked children, half cherubs, half cupids, playing with the sacred instruments of the Lord's Passion; nails, sponge, lance, and crown of thorns.

The fierce wind howled in the chimney, but within the dainty *studiolo* all was comfort and luxury. Madonna Lucrezia, seated on a cushion at the Duke's feet, was sorrowful, for he had chided her, the ground of his complaint being that she did not visit Beatrice, his duchess.

"Your Excellency!" cried the girl, with drooping eyelids, "I beseech you, constrain me not! I am incapable of lying."

"Lying?" echoed Il Moro; "but this is concealment, not lying! Did not the Thunderer himself hide his pranks from his jealous spouse? And Theseus? and Phædra? and Medea? All the gods and heroes of antiquity! We, poor mortals, cannot resist the might of the god of Love. But would it be well to have the evil flagrant? Then you lead your neighbour into temptation, which is contrary to all Christian charity. And charity, you know, covers a multitude of sins."

He laughed; but Lucrezia shook her head and looked at him with her large eyes, innocent and pensive as a child's.

"You know, my lord, I am happy in your love; but sometimes I fall into such a remorse, remembering that I am deceiving Madonna Beatrice, who loves me as a sister, that I know not how to endure it."

"Enough, enough, my child!" cried the Duke, and drew her to his knee, throwing one arm round her waist, and with the other hand caressing her smooth raven tresses, which were confined by the *ferroniera*, a thread of gold fastened over the brow by a diamond, which glistened like a tear. Lowering her eyelashes she permitted his caresses coldly, and without returning them.

"Ah, if you knew how I loved thee, my gentle one! so sweet, so modest! Thee only!" he sighed, breathing again that odour of violet and musk.

The door opened, and a frightened maid-servant rushed in.

"Madonna! madonna!" she cried; "there! down by the great door! O Lord, have pity on us sinners!"

"Speak!" said the Duke, "who is at the great door?"

"Beatrice, the Duchess."

Il Moro turned pale.

"The key! Quick, the key of the little door! I will go through the courtyard. Give me the key—at once."

"But the cavaliers of Madonna Beatrice are surrounding the house!" cried the servant, wringing her hands.

"Then it's a trap," said the Duke rubbing his brow. "But how has she come by the knowledge? Who can have told her?"

"Surely Monna Sidonia, the accursed witch who creeps in to vex us with her unguents and her phials. I warned you, Madonna, to beware of her."

"What's to be done? *Dio mio!* What's to be done?" muttered the Duke, ever paler.

From the street came a violent knocking on the great door and the servant rushed to the staircase.

"Hide me, Lucrezia. Hide me!"

"Most Excellent, if Madonna Beatrice suspects, she will search the house. Were it not better that you went straight up to her?"

"God forbid! You know not the manner of woman she is. Good Lord, to think what may come of this! Remember her state—the danger to the infant! Hide me; hide me at once—no matter where."

At this moment the Duke more nearly resembled a thief detected than a descendant of Anglus, the companion of Æneas.

Lucrezia took him to her dressing-chamber and hid him in the wardrobe, a large press let into the wall, with white doors inlaid with gold; here he effaced himself in a corner among the dresses.

"What a position!" he said to himself. "Exactly like the ridiculous heroes of Boccaccio or Sacchetti."

Il Moro was, however, in no mood to appreciate the ridiculous side of the adventure. He drew from his bosom a small case with relics of St. Christopher; another containing a morsel of Egyptian mummy, a talisman much in vogue. In the dark he could not distinguish which was which of these treasures, so he kissed them both, crossing himself and praying.

Hearing the voices of his wife and his mistress entering the closet together, he turned cold with fear. But they were talking amicably as though nothing were amiss. Lucrezia was showing the Duchess her new house, at her own urgent request. Probably Beatrice had no clear proofs of her case, and therefore was dissembling her suspicion. It was a duel of feminine cunning.

"What! gowns here, too?" said the Duchess indifferently, as she approached the press in which her husband had settled himself down half dead with fear.

"Yes, old gowns. What I wear at home. Would your Excellence like to look?" said Lucrezia, also indifferently, and she partly opened the door.

"Hearken, my dear. Where do you keep that robe I was so fond of—don't you remember?—which you wore at the Pallavicini fête last summer? Little golden caterpillars sparking like fireflies on a purple ground."

"I don't remember," said Lucrezia. "Oh, yes, though—it must be here," and she moved away from her lover's hiding-place, leaving its door ajar, and drew the Duchess to the other wardrobe.

"And she declared she could not deceive!" thought the duke, pleased notwithstanding his terror. "What presence of mind! Oh, women! 'tis from you princes should learn diplomacy."

Presently the ladies moved away into the adjoining apartment, and Il Moro breathed more freely, though he still convulsively clutched at the relics of St. Christopher and the morsel of mummy.

"Two hundred imperial ducats to the monastery of St. Maria delle Grazie for oil and candles, if it ends well!" he vowed.

At last the maid came running, opened the press, and with an air both respectful and sly let the prisoner out, telling him the danger was passed, and the most excellent Madonna Beatrice had been pleased to retire, after taking a gracious leave of Madonna Lucrezia.

Having crossed himself, he returned to the *studiolo*, drank a glass of the *Balnea aponitana* water, looked at Lucrezia, who sat by the fireplace as before, her head drooping, and smiled. Then he stepped cautiously to her side, bent down and took her in his arms. The girl shuddered.

"Leave me! Leave me, I pray you. I beseech you to go away. How can you do this after what has happened?"

But the Duke unheeding, covered her face and neck and hair with ardent kisses. He had found a new charm in her unsuspected talent for deception, and never had she seemed to him more lovely.

The December storm still howled in the chimney; but the glow of the fire illuminated the chain of laughing naked children who, among the vine-branches of Bacchus brandished nail, hammer, spear, and crown of thorns.

IV

For three months, under the direction of Bramante, Caradosso, and Leonardo da Vinci, preparation had been making for the great ball, decreed by the Duke for New Year's Day. No less than two thousand persons had been invited. On the appointed day, at about five o'clock in the afternoon, the guests assembled at the palace. A snowstorm had damaged the roads; the castle towers and battlemented walls with the loop-holes for the mouths of cannon showed with ghastly whiteness against the heavy clouds. Fires had been kindled in the wide courtyard, and round these were assembled noisy groups of equerries, palanquin-bearers, grooms, couriers, outriders, and their like. Gilded chariots and coaches, very cumbrous, and drawn by cart-horses, were setting down fur-wrapped ladies and cavaliers at the entrance of the palace, or crossing the drawbridge which led to the inner court of the Rocchetta. The frosted windows glittered in the festal illuminations within.

Entering the vestibule, the guests passed between two long rows of ducal guards, Turkish *mamelukes*, Greek *stradiotes*, Scotch bowmen, Swiss *lanzknechts*, all in armour, and bearing heavy halberts. In front of them stood the pages, pretty as maidens, in parti-coloured liveries, the right side pink velvet, the left blue satin, trimmed with swan's-down, and silver-embroidered with the arms of Sforza and Visconti. Their garments were so tight as to display every outline of their lithe and graceful bodies; and in their hands these charming candlebearers held torches of red and yellow wax, such as were used in the churches. As each guest entered the great hall, a herald, attended by two trumpeters, proclaimed his style and titles; then a vista opened before him of vast dazzlingly-lighted saloons; "the hall of the white doves on a red field"; "the hall of gold," with the ducal hunting trophies; "the hall of purple," hung with gold-embroidered purple satin, adorned with buckets and firebrands (the insignia of the Dukes of Milan, who at pleasure could blow up the fire of war, or quench it with the waters of peace). Last was the small and exquisite "black saloon," designed by Bramante, and adorned on walls and ceiling with frescoes by Leonardo, still unfinished.

The richly-dressed crowd buzzed like a swarm of bees. Their attire was iridescent, gorgeous, not seldom tasteless through over-richness, in fashions borrowed from many lands, so that a witty writer of the day said that he read the invasion of foreigners, and the enslavement of Italy, in the garb of his own countrymen. The robes of the ladies, hanging in heavy folds, and stiff with gold and jewels, suggested ecclesiastical vestments. Many were heirlooms handed down from long-forgotten grandmothers. There was ample display of fair shoulders and bosoms, and hair was confined in golden nets, and plaited in thick strands, artificially lengthened by ribbons and false hair. Fashion proscribed eyebrows; therefore ladies whom nature had disfigured by those superfluities carefully removed them, hair by hair, with steel tweezers called "*pelatoio*." Rouge, and heavy perfumes such as musk, amber, viverra, and cypress powder, were regarded as mere necessary decencies.

Here and there in the crowd might be seen girls and women inheritors of that peculiar charm only seen in Lombardy, that beauty, as it were, of vaporous shadows, melting like mist into the transparent pallor of the skin; of oval faces, and delicate chiselling of features such as Leonardo delighted to paint.

Madonna Violante Borromeo was by universal consent acclaimed queen of the festival, with her black and brilliant eyes, her tresses dark as night, her triumphant beauty patent to all. Her dress was embroidered with moths burning their wings in flames—a warning to all heedless admirers. Yet it was not Madonna Violante who attracted the eyes of veritable connoisseurs in female loveliness so much as the graceful Diana Pallavicino. Her eyes were clear and cold as ice, her fair hair was almost colourless, her smile calm, her voice slow, melodious, and thrilling as the strings of a viol. She wore a simple dress of white damask with long floating lines, trimmed with ribbons of palest green: amid the noise and splendour of the feast she seemed a being apart, alien, solitary, like a water-lily slumbering on some silent moonlit pool.

Suddenly the horns and trumpets sounded, and all the guests moved to the great Hall of the Tennis Court. Here waxlights burned in fiery clusters upon huge candelabra, and woke sparkles in the golden stars which strewed the azure ceiling-vault. The balcony, in which the choir was concealed, was hung with silken carpets, and with garlands of evergreens.

Punctual to the moment prescribed by the astrologers (for the Duke never moved a step nor, as the wits had it, changed his shirt nor kissed his wife, without first consulting the stars), Il Moro and Beatrice made their entry, robed in ermine-lined brocaded mantles, followed by pages, chamberlains, and lords-in-waiting. On the breast of the Duke, set as a brooch, glowed a ruby of extraordinary brilliance and size, taken from the treasure of Gian Galeazzo.

As for Beatrice, she had of late greatly declined in beauty; her unformed still girlish expression and manner had a strange pathos, contrasted with the state of her health and evident sufferings.

The Duke gave the signal, the seneschal raised his staff, the music struck up, and the guests took their allotted seats at the splendid banquet.

V

And now a commotion arose. The ambassador of the Grand Duke of Muscovy, Danilo Mamiroff, refused to sit below the envoy of the Most Serene Republic of St. Mark. To all explanations, persuasions and entreaties the old man was obstinate, and only repeated:—

"I will not sit down. I will not sit down. 'Tis an affront!" Nor recked he of curious looks and ironical smiles turned on him from every side.

"What's the matter? More trouble with the Muscovites? Good Lord, what barbarians they show themselves! They always expect the best places, and won't listen to reason. They are forever in the way. Mere savages! And such a language! They might as well be Turks! A nation of wild beasts!"

Messer Boccalino, the interpreter, a Mantuan of great resource, hurried to the ambassador:—

"But Messer Daniele, Messer Daniele!" he cried in broken Russian, bowing low, and making gestures of perfect servility, "Messer Daniele, you really must sit! 'Tis a mere Milanese custom. Sit down, I beseech you, or his Highness will be offended."

Nikita Karachiarov, Mamiroff's young secretary, had come likewise to the old man.

"Danilo Kusmitch, little father, do not, I pray you, be wroth. No one can keep his own rule in a strange monastery! What would you have? These foreigners are ignorant of our usages. Pray you beware lest they take you by the arms and exclude you from the banquet. Think what a figure we should cut!"

"Nikita, hold your tongue. 'Tis not for you to teach a man of my years. I know very well what I am about. I am not going to give in. I will never sit below that man from Venice. I represent my sovereign; and my sovereign is the Autocrat of all the Russias. . ."

"Messer Daniele! Messer Daniele!" stammered Boccalino.

"Leave me alone, you monkey-face. What are you squeaking about? Get away. I have said I will not sit down, and sit down I will not!"

The old man's small eyes, gleaming like those of a bear under his frowning brows, flashed fires of pride, fury, and indomitable obstinacy. His emerald-studded staff trembled in the tight grasp of his nervous fingers. It was clear that he was not to be subdued by any human force. The Duke summoned the Venetian envoy, and with that happy courtesy which was his characteristic, he begged as a personal favour to himself that the Italian guest would consent to the change in his seat. He added that no one attached the slightest importance to the childish arrogance of these utter barbarians. Yet in point of fact Ludovico greatly prized the favour of the Grand Duke of Muscovy; he reckoned on his countenance to conclude an advantageous treaty with the Sultan. The Venetian looked at Mamiroff, contemptuously shrugged his shoulders, remarked that his Excellency spoke well, and quarrels over precedence were unworthy of educated persons; then calmly seated himself in the chair allotted. Danilo Kusmitch had not understood the conversation, nor would it have altered his sense of his own importance. Unconcerned at the fire of hostile eyes, complacently stroking his beard and adjusting the sash and the sable-trimmed satin pelisse upon his corpulent person, Danilo seated himself heavily and majestically upon the chair he had conquered; while Nikita and Boccalino retired to the lower table, and sat beside Leonardo da Vinci.

The boastful Mantuan told tales, half fact, half fiction, of the wonders he had seen in Muscovy; but Leonardo, desiring more dependable information about the far-off land which, like all things vast and mysterious, excited his immediate interest, addressed himself to Karachiarov, asking questions about its boundless plains, its immense rivers and forests, the flood-tide in its Hyperborean ocean and its Hyrcanian sea, the sunlit northern nights; finally about certain of his friends who had gone thither—Pietro Solari, who was engaged in the building of the Granite Palace in Moscow, and Fioravanti of Bologna, who was putting up certain fine edifices in the square of the Kremlin.

"Messere," said the lovely Madonna Ermellina to the interpreter at her side, "I have heard that astonishing country of which you speak called 'Rossia' because of its wondrous abounding in roses. Pray you, is this to be credited?"

Boccalino laughed, and assured her that in "Rossia" there was, on the contrary, sad lack of the queen of flowers, on account of the intolerable cold; and he told the following tale:—

"Certain Florentine merchants once went to Poland, but were not allowed further into 'Rossia' because of the state of war between Poland and the Grand Duke of Muscovy. The Florentines, desirous of buying sables, invited Russian merchants to the bank of the Borysthenes, which flowed between the two countries; and bargaining began across the river, each party shouting their loudest. But so great was the cold that the words froze in the air and reached not the opposite bank. Certain ingenious peasants then made a huge fire on the midmost point of the ice-bound river; and presently, lo! the words which had remained a whole hour in mid-river air unable to move, began to thaw and to drip, gurgling and clattering like the droppings in the melting time of spring; and at last they were distinctly heard on the far shore by the Florentines, notwithstanding the fact that the Muscovites who had uttered them had long since left the opposite bank."

After listening to this anecdote, the ladies looked with great compassion at Nikita, the inhabitant of so unpleasing a country. Nikita, however, did not respond to their glances, for his attention had been arrested by a wondrous dish just served; a naked Andromeda, made of the breasts of capons, bound to a rock of cream-cheese, and about to be loosed by a winged Perseus of veal.

The meat courses had all been served on plates of gold, but the fish was eaten off silver, as more appropriate to the watery element; silvered bread and silvered lemons were handed round, and then among oysters, lampreys, and trout appeared Amphitrite herself, made of the white flesh of eels, riding in a mother-o'-pearl chariot drawn by dolphins over an ocean of quivering blue jelly.

After this came the sweets, marchpane, pistachios, cedar-cones, almonds, and burnt sugar, edifices designed by Bramante and Leonardo—Hercules in the garden of the Hesperides, Hippolytus and Phædra, Bacchus and Ariadne, Danae and Zeus—a whole Olympus of resuscitated gods.

Nikita stared with childish enjoyment, but Danilo was so much shocked that he lost his appetite, and growled between his teeth—

"Antichristian abominations! Horrible paganism! Horrible!"

VI

Dancing began; slow and stately measures known as "Venus and Zephyr," "Cruel Destiny," "Cupid," etc.; the dresses of the ladies, being long and heavy, did not admit of rapid motion. The music was tender and soft, full of passionate languor like the sonnets of Petrarch, and to it moved dames and cavaliers, meeting and parting with bows, sighs, and smiles, all the perfection of dignity and grace.

Messer Galeazzo Sanseverino, the young commandant of Il Moro's guards, was the cynosure of the ladies' eyes; he was attired in white, with open-work sleeves upon a pink lining; his white shoes had diamond buckles, and his face was handsome, but fatigued, dissipated, and effeminate. An approving murmur ran through the crowd when in the dance, "*Sorte crudele*" he dropped (of course accidentally), first his shoe, and then his mantle, but continued gliding and circling with that air of saddened negligence which was considered the mark of breeding. Danilo Mamiroff watched him in astonishment, spat contemptuously, and exclaimed—

"Good Lord, what a fool!"

The Duchess was not dancing; her heart was heavy, and only long practice enabled her to play her part of amiable hostess, to receive the New-Year's congratulations, and to respond with suitable banalities to the fine speeches of the courtiers. At times she felt unable to carry the business through; she longed to escape into some corner where she could burst into sobs.

Presently she entered a small and secluded apartment, where by a fire certain young ladies and courtiers were talking in a close ring. She asked them of what they spoke.

"Of platonic love, your Excellency," replied one of the ladies. "Messer Antoniotto Fregoso maintains that a lady does no violence to her modesty by kissing a man on the lips so it be by the way of ideal love."

"And how does he prove that?" asked the Duchess absently.

Messer Antoniotto answered eagerly himself.

"With your Grace's permission, I maintain that the lips are the gates of the soul, and when they meet in a platonic salutation the souls of the lovers rise as to their natural outlet. Plato condemns not a kiss; and Solomon, in the Song of Songs, typifying the mystical union of the soul with God, says, 'Let him kiss me with the kisses of his mouth.'"

An old baron, a country knight, with a blunt and honest face, objected from the point of view of a husband; but the pretty lady, Fiordiligi, shrugging her graceful bare shoulders, reproved his barbarism.

"*Dio mio!* we speak of love, not of marriage! Would you profane the sacred names 'Lover' and 'Beloved' with those ignoble, rude, shameless titles, 'husband' and 'wife'?"

The baron would have answered her, but Messer Antoniotto interrupted with further descant; the Duchess, however, was tired, and moved away.

In the next saloon, verses were being recited by a noted poet from Rome, Serafino d'Aquila, surnamed the Unique; a little man very carefully washed, shaved, curled, and scented, with pink cheeks and a languishing smile, irregular teeth, and wily eyes.

Seeing Lucrezia in the circle of ladies surrounding this servant of the Muses, Beatrice paled, but instantly recovering herself, she advanced and kissed her with her usual graciousness. Before she could speak, however, an interruption occurred in the entry of a stout and gorgeous lady, who was suffering from bleeding of the nose.

"'Tis an event upon which even Messer Unico himself could scarce make love-verses," observed one of the courtiers contemptuously, for the sufferer was old and ugly.

Messer Unico, feeling his reputation at stake, sprang to his feet, passed his hand through his hair, threw back his head, and raised his eyes to heaven.

"Hush! hush!" murmured the ladies. "Messer Unico composes! If your Excellency would move a little further she would hear better!"

Madonna Ermellina took a lute and ran her fingers over the strings; thus softly accompanied, the poet, in a voice guttural and majestic as that of a ventriloquist, declaimed his lines. They were to the effect that Love, moved by a lover to shoot at the heart of a fair one, had, owing to the bandage over his eyes, shot awry, and wounded not the heart but the nose of the unfortunate lady.

The audience applauded.

"Most beautiful! Stupendous! Unsurpassable! What conceits! What facility! Not like our Bellincioni who melts away under the exertion of putting a sonnet together! Truly, when he raised his eyes I felt the very wind of his inspiration making me wellnigh afraid!"

One lady offered him wine, another cooling tablets of mint; another placed him in an armchair and fanned him. He drooped and languished and blinked his eyes like a gorged cat in the afternoon sunshine.

Then he produced another sonnet in praise of the Duchess, which told how the snow, put to shame by the whiteness of her skin, had in vengeance turned itself to ice, and caused her to slip and wellnigh to fall upon the courtyard pavement.

Then he celebrated a lady who had lost a front tooth; 'twas the device of Love, who, dwelling in her mouth, required a loophole for the shooting of his arrows.

"But this man is a genius!" cried the ladies; "his name will go down to posterity linked with that of Dante!"

"Nay, higher than Dante's. Where in the verses of Dante will you find these subtleties of our Unique one?"

"Ladies," said the poet humbly, "methinks you go too far. Dante has his special merits. Everyone has his own qualities! As for me, I would give Dante's glory for your applause."

He began another sonnet; but the Duchess had lost patience, and went away.

Returning to the main saloon, she commanded her page, Ricciardetto, a faithful lad, enamoured of her she sometimes fancied, to attend with a torch at the door of her bedchamber. Then she hurried through the long line of brilliant and crowded rooms, passed along a distant and deserted gallery, and ascended the winding stair. The immense vaulted apartment, now used as the ducal bedchamber, lay in the rectangular northern tower of the castle; she entered, took a candle, and went to a small oaken cupboard let into the thickness of the wall, in which the Duke kept important papers and his private letters. She had stolen the key from her husband, and now, nervous and agitated, fitted it to the lock. However, the attempt showed the lock to be broken, and she tore open the brass fastenings, only to find that the shelves had been emptied of their contents. Obviously Il Moro, noting the loss of his key, had transported his letters elsewhere. Beatrice stood motionless.

Snowflakes were fleeting past the window like white phantoms. The wind whistled, and howled, and moaned, and the lady shuddered as she listened, for these voices of the storm and of the night recalled to her mind a something terrible which she was never able to forget for long.

Her eye fell on the round lid of iron which covered the aperture to the Dionysius ear, the hearing-tube which Leonardo had run from the lower chambers of the palace to the Duke's bedchamber. She put her ear to it now and listened. Waves of sound reached her like the rolling of the sea heard in shells. She listened to the festal cries of the company, the laughter, the revels, the passionate sighing of the music, but with it mingled the whistle and roar of the storm.

Suddenly it seemed to her that, close by her side, someone murmured "Bellincioni! Bellincioni!"

She gave a cry, the colour leaving her cheeks.

"Bellincioni! Of course! Why did I never think of him before? He is the one who will tell me everything. I must go to him this minute. Only so that no one shall notice me! Yet, truly, I care not if I am seen. I must *know*! I can endure this atmosphere of deceit no longer."

She remembered that Bellincioni, on the pretext of indisposition, had not come to the ball. At this hour he would be at home, and alone!

So she called Ricciardetto, who was at the door.

"Tell two runners, with a litter, to await me below at the private gate. Despatch. Only see, if you desire my favour, that the matter is not known. Hear you? It must be known to none."

He kissed her hand and set off with the message.

Beatrice threw on a sable pelisse and a mask of black velvet. A few minutes more and she was in the litter, being carried toward the Porta Ticinese, where the court poet had his lodging.

VII

Bernardo Bellincioni called his old ruinous house "the lizard's hole." He was the recipient of many munificent gifts, but his life was irregular; he drank, and gambled away whatever he had, so that "misery," as he was accustomed to say, "followed him like a wife, unloved and faithful."

Lying on a broken couch, of which the fourth leg was replaced by a billet of wood, and the mattress thin as a girdle-cake, he was sipping his third glass of sour wine, and composing an epitaph for Madonna Cecilia's deceased lapdog. Listening to the north wind, and making gloomy prognostications as to the sort of night he was going to spend, he watched the dying-out of the remnant of fire, and vainly tried to warm his thin legs in the moth-eaten squirrel cloak, which he had thrown over them. He had not presented himself at the court ball (where his masque, *Paradiso*, was to be performed) for other reasons than illness; though indeed he had been ill for some while, and was so lean that, as he said, "in his body it were possible to study the anatomy of the bones, muscles, and veins of the human subject." Had he been dying he might still have dragged himself to the festival; more potent than illness was, however, jealousy; he preferred freezing in his kennel to witnessing the triumph of his rival, that interloping and pretentious humbug, Messer Unico, who had turned the heads of all the silly women. The mere thought of Messer Unico overflowed his heart with black bile; he clenched his fist, gnashed his teeth, and jumped frantically from his bed. But the room was so cold that he returned to its inadequate shelter, coughed, shivered, and rolled angrily from side to side.

"The villains!" he grumbled; "have I not written four sonnets in the best rhyme praying for firewood, and not a stick has come. I shall certainly be reduced to burning my banisters: no one comes to visit me save Jews, and if they break their necks so much the better."

However, he spared the banisters. His eye fell on the makeshift leg of his bed, and he considered which were the more dangerous, a fireless room or an insecure sleeping-place. The storm swept through the room, blowing in at the chinks and shrieking in the chimney like a witch. With desperate decision Bernardo tore away the support of his couch, chopped it up and cast it on the hearth. The fire blazed up anew, and he sat before it on a stool, putting his blue fingers to the flame, and apostrophising the last warm friend of a lonely poet.

"A dog's life!" he muttered presently; "and of a truth I merit these castigations less than others. Was it not of my forefather, the Florentine, who lived before the house of Sforza had been heard of, that the divine poet wrote:—

'Bellincion Berti vid' io andar cinto
Di cuoio e d'osso'?

Good Lord, when I came to Milan this herd of creeping animals did not know a sonnet from a *strambotto*. Who is it has taught them the elegancies of the new poetry? Was it not through my facile fingers that the waters of Hippocrene enriched the Lombard plain, and even threatened an inundation? And this is my reward! To lie like a dog in a kennel! To be neglected by all because, forsooth, I am poor! A poet situated as I am, is unknown as he whose face is hidden by a mask or deformed by the smallpox."

And he recited certain lines from his epistle to Ludovico, the Duke:—

"I cry for aid to everyone,
But each in turn replies, 'Begone!'
Ah, wretched poet! for his pains,
Thou generous lord, what meed remains?
The very cap and bells to him denied,
Among the beasts of burden harness thou his pride!"

And he hung his bald head, smiling bitterly; on his stool by the fire, crouching, and very thin, with a long red nose, he looked like some melancholy roosting bird.

Presently a knock was heard at the house-door below; then the sleepy grumbling of the surly old woman who was the poet's sole attendant; and then steps upon the brick floor.

"What, the fiend!" wondered Bellincioni; "can it be that abominable Jew come again after his money? The infidel hound! Can he not leave me in peace even at night?"

The staircase creaked, the door opened, and into the wretched room came a woman in a sable mantle and a black velvet mask. Astounded and staring, Bernardo sprang to his feet. The lady, without a word, was about to seat herself on a chair.

"For God's love, be careful, madam!" cried the poet, "the back is broken!" Then in the ceremonious tone of a courtier he added; "To what good genius am I indebted for the happiness of seeing an illustrious lady in my poor abode?"

"Surely," he thought, "'tis a customer come to order a madrigal! Well, it brings money, and that brings firewood! Yet the hour is strange for a lonely lady! 'Tis clear my name is not unknown. And if this one, who knows how many more are my admirers?"

With reviving spirits he threw the rest of the wood on the flame, which already had begun to languish.

The fair unknown raised her mask.

"It is I, Bernardo."

In his astonishment he staggered against the doorpost.

"Jesus! Holy Virgin! Angels and martyrs!" he exclaimed. "What? Your Excellency! Most shining lady—"

"Bernardo, you can do me a great service," she looked round uneasily; "but can anyone hear us?"

"Be at ease, madam. No one except the rats and the mice."

"Listen!" said Beatrice slowly, fixing her piercing eyes on his. "I am aware that you have composed verses for Madonna Lucrezia; doubtless you have kept the letter of commission from the Duke."

He turned pale, and observed her silently, consternation in his eyes.

"Fear nothing," she continued; "no one shall know. I shall study how to reward you, Bernardo."

"Your Excellency!" stammered the unlucky poet, whose tongue had lost its glibness, "do not believe—nay, 'tis all calumny! No letters—before God, I swear there are no letters!"

Her eyes flashed, and her brows contracted in an ominous frown. She rose and drew nearer, still fixing him with her gaze.

"Lie not. I know all. As you value your life, give me the Duke's letters. Give me them! Hear you? Bernardo, be careful, my servants are at the door. Think you I have come to jest with you?"

He fell before her on his knees.

"But, most illustrious lady, I have no letters!"

"You say you have no letters?"

"None."

Fury overcame her. "Wait then, accursed pander, till I tear the truth from your lips. Oh, I'll wring confession from you! I'll strangle you with my own hands, you rubbish, you rogue!" she cried: in good sooth driving her slender fingers into his throat with such force that the veins swelled on his forehead. Unresisting, rolling his eyes and hanging his hands helplessly, he more than ever resembled a sick bird.

"She is strangling me!" thought Bellincioni; "well, it can't be helped. Not for so poor a reason will I betray my lord!"

Dissipated rascal, and venal flatterer the poetaster had always been, but never traitor. In his veins flowed better blood than that of the Sforzas, and the moment had come for showing it.

The Duchess, however, recovered herself. With a gesture of disgust she flung him from her, snatched up the little lamp with its broken sides and charred wick, and made for the adjoining cabinet, which she guessed to be the poet's working *studiolo*. Bernardo, placing himself against the door, barred the entrance. But the haughty glance of the Duchess awed him, and he withdrew. She swept past and entered the poor refuge of his threadbare muse. A smell of mould came from the books, great patches of damp showed on the plaster walls. The broken glass of the frosted windows was repaired with tow. On the sloping ink-splashed board were quills, gnawed and twisted in the agony of finding rhymes, and papers, doubtless rough copies of poems.

Heedless of the author, Beatrice stood the lamp on a shelf and began to rummage among these sheets. She found sonnets addressed to chamberlains, treasurers, and dispensers, with burlesque complaints and prayers for firewood, clothes, wine, and bread. In one he asked of Messer Pallavicini a roast goose for the due celebration of All Saints' Day. In another, headed "*Del Moro a Cecilia*," the poet recounted how Jupiter, returning from his mistress, had been forced to brave the storm lest *jealous Juno* should guess his treachery, and tearing the diadem from her brow scatter its pearls like hailstones and raindrops from the sky.

Presently the search brought the Duchess to a dainty case of black wood; she opened it, and saw a carefully tied-up packet of letters. Bernardo, watching her, wrung his hands in dismay. The Duchess looked at him, then at the letters; read the name of Lucrezia, recognised the handwriting of her husband, and knew she had found the thing she sought, his letters—the rough draft of the love-verses he had commanded for Lucrezia. She thrust the packet into the bosom of her dress, flung a bag of ducats at the poet, as one might fling a bone to a dog, and departed.

He heard her descend the stair, heard the bang of the door, and stood motionless in the centre of the room as if thunderstruck, though the floor seemed shaking under him like the deck of a ship in storm. At last, exhausted, he flung himself on the three-legged couch, and sank into a deathlike slumber.

VIII

The Duchess returned to the castle, where the guests had noticed her absence with surprise, and the Duke himself become alarmed. He met her in the hall, and she accosted him, her face somewhat blanched, and explained that having felt fatigued after the banquet she had gone into an inner room to snatch some repose.

"Bice!" cried the Duke, taking her hand, which was trembling and cold, "you are ill! Tell me, for pity's sake, what is the matter. Shall we put off the second part of this entertainment? Dear one, did I not arrange it solely to give pleasure to thee?"

"There is nothing the matter," replied Beatrice. "Why this anxiety,

Vico? I have not felt so well this many a day. I wish to see the *Paradiso*. I intend to dance."

Il Moro was partly reassured.

"God be thanked, beloved," he said, kissing her hand.

The guests now streamed into the *Sala del giuoco alla palla*, which had been arranged for the representation of the *Paradiso*, by Leonardo da Vinci, the court mechanician. When everyone was seated, and the lights had been extinguished, it was his voice which cried "Ready!" Then a train of powder exploded, and crystalline globes, like planets, were seen disposed in a circle, filled with water, and illumined by a myriad of living fires sparkling with rainbow colours.

"See!" said the lively Madonna Ermellina, pointing out Leonardo to her neighbour; "see that face! He is a wizard capable of carrying away the castle bodily, as one reads in the romances."

"I mislike this playing with fire," replied the other. "Heaven grant we have not a real fire presently!"

Presently, from a black chest concealed behind the fiery globes, a white-winged angel arose and recited the prologue. At the line—

"The great King makes his spheres revolve"—

he pointed to the Duke, as if indicating that he governed his people with the same wisdom shown by the monarch of heaven in turning his celestial spheres. At the same moment the crystal globes began to turn to the accompaniment of a low strange music, representing the celestial harmony told of by Pythagoras. Again the planets stood still; upon each appeared its presiding deity, and each one recited a hymn in praise of Beatrice.

Mercury said:—

"Thou Nature's miracle! Diviner Sun!
Lightning, by whom the clouds are overrun!
Thou Lamp, by whom the stars are all outshone!
The pride and glory of a future race!

In that angelic figure, half concealed,
The secret of the higher world lies sealed,
And all of heaven's glory is revealed
In that fair face."

And again Venus, kneeling before the Duchess, exclaimed:—

"O Jove! whose justice never errs,
And at whose voice all nature stirs
And quickens to a goodly heritage,
I bless thee for thy coming unto earth,
Since thus fair Beatrice was given birth,
Whose fruit is nurtured by the Hesperides,
My beauty at her feet in ashes lies,
Despoilèd Venus none shall recognise."

And Diana prayed that she might be given as a slave to Beatrice the beauteous, since never had a star like her shone in the heavenly firmament. Then came the epilogue, in which Jove presented to Beatrice the three Hellenic graces and the seven Christian virtues; and the whole Olympus and Paradise, under the shadow of the radiant angelic plumes, and of a cross gleaming with green lamps, symbols of hope, once more began to revolve, while gods and goddesses sang hymns in praise of Beatrice, accompanied by the music of the spheres and by the acclamations of the spectators.

"And why," asked the Duchess of Messer Gaspare Visconti who sat at her side; "why is there here no jealous Juno to tear the diadem from her brow, and to rain pearls upon the earth in the form of hailstones and raindrops?"

On hearing these words Il Moro turned quickly and looked at her. She laughed a laugh so wild and forced that the Duke felt ice fall round his heart; but immediately Beatrice composed herself, and turned the conversation; Only she pressed the incriminating letters more closely to her bosom, intoxicated by the hope of revenge, strong, calm, almost gay, in her mood of triumph.

The masque ended, the guests passed into another hall where a new spectacle awaited them. The triumphant chariots of Numa Pompilius, Cæsar, Augustus, and Trajan crossed the stage, drawn by negroes, leopards, griffons, centaurs, dragons, and adorned with allegorical pictures and inscriptions, which set forth that all these heroes were but precursors of Ludovico of Milan. Then a chariot came alone, drawn by unicorns, and bearing an immense globe representing the earth, upon which was stretched a warrior in a cuirass of rusty iron; a naked and gilded child, holding a branch of mulberry (*moro*) in his hand, issued from a cleft in the cuirass, to signify the death of the Age of Iron and the birth of the Age of Gold under the sage rule of Ludovico. To the delight of the spectators the Golden Age proved to be a living child; he was, however, in great discomfort from the plaster of gold which covered his little body, and tears shone in his frightened eyes. In a tremulous and miserable voice he whined a *canzonetta*, praising the Duke, with the monotonous and lugubrious refrain:—

"Tornerà l'età dell' oro,
Cantiam tutti: 'Viva il Moro!'"

(The age of gold shall brighten as of yore,
And all exulting sing, "Long live the Moor.")

Around the chariot of the Golden Age the dancing was renewed, and though no one heeded him any longer, the unhappy golden child still sobbed out his piteous song:—

"Tornerà l'età dell' oro,
Cantiam tutti: 'Viva il Moro!'"

Beatrice was dancing with Gaspare Visconti. At times she laughed and sobbed hysterically, and her throat convulsively contracted. With unsupportable agony the blood throbbed at her temples, and a mist rolled before her eyes; yet her face was calm, and she even smiled.

At the dance's conclusion she again slipped unnoticed from the revelling crowd, and sought seclusion in her private apartments.

IX

She went to the retired *Torre della Tesoreria*, where no one ever came save the Duke and herself. Taking the candle from Ricciardetto and bidding him await her at the entrance, she passed into a lofty hall, dark and cold as a cellar, sat down, drew forth the packet of letters and was about to read. But suddenly a strange and eerie gust of wind swept shrieking round the tower, howled in the chimney, invaded the room with an icy breath almost extinguishing the candle. There was a great hush; it seemed to her she could hear the distant music of the ball, the murmur of voices, the patter of dancing feet, the sound of iron fetters from the vaults below, where was the prison.

And at the same moment she felt a presence in the room with her: there, in the dark angle of the wall, with eyes fixed upon hers. An anguish of terror seized her soul. She felt she must not move, must not look. But it was unendurable, and she did look. He stood there, as once she had seen him before, a long, long, black figure, blacker than the investing darkness, his head bent, and shrouded in the cowl of a monk. She tried to scream, to call Ricciardetto, but her voice failed. She rose to flee and her legs refused to support her; she fell on her knees groaning:—

"Thou? Again? And wherefore?"

He raised his head slowly and threw back the cowl, and showed the visage of Gian Galeazzo Sforza, *the murdered duke*. The face had nothing in it corpse-like, nothing appalling, and he spoke gently and distinctly:

"Poor thing! Poor woman! Pardon me!"

He made a step towards her, and she felt a freezing and unearthly cold. She shrieked, and fell unconscious to the earth.

Ricciardetto heard the cry and ran to her succour. When he saw his beloved mistress stretched senseless, he too shrieked, rushed away along the dark galleries, where at long intervals sentries stood holding dim lanterns, then into the crowded guest-chambers seeking the Duke, and crying wildly:

"Help! Help!"

It was midnight, and the revelry was at its height. The modish dance called "*Fedeli Amanti*" had just begun. In it lady and cavalier must pass under an arch upon which stood the Genius of Love blowing a trumpet; at its foot were judges; and when true lovers approached, the Genius greeted them with tender strains, and the judges smiled and applauded and let them pass; but the untrue were hindered, and the trumpet stunned them with terrible noise, the judges pelted them with hail of *confetti*, and the luckless couple, loudly bemocked, were forced to turn and flee.

The Duke, to sweetest strains like the cooing of doves, had just made his passage of the arch, when, the crowd parting in dismay to admit his approach, Ricciardetto hurled himself at his master, still shrieking his wild, "Help! Help!"

Ludovico laid a hand upon his shoulder.

"What is it? What has happened?"
"The Duchess! She is dying! Help!"
"The Duchess is ill? Where? Speak, in the name of God!" cried the Duke.
"In the *Torre della Tesoreria*."
The Duke rushed from the hall, his golden chain rattling, his hair flying.
The Genius of the arch of true lovers went on blowing his trumpet, but now the dancers left him and he stopped. Some had followed the Duke—in a moment the whole brilliant throng had scattered like a flock of frightened sheep. The arch was overthrown and trampled, the trumpeter nearly fell, was hustled, and sprained his ankle.
Some cried "Fire!"
"I said it was madness to play with fire," wailed the lady who had disapproved Leonardo's rotating planets; and others fainted.
"Calm yourselves, ladies. There is no fire!" said the seneschal.
"Then what is it?"
"The Duchess is indisposed."
"Nay, she is dying! She has been poisoned!"
"Impossible! Her Grace was here but now. She was dancing!"
"But don't you see? Isabella of Arragon, to avenge her lord, has with slow poison—"
"*Oh Dio! Dio!*"
But in the next saloon the music continued, for there nothing was known of the disturbance. The dance "Venus and Zephyr" was in progress, the smiling ladies leading their cavaliers by golden chains, and when these fell on their knees with lamentable sighs, placing their feet upon their necks. But a chamberlain now entered, waving his hand to the musicians.
"Silence! The Duchess is ill."
There was an instant hush, save for one viol played by a deaf and purblind old man, which long continued to pour forth its plaintive quiverings.
The servants passed through the hall carrying a bed, long and narrow, with hard stuffing, and bars at sides and ends, kept from time immemorial in the wardrobes of the palace, and *de rigueur* for the birth of the princes of Milan. Strange and ill-omened seemed this portentous couch in the midst of the festivity, the lights, the crowds of gorgeous ladies. They looked from one to the others mysteriously.

"'Tis from a fall or, mayhap, a fright," said one of mature age. "She should have swallowed at once the white of an egg in which were lengths of scarlet silk, cut small."

From the upper room, meantime, (Ricciardetto being stationed in the adjoining closet) came such a terrible cry, that the page seized the arm of one of the women who were passing with warming-pans, baskets of linen, and so forth, and cried in an agony:—

"For God's sake, tell me what is the matter?"

She did not answer, and another, clearly the midwife, ordered him away.

"'Tis no place for boys," she said sternly.

Yet the door was left ajar for a moment, and looking into the disordered room he saw the suffering face of her whom he loved with his hopeless boy's love, her lips parted in a continuous groan.

He turned pale, and hid his face in his hands.

Beside him chattered a group of gossips each with her infallible recipe; snake's skin, a bath in a heated cauldron, decoctions of cochineal and of stag's antlers, the tying of her husband's *berretto* round the neck of the patient, and so forth.

The Duke entered hurriedly and sank upon a chair, clutching his head with his hands and weeping distractedly.

"Lord God! What torture!" he murmured. "I cannot support it! I cannot! Ah Bice! Bice! And 'tis all my doing! mine!" Still echoed in his ears the furious cry with which she had greeted his approach.

"Go away! Go away! Go to your Lucrezia!"

One of the busybodies brought him a pewter plate piled with meat.

"Your Excellency will be pleased to eat it."

"Good Lord, what are you giving me?"

"Wolf's flesh. 'Tis of great benefit to the wife in her labour, if the husband will eat the flesh of wolves."

The Duke, submissive and self-denying, did his best to swallow the repulsive black substance, which was so hard as to stick in his throat, and the old woman gabbled as she bent over him:—

"Our Father which art in Heaven,
Seven wolves and the mate of one,
Blow the wind from us this even,
Praise Thy name, the storm is done!

Holy, Holy, Holy, in the name of the Trinity, one and eternal.
Let the word stand forever! Amen."

She was interrupted by Messer Luigi Marliani, the first of the court physicians, who came from the sick room, followed by his colleagues.

"Well? well?" asked Ludovico.

There was a silence; then Messer Luigi spoke.

"Your Excellency, we have done all that is possible. Now we must put our hope in the clemency of the Lord."

"No! No!" cried the Duke seizing his hand, "there must be some means! It is unendurable! Try something!"

The physicians exchanged glances like augurs, hoping thus to reassure him. Then Marliani, knitting his brows, said in Latin to the young doctor beside him:—

"Three ounces of river snails, with nutmeg and red coral,"

"A bleeding, perhaps?" suggested another, an old man, with a gentle and diffident face.

"I had thought of it," said Marliani; "but Mars is in Cancer and in the fourth house of the sun. And, further, today's date is an uneven number."

The old man sighed, shook his head and forbore to urge his point. Various other loathsome medicaments were proposed, till the Duke could no longer contain himself. He turned furiously to the doctors.

"To the devil with all your science!" he exclaimed; "she is dying, do you hear me? She is dying! and you have nothing better to propose than three ounces of snails and a plaster of cow's dung! Rascals, charlatans, fools! I will hang everyone of you!"

He paced the room a prey to mortal anguish, listening to the sufferer's unceasing groans. Suddenly his eye fell on Leonardo and he drew him aside.

"Listen," he cried wildly, "Leonardo, you are master of great secrets. No, no, deny it not, I *know*. Ah, my God! my God!—that cry! What was I saying? Yes, yes! Help me, Leonardo! Do something! I would give my soul to succour her—even for a short space—only to still that cry!"

Leonardo would have replied; but the Duke, forgetting that he had appealed to him, hurried to meet the chaplain and two monks entering at that moment—

"At last! God be praised. What have you brought? Ah! a particle of the remains of St. Ambrose, the belt of St. Margaret—is she not the patroness of women in childbed?—and a hair of the Blessed Virgin! Ah, how I thank you! And surely your prayers—"

Following the monks he was entering the sick-chamber when the continual low groaning suddenly gave place to shrieks so appalling that, stopping his ears, he turned and fled, passing through the dark galleries like one possessed. He hurried to the chapel and cast himself on his knees before the most revered picture.

"Holy Mother of God," he implored with clasped hands and streaming eyes, "I have sinned—I have sinned horribly—I have slain an innocent youth—my lawful sovereign. O thou merciful Mediatress, have mercy upon me! Take my life—take my soul; but in pity, O Holy Mother, save Beatrice!"

Shreds of thoughts and senseless fancies crowded in his brain and stole his attention from his prayers. He remembered a story of a drowning sailor who had thought to buy salvation by the promise of a candle as big as the mast of a ship; and when asked how the wax for this colossus was to be provided, had answered; "Hold your tongue; our present task is to get saved, and afterwards we'll get the Virgin to be content with a smaller candle."

"Oh God, where are my thoughts!" cried the Duke bethinking himself. "I must be going mad! God help me!" And he fell a-praying with renewed fervour; but now visions of Leonardo's crystal globes tormented him, and the tiresome chant of the gilded boy—

"Tornerà l'età dell' oro,
Cantiam tutti: 'Viva il Moro!'"

Then all vanished, and he sank in a profound slumber. When he awoke he fancied but two or three minutes had elapsed. He left the chapel, and saw through the frosted window-pane the grey light of the winter's dawn.

X

Il Moro returned to the *Sala della Rocchetta*, where reigned a mournful silence. A woman passing with a basket of swaddling clothes, approached him and said.

"Her Excellency has been delivered."

"Does she live?" he stammered, very pale.

"Yes, she lives; but the infant is still-born. She is very weak; and she desires to speak with your Highness."

He went to her room; and there on the pillows he saw a small shrunken face like a child's, pallid and calm, with great eyes surrounded by livid circles, and turbid as if a spider's web were drawn over them; familiar and yet strange. He bent over her silently.

"Send for Isabella! Quickly!" she gasped.

He gave the order; and presently the tall, young, graceful woman with the proud sad look, the widow of Gian Galeazzo, entered the room and approached the dying Beatrice. All retired except Ludovico and the confessor.

For a few minutes the two women whispered together. Then Isabella kissed the other's cold forehead, knelt by the bedside and prayed, covering her face with her hands.

Beatrice signed to her husband.

"Vico, forgive me! Weep not. Remember my spirit will be always with you. I know it was I only—I only whom—"

She could not complete the sentence, but he understood her meaning.

"It was I only whom you loved." Slowly she turned her eyes to him, eyes already darkening, and murmured:—

"One kiss—on my lips. . ."

The monk was reciting the last prayers for the dying, and the attendants, who had re-entered, responded in chorus.

The Duke felt the lips beneath his own turn cold and stiff; in that long kiss she had breathed her last faint sigh.

"She is dead," said Marliani.

All knelt, making the sign of the cross. Il Moro raised himself very slowly, his face rigid, expressive less of grief than of extreme tension of spirit; he breathed heavily and loud like one toiling up the steep hillside. Suddenly he stretched out his arms, gave one wild cry:—

"Bice!" and fell senseless upon the corpse.

Of the spectators Leonardo alone had remained calm; his clear searching eyes were fixed upon the Duke. The look of supreme suffering in a human face, or its expression in the gestures of the body, was to his eyes a rare and beautiful manifestation of nature, an exceptional experience. Not a wrinkle, not the quivering of a muscle escaped his passionless all-seeing eyes. Presently, over-mastered by the desire to draw, he slipped from the room to fetch his sketch-book.

In the lower halls, whither the artist bent his steps, the candles were dying out in black smoke and gutterings of wax. The chariots of Numa and Augustus, and all the pompous allegorical paraphernalia employed to glorify Il Moro and his Beatrice, were unspeakably melancholy and wretched in the morning brilliance. In one room he saw the overthrown and trampled *Arco dell' Amore*.

Standing by the moribund fire he was beginning his sketch, when in the chimney-corner he noticed the boy who had personified the Golden Age. He had fallen asleep, huddled up, his hands clutching his knees, his head dropped upon them. The faint heat from the dying embers had not sufficed to warm the poor little naked and gilded body. Leonardo touched him on the shoulder, but the child did not look up. He moaned piteously and the artist took him in his arms. Then he opened frightened eyes, blue as violets, and wailed.

"Let me go home! Let me go home!"

"What is your name?" asked Leonardo.

"Lippi. Let me go home! Let me go home! I am so cold. I feel so sick."

His eyelids fell heavily, and he babbled deliriously.—

"Tornerà l'età dell' oro,
Cantiam tutti: 'Viva il Moro!'"

Leonardo wrapped the boy in his own cloak, laid him in a chair and roused the servants in the ante-chamber who were sleeping off the effects of their cups. He learned from them about the child: that he was motherless, the son of a tinker in the *Broletto Novo*, who, for twenty scudi, had sold his child to the mumming, though warned that he might die of being gilded. Leonardo returned, wrapped the boy snugly in his furs, and was carrying him out of the palace to the nearest drug shop that the paint might be removed from his skin. Suddenly, however, he paused, for he remembered the drawing he had just commenced, and the interesting look of despair in Ludovico's face.

"Ah, well," he thought, "I shall scarce forget it. The chief thing is the wrinkle over the arched eyebrows, and the strange smile which one might think full of serenity, even of enthusiasm. The expression of immense grief is like enough to that of immoderate joy; and truly Plato has said that the two emotions, rising upon different bases, converge at their apex."

Then feeling the tremble of the frozen child, he added to himself ironically—

"Poor little sick bird—our Age of Gold!"

And he pressed him with such tenderness to his heart that the little lad fancied his mother had risen from her grave, and was comforting him.

XI

Beatrice Sforza d'Este died on Tuesday, the 2nd of January 1497, at six in the morning. The Duke remained by her corpse for twenty-four hours, refusing food and sleep. It was feared his reason would give way. On Thursday morning he called for writing materials and wrote to Isabella d'Este, sister of the dead Duchess, a long letter breathing bitterest grief.

"It had been easier for me to have died myself," he wrote; "I pray you send me no condolence nor messenger."

After writing he was induced to eat a little, not presenting himself at table but being served in solitude by Ricciardetto.

He had proposed to leave the disposing of the funeral to Bartolomeo Calco, his secretary; arranging himself merely the order of the procession. But his interest became aroused, and presently he was planning details of the ceremonial with the same zeal he had shown in ordering the magnificent festival of the Golden Age. He fixed the precise weight of the funeral tapers; the number of *braccia* of gold brocade and of black cramoisie for the altar cloths; the largess of small coin, pease, and tallow to be distributed among the poor in the name of the deceased. Choosing the cloth for the mourning of the court functionaries, he did not omit to feel its weight with his fingers, and to make sure of its quality by holding it to the light. For himself he ordered a special mourning garb (*abito solenne di lutto profondo*) having holes torn in it to simulate the rendings of despairing frenzy.

A few days later Il Moro caused the tomb of the still-born child to be inscribed with a pompous epitaph composed by himself and translated into Latin by Merula.

"I, unhappy child, have perished before I have seen the light; more unhappy in that, dying, I have ravished life from my mother—from my father his consort. In this adverse fate but one consolation remains to me; that I was born of parents equal unto gods. In the year 1497, the third of the Nones of January."

Il Moro stood a long time contemplating this inscription, cut in gold letters upon a slab of black marble covering the infant's grave. It was in the Monastery of Santa Maria delle Grazie, where Beatrice also slept her last sleep. The Duke shared the naïve enthusiasm of the stone-mason, who having finished his work drew back and admired it from a distance, putting his head on one side, closing one eye, clucking his tongue, and murmuring in an ecstasy of satisfaction:—

"This is no tomb, but a jewel."

One morning when the snow on the housetops shone white against the rich blue of the sky, and in the crystal air was that freshness like the fragrance of lilies which seems to be the perfume of snow, Leonardo da Vinci passed from the sunlit frost into a dark close chamber hung with black taffeta, where the shutters were rigorously closed, and funeral tapers were still alight—the chamber of Ludovico, who for many days had refused to leave it.

The Duke spoke of the *Cenacolo* which was to glorify the place where Beatrice was laid. Then he said:—

"Leonardo, they tell me you have taken under your wing that urchin who played the Golden Age at our ill-omened feast. What of him?"

"He is dead, Most Illustrious. He died on the day of Her Grace's funeral."

"Died!" echoed the Duke. "Nay, but that is strange!" And he dropped his head on his hands, sighing heavily. Then he stretched his hand to Leonardo.

"Yes! yes!" he cried; "'twas destined to fall out thus. Truly our Golden Age is dead; dead together with my incomparable one, for it could not, it should not, survive her. Is it not a truth, *amico mio*, that here we have a strange coincidence—theme for a tremendous allegory?"

XII

The whole year was passed in the deepest mourning. The Duke did not lay aside his garment of woe, nor did he present himself at table, but ate off a tray held before him by courtiers.

"Since his lady's death," wrote the Venetian ambassador, Marin Sanuto, "Il Moro has become very devout, is present at all church ceremonies, fasts, and lives continently (so at least they say), and has in his plans the fear of God constantly before his eyes."

In the daytime the Duke was able to forget his bereavement in the affairs of state, though even here he felt the lack of Beatrice; during the night the intensity of his grief redoubled. Often in dreams he saw her as she had been when he had married her; sixteen, childish and wilful, slim, dark; almost like a boy; so untamed that sometimes she hid herself in cupboards to avoid assisting at state ceremonials, and for three months after their marriage defended herself with her teeth and her nails from her husband's caresses. One night, five days before the first anniversary of her death, he dreamed of her as she had been one day long ago when there had been a fishing party on the banks of the lake in her favourite country house of Cusnago. Fish had been plentiful, and the buckets were filled to the brim. Having turned up her sleeves, the young Duchess had amused herself throwing the creatures by handfuls back into the water, laughing and delighting in the joy of the released captives, in the flash of their scales as they plunged deep into the clear water. The perch, the roach, the bream wriggled in her bare hands, then catching the sun they glowed like brilliants; and the smooth olive cheek of the beautiful girl glowed too. Upon awaking, Ludovico found his pillow wet with tears. He rose and went to the Convent delle Grazie, and prayed long at his wife's tomb; then he dined with the prior and disputed with him upon the burning theological question of the hour, the Immaculate Conception of the Blessed Virgin. When it grew dark, Il Moro left the monastery, and went straight to the dwelling of Madonna Lucrezia.

His grief for his wife, his fear of God, in no wise militated against love for his mistresses. On the contrary, he clung to them more closely than before; the more so that of late the Countess Cecilia and Madonna Lucrezia had become bosom friends. Cecilia, though a blue-stocking or *dotta eroina*, as it was then called, and famed as the "new Sappho," was at bottom a simple good-hearted creature, somewhat easily run away with by enthusiasms. Upon the death of the Duchess she found opportunity for one of those exploits of love of which she had read in romances; she would make common cause with Lucrezia, her young rival, that together they might comfort the duke! At first Lucrezia was jealous and hard to win, but the magnanimity of the *dotta eroina* finally disarmed her, and she opened her heart to this anomaly in female friendship.

In the summer Lucrezia bore a son; the Countess desired to be his godmother, and though herself the mother of children by the Duke, lavished on the infant extravagant tendernesses and called herself his grandam. Thus Il Moro's prophetic dream had been realised, and his mistresses were friends. To celebrate the auspicious arrangement, he caused Bellincioni to write a sonnet in which Lucrezia and Cecilia were figured as the Morning and the Evening glow; while he, disconsolate widower, stood between them.

This evening, entering the familiar luxurious chamber of the Palazzo Crivelli, he found the ladies side by side before the fire. Of course, like the rest of the court, they were dressed in the deepest mourning.

"How is your Excellency in his health?" asked the Evening Glow. She was quite unlike her rival, but no less attractive, with her white skin, flame-coloured hair, and hazel eyes clear as the water in a mountain tarn.

The Duke had complained of ill health lately, and though this evening he felt rather better than usual, languidly answered, from force of habit:—

"Ah, madam, you can easily conceive to what condition I am reduced. My mind is occupied but with one subject, how soonest I may be laid to rest beside my dove."

"Nay, nay, your Excellency must not speak so!" said Cecilia with deprecating hands. "Think, if Madonna Beatrice could hear you! All sorrow comes from God, and must be accepted even with thankfulness."

"You speak well," replied Il Moro, "I would not murmur. Nay, then, God forbid! Blessed are they that mourn, for they shall be comforted."

And he raised his eyes to heaven, pressing closely the hands of the two ladies.

"May the Lord reward you, my dear ones, that you have not abandoned the poor widowed one!"

He wiped his eyes, and then drew two papers from the pocket of his mourning attire. One was a deed of gift by which he gave the rich lands of the Villa Sforzesca to the Monastery delle Grazie.

"But," said the Countess, astonished, "I had thought your Highness adored this villa."

"My love for terrestrial things is dead. And, madam, what need has one man with lands so large?"

Cecilia laid her rosy fingers on his lips with sympathetic reproach. Then she asked curiously:—

"And this other paper, what is it?"

At this his face cleared, and the old, gay, somewhat cunning smile appeared on his lips.

He read the second document aloud, also a deed of gift, with recital of the lands, woods, hamlets, hunting rights, and other advantages which he, Ludovico, Duke of Milan, was conferring on Madonna Lucrezia Crivelli and his natural son Giampaolo. With the rest was included the villa of Cusnago, Beatrice's favourite country house, renowned for its fisheries.

The last words of the document Ludovico read in trembling tones:—

"In the wondrous and rare bonds of great love, this lady has showed unto us entire devotion and displayed such loftiness of sentiment that often in our intercourse with her we have experienced an entrancing and exceptional delight, added to great lightening of our cares."

Cecilia clapped her hands and fell on her friend's neck, her eyes wet with maternal tenderness.

"Did I not tell you, my sweet sister, that he had a heart of gold? Now my little grandson, Giampaolo, has the richest inheritance in Milan."

"What date have we?" asked Il Moro.

"'Tis the 28th of December," replied Cecilia.

"The 28th!" he echoed pensively.

It was the day, the hour, when a year ago Beatrice had surprised her husband with his mistress. The room was unchanged; the same winter wind howled in the chimney; the bright fire burned on the hearth, and above it danced the chain of naked cupids or cherubs. On the round table with the green covering stood the same crystal goblet of *Balnea aponitana*; the same mandoline, the same sheets of music littered the floor. The doors opened into the bedroom, and there was the wardrobe in which he had taken refuge.

What would he not give, so he thought, if he might at this moment hear the rap of the knocker on the great door, if the frightened maid should run in with the cry, "Madonna Beatrice!" Yes, he would gladly once again tremble in the wardrobe like a caught thief, hearing in the distance the indignant voice of the lady of his love. Alas! it could not be, that time had gone by forever! His head sank and tears filled his eyes.

"Oh, *Santo Iddio*!" said Cecilia, turning to her friend, "he weeps anew. Rouse yourself! Coax, comfort him! Console him! How can you be so cold?"

And gently she pushed her rival into the Duke's arms.

Lucrezia had long felt sickened by this unnatural friendship. She would have liked to get up and go away; nevertheless she took the Duke's hand. He smiled at her through his tears and laid it upon his heart.

Cecilia took the mandoline, and, assuming the pose in which twelve years ago Leonardo had painted her, sang one of Petrarch's lyrics for Laura:—

"Levommi il mio pensiero in parte ov' era
Quella ch'io cerco e non ritrovo in terra."

The Duke, much moved, wiped his eyes, and stretching out his hands as to a dissolving vision, he repeated the last line:—

"E compie' mia giornata innanzi sera."

"Ah, yes, my dove, thou didst indeed finish thy day before the evening! . . . Ladies, sometimes it seems to me as if she smiled upon us three from heaven. Ah, Bice, Bice, *mia adorata!*"

He drew Lucrezia to him, and presently Cecilia rose and left them together. The "Evening Glow" was not jealous of the "Dawn"; from long experience she knew that soon again her turn would come. Her mandoline sounded from the next room.

And above the merry firelight, the naked cupids of Caradosso's moulding prolonged their eternal dance, laughing madly around the nails, the lance, the crown of thorns.

Book IX

THE SIMILITUDES—1498–1499

"I sensi sono terrestri, la ragione sta fuor di quelli,
quando contempla."

—LEONARDO DA VINCI

*(The Senses belong to earth: Reason, when she contemplates,
stands outside them.)*

(Greek: "Ouranhos anô ouranhos katô.")
(Heaven above—heaven below.)

—TABULA SMARAGDINA

I

"SEE HERE! ON THE MAP of the Indian Ocean, westward of the island of Taprobane, we find a note—'The Sirens: prodigies of the sea.' Christopher Columbus told me that having come there and found no sirens, he was greatly astonished. But you smile. Why?"

"Oh, nothing! Go on, Guido; I am listening."

"I know very well, Messer Leonardo, that you don't believe in sirens! Well, and what would you say of the skiapodes, who use their feet as parasols; or the pygmies, whose ears are so large that they make one a bolster, the other a blanket; or of the tree which bears eggs for its fruit, from which come yellow downy chickens, so fishy-flavoured they may be eaten on fast-days; or of that marine monster upon which certain mariners, believing it an island, disembarked and lighted a fire for the cooking of their supper? This last is a very true tale, related by an aged mariner from Lisbon, a man in no wise given to wine, and who swore and swore again by the blood and the body of Christ, that he spoke what was true."

This conversation took place six years after the discovery of the New World, on Palm Sunday, at Florence, in a room above the storehouse of Messer Pompeo Berardi, a shipbuilder, who had a branch establishment at Seville, and superintended there the building of ships for sailing to the New Continent. Messer Guido Berardi, Pompeo's nephew, was an impassioned seaman; he had prepared to take part in Vasco di Gama's expedition, when he was stricken by the terrible disease called French by the Italians, and Italian by the French; German by the Poles, Polish by the Muscovites, Christian by the Turks. In vain he had consulted all physicians, in vain he had made waxen offerings at every wonder-working shrine; paralysed, condemned to eternal immobility, he preserved an extraordinary activity of mind, and by listening to sailors' stories, and sitting up all night over books and maps, he sailed the oceans of imagination, and made discoveries by proxy. His room, which sextants, compasses, astrolabes, made like a ship's cabin, opened on to a balcony, a Florentine loggia. The clear sky of a spring evening was already darkening; the flame of the lamp flickered in the wind; from the storehouse below were wafted odours of spices—cinnamon, ginger, nutmeg and cloves.

"And so, Messer Leonardo," he concluded, rubbing his unhappy legs under their coverlet, "'tis not meaningless the saying that faith removes mountains. Had Columbus doubted like you, he had accomplished naught. Confess, I pray you, is it not worth grey hair at thirty to have found the Earthly Paradise?"

"Paradise?" said Leonardo; "nay, how is that?"

"What? Have you not heard? Know you not that by observations on the Pole Star, taken by Messer Cristoforo near the Azores, he has proved that the world has not the shape of an apple, as is commonly supposed. 'Tis a pear, with a protuberance like the nipple of a woman's breast. On this nipple, a mountain so high that its summit leans against the lunar sphere, lies the Earthly Paradise."

"But, *caro* Guido, science. . ."

"Science!" cried the other contemptuously. "Know you, Messere, what Columbus says of science? I will quote you his words in his *Libro de las Profecias*. He says: 'Not mathematics, nor the charts of geographers, nor the arguments of reason, helped me to my deed, but solely the prophecy of Isaiah touching a new heaven and a new earth.'"

Here Guido fell silent, for at this hour began the nightly racking of his joints. He was carried to his bed; and Leonardo, left alone, entertained himself verifying those observations upon the Pole Star which had led to so singular a delusion; and, in truth, he found errors so gross that he could not believe his eyes.

"What ignorance!" he said to himself more than once; "it would seem he has discovered the New World by chance, groping at random. He himself sees no more than a blind man, nor doth he know what it is he has discovered; he thinks it is China or Solomon's Ophir; or, by my faith, the Earthly Paradise! Death will overtake him before he has learned the truth."

He read the first letter, dated April 29th 1493, in which Columbus informed Europe of his discovery; "the letter of Christopher Columbus, to whom our age oweth much touching the newly-found islands beyond the Ganges."

Leonardo spent the whole night over the calculations and the maps. At times he went out upon the loggia and looked at the stars, thinking of this finder of the new heaven and the new earth—that strange dreamer with the mind, and the heart, of a child. Involuntarily he compared this man's destiny with his own.

"How little he knew; how much he did! And I, with all my knowledge, am helpless as the paralysed Berardi. I, too, have aimed at unknown worlds, but have made no step towards them. Faith, say they, faith! But is not perfect faith the same as perfect knowledge? Cannot these eyes of mine see farther than those eyes of Columbus, the blind prophet? Or is it the caprice of Fate that men must see to know; must be blind to act?"

II

Leonardo did not notice that the night was passing. The stars went out one by one; rosy light overspread the sky and shone upon the tiled roofs and the wooden cross-beams of the old brick houses; the street became gay with the hum of the people going forth to their daily toil. Presently a knock came to the door, and Giovanni Boltraffio entered, to remind his master that this was the day for the "Trial by fire."

"What trial?" asked Leonardo.

"Fra Domenico on behalf of Fra Girolamo, and Fra Giuliano Rondinelli on behalf of his enemies, will pass through the fire. That one who is unhurt will be proved by God to be in the right."

"Very good; you can go, Giovanni, and I wish you good entertainment."

"Will you not come also, Master?"

"No. I am busy."

Giovanni took a step towards the door; then, trying to appear indifferent, he said:—

"I am sorry you are so occupied. As I came hither I met Messer Paolo Somenzi, who promised to bring us to a place where we could see excellently. The trial is not till mid-day. If you could finish your work by then, we might yet be in time."

Leonardo smiled. "You want me so much to see the prodigy? Very well, then; we'll go together."

At the appointed time Messer Paolo Somenzi arrived. He was a spy in the pay of the Duke of Milan, and a bitter enemy of Savonarola's: a restless, fussy little man, with brains of quicksilver.

"How is this, Messer Leonardo?" he began in a harsh disagreeable voice, with much gesticulation. "You thought of refusing your presence? Has this physical experiment no attraction for the devotee of natural science?"

"But will the magistrates really permit them to go into the fire?" asked Leonardo.

"*Chi lo sa?* But one thing is certain, that Fra Domenico will not shrink from the flames. Nor is he the only one! More than two thousand of the citizens, rich and poor, wise and simple, women and children, declared last night at the Convent of San Marco that they were ready to follow Fra Domenico to this singular test. I tell you there is such a frenzy abroad that the most sensible feel their heads go round. The very philosophers are taking fright, and asking themselves if there is not a chance of neither champion being burned. But for my part, I am wondering how the Piagnoni will look when, on the contrary, the two poor fools are slain before their eyes!"

"Does Savonarola really believe?" exclaimed Leonardo, as if thinking aloud.

"I suspect he has his doubts and would fain draw back. But 'tis too late. To his own hurt he has so debauched the imagination of this people that now they require a miracle at all costs. See you, Messere, 'tis a pure question of mathematics, and of a kind no less interesting than yours: if God really exist, why should he not do a miracle—why should he not cause two and two to make five? as, verily, the faithful daily request, that the impious like you and me, Messer Leonardo, may be put to eternal confusion."

"Well, let us set forth," said Leonardo, interrupting Messer Paolo with ill-concealed aversion.

"Soft, though," said the other; "one little whisper more. You and I, Messer Leonardo, are of one mind in this matter; and at the day's end we shall cry 'Victory!' whether God exist or no. Two and two will always make four. *Viva la Scienza!* and long live logic!"

The streets were crowded, and on all faces was that air of curiosity and happy expectation which Leonardo had already remarked in Giovanni. The press was greatest in the Via de' Calzaioli before the Orsanmichele, where was a bronze statue by Andrea Verrocchio:—the apostle Thomas thrusting his fingers into the wounds of his Lord. Here the eight theses, the truth or falsity of which was to be demonstrated by the fire, were appended to the wall, "writ large" in vermilion letters. Some of the crowd were spelling them out, others listening and making their comments.

I. The Church of the Lord needs to be born again.
II. God will chastise her.
III. God will transform her.
IV. After the chastisement, Florence also shall be renewed and shall rise above all peoples.
V. The infidels shall be converted.
VI. All this shall happen forthwith.
VII. The excommunication of Savonarola by Pope Alexander VI is invalid.
VIII. He committeth no sin who holds this excommunication invalid.

Jostled by the crowd, Leonardo and his companions stopped to listen to the remarks of the people.

"It is all gospel truth," said an old artisan; "nevertheless deadly sin may come of it."

"What sin is stinking in your old nostrils, Filippo?" asked a lad, smiling contemptuously.

"There can be no sin in it," said another.

"It's a trap of the Evil One," said Filippo undaunted. "We are demanding a miracle. But we may be unworthy of a miracle. Is it not written in Scripture, 'Thou shalt not tempt the Lord thy God?'"

"Hold your tongue, old man! Is not a mustard-seed of faith able to raise mountains? God cannot avoid a miracle once we have faith."

"No! He can't! He can't!" cried many voices.

"But who is to go into the fire first? Fra Domenico or Fra Girolamo?"

"The two together."

"No, Fra Girolamo will only pray. He is not going in."

"You don't know what you are talking about. 'Twill be first Fra Domenico, then Fra Girolamo, and then all of us who wrote ourselves down last night at the convent."

"Is it true that Fra Girolamo is going to raise a dead man?"

"Of course it is true! First the trial by fire, and then the resurrection of the dead. I, myself, have seen his letter to the pope. He challenges him to send a man who shall descend into a tomb with Fra Girolamo, and say to the dead, 'Come forth!' He who shall resuscitate the corpse shall be the true prophet; and the other the deceiver."

"Have faith, brothers, only have faith! Many miracles await you. Ye shall see the Son of Man in his flesh and bones coming on the clouds, and other wonders, of which ancient times had not even the conception!"

At these words several cried "Amen"; and all faces grew pale, and all eyes burned with the wild fires of fanaticism. The crowd moved on, carrying Messer Paolo and the others with it. Giovanni threw one more look at Verrocchio's bronze figure. In the good-humoured, half-contemptuous smile of the incredulous apostle, he seemed to see the smile of Leonardo.

III

As THEY APPROACHED THE PIAZZA della Signoria, the press was so great that Paolo requested one of the mounted guards to escort them as far as the balcony, where places were reserved for the orators, and for the more important of the citizens.

Never, thought Giovanni, had he seen so great a multitude. Not only was the square packed with spectators, but the loggias, the towers, windows, and roofs of the houses. Like limpets, they clung to the iron lamp-brackets, gratings, gutters, eaves, rain-pipes. They hustled each other and fought for room, and some fell and were trampled out of life. All the approaches to the piazza were rigorously barred with iron posts and chains; at three places only, men of full age and unarmed were permitted to pass singly.

Messer Paolo explained to his companions the manner in which the pyre was constructed. There were two long narrow piles of wood smeared with tar and sprinkled with powder, which extended from the Ringhiera or rostrum, where stood the Marzocco (the ancient lion of Florence), as far as to the Tettoia del Pisani. Between the two piles was a narrow lane, paved with stones, sand, and clay, along which the two friars were to pass.

At the appointed hour the Franciscans appeared from one side, the Dominicans from the other; the procession was closed by Fra Domenico, in a velvet habit of brilliant red, and Fra Girolamo dressed in white, and bearing the *Ostensorio*, which glittered in the sunlight. The Dominicans intoned a Psalm:—

"Come and see the works of God, he is terrible in his doing toward the children of men!"

And the crowd responded, "Hosanna, Hosanna! Blessed is he who cometh in the name of the Lord!"

The enemies of Savonarola occupied half the Loggia dei Lanzi, his followers the opposite half, a partition having been erected between them. All was now ready; nothing remained but to light the fire and call forth the champions.

At last the judges of the trial came from the Palazzo Vecchio, and everyone held his breath and watched what they would do; but after speaking a few words in a low voice with Fra Domenico they retired again, and suspense reigned as before. Fra Giuliano Rondinelli had gone out of sight. Then the tension of spirit became almost insupportable, and the crowd stood on tiptoe, and craned their necks, making the sign of the cross and telling their beads, and murmuring childish prayers; "Lord, Lord! perform us a miracle!"

The air was sultry; a thunderstorm was drawing nearer, and growls of thunder which had been heard at intervals all day, were becoming louder and more insistent. Certain members of the council, in long robes of red cloth, like the togas of ancient Rome, issued from the Palazzo Vecchio and took places on the Ringhiera; an old man with spectacles and a quill behind his ear, evidently the clerk, tried to recall them with shouts of:—

"Messeri! Messeri! the sitting is not ended! the voting is in progress!"

"To the devil with the voting," said one of the magistrates; "I have had my fill of this stupid discussion. The noise has broken my ear-drum."

"What is the use of deliberation?" said another. "If they wish to burn themselves let them do it, and Goodnight to them!"

"By my troth, it were homicide!"

"And an excellent homicide, too! Two fools less on earth."

"But they must be burned according to the rule and canon of the Holy Church. It's a delicate theological question."

"Well, then, propose the question to the pope."

"What have we to do with the pope? We are concerned with the people. If by such means one could restore the people to sanity, there would be no great evil in sending all the priests and friars in the world, not only into the fire, but into the water and under the ground likewise."

"Water will serve. Throw them both into a tub of water, and let him who comes forth dry be the victor. 'Twould be a thought less dangerous than these pranks."

"Have you heard, most honourable signiors," said Messer Paolo with deep reverences, "that poor Fra Giuliano has fallen sick in his stomach? 'Tis a malady caused by fear, and he has been bled for it."

"Sir," exclaimed an old man of imposing aspect, his face showing at once distress and intelligence, "you make a jest of everything. But I, when I hear such talk from the men highest in the state, I ask myself whether it were not better to die. Truly, if the founders of this city could rise from the dead and see the folly and the infamy of this day's proceedings, they would flee back into their graves for shame."

The judges, meanwhile, came and went incessantly from the Loggia to the Palazzo, from the Palazzo to the Loggia, and it seemed as if the deliberations were to have no end.

The Franciscans first accused Savonarola of having enchanted Fra Domenico's habit; he therefore removed it, but it was alleged that sorcery might have influenced his under garments. He retired into the Palazzo Vecchio, stripped himself naked, and donned the vesture of another. Then the Franciscans demanded that he should hold aloof from Savonarola, lest his new garments should be enchanted; and that he should give up the cross which he held. To this Domenico consented, but protested that he would not enter the flames without the Holy Sacrament in his hands. The Franciscans at this swore that Savonarola's disciple wished sacrilegiously to burn the body and blood of Christ. In vain Domenico and Girolamo replied that the Holy Sacrament could not be reduced to ashes; the material part (*modus*) might indeed be burned, but not the eternal and incorruptible part (*substantia*). An interminable scholastic dispute now began between the two parties.

The crowd in the piazza was beginning to murmur, and dense black clouds were spreading over the sky. Suddenly from behind the Palazzo Vecchio and the Via de' Leoni where the lions of Florence were kept in cages, a prolonged and hungry roar was heard. The mob imagined that the bronze Marzocco, indignant with his city, was roaring out his wrath. They responded with a sound no less furious, no less hungry.

"Have done! Have done! To the fire at once! Fra Girolamo! We *will* have the miracle! We *will* have the miracle!"

At this cry Savonarola, who had been kneeling in prayer, rose, shook himself, approached the parapet of the Loggia, and with imposing gesture commanded silence. But the people refused to be silent. And then someone from under the Tettoia de' Pisani cried:—

"He's afraid!"

And this cry was taken up and passed along.

A company of horsemen of the Arrabbiati tried to push their way to the Loggia to fall upon Savonarola and seize him, making their profit of the confusion.

"Kill him! Kill him! Down with the cursed schismatic!" was the shout.

Boltraffio closed his eyes that he might not see those furious faces which had now lost all look of humanity; nothing, he thought, could save Savonarola from being torn to pieces.

At this moment the storm broke. Rain descended, the like of which had not been seen in Florence.

It endured but a short time, and when it was over the trial by fire had become an impossibility. For between the twin piles of faggots the water ran with the fury of a channel hemmed in between dykes.

Some laughed.

"Well done, friars! They undertook to tread the fire, but they've got to swim for it! That's their miracle, eh?"

Cursed by the crowd, Savonarola on his return to his convent was escorted by soldiers, and Giovanni's heart bled as he watched the deposed prophet, kicked and buffeted, making his way with faltering step, his eyes on the ground, his white garb splashed with the mire of the streets. Leonardo saw his disciple's wan face, and, as before at the "Burning of Vanities," took his hand and led him away.

IV

Next day in the Casa Berardi, sitting in the chamber which was so like a ship's cabin, Leonardo tried to prove to Messer Guido that Columbus had erred in locating Paradise on a swelling upon a pear-shaped earth. At first Guido listened and argued, then mournful silence fell on him. He was vexed with his friend for telling him the truth. Presently he discovered pains in his legs, and had himself carried away.

"Why have I hurt him?" thought Leonardo; "He wants a miracle too!"

Turning over his note-book, his eyes fell on the words he had written that night when the Milanese mob had attacked his house for the seizure of the Holy Nail; "O marvellous justice of Thee, Thou Prime Mover, who hast denied to no force the order and the qualities of its necessary effect!"

"There!" he exclaimed, "there is the miracle!"

And his thoughts turned to his *Cenacolo* and to the face of Christ, still sought for, not yet found; and he felt that between this inviolable law of Necessity, and the perfect wisdom of Him who said, "One of you shall betray me," there existed a deep correlation.

In the evening Giovanni came with the day's news. The Signoria had exiled Fra Girolamo and Fra Domenico from the city; and the "Enraged," brooking no delay, had besieged San Marco with a countless throng of armed persons, and had broken into the church where the brothers were at vespers. They defended themselves, fighting with burning tapers, candlesticks, and crucifixes; in the cloud of smoke they seemed ridiculous as angry doves. One climbed on the roof and hurled stones down from it. Another fired an arquebus from the altar, shouting at each discharge "*Viva Cristo!*" Presently the monastery was taken by storm.

The brethren entreated Savonarola to flee, but he, together with Domenico, gave himself up, and they were haled to prison. The guards were unable or unwilling to defend them from the insults of the crowd, who struck Fra Girolamo from behind, crying:—

"Prophesy unto us, thou man of God, who is he that smote thee?"

Others crawled at his feet as though seeking something, and cried; "The key? The key? Where is Fra Girolamo's key?"

—in allusion to the key often spoken of in his sermons, with which he would unlock the secrets of the abominations of Rome.

The very children who had belonged to the Sacred Troop of inquisitors now pelted him with apples and rotten eggs. Those who could not penetrate the crowd howled from a distance, reiterating their abuse till their throats were hoarse.

"Dastard! Coward! Judas! Sodomite! Sorcerer! Antichrist!"

Giovanni followed him to the doors of the prison of the Palazzo Vecchio, whence he was not to issue till the day of his execution.

On the following morning Leonardo and Boltraffio quitted Florence.

At once, on arrival in Milan, the painter set himself to the task which had baffled him for eighteen years—the face of the Christ in the "Last Supper!"

V

On the very day of that trial by fire, which in Florence had had such bad results—Charles VIII, King of France, died very suddenly. The news was of sinister import to Il Moro, for the Duke of Orleans, who was now to ascend the throne as Louis XII, was descended from Valentina Visconti, daughter of the first Duke of Milan. He claimed to be the only legitimate heir of the dominion of Lombardy, and now proposed to reconquer it, annihilating "the robber nest of the Sforzas."

Shortly before the change of sovereigns in France, there had taken place at the Milanese court what was called a "scientific duel," and Il Moro had found so much entertainment that he proposed another for a day two months later. Now that war was impending some supposed he would postpone this duel, but Ludovico, who was an adept in the arts of dissimulation, had no such intention. He wished his enemies to think he cared little for their designs, but was absorbed in that revival of art and learning, "the fruit of golden peace," which flourished under his mild rule, and brought him the fame of being the most enlightened Italian potentate, the protector of the Muses, protected not merely by the arms but by the admiration of his people.

Accordingly on the appointed day, in the Great Hall of the Rocchetta, which was called the *Sala per il giuoco della palla*, there assembled all the doctors, deans, and masters of the University of Pavia, wearing their scarlet four-cornered *berrette*, their ermine-bordered hoods, their violet gloves, and pouches of gold embroidery. Ladies were present dressed in sumptuous festal robes, amongst them Lucrezia and Cecilia, sitting together at the foot of Ludovico's throne. The proceedings were opened by a pompous oration from Giorgio Merula, in which the Duke was likened to Pericles, Epaminondas, Scipio, Cato, Augustus, Mæcenas, and other worthies, while Milan was celebrated as the new Athens, of surpassing glory. Then followed a theological dispute on the Immaculate Conception, then medical discussions on the following questions:—

"Is a handsome woman more prolific than an ugly one?"

"Was the healing of Tobias natural?"

"Is woman an incomplete creation?"

"In what part of the body was formed the water which issued from the side of the crucified Christ?"

"Is woman more sensual than man?"

Then came the turn of the philosophers, on the unity or the plurality of primal matter.

"Be good enough to expound me this apophthegm," said a toothless old man with venomous smile, and eyes dull and troubled as those of a sucking babe; a great doctor of scholastics, who thoroughly understood the confounding of opponents by subtle distinctions (*quidditas et habitus*) which nobody could understand.

Alone and thoughtful as was his custom, Leonardo was listening, and now and then his lips curled.

VI

POINTING TO LEONARDO, THE COUNTESS Cecilia whispered to the Duke, who called up the artist, and begged him to take part in the discussion.

"Be kind," insisted the countess. "Do it for my sake—"

"Lay aside your bashfulness," said Ludovico, "and tell us something entertaining. Speak to us of your observations upon nature. Do we not know that your brain is always stuffed with chimeras?"

"Your Excellency must excuse me. Madonna Cecilia, I would gladly please a lady, but, truly, I cannot—"

Leonardo was not feigning. He was neither able nor willing to speak before a crowd. An insuperable barrier seemed to lie between his thought and his word, as if speech must either exaggerate or be inadequate to the sense, modify or vitiate it. In his note-books he continually cancelled, erased, corrected, and revised; in conversation he stammered, lost the thread, sought for words and could not find them. He called both orators and authors "babblers," but in secret he envied them. The frequent glibness of insignificant persons was a wonder and an annoyance to him.

"That God should give such men such skill!" he would say, with a kind of ingenuous admiration.

However, the more firmly Leonardo declined the task offered him, so much the more did the ladies insist.

"We beseech you, Messere! We all pray you with one voice. Tell us, tell us something entertaining!"

"Tell us how men are to fly!" suggested Madonna Fiordiligi.

"Nay, but speak to us of sorcery!" cried Madonna Ermellina; "something of black magic! 'Tis so interesting, this necromancy. Explain to us how they raise the dead men from their graves!"

"I assure you, Madonna, I have never raised any dead person from his grave."

"Then take someother theme, so it be terrible, and have no savour of mathematics."

Leonardo was always hard put to it to refuse a beggar, and he could only repeat with embarrassment:—

"Truly, Madonna, I am incapable—"

But Ermellina interrupted him, clapping her hands.

"He consents! He consents! Silence for Messer Leonardo! Listen ye all!"

"Eh? Who? What?" asked the dean of the theological faculty, who was deaf, and somewhat fallen into dotage.

"'Tis Leonardo!" shouted his neighbour into his ear.

"Leonardo Pisano, the mathematical professor?"

"No, Leonardo da Vinci himself."

"Is he doctor or master?"

"No, nor even bachelor. Leonardo, the painter of the *Cenacolo*."

"Is he going to speak of painting?"

"It seems he will speak of natural science."

"Are the painters so learned? I have never heard of this Leonardo. What has he written?"

"Nothing that I know of."

"Nay," said another, "'tis certain that he writes, for they say he uses his left hand, and produces a caligraphy proper only to himself, which none can read."

"Which none can read? With his left hand?" said the old dean.

"I take it, gentlemen, this speech will be some jest; an interlude to entertain the Duke and the ladies."

"Very like 'twill be ridiculous. We shall see."

"Just so, just so. 'Tis necessary to amuse the folk of the court. And painters are witty fellows enough. Buffalmacco, now—they said he was a perfect jester. Well, let us see what this Leonardo is good for."

And the old man polished his spectacles, the better to enjoy the comedy.

Leonardo was still looking supplicatingly at the Duke, but though smiling, Ludovico was determined; and the Countess Cecilia menaced the hesitant with her finger.

"If I refuse I shall offend them," thought the artist; "and very soon I shall be requiring bronze for the Cavallo. Well, I will say the first thing that comes into my head, just to be quit of the business."

And with desperate resolution he mounted the tribune and threw a glance upon the learned assembly. Then, blushing and stammering like a boy who does not know his lesson, he began:—

"I must warn you, gentlemen, I am not prepared. . .'Tis to please the Duke. I would say—I mean—in fine, I will speak to you about shells."

And he told of petrified marine animals, the imprints of coral, and water-plants found on hills and in valleys far removed from the sea, evidence of how the face of the earth has been changing from time immemorial. There, where now are hills and dry land, once was the ocean. Water, the mover of Nature, her "charioteer," creates and destroys the very mountains; the shores gradually remove into the centre of the sea, and the inland seas lay bare their beds, traversed by some river which ever hurries towards the sea, scoring for itself a deep channel. Thus the Po, which now rushes across the dried-up lake of Lombardy, will eventually score itself a deep channel across the dried-up Adriatic; and the Nile, when the Mediterranean has become a country of hills and plains like Egypt and Libya, will empty itself into the Atlantic Ocean beyond the Pillars of Hercules.

"I am convinced," said Leonardo in conclusion, "that the study of petrified plants and animals, which we have hitherto neglected, will lay the foundation of a new science of our earth; of its past, and of its future."

Notwithstanding the awkwardness of his delivery, Leonardo's ideas were so clear and precise, his faith in knowledge was so sure, all he had said was so unlike the Pythagorean ravings of the previous disputant, and the dry bones of logic in the mouths of the learned doctors, that when he stopped speaking a stupor of amazement was seen on the faces of the audience. Were they to laugh or to applaud? Was this talk of a new science the vain chatter of a presumptuous fool?

"Truly, my Leonardo," said the Duke condescendingly, as if speaking to a child, "it would be famous fun if the Adriatic were to dry up and leave our enemies, the Venetians, stranded like crabs on a sandbank."

At this they all laughed, well pleased to be told the line they were to take, for courtiers are ever weathercocks turned by the wind. Messer Gabriele Pirovano, the Rector of the University of Pavia, an old gentleman with silver hair, fine manners, and a dignified but somewhat foolish face, thus delivered himself, reflecting in his smile the condescending kindness of the Duke:—

"Messer Leonardo, the information you have given us is very interesting; but were it not perhaps simpler to explain the origin of these little shells, as a charming (we might even say poetic) but wholly accidental freak of nature, rather than as the foundation of an entire new science? Or, as others have done before us, we might account for their presence by the catastrophe of the universal Deluge."

"Oh, the Deluge!" said Leonardo, who had conquered his shyness and now spoke with a freedom which to many appeared excessive and even irreverent; "I know that explanation, but it won't do at all. Judge for yourself, Messer Gabriele. According to the man who measured it, the level of the waters of the flood exceeded by ten cubits the tops of the highest mountains. The shells would have settled on the summits, not on the sides or the feet of the mountains, nor within caverns; and, withal, they would have settled at haphazard according to the pleasure of the waters, and not everywhere at the same level, not in consecutive layers, as we find by observation. And further, here is a wondrous thing. We find collected together all those creatures which are used to live in societies, such as oysters, cuttlefish, molluscs; while those which are used to be solitary are scattered singly in their fossil state just as we find their descendants now on the seashore. I myself have often noted the position of these petrified shells in Tuscany and in Lombardy and in Piedmont. And if you tell me 'twas not the waves carried them, but that of themselves they gradually rose in crowds above the water as it grew higher, that, too, is easily refuted, for a shellfish is as slow a beast as a snail. It floats not, but crawls with its valves over sand and stones, and the furthest it can go in a day's hard journeying is some three or four arm-lengths. How then, Messer Gabriele, would you explain, that in the forty days of the flood's duration, your shellfish could creep the two hundred and fifty miles which divide the hills of Monferrato from the shores of the Adriatic? Only he who, despising experiment and observation, judges of Nature from books, can maintain such an argument; not he who has had the curiosity to see with his own eyes those things of which he speaks."

An uncomfortable silence followed; all felt that the Rector's reply had been a trifle weak. Then the court astrologer, Ambrogio da Rosate, a great favourite of the Duke's, advanced another explanation based on Pliny's natural history; which was that the petrified shapes which looked like marine animals had been formed in the interior of the earth by the magic working of the stars.

At the word magic, a resigned smile played over Leonardo's lips. "Then, Messer Ambrogio," he replied, "how would you explain the fact that the stars in the one place should make animals not only of many kinds but of various ages? (for the age of shells can be ascertained no less than the age of horns or of trees). What say you to finding some of these shells entire, some broken, some mixed with sand, mud, the claws of crabs, fish-bones, and rubble, such as you may see any day on the seashore; and the delicate imprint of leaves on the rocks of the highest mountains, and marine weeds clinging to the shells, petrified and blended into one lump with them? From the working of the stars, say you? If this is to be our reasoning, Messere, then in all Nature there will be no phenomenon for which you cannot account by the starry influences, and all science outside astrology is useless."

Here an old Doctor of scholastic interposed, saying that the dispute was irregular.

"For," he exclaimed, "either this question of fossils belongs to a vulgar, mechanical science, alien to metaphysic, and hence not to be discussed in an assembly met to contend solely about philosophical questions, or it verily pertains to the true, the sublime science of dialectic; in which case it must be discussed according to the laws of dialectic, which alone allows theory to ascend to the sphere of pure speculation."

"I understand you, Messere," said Leonardo patiently; "I have thought of what you say. But the alternative is not as you state it."

"Not as I state it?" cried the veteran smiling angrily, "not as I state it? Then, sir, pray let us hear how *you* propose to state it!"

"Nay, nay; I had no wish to offend. In fine, I spoke but of shells. I think—nay, Messere, but there is no vulgar science, nor is there sublime science. There is but one science; that which is based upon the experience of the senses."

"The experience of the senses? Then where would you put the metaphysic of Aristotle, of Plato, of Plotinus, and of all the ancient philosophers who speculated upon God, upon the soul, and upon the essences? Would you say of all this—?"

"That it is not science," replied Leonardo calmly. "I recognise the greatness of the ancients, but not in that respect. In science they mistook the road. They wished to learn what was beyond the reach of knowledge, and what was within their reach they despised. They led men astray for many ages. Discussing matters which admit not of proof, it is impossible for men to agree; the less so if they would make up for the lack of proof by vehemence of clamour. He who truly *knows* has no occasion to shout. The voice of truth is unique; and when it has spoken, all the noise of dispute must be hushed. If the cries continue, it means that the truth has not yet been found. Do we need mathematical dispute as to whether twice three be six or five? or whether the angles of a triangle be or be not equal to two right angles? In these instances doth not contradiction cease in the presence of truth? and is not truth to be enjoyed as it never can be enjoyed in sophistical and imaginary sciences?"

Leonardo would have spoken further, but after a glance at the face of his opponent he became silent.

"Ah!" said the doctor of scholastic, ironically, "I thought we should arrive at an agreement! You and I were certain to understand one another! But one thing I do not understand. Pardon the ignorance of an old man! If our knowledge of God and of a future life, not being confirmed by the testimony of our senses, but by the testimony of Holy Writ—"

"I spoke not of this," interrupted Leonardo; "I leave out of the dispute the books inspired by God, for they are of the substance of supreme truth."

He was not allowed to continue; uproar ensued. Some shouted, some laughed; some, springing from their chairs, turned wrathful faces on him, while others, shrugging their shoulders, left the assembly.

"Make an end! Make an end!"

"But, gentlemen, permit me to reply—"

"There is no occasion for reply."

"When things are stated contrary to sense—"

"I desire to speak!"

"Plato and Aristotle!" . . .

"Not worth a rotten egg!"

"But I ask, shall this be permitted? The truth of our Holy Mother Church—"

"Heresy! Heresy! Atheism!"

Leonardo remained silent, his face calm and sad. He was alone among these men who believed themselves the servants of knowledge, and he saw the impassable gulf which separated him from them. He was displeased, not with his opponents, but with himself for having broken his accustomed silence, and become entangled in an argument; for having conceived (in defiance of experience) that it were possible to reveal the truth unto men, or that they were able to receive it.

As for the Duke, though he had long lost the thread of the argument, he continued to follow the disputation with delight.

"Good! Really good!" he applauded, rubbing his hands. "Madonna Cecilia, will they not, think you, presently come to blows? Look at that old fellow, shaking all over, brandishing his cap, clenching his fists! And the little black one behind him, foaming at the mouth! And all about a few fossil shells! Fine madmen, these scholars! kittle cattle! And our Leonardo, who pretended to be possessed by a dumb devil!"

And they laughed, watching the scientific duel as if it were a cock-fight.

"I shall have to save my Leonardo," said Il Moro at last, "or these red-capped folk will claw him."

And he rose and passed through the crowd of infuriated philosophers, who suddenly were hushed into silence as they made way for him. Soothing oil had been poured upon stormy waves; one smile from the prince sufficed for the reconciliation of metaphysics and natural science. He closed the discussion by a courteous invitation to supper.

"I am glad," he said with his usual gaiety, "that the Adriatic is not yet dry; because I trust that its oysters, which I have had cooked for your entertainment, may give rise to less contention than the shells of Messer Leonardo."

VII

During the supper Fra Luca Pacioli, who was sitting beside Leonardo da Vinci, whispered in his ear:—

"Forgive me, friend, that I kept silence when they attacked you. They did not understand your meaning, but you might easily make an alliance with them, for the one opinion does not exclude the other. Avoid extremes."

"I entirely agree with you, Fra Luca," replied Leonardo.

"That's the way; love and concord. What is the object of dissension? Metaphysics are good, and mathematics are good! Room for both. Is it not so, dear friend?"

"Precisely so, Fra Luca."

"I was sure you would agree. You give in to me, I give in to you; we are allied, you with us, we with you."

Leonardo looked at the astute countenance of the mathematical monk, who reconciled Pythagoras and Thomas Aquinas so easily; and he thought—

"The calf sucks from two dams."

Then the alchemist, Galeotto Sacrobosco, raising his glass and bending towards Leonardo with the air of an accomplice, said—

"To your good health, Master! How skilfully you played them on the line! What a subtle allegory!"

"Allegory?" repeated Leonardo, stupefied.

"To be sure, Messere. No call for mystery with me. We shall not betray one another. By dry land you meant sulphur; by the sun, salt; by the ocean which overflowed the mountains, quicksilver. Do I catch your meaning?"

"Precisely, Messer Galeotto."

"You see even we are good for something! As for the shells, by them you intended the philosopher's stone, the alchemist's secret, composed of what? why of sulphur, salt, and quicksilver!"

And he laughed his jolly childlike laugh, raising his forefinger and arching his brows, which were scorched by the fury of his immense furnaces.

"And all these great doctors with their red caps understand not a word of it! To your health, Messer Leonardo, and to the glory of alchemy, our common mother!"

"I honour the toast, Messer Galeotto. And as I see nothing can be concealed from you, I will vex you with no further mysteries."

After supper the party broke up: only a small and selected company were invited by the Duke into a cool snug room, where wine and fruits were served.

"Most charming! Insurpassable!" cried Madonna Ermellina. "I should never have conceived it could be so diverting. Better than a *festa*! How they shouted at Leonardo! Pity he might not finish—he would have told us of his spells and necromancy."

"Perchance 'tis calumny," said an old courtier; "but I am told the infection of heresy has so taken hold of Leonardo, that he scarce credits the existence of God. He holds it of greater moment to be a philosopher than a Christian."

"'Tis mere babble," said the Duke. "I know the man well, and I swear he has a heart of gold. He is violent in word, but in practice would not hurt a flea. He dangerous! Would that all dangerous ones were as he! The Father Inquisitors would have him, but let them roar! None shall hurt a hair of my Leonardo!"

"And our posterity will praise your Excellency for having protected a genius so extraordinary," said Messer Baldassare Castiglione, a very elegant cavalier from the court of Urbino. "'Tis pity," he added, "that the man should neglect his art to give himself to dreams and chimeras."

"True, Messer Baldassare; I have often reproached him. But painters, you know, are an unmanageable race."

"Your Excellency speaks well," said the Commissioner of the Salt Tax, who was burning to tell a tale of Leonardo; "painters are impracticable folk. T'other day I came to his studio seeking an allegorical drawing for a marriage chest. 'Is the master at home?' say I. 'No,' is the reply, 'he hath gone forth, greatly busied, to measure the weight of the air.' Truly, I thought the youth mocked me; but when I met Leonardo himself and taxed him with this folly, he confessed it, looking at me as if he thought I were a fool. Ladies, how like you the notion? and how many grains will you find in the spring zephyr?"

"I know worse of him than that," said a young lord with a vulgar self-complacent face; "he has invented a boat which travels up stream, yet without oars."

"How doth it travel?"

"On wheels, by steam."

"A boat with wheels? Nay, sir, this must be your invention of this moment!"

"I had it of Fra Luca Pacioli, who had seen the design. Leonardo conceives that in steam lies a force able to move large ships, let alone little boats."

"You see! You see! Did I not tell you!" cried Madonna Ermellina, "this is his necromancy, black magic pure and simple!"

"'Tis not to be denied he is mad!" said the Duke with his urbane smile; "for all that I wish him well. In his company I never weary!"

VIII

Leonardo went homewards by the quiet suburb of Porta Vercellina. It was a lovely evening. Goats were contentedly browsing along the edge of the road; and a rugged sunburnt little lad was driving a flock of geese. Storm-clouds, lined with gold, were rising in the north over the unseen Alps, and high up in the clear sky there burned a single star.

The artist walked slowly; he was thinking of the scientific dispute which he had just left, and then his thoughts went back to the trial by fire at which he had been present in Florence. He could not but think the two duels resembled each other like twins.

A little girl of six was eating rye-bread and onions on the outside staircase of a cottage. He called her, and after a moment's hesitation, reassured by his smile, she trotted to him, smiling herself. He gave her a sugared and gilded orange which he had brought from the supper.

"Gold ball!" said the child.

"No, not a ball. A sort of apple. Try it; 'tis sweet within."

She continued to stare ecstatically at the unfamiliar dainty.

"What is your name?" he asked.

"Maia."

"I wonder, Maia, if you know how the cock, the goat, and the donkey went a-fishing together?"

"No."

"Shall I tell you?"

And he fondled her soft wild curls with his delicate, almost womanish, hand. "Come here then! Let us sit down! Wait a minute, though, I think I have some nice cakes also, as you won't try my golden apple!" And he turned out his pockets. A young woman now appeared, looked at Maia and at the stranger, nodded approvingly, and seated herself with her distaff. Then came also the grandmother, a bent old woman with eyes like Maia's. She, too, looked at Leonardo; but suddenly, as if recognising him, she made a sign with her hands and whispered to her daughter, who sprang up saying:—

"Maia! Maia! Come away at once!"

The child hesitated.

"Come, run, naughty one; unless you wish—"

The little girl was frightened and fled to the grandmother, who snatched the orange from her and flung it over the wall to the pigs. The child cried, but the old woman whispered something in her ear which at once checked her sobs, and she sat gazing at Leonardo with wide eyes full of terror. The painter turned away, well understanding. The old woman thought him a sorcerer capable of bewitching the child. A sad smile on his lips, still mechanically searching for the cakes no longer needed, pained at heart by the little one's needless fear, he felt himself more of an outcast than in face of the crowd which had sought to kill him, the learned men who fancied his truths the ravings of a madman. He felt himself as far removed from his fellows as was that solitary star shining in the still undarkened sky.

He went home and shut himself into his study. With its dusty scientific instruments and its dull books, it seemed to him gloomy as a prison. However, he lighted a candle, seated himself, and became immersed in his latest research, in inquiry into the laws of the motion of bodies travelling on an inclined plane. Like music, mathematics had ever for him a soothing influence; and tonight, they brought him the hoped-for consolation. Having finished his calculations, he took his diary, and writing with his left hand, and from right to left, so that reading must be in a mirror, he recorded a few thoughts roused by the scientific disputation.

"The disciples of Aristotle, men of words and of books, because I am not a *letterato* like themselves, think me incapable of speech on my own subjects. They perceive not that my matters are to be expounded rather by experience than by words; experience, which truly was mistress of all those who have written well; which I will take for my mistress, by which, in all cases, I will stand or fall."

The candle had burned low; and the cat, faithful comrade of his sleepless nights, sprang on the table, purring and rubbing herself against him. The solitary star, seen through the undusted windows, seemed still farther away, still less attainable. He remembered Maia's frightened eyes, but he had vanquished his melancholy. He was solitary, yes, but undaunted and serene. Nevertheless, unknown to himself, there was bitterness in the secret depth of his heart like a hot spring beneath the ice of a frozen river; there was almost remorse, as if, verily, he were guilty concerning Maia; as if there were something for which he was unable entirely to forgive himself.

IX

Next morning Leonardo, with Astro carrying sketch-books, paint-boxes and brushes, was on his way to the monastery for a day's work on the figure of the Saviour. He stopped in the courtyard to speak to Nastasio, who was busily grooming a grey mare.

"Bravo!" said the master, "and how is Giannino today?" Giannino was his favourite horse.

"Giannino is all right," answered the groom, "but the piebald is lame."

"The piebald?" said Leonardo, vexed; "and since when?"

"Since four days agone," replied Nastasio surlily; and without looking at his master, he continued curry-combing the mare's hindquarters with such energy that she changed her feet.

Leonardo, however, wished to see the piebald, and the groom took him to the stable. When Giovanni Boltraffio, a few minutes later, came to the courtyard fountain for his morning wash, he heard the master talking in loud piercing tones almost feminine in their shrillness, which he used in rare passions of sudden, violent, but not dangerous anger.

"Tell me this instant, you fool, you drunken ape, tell me who bade you summon the horse-leech?"

"I pray you, Messere, could a sick horse be left without a leech?"

"A pretty leech! Think you, fool, that stinking plaster—"

"'Tis not so much a plaster as a charm. You are not learned in these matters, and that is why you are so wroth."

"The devil take you and your charms together! How could that ignoramus cure anything when he knows naught of the structure of the body, and has never heard the name of anatomy?"

"Anatomy, forsooth!" said Nastasio, raising lazy contemptuous eyes to his master.

"Ass!" shouted the latter; "take yourself off out of my service!"

The groom did not move an eyelash.

"I was on the stroke of leaving you on my own account. Your Excellency owes me three months' wages; and as regards the oats, 'tis no fault of mine. Marco gives me no money for oats."

"What's the meaning of all this? Once I issue my orders—"

Nastasio shrugged his shoulders and returned to his grooming of the grey mare, working violently as if venting his spleen on the dumb animal.

Meantime Giovanni, amused by the altercation, was smiling as he scrubbed his face with a coarse towel.

"Shall we set out, Master?" asked Astro, wearied by the delay.

"Wait," replied Leonardo; "I must ask Marco about the oats. I would know how much truth is in the words of this scoundrel."

And he returned to the house, Giovanni following him. Marco was in the studio, working as usual by rule and with mathematical accuracy, perspiring and panting as if he were rolling a weight uphill. His closely compressed lips, the disorder of his red hair, his red fat ineffectual fingers, seemed to say, "Patience and perseverance will conquer all things."

"Marco! Is it true you give out no money for the horses' oats?"

"Of a surety it is true."

"How is that, friend?" exclaimed the painter, his look having already become timorous before the stern face of him who was steward of the household. "I bade you, Marco, take heed to remember the oats. Have you forgotten?"

"No, I have not forgotten; but there is no money."

"I guessed as much. There is always this lack of money. None the less, Marco, I ask you, can horses live without oats?"

Marco threw his brush away angrily. And Giovanni noticed how the master and the scholar seemed to have changed places.

"Hearken, Master!" said Marco. "You bade me take charge of the housekeeping, and not trouble you. Why do you yourself re-open the matter?"

"Marco!" said Leonardo, with gentle reproach, "'twas but a week ago that I gave you thirty florins."

"Thirty florins! Pr'ythee count it up. Of this thirty, four were a loan to Pacioli, two to that eternal sponge, Messer Galeotto Sacrobosco; five went to the body-snatchers for your anatomy studies; three for mending the glass and the stoves in the hot room for your reptiles and fishes; and six golden ducats went for that spotted devil—"

"Do you mean the camelopard?"

"Precisely; the camelopard. We have nothing to eat ourselves, but we feed that cursed beast. And whether we feed him or not, 'tis clear that he will die."

"Never mind, Marco," said Leonardo gently; "if he die I will dissect him. The neck vertebræ of these animals are very curious."

"The neck vertebræ! Oh, Master! Master! if you had not all these fancies for horses, and corpses, and giraffes, and fish, and every sort of beast, we might live as lords, asking alms of no one. Is not daily bread better than caprices?"

"Bread? Have I ever asked for anything better than bread? Oh, I know very well, Marco, you would like to see the death of all my creatures, though they cost me so much trouble and expense to obtain. They are indispensable to me—more so than you can imagine. You want to have everything your own way."

Helpless injury trembled in the voice of the Master; and Marco maintained a sulky silence.

"But what is to become of us?" continued Leonardo. "Already a famine of oats? We were never in such straits before."

"We have always been in straits," said Marco, "and we always shall be. What can you expect? For a year we have not had a *quattrino* from the Duke. Messer Ambrogio Ferrari says daily, 'tomorrow! tomorrow!' and to my thinking he but mocks us."

"Mocks us! Well, I will show him how to mock at me! I will complain to the Duke! I will give that scurvy piece, Ambrogio, a lesson he shall not forget! the Lord send him an evil Easter!"

Marco made a vague gesture, as if to say it was not Leonardo who would teach lessons to the Duke's treasurer. Then an expression of kindness and love came over his hard features, and he added soothingly:—

"No, no, Master, let it be! God is merciful, and we shall get along in some fashion. If you really take it to heart, I will find the money even for your oats."

And Marco reflected that he could use some of his own money, a little hoard he had been making for his mother.

"The oats are not the major question," said Leonardo, sinking wearily on a chair, and defending his eyes as if from a cruel wind. "Hearken, friend, there is a thing I have not yet told you; next month I shall absolutely require eighty ducats, which I have had on loan. There is no need to stare at me with those eyes, Marco."

"Of whom had you the loan?"

"Of the money-changer, Arnoldo—"

"Of Arnoldo! Oh, Master! what have you done? Don't you know he is worse than any infidel or any Jew? Why did you not tell me at once?"

Leonardo hung his head.

"I wanted the money—be not so wroth, Marco!" he said; and added piteously, "Bring the reckonings, perhaps we shall be able to devise something."

Marco was convinced they could devise nothing; however, finding absolute obedience the best way of influencing the Master, he fetched the account-books. Leonardo's brow contracted in a look of disgust, and he watched the opening of the too familiar green volume with the air of one looking into a gaping wound; then together they plunged into calculations, and it was wonder and pity to see the great mathematician making the blunders of a child in the additions and the subtractions. Now and then he suddenly remembered some mislaid account of a thousand ducats, sought it, fumbled in cases and boxes, and dusty piles of papers, but found in its place trifling and useless memoranda written in his own hand, such, for instance, as that one of Salaino's cloak:—

Silver brocade,	Livre	15	soldi	4
Crimson velvet for trimming,	"	9	"	0
Braid,	"	0	"	9
Buttons,	"	0	"	12

He tore them angrily, and blushing and swearing threw them under the table.

Giovanni, seeing on the great man's face these marks of human weakness, murmured to himself:—

"A new Hermes Trismegistus halved with a new Prometheus? Nay, neither god nor Titan, but a simple mortal like the rest of us! And to think that I feared him! the poor kind soul!"

X

Two days passed, and as Marco had foreseen, Leonardo forgot the money question completely. He demanded three florins for the purchase of a fossil with so confident an air that Marco lacked courage to refuse him, and handed out the money from his private hoard. The ducal treasurer, deaf to Leonardo's entreaties, had still not paid the year's salary, and was the less likely to do so that Ludovico himself required great sums to spend in preparation for war with France. Leonardo was obliged to borrow wherever he could, even from his own pupils.

Nor was the money forthcoming for the completion of the Sforza monument. The plaster cast, the mould, the receiver for the molten metal, the furnace—all were ready; but when the artist presented his estimate for the bronze, Il Moro was alarmed, and even refused him an interview.

At last, in the end of November, urged by want, he wrote a letter to the Duke; sentences fragmentary, disconnected, like the stammering of one overcome by confusion, who does not know how to beg.

"Signore, knowing that the mind of your Excellency is occupied with affairs of greater moment, yet fearing that silence may be a cause of anger to my most gracious patron, I take freedom to remind your Excellency of my humble necessities, and of the needs of my art, now condemned to inactivity. . . Two years have passed since I have received my salary. . .

"Some persons in your Grace's service can afford to wait, since they have other revenue, but I with my art, which, however, I would gladly abandon for one more lucrative. . .

"My life is at your Excellency's service; and I shall always be prompt in obedience.

"I speak not of the monument, for I know that the times. . .

"It irks me that owing to the necessity of earning my livelihood I must break off my work, and occupy myself with trivialities.

"I have had to provide for six persons during fifty-six months, with only fifty ducats. . .

"I know not to what I must dedicate my activity. . .

"Am I to study glory, or only my daily bread. . . ?"

XI

One November evening, after a day spent in soliciting the munificent Gaspare Visconti, and Arnoldo the usurer, and in coming to terms with the hangman—who demanded payment for two corpses (used by the artist for studies), threatening in default to denounce the purchaser to the Holy Inquisition—Leonardo came home greatly wearied and out of heart. Having dried his clothes by the kitchen fire, and received the key of his workshop from Astro, he was proceeding thither when he was surprised by the sound of voices behind the door.

"What?" he said, "is it not locked? Can it be thieves?"

Recognising the tones of his pupils, Giovanni and Cesare, he suspected them of prying into his private papers. About to throw open the door, he was arrested by a vivid imagination of their confusion, and the wide eyes of terror with which they would greet him. He felt ashamed for them, and went away, walking on tiptoe as if himself the culprit; presently he called from the studio:—

"Astro! Astro! Bring me a light! Where have you all got to? Andrea! Marco! Giovanni! Cesare!"

The voices in his room were silenced, some glass thing fell with a crash, there was a shutting of windows. Leonardo still hesitated, unable to resolve upon entry. In his heart was not so much anger as disgust.

His suspicions were not amiss. Having entered by the courtyard window, Giovanni and Cesare had searched his drawers and opened his papers, drawings, and diaries. Boltraffio, very pale, held a mirror, and Cesare read the master's inverted writing:—

"*Laude del Sole. I cannot but blame Epicurus, who maintained that the sun's magnitude is no other than it seemeth. Socrates astounds me, who, depreciating so great a light, calls it but a molten stone. And would I had vocables strong enough to confound those who prefer the apotheosis of man to the apotheosis of the sun!*"

"Shall we pass on?" asked Cesare.

"Read to the end," said Giovanni.

"*Those who worship men for gods,*" continued the reader, "*are greatly in error; for man, though he were of the magnitude of the earth, would appear smaller than the smallest star, a scarce visible spot upon the universe; and seeing, further, that men in their sepulture are subject to putridity and decay—*"

"Strange," observed Cesare, "that he can reverence the sun, but appears not to recognise Him who, dying, was the vanquisher of death."

He turned the page. "Let us try this."

"*In all parts of Europe, by great peoples, will be bewailed this day the death of a man who died in Asia—*"

"You don't understand, Giovanni. I will explain: he treats of Good Friday. Shall I go on?"

"*O mathematicians, throw light upon this error! Spirit exists not without body, and where is no flesh, nor blood, nerves, tongue, bone, and muscle, can be neither voice nor movement.*"

"I can't make it out; the next lines are erased. We will pass to the end."

"*Other definitions of spirit I leave to the Holy Fathers, who know the secrets of Nature by revelation from above.*"

"H'm, I would not be Messer Leonardo if these lucubrations should fall into the hands of the Holy Fathers! Here we have another of his prophecies."

"*Enough shall there be, who, leaving the ascesis of labour and poverty, think to serve God by living luxuriously in buildings like palaces, and in amassing visible wealth at the expense of the wealth invisible.*"

"I conclude he here treats of Indulgences. Quite in Savonarola's vein! A stone slung at the pope."

"*Those who have been dead a thousand years will be the food of the living.*"

"That passes me! Nay, though, the thousand-year dead must be the saints in whose name the monks collect money. A pretty riddle!"

"*They shall adore those who do not hear; they shall burn lamps before those who do not see.*"

"Images of saints."

"*Women shall disclose to men their passions, their secret and shameful deeds.*"

"The confessional! How does it like you, Giovanni? A strange man, is he not? But there is no real malice in these riddles. It is only jest—sporting with blasphemy."

"*Many who cozen the simple by dealing in pretended miracles, punish those who unmask their deceits.*"

"The trial by fire, of which the reckless Savonarola was the victim."

He laid down the book and looked at his companion.

"Well, is it enough? or do you want further proof?"

Boltraffio shook his head; "No, Cesare, it is not enough. Could we but find a place where he speaks *plainly*!"

"Plainly? Ask not for that. Such is his disposition. He deals ever double, conceals himself, feigns like a woman. Riddles are his nature. Nor does he know himself. He is his own greatest enigma."

"Cesare is right," thought Giovanni. "Better open blasphemy than these mockings—this smile as of the unbelieving Thomas, who thrust his fingers into the wounds of the Lord."

Then Cesare showed a drawing in red chalk, tossed carelessly among the machines and the tables of calculations—the Virgin with the Child in the desert; seated on a stone, she was drawing triangles and circles with her finger on the sand—the Mother of God teaching the Divine Son geometry, the principle of all knowledge.

Giovanni gazed long at this strange drawing; then he held it to the mirror that they might decipher the inscription. Cesare had scarce read the first words, "*Necessity, the eternal teacher*," when Leonardo's call was heard:—

"Astro! Bring me a light! Andrea! Marco! Giovanni! Cesare!" Then Giovanni turned pale. The mirror fell from his hands, breaking into pieces.

"An evil omen," said Cesare with a smile.

Like thieves caught in the act they pushed the papers into their places, picked up the fragments of the mirror, opened the window, sprang to the ledge and, clinging to the water-pipe and the branches of the vine, dropped into the court. Cesare missed his hold, fell, and sprained his foot.

XII

THAT EVENING LEONARDO DID NOT find his accustomed solace in his mathematics. He walked the room, seated himself, began a drawing, flung it aside. His mind was vaguely uneasy; there was something he must decide, yet could not. His thought reverted continually to the same thing; how Boltraffio had fled to Savonarola, had returned, and for a time had settled down to work, recovering his calm in the pursuit of art; but ever since that disastrous trial by fire, and especially since the news of the prophet's approaching execution had reached Milan, he had again been racked by doubts and regret. Leonardo understood how he suffered; how again he felt the necessity to go away, yet could not make up his mind to leave; how terrible was the struggle in a nature too deep not to feel, too weak to overcome its own contradictions. Sometimes Leonardo fancied he must himself drive his disciple away in order to save him.

A bitter smile came to his lips as he thought:—

"It is true that I—I only—have ruined him! 'Tis a just accusation that I have the evil eye! How am I to help him?"

He rose and mounted the steep dark stair, knocked at a door, and receiving no answer opened it and went in. In the narrow room the darkness was scarce broken by the little lamp burning before the figure of the Madonna; rain was splashing on the roof, and the autumn wind howled mournfully. A black crucifix was suspended against the white wall. Giovanni, still dressed, his face hidden in the pillow, lay in the unrestful position of a suffering child.

"Are you asleep?" asked the Master, bending over him.

He started up, with a faint cry, gazing with the same terror-struck eyes and defensive hands that Leonardo had seen with the little Maia.

"Why, Giovanni! Giovanni! What is the matter? It is only I!"

Boltraffio came to himself, passing his hand slowly over his eyes.

"Ah! it is you, Messer Leonardo! I fancied—I have had a terrible dream! But is it really *you*?" he repeated, his brows contracted as if he could hardly believe his eyes.

The Master sat on the bedside and touched the lad's forehead.

"You have fever. Why did you not tell me?"

Giovanni would have turned away, but looking afresh at Leonardo, and joining his hands supplicatingly, he said:—

"Drive me out! Drive me from you, Master! I shall never myself have the courage to go. I am guilty towards you—a vile traitor."

For answer Leonardo embraced him, drawing him to his breast.

"What say you, my son? Do you think I have not seen your distress? If there is anything in which you think you have wronged me, I pardon it. Perhaps some day you will be asked to pardon me!"

Astonished, Giovanni gazed at him with dreaming eyes, then suddenly hid his face in his breast, sobs shaking his frame as he murmured:—

"If ever again I am obliged to leave you, oh, Master, do not think it is for lack of love! I myself know not what has happened to me. Sometimes I fear I am losing my reason. God has forsaken me! Oh, never, never suppose—for truly I love you more than all else in the world! I love you more than Fra Benedetto, who is as my father. Never will anyone love you as do I!"

Leonardo soothed him like a child. "Enough! Enough! Think you I credit not your love, my poor lad? Has Cesare suggested—but why do you heed Cesare? He is clever, and he, too, loves me well, for all he thinks to hate me; but there are matters beyond him."

The disciple had become calm, and his tears were dry. Raising himself, and fixing scrutinising eyes on the Master, he shook his head.

"No; it was not Cesare. 'Twas I myself. And yet no; it was not I, but *he*."

"Who is *he*?"

Giovanni again trembled, and pressed closer to his friend. "No, no! For God's sake let us not speak of *him*!"

"Listen, my son," answered Leonardo, in that soothing yet severe and almost rough tone in which a doctor speaks to a sick child; "I see you have a weight upon your heart. You must tell me all; all, do you hear? Thus only shall I be able to help you"; and after a pause he added; "Tell me of whom you spoke just now."

Giovanni looked round as if in fear; then whispered in low, awestruck tones:—

"Of your Semblance."

"My Semblance? How mean you? Did you see it in a dream?"

"No; in reality."

For a moment Leonardo thought him delirious.

"Messer Leonardo, three nights ago you, yourself, came to me as you have come tonight?"

"No, I did not come. Why do you ask? Can you not remember yourself?"

"I do remember. Master, now I am certain it was *he*!"

"But what has given you this idea? What happened?" He felt that Giovanni wished to speak, and sought to force him to do so, in the hope it would afford him relief.

"This is what happened. Three nights ago he came to me as you have come today at this very hour, and he sat on the edge of the bed as you do now, and in every word, in every motion he was as you; and his face was like yours, only as if seen in a glass, nor was he, like you, left-handed, so I thought at once within myself, perchance it was not you; and he knew my thought, yet dissembled and made no sign, but pretended that we both knew naught. Only on leaving he turned himself round to me and said: 'Hast thou never, Giovanni, seen that one in my likeness? If so be thou dost see him, be not at all afraid.' And from his saying this I understood all."

"And you still believe this, my poor boy?"

"How should I not believe it, when I saw him as now I see you? Ay, and he spoke with me!"

"Of what did he speak?"

Giovanni covered his face with his hands, and did not answer at once.

"It was not good," he said at last in deprecating tones; "he said terrible things to me. He said that there was nothing in the world but Mechanics—things like that terrible spider with the bloody revolving arms, which he—no, not he—which *you* have invented."

"What spider? Ah yes, yes! I understand; you have seen my drawing of the scythed chariot?"

"And he said," resumed Giovanni, "that what men call God is the eternal force by which the hideous spider is moved, by means of which its blood-stained arms revolve; and that this God cares nothing for truth or untruth, for good or evil, for life or death. And that praying to him is bootless, for he is inexorable as mathematics; two and two will never, never make five."

"I see. I see. You torture yourself uselessly. I know how it is."

"No, Messer Leonardo, you do not yet know all. He said that Christ had died in vain, had not risen triumphant from the grave, had not vanquished death, but that His body lay mouldering in the tomb. And when he said this, I burst into weeping, and he had compassion on me, and tried to bring me comfort. And he said: 'Weep not! There is no Christ, but there is Love, Great Love, the daughter of Great Knowledge. Who knoweth all, loveth all.' Master, he used your very words! 'Of old,' he said, 'they taught that love came of weakness, of wonder, of ignorance; but I tell you it comes of strength, of truth, of wisdom; for the serpent lied not when he said, Eat of the tree of the knowledge of good and evil, and ye shall be as gods.' And then I knew him that he came of the devil! I cursed him, and he withdrew himself; but he said he would come again."

Leonardo listened with as much interest as if this were no longer the delirium of sickness. He felt the gaze of his disciple, now almost calm, but terribly accusatory, sink into the secret depths of his soul.

"And the most fearsome thing," continued Giovanni, slowly withdrawing himself from the Master, and looking him full in the face with fixed and piercing eyes; "the most fearsome was that, as he spake to me thus, he smiled. Yes, he could smile! He smiled, as you smile upon me now—*you*!"

And his face became suddenly pale as wax, and with starting eyes and contorted features, he pushed Leonardo from him, and cried in a wild shout of terror:—

"Thou! Thou again! Thou hast cozened me! In the name of God, begone. Get thee behind me, Accursed One!"

At these words the Master rose, and with compelling eyes fixed on his disciple, he said:—

"Giovanni, of a truth you will do well to leave me. You remember it is said in the Scripture, 'He that feareth is not made perfect in love.' If you loved me with perfect love you would have no fear; you would know that all this is delusion and madness; that I am not what men suppose; that I have no Semblance; and that, perchance, I believe more truly in Christ my Saviour than do those who call me Antichrist. Farewell, Giovanni."

His voice shook with inexpressible bitterness, which was, however, unresentful. He rose to go.

"Have I spoken truth?" he asked himself, and felt that if his pupil could only be saved by lies, he still was unable to lie. Boltraffio flung himself upon his knees at Leonardo's feet.

"Master! pardon me. Nay, I know it is madness! I will drive away these hideous thoughts! Only forgive me. Let me stay!"

Leonardo looked at him, his eyes glistening with tenderness; then he bent over him and kissed his brow.

"Then forget not, Giovanni, that you have promised!" he exclaimed; and added calmly, "Now let us go down; the cold is too nipping here. I cannot leave you in this room till you are completely cured. I have some urgent business on hand, in which you can help me."

XIII

He took his disciple into his own sleeping-chamber, which adjoined the studio, blew up the fire, and when the crackling flame had diffused a pleasant light upon everything, bade Giovanni prepare him a panel for a picture. He hoped that work would calm the sick youth, nor was he mistaken; by degrees Giovanni became completely absorbed in his occupation.

With concentrated and serious attention, as if the task were of the most curious and important in the world, he helped the Master to soak the wood in acquavita, bi-sulphate of arsenic and corrosive sublimate, to keep it from becoming worm-eaten; they filled in the dents and chinks with alabaster, cypress lac, and mastic, and smoothed the unevenness with a plane. As usual, under the hands of Leonardo, the work went on easily as child's play. He talked also, and gave instruction on the making of brushes, the coarser of pigs' bristles fixed in lead, and the finer of squirrels' hair set in goose-quill; of varnish also, and the driers to be used, of Venetian green and ferruginous ochre. A pleasant, pungent, business-like scent diffused itself through the room, and as Giovanni rubbed the panel lustily with linseed oil, the exertion made him hot. His fever had disappeared. Once, stopping to take breath, he looked at Leonardo, but the latter cried:—

"Make haste! make haste! if you let it grow cold the oil won't sink in!"

And Giovanni, bending his back, compressing his lips, and straining his legs, rubbed on with increased energy and good will.

"How do you feel now?" asked Leonardo.

"Well!" replied the other smiling.

The rest of the pupils gathered also in the bright room. The comfort and warmth within was redoubled by the howl of the wind and the patter of the rain outside. Salaino came, shivering but light-hearted; Astro, the one-eyed Cyclops; Jacopo and Marco; but Cesare da Sesto, as usual, kept aloof from this friendly circle.

Then the panel was laid aside to dry, and Leonardo discoursed on the purest oil for painting. An earthen dish was brought, in which was white walnut juice covered with amber-coloured grease. Long coils, like lamp-wicks, were laid in it and allowed to drip into a glass vessel.

"See, see!" cried Marco, "what purity! Mine is always turbid, however often I strain it!"

"Do you skin your nuts?" said Leonardo; "if you do not, your colours will turn black."

"Then," said Marco, "the thin peel of a nut might ruin the best painting in the world! Hear you, lads? you who mock me because I carry out the Master's instructions with mathematical rigidity!"

The pupils laughed and talked and jested while they watched the preparation of the oil. It was late, but no one cared for sleep, and without heeding the protests of Marco the steward, they continually threw new logs upon the fire. All were unaccountably merry.

"Let us tell stories," said Andrea; and began with the tale of the priest who on Holy Saturday took upon himself to sprinkle a particular picture with holy water. "Why so?" asked its painter. "Because it is written that for a good work one shall receive a hundredfold," replied the priest. And presently, as he left the house, the painter from an upper window poured a pail of water on his head and cried—"Here is the hundredfold for the good you have done me in spoiling my best picture."

Other tales followed, and none enjoyed them more than Leonardo, who indeed laughed like a child, nodding his head and wiping tears from his eyes, and cackling with a strange thin laugh, incongruous with his great height and powerful build.

About midnight they agreed it were impossible to go to bed without eating, especially as they had supped sparingly, for Marco kept them on short commons. Astro brought all there was in the pantry, some stale ham, cheese, a few olives, and some bread. Wine there was none.

"Have you tilted the cask?"

"In all directions. There is not a drop."

"Ah, Marco! Marco! what are we to do? How can we go without wine?"

"Can I buy wine without money?" said Marco.

"There is money, and there shall be wine!" cried Jacopo, tossing a gold piece.

"How got you it, imp of the devil? Marry, stealing again. I suppose! Come here and I'll box your ears for you," said Leonardo, shaking his finger at him.

"I swear by God, Master, I did not steal it. Cut out my tongue and send me to the pit if I did not win it at dice."

"Well, stolen or not, fetch us some wine."

Jacopo ran off to the Golden Eagle hard by, much frequented by the Swiss mercenaries, and kept open all night; presently he returned with pewter cans. The wine increased the mirth; the little Ganymede holding the vessel high so that beaded bubbles winked on the red liquid; and overflown with pride in entertaining the company at his own expense, he played pranks and jested and jumped; and mimicking the hoarse voice of a confirmed toper, he sang the song of the unfrocked monk:—

"To the devil with cowl and with frock, oh!
With hood and with scapularie!
Pretty nun, the lord Abbot bemock, oh!
And dance at the junket with me!
Ha! ha! ha! Ho! ho! ho!"

and then the solemn chorus from the Bacchanalian Mass, written in Latin, and sung by the students on festive occasions:—

"Who waters wine at this high feast supernal
Shall drown in it for ages sempiternal,
And after roast at fires of realms infernal!"

They drank toasts to the Master's health, to the glory of his studio, to the hopes of future wealth; and Giovanni never supped so much to his liking as at this beggars' feast, on cheese hard as rock, stale bread, and Jacopo's stolen wine. Presently Leonardo said with a smile—

"I have heard, friends, that St. Francis called melancholy the worst of sins, and preached that whoso wished to please God must be cheerful. Let us drink to the wisdom of Francis and to eternal cheerfulness in God."

These words were surprising to all the youths except Giovanni, who understood their intention.

"Eh, Master," said Astro, shaking his head, "it is very well to speak of cheerfulness, but how can we be cheerful while we crawl along the ground like grave-worms? Let the others toast what they please, but I will drink to wings and to the flying-machine. May the devil carry away the laws of gravity and of mechanics which interfere with us."

"Without mechanics you won't fly far, my friend," said the Master laughing.

After this the party broke up, and Leonardo would not allow Giovanni to return to his cold attic; he aided him to improvise a bed in his own room as near as might be to the hearth, where a few cinders still glowed red.

XIV

GIOVANNI HAD LEARNED FROM CESARE that the master had all but finished the face of the Christ in the "Last Supper"; he had asked several times to be allowed to see it, but Leonardo had always postponed the matter.

At last, one morning he took the lad to the Refectory, and there, in the place which had been vacant for sixteen years, between St. John and St. James, against the square of the open window, with the background of the quiet evening sky and the blue hills of Zion, Giovanni saw the Christ.

A few days later Leonardo sent him for a rare mathematical book to the house of the alchemist, Sacrobosco. He was returning late in the evening. The air was frosty and still, after a day of high wind and thaw; the pools and the ruts of the road were coated with ice; the low clouds seemed to cling motionless to the purple tops of the larches, in which were a few ruined and deserted nests. Darkness came on apace; on the dim verge of the horizon stretched the long copper and golden streak where the sun had gone down. The water in the Cantarana Canal, still unfrozen, seemed heavy, black as iron, and unfathomably deep.

Giovanni did not own it to himself, and indeed used every effort to suppress the thought, but he was comparing, not without dismay, Leonardo's two renderings of the Lord's face. If he shut his eyes, both rose before him like living things; the one face that of a brother, and full of human weakness, the face of Him who had agonised in bloody sweat, and prayed a childlike prayer for a miracle; the other, superhuman, calm, wise, alien, and terrible.

And Giovanni thought that, perhaps, notwithstanding their inexplicable contradiction, the one was a likeness no less true than the other.

He grew confused, as if delirium were returning, and sitting on a stone above the black canal waters, he bowed himself in exhaustion, and buried his head in his hands.

"What are you doing here, like a shade on the banks of Acheron?" cried a mocking voice; and he felt a hand on his shoulder, turned, and saw Cesare, like some ill-omened ghost, in the wintry twilight; a long, lean figure, with a long, lean, pale face, and muffled in a long grey cloak. Giovanni rose, and they moved on together, the dead leaves rustling under their feet.

"Does he know we ransacked his papers?" asked Cesare.

"Yes."

"And is not angered. That I expected"; and Cesare laughed maliciously. "Everlasting pardon, of course!"

There was a silence; a crow flew across the canal, cawing hoarsely.

"Cesare," said Boltraffio in a loud voice, "have you seen the face of the Christ in the *Cenacolo*?"

"I have,"

"And—what think you of it?"

"What think *you*?" said Cesare, turning abruptly to his companion.

"I can hardly say; but it seems to me—"

"Speak frankly. It does not satisfy you?"

"That is not what I mean. But it seems to me, perhaps, that it is not Christ."

"Not Christ? Who then else?"

Giovanni did not reply; his eyes were on the ground, and without knowing it, his pace slackened. At last he said—

"That other sketch in coloured chalk, the young Christ—have you seen that?"

"Yes. A Jewish boy with chestnut curls, full lips and a low brow; the son of old Barucco. You like it better?"

"No. But I was thinking how little alike they are, those two pictures!"

"Little alike? But it is the same face—fifteen years older, that is all! However, it may be you are right. They may be two Christs, but as like each other as a man and his own phantom."

"As a man and his own phantom!" echoed Giovanni, shuddering and stopping. "What say you, Cesare? A man and his own phantom?"

"Well, what is so alarming in those words? Don't you agree with me?"

They walked on.

"Cesare!" cried Boltraffio suddenly and impulsively, "do you not see what I mean? How could He, the Omnipotent, the Omniscient, whom Leonardo has painted in the *Cenacolo*, how could He have been tortured on the Mount of Olives, not a stone's throw away, till He sweated blood and prayed a human prayer for a miracle? 'Let not that take place, to accomplish which I came into the world, that which I know cannot fail to be! Father, let this cup pass from me!' Cesare, everything is contained in that prayer! Without it there is no Christ, and I would not relinquish it for all the wisdom of Solomon! The Christ who prayed not that prayer was never a man; He did not suffer and die like us!"

"I see your meaning," replied Cesare slowly; "certainly the Christ of the *Cenacolo* never prayed that prayer."

The darkness was falling around them, and Giovanni could not accurately see the face of his companion, which, however, seemed strangely illuminated. Suddenly Cesare stopped, raised his hand, and spoke in a low solemn voice.

"You wish to know whom he has painted, if 'tis not the weaker Christ who prayed for a hopeless miracle in the garden of Gethsemane? Well, I will tell you. Remember that beautiful invocation of Leonardo's when he spoke of the laws of the mechanical sciences, 'O divine justice of Thee, Thou Prime Mover!' His Christ is the Prime Mover, who, principle and centre of every movement, is Himself moveless. His Christ is the eternal necessity, which is divine justice, which is the Father's will. 'O righteous Father, the world hath not known Thee, but I have known Thee and I have declared unto these Thy name, that the love wherewith Thou hast loved Me may be in them, and I in them.' Do you see? Love born of knowledge. '*Grande amore è figlio di grande sapienza.*' Great love is the child of great knowledge. And Leonardo, who alone of men has understood this saying of the Lord's, has incarnated it in his Christ, who loves all because he knows all."

Cesare ceased, and for long they walked silently in the profound calm of the winter twilight. At last Boltraffio said:—

"Do you remember, Cesare, how four years ago, you and I, walking along this path together, were discussing the Cenacolo? Then you mocked at the Master, and said he would never finish the face of the Christ, and I contradicted you. Now it is you who defend him against me. Of a surety I should never have believed that you—*you*! would one day speak of him as now you have spoken!"

And Giovanni tried to see his companion's face, but the other turned away.

"Now, I see with joy, Cesare, that you also love him! Yes, you love him, you who wish to hate him; you love him perhaps better than do I!"

"Did you imagine anything else?" replied Cesare, slowly turning to his companion a pale moved face; "and yet I would indeed be glad to hate him, but instead I must love him, for he has done, in the "Last Supper," what no one has ever done, what perhaps he himself does not understand so well as I—I, his most mortal enemy." And Cesare laughed a forced laugh. "How odd is the human heart!" he went on. "I will confess the truth, Giovanni; perhaps I love him less today than I did at the time you have alluded to."

"Why so, Cesare?"

"Perchance because I value my own individuality. To be lowest among the lowest—yes, better that than to be but a member of his body, a toe of his foot! Let Marco find contentment in ladles for the measuring out of paint, and rules for the proportions of noses. *I* should like to ask with which of these Leonardo made that countenance of Christ! True, he does his best to teach us, poor chickens, to fly like eagles from the eagles' nest; for he is compassionate, and sorry for us, as he is sorry for the blind pups in the yard, or for a lame horse, or for the criminal whom he accompanies to execution that he may watch his dying convulsions. Like the sun, he shines upon everything. Only, see you, my friend, each man hath his own fancy; you may like to be the worm which, in St. Francis' fashion, Leonardo lifts from the highway and sets on a green twig; I'd sooner be crushed by him!"

"Then, Cesare, if you feel thus, why do you not leave him?"

"And you—why do *you* not leave him? You have burnt your wings like a moth in a candle, and still you flutter round the flame. Perchance I also am fain to burn myself in that flame. Yet, maybe, one hope remains to me!"

"What hope?"

"A foolish hope. The dream of a madman! Yet I often dwell upon it. The hope that one day a man shall arise, unlike him, yet his equal; not Perugino, nor Borgognone, nor Botticelli, nor the great Mantegna—Leonardo surpasses all these; but another, one who is still unknown, reserved for a later day. I would fain see the glory of this new one immense! I would fain look in the face of Messer Leonardo and remind him that even a spared worm like me can prefer another to him, can be pleased in the humiliation of his pride; for, Giovanni, he is proud as Lucifer, in spite of his lamb-like meekness and his universal charity."

He broke off abruptly, and Giovanni felt his hand tremble.

"Hark you, Giovanni," he said in a changed voice, "who told you I loved him? You never guessed it?"

"He told me himself."

"He? Then he believes—"

His voice broke. Nothing remained to be said, and each was lost in his own thoughts, his own griefs. At the next cross-road they parted.

Giovanni, with eyes on the ground, walked mechanically along the narrow path skirting the canal in whose dark waters no star was reflected. He repeated to himself, scarce consciously, "As like as a man and his own phantom! His own phantom!"

XV

At the beginning of March 1499, and at the moment when he least expected it, Leonardo received his salary, which had been for two years unpaid. It was reported at this time that Il Moro, overwhelmed by the news of the alliance concluded against him by the Doge of Venice, the Pope, and the King of France, intended to flee to the German Emperor upon the first appearance in Lombardy of the French forces; and that it was in order to secure the fidelity of his subjects during his absence that he lightened the taxes, paid his creditors, and heaped largesses upon his friends. A little later Leonardo received a fresh mark of his patron's favour: the gift of sixteen perches of vineyard land, acquired from the monastery of San Vittore near the Porta Vercellina, "which," so ran the deed of gift, "Ludovico Maria Sforza, Duke of Milan, confers on Leonardo da Vinci, the Florentine, most famous of painters."

Leonardo went to express his thanks to the Duke, and was not granted an interview till very late in the evening, owing to the pressure of state affairs. Il Moro had passed the whole day in tedious conversation with secretaries and treasurers, in verifying accounts for munition of war, in loosing old knots and tying new ones in that web of deceit and treachery, which had pleased him well when he had been the spidery master of the threads, but which was another matter now he found himself in the position of a fly.

His business despatched, the Duke went to the Gallery of Bramante, which looked down upon the castle moat. The stillness of the night was broken at times by the blare of a trumpet, by the challenge of sentinels, by the clank of the drawbridge chains. As soon as he had entered the gallery, his page, Ricciardetto, fixed torches in iron sconces against the wall, and handed his master a gold platter with small pieces of bread. These Ludovico threw to the swans which, attracted by the reflection from the windows, had come sailing over the black mirror of the water in the moat. Isabella d'Este, his lost Beatrice's sister, had sent him these swans from Mantua, where the flat shores of the Mincio, thick with reeds and willow-trees, were a renowned breeding-place for great flocks of these beautiful birds. Feeding them was his chief recreation after the business and anxieties of the day. They reminded him of his childhood, by the weed-grown pools of Vigevano; and here in the gloomy castle moat, among frowning embrasured walls, high towers, cannon balls, and bombards, the noiseless snow-white creatures, gliding like phantoms through the silver moonlit mist upon the scarce visible water in which stars were reflected, seemed to him full of mystery and charm.

Leaning out of the window, and still absorbed in his amusement, the Duke did not hear the creak of a small door, nor notice the approach of a chamberlain, until, with a deep reverence, the man had handed him a paper.

"What is this?" asked the Duke.

"Messer Borgonzio Botta sends your Excellency the account for munition of war, powder and bullets; he is grieved that he must trouble your lordship, but at dawn the convoy starts for Mortara."

Il Moro snatched the paper angrily, crumpled it, and threw it aside.

"How many times have I said I transact no business after supper? Good God! soon I shall not be allowed even to sleep!"

The chamberlain, still bowing, retreated backwards, announcing in a low voice which the Duke need not hear unless it so minded him:

"Messer Leonardo."

"Leonardo! Why not have brought him in before? Conduct him hither at once."

And returning to the feeding of his swans, he added to himself, "Leonardo will not worry me!"

When the painter entered, Il Moro smiled at him much as he smiled at his pets; and when Leonardo would have knelt, restrained him, and kissed his forehead.

"Welcome! 'Tis long since I have seen you. How fare you, friend?"

"I have to thank your Excellency—"

"Enough! Enough! You are worthy of better gifts. Give me time, and I will recompense you properly."

Then they talked of the diving-bell, the shoes for walking the water, the wings. But when Leonardo would have diverted the conversation to business, to the fortifications, the Martesana Canal, the casting of the great *Cavallo*, Ludovico evaded the subject with an air of disgust. Suddenly, as if remembering something, he fell into a fit of abstraction, oblivious of his companion's presence, sitting quite silent, with eyes on the ground, and Leonardo, supposing himself dismissed, would have taken his leave. The Duke nodded absently, but when the painter had reached the door he recalled him, and laying both his hands on his shoulders, looked at him with a long sad gaze.

"Farewell, my Leonardo. Who knows if ever again we shall see each other, we two alone, face to face, as at this minute!"

"Is your Excellency going to abandon us?"

Il Moro sighed heavily and paused before replying.

"We have been together for sixteen years," he said at last, "and in all that time I have never disapproved you, nor, I think, have you disapproved me. The vulgar may murmur; yet I think in after ages, when they speak of Leonardo, they will have a good word for Il Moro, his friend."

The painter, who did not like outbursts of tenderness, replied in the one courtly phrase which he reserved for moments of necessity:—

"I would I had more than a single life to dedicate to the service of your Highness."

"I believe it," said Ludovico; "some day, Leonardo, perhaps you will remember me, and will weep—"

And himself scarcely restraining a sob, he embraced him, kissing his lips.

"Leave me now, and may God go with you!" he said; and after Leonardo had gone he remained long in the Bramante Gallery, where no sound broke the stillness save the slow droppings from the torches, watching his swans, and thinking strange thoughts. He fancied that across his dark, and even criminal, life Leonardo had passed like these white swans across the black waters of the castle moat, under those embrasured walls, towers, and magazines; Leonardo, useless as they, delightful, immaculate, and pure.

XVI

Late as was the hour, the artist, having left the Duke, went to the Convento of Saint Francis to inquire for his pupil, Giovanni Boltraffio, who was lying there grievously sick of a brain fever.

Visiting his former teacher, Fra Benedetto, in December 1498, Giovanni had found Fra Paolo, a Dominican from Florence, with him, and this man had given them the account of Savonarola's death.

The execution—thus Fra Paolo related—had been appointed for nine of a May morning, to take place in the Piazza della Signoria, exactly where had been the burning of vanities and the ordeal by fire. A pyre was raised at the end of a long platform; and above it a gibbet—a stout beam driven into the ground, with a crosspiece, from which dangled three halters and iron chains. No effort of the carpenters could prevent this erection from looking like a cross. The square, the loggias, the windows and roofs of the houses were thronged by as great a multitude as had assembled for the trial by fire. The condemned—Fra Girolamo Savonarola, Fra Domenico da Pescia, and Fra Silvestro Maruffi—issued from the Palazzo Vecchio, advanced along the platform and stood before the Bishop of Pagagliotti, the papal nuncio. The bishop rose, took Savonarola's hand, and in trembling tones, not daring to meet the unfaltering gaze of the monk, he pronounced the ritual of degradation. Almost hesitatingly he uttered the concluding words; "*Separo te ab Ecclesia militante atque triumphante*." (I cut you off from the Church militant and triumphant.)

To which Fra Girolamo replied:—"*Militante, non triumphante; hoc enim tuum non est.*" (From the Church militant, yes; from the Church triumphant, no; that is not within your power!)

The three brothers were unfrocked; then, covered merely with their under-tunics, they advanced further and stood before the tribune of the Apostolic Commissaries who pronounced them heretics and schismatics; and then again before the "*Otto Uomini della Repubblica Fiorentina*" (The Eight of the Florentine Republic), who solemnly, in the name of the people, pronounced the death sentence. During this last progress, Fra Silvestro stumbled and nearly fell, and Fra Domenico and Savonarola likewise were seen to totter. Later it was discovered that this was due to a jest of certain of the Sacred Troop of Youthful Inquisitors, who had crept under the planks and run nails through them, so as to wound the naked feet of the condemned.

Fra Silvestro, the imbecile, was the first taken to the scaffold. With his customary apathetic expression, seemingly unconscious of what was befalling him, he ascended the steps; yet when the hangman put the noose upon his neck he cried, raising his eyes to heaven; "Lord, into Thy hands I commend my spirit." And not waiting for the executioner's thrust, he leaped deliberately and fearlessly from the ladder. Then Fra Domenico, who had expected his turn with joyous impatience, immediately on receiving the signal, sprang to the scaffold smiling ecstatically as if summoned to Paradise.

Fra Silvestro's body hung from one end of the crossbeam, Fra Domenico's from the other; the centre was for Savonarola. As he neared the place, he stood still, and looked down upon the crowd. Then there was a silence, profound as once in the Cathedral of Santa Maria del Fiore, when his expectant followers awaited the commencement of his preaching. But now he said no word; and the halter was adjusted; then a voice called out (and no one knew if it were mockery or the wild cry of agonising faith); "Perform a miracle, O prophet! Perform a miracle!" But the executioner had already swung off the martyr from the ladder.

Then an old workman, whose face was resigned yet full of ascetic fervour, and who for several days had had the custody of the pyre, crossed himself hurriedly and threw the lighted torch upon the pile, exclaiming, as Savonarola had done when he had set fire to the "vanities and anathemata"—"In the name of the Father, the Son, and the Holy Ghost!"

The flames leaped into the air; but the wind blew strongly and drove them in the contrary direction from the scaffold. Wherefore the crowd, smitten with a sudden fear, fell into tumult, and swayed hither and thither, pressing upon and trampling one another, and bursting into the cry; "They burn not! Lo! a miracle! a miracle!" But the wind fell and the flames rose straight and high, and licked round Fra Girolamo's corpse. And the cord wherewith his hands had been tied was sundered by the fire, and the hands fell loose and dropped and moved in the flame; and to many of the people it seemed that for the last time he blessed them.

When the fire was spent, and of the three brothers there remained only charred bones and morsels of blackened flesh quivering on the iron chains, then the faithful pressed forward and would have collected relics of the martyrs. But the guards, driving them away, piled the ashes into a cart and took them to the Ponte Vecchio with intent to cast them into the river. And on the way thither the Piagnoni succeeded in snatching some few handfuls of the sacred ashes, and certain rags of flesh which they believed to have been the heart of their murdered prophet.

Fra Paolo ended his recital; and he showed his hearers a little purse in which he had saved some of these sacred ashes. Fra Benedetto kissed it again and again, watering it with his tears; then the two monks went together to vespers. When they returned to the cell, they found Giovanni lying senseless on the ground before the crucifix, clutching the little casket of ashes in his frozen fingers.

For three months the young man lay between life and death; and Fra Benedetto never left him day nor night. He was long delirious, and the good monk shuddered as he listened to his wanderings. He raved of Savonarola, of Leonardo, of that blessed Mother of God, who, drawing with her finger on the sand of the desert, taught the divine Child geometrical figures and the laws of eternal necessity.

"For what dost Thou pray?" the sick man would repeat with unutterable grief; "Knowest Thou not that there is no relief—no miracle—? The cup cannot pass from Thee; even as a straight line cannot fail to be the shortest way between two points."

He was haunted by the vision of the two faces of the Lord, unlike, yet like as a man and his own phantom; the one overborne with human woe and weakness, who in His agony had prayed for a miracle; the other the face of the Omnipotent, of the Omniscient; of the Word made flesh, of the Prime Mover. They were turned towards each other like irreconcilable and eternal foes. And while Giovanni gazed at them, gradually the one Face, that of the Lamb of God, gentle, sorrowful, long-suffering, became obscured; and changed into the face of the demon which Leonardo had once drawn, caricaturing Savonarola. And this demon-face, denouncing the semblance of the Omnipotent, named him Antichrist.

Fra Benedetto's loving care saved the life of his adopted son. By the beginning of June Giovanni had so far recovered as to be able to walk; and then, notwithstanding all the warnings and the entreaties of the affectionate monk, he returned to Leonardo's studio.

Towards the close of July the army of Louis XII of France, commanded by Marshal d'Aubigny, Louis of Luxemburg, and Gian Giacomo Trivulzio, crossed the Alps and burst down upon the plains of Lombardy.

Book X

Calm Waters—1499–1500

"Le onde sonore e luminose sono governate dalle stesse leggi che governano le onde delle acque: l'angolo incidente deve eguagliare l'angolo riflettente."

—Leonardo Da Vinci

(The waves of light and sound are governed by the same mechanical law as that governing waves of water: the angle of incidence equals the angle of reflection.)

"Il duca ha perso lo Stato e la roba e la libertà; e nessuna sua opera si fini per lui."

—Leonardo Da Vinci

(The duke has lost state, wealth, and liberty; not one of his works will be finished by himself.)

I

The Duke's treasury, a subterranean chamber very long and narrow and piled with huge oak chests, was entered from the north-west tower of the Rocchetta by a small iron door set in the thickness of the wall and adorned with an unfinished painting by Leonardo. On the first night of September 1499, Messer Ambrogio Ferrari the court treasurer, and Messer Borgonzio Botta the comptroller of the ducal revenue, with their assistants, shovelled coins, pearls, and other treasures hastily from the oak chests, threw them into leathern bags, which they sealed with the ducal seal, and consigned to servants to be packed upon mules. Already two hundred and forty bags had been sealed and thirty mules had been loaded, yet the guttering candles still showed that the chests contained great heaps of silver. Il Moro, meanwhile, sat at a portable writing-desk heaped with registers and account-books, but gazed blankly at the flame of the candle, and paid no attention to the work of the treasurers. Since the terrible news had reached him of the defeat of Galeazzo Sanseverino, the commander of his forces, and of the inevitable nearing of the French, he seemed to have fallen into some strange torpor which resembled insensibility.

Presently Ambrogio Ferrari inquired whether the Duke wished to take the gold and silver plate also; but Ludovico, after frowning and apparently making an effort to attend, turned away, waved his hand, and once more fixed his eyes upon the candle. The question was repeated, but this time he did not even feign attention; and presently the treasurers, unable to obtain an answer, went away. Il Moro remained alone.

A few minutes later, the old chamberlain announced Messer Bernardino da Corte, the newly appointed commandant of the fortress. The Duke roused himself, passed his hand over his brow, and bade his approach.

Ludovico, distrustful of the scions of great families, liked raising men from nothing, making the first last, and the last first. This Bernardino was the son of a footman, and had himself in his boyhood worn the court livery. The Duke had, however, exalted him to the highest offices of state, and now, as a proof of final confidence in his ability and good faith, had charged him with the defence of the castle of Milan, his last stronghold.

The Duke received the new governor graciously, bade him sit, spread before him the plan of the castle, explained the signals concerted between the fortress and the town. For example, in the daytime a curved gardening knife (or at night a flaming torch) displayed from the main tower of the castle was to show the need for instant help; a white sheet, hung on the tower of Bona, signified treachery within the walls; a chair suspended by a rope meant lack of powder; a petticoat, lack of wine; a pair of breeches, scarcity of bread; an earthenware pot, the need of a doctor.

Il Moro had himself invented this code, and was childishly pleased with it, as if in it lay somehow his chief hope of safety.

"Remember, Bernardino," thus he concluded his exordium, "everything has been foreseen. You have sufficiency of money, powder, provisions, fire-arms; the three thousand mercenaries are already paid; the fortress is in your hands, and should be able to stand a three years' siege. I, however, only ask you to hold it for three months; if at the end of that time I have not returned to your relief, you must do what you think best. Now you know all. Farewell, my son; may the Lord protect you!" And he favoured him with an embrace.

The governor of the castle dismissed, Il Moro bade the page prepare his camp bed. He prayed, and laid himself down, but sleep proved impossible. He lighted a candle, took a packet of papers from his wallet, and found a poem by one Antonio Cammelli da Pistoia, Bellincioni's rival, who on the first appearance of the French had deserted his patron. The poem represented the war between Ludovico and Louis XII as a conflict between a winged serpent and a cock:—

"Italia's lord, we lay to heart thy fate,
For good it is to learn by other men's undoing.
O bitter word to speak, the loss of all things rueing—
When fickle fortune smiled, I was a potentate!
The world to Ludovico seemed a fief but late;
Itself and all its glory appeared but of his doing;
Yet Heav'n, his stomach high and proud presumption viewing,
His every hope and scheme did suddenly frustrate."

The Duke's soul was pervaded by melancholy, which was not, however, entirely disagreeable. It was partly the pride of a martyr. He remembered the servility of the sonnets the same poet had dedicated to him not long ago:—

"Speak, potent lord, and say, The world to me is given!"

It was midnight, and the flame of the dying candle flickered and grew dim, but still the Duke continued to pace the gloomy room, thinking of his griefs, of the injustice of blind fortune, of the ingratitude of men.

"What wrong have I done them? Why do they hate me? They call me a villain and an assassin; but what have I done more than Romulus who killed his brother, and Cæsar, and Alexander, and all the heroes of antiquity? Were *they* villains and assassins? My desire was to give them a new age of gold, such as had not been seen since the days of Augustus and the Antonines. A little longer, and under my rule Italy would have been united; the laurels of Apollo would have bloomed, and the olives of Pallas; the reign of peace would have begun, and the worship of the muses. First among princes, I sought greatness not in deeds of war, but in the fruits of golden peace, in the protection of talent, Bramante, Pacioli, Caradosso, Leonardo, and how many others! In days to come, when the noise of arms shall be forgotten, their names will be remembered, together with the name of Sforza. To what a height should not I, the new Pericles, have raised my new Athens, but for this horde of northern barbarians who have cut short my work? Why, O my God *why* is this permitted?"

And, his head drooping on his breast, he thought again of the lines:—

"O bitter word to speak, the loss of all things rueing—
When fickle fortune smiled, I was a potentate!"

The candle flared for the last time, illuminating the vaulting of the roof, and the fresco of Mercury above the treasure-house door. Then it sank down and went out. The Duke shuddered, for he thought it a bad omen. Fearful of awakening Ricciardetto, he groped his way to the bed, lay down again, and this time fell asleep at once.

He dreamed that he knelt to Madonna Beatrice, who having discovered his intrigue with Lucrezia was taxing him with it, and striking him full in the face. He was pained, yet rejoiced that she had returned to life. He submitted to her chastisement, caught her hands that he might kiss them, and wept for love. But suddenly there stood before him, not Beatrice, but the Mercury of Leonardo's fresco over the door. The god seized him by the hair, crying:—

"O fool, and blind! In what dost thou yet hope? Will all your deceits save you from the just punishment of God? Murderer and villain!"

When he awoke, the morning light was shining on the windows. The lords, the knights, the captains, the German mercenaries, who were to escort him to the court of Maximilian, in all, some three thousand horsemen, were awaiting his presence by the main road which led north—towards the Alps.

Ludovico mounted, and rode to the Monastery delle Grazie, that he might pray for the last time beside the grave of his lost Beatrice. Later, when the sun was high in the heavens, the cortège began its march through Como, Bellaggio, Bormio, Bolzano, and Brisina, to the Tyrol, and the city of Innsbrück.

II

THE JOURNEY TOOK OVER A fortnight, for a rainy autumn had spoiled the roads. On the 18th of September, the Duke, being fatigued and indisposed, determined to pass the night in a mountain cave, which afforded shelter to a few herdsmen. It would not have been difficult to find a more commodious resting-place, but Il Moro deliberately chose this wild spot for his reception of the ambassador from Maximilian. The watch-fires illumined the stalactites and the natural vaulting of the cavern; pheasants were roasting for supper; and the Duke, seated on a camp-chair, his feet on a brazier, and his head muffled—for he was suffering from toothache—reflected, not without a certain satisfaction, on the greatness of his misfortunes. Lucrezia Crivelli, bright and gentle as ever, was preparing an anodyne of wine, pepper, cloves, and other potent spices for the illustrious sufferer.

"So, then, Messer Odoardo," said Il Moro to the Emperor's envoy, "you can tell his Majesty where, and in what condition you found the legitimate ruler of Lombardy."

Ludovico was in one of the fits of loquacity which sometimes succeeded to long periods of silence and dejection. "Foxes have holes," he went on, "and birds of the air have nests, but I have not where to lay my head. Corio," he turned to the chronicler, "in compiling your annals omit not description of this lodging, the refuge of the last heir of the great Sforzas, of the descendant of Anglus, the Trojan, the comrade of Æneas."

"My lord," said Odoardo, "your misfortunes deserve the pen of a new Tacitus."

Lucrezia brought the anodyne, and the Duke paused to look at her admiringly. Her pale clear face was bright in the rosy glow of the firelight, her black hair coiled smoothly above her pure forehead, upon which glowed the single diamond of the *ferroniera*. She looked at her lover with her grave, innocent, and observant eyes; on her lips was a smile of almost maternal tenderness.

"Sweet heart!" thought Ludovico, "here is one who will never betray me!" and receiving the medicament from her hand, he again turned to the chronicler and said, with swelling sententiousness; "Corio, set down likewise this; 'true friendship is proved in the furnace of affliction, as gold is proved in the fire.'"

"Eh, old fellow, why so gloomy?" cried Janachi, seating himself at the Duke's feet, and slapping his knee, "a truce to this black bile! There's remedy for every ill save death, and trust me, old man, it's better to be a living ass than a dead prince! Kiki riki! Look! look! what a throng of ass-saddles we have here!"

"Well, what of it?" asked the Duke, wearily.

"*Moro mio, moro mio*, there's an old Story which says—"

"Well—go on; relate the story!"

The fool jumped to his feet, ringing his bells and shaking his rattle.

"Once upon a time there was a king in Naples, and he bade Giotto the painter make him a wall-picture of his kingdom. And the saucy painter drew a stout Ass carrying on his back a Saddle with the royal arms, the sceptre, and the crown; and the Ass was sniffing at another Saddle, also emblazoned with arms, sceptre and crown. Wherefore, dear Sir, I say to thee, today the people of Milan are sniffing at the French Saddle. Let them alone! Soon enough will it gall their backs, and they'll wish to be quit of it!"

"*Stulti aliquando sapientes*," said the Duke, with a melancholy smile at this piece of imbecility. "Corio, write in the chronicle—"

But he did not finish the phrase, for the snorting of horses, the tramp of hoofs, and the buzz of voices were heard outside the cavern. Mariolo Pusterla the chamberlain, his face pale and agitated, entered hastily, and whispered with Calco the chief secretary.

"What has happened?" asked the Duke.

No one was willing to reply, and all eyes fell.

"Your Excellency—" began the secretary, in trembling tones, and broke off.

"May the Lord support your Excellency!" said Luigi Marliani. "Be prepared; bad news has arrived from Milan."

"Speak, then; speak! For God's sake, speak!" cried Ludovico, turning pale. Then looking towards the entrance, he caught sight of a man splashed with mud, and travel-worn. The Duke brushed Marliani aside, hurried to the messenger, and snatching a letter from his hand, broke the seal, read with lightning glance, uttered a cry, and sank senseless to the ground. Marliani and Pusterla were barely in time to break his fall.

On the 17th of September, the feast of San Satiro, the traitor Bernardino da Corte had opened the gates of the Castle of Milan to the French marshal, Gian Giacomo Trivulzio.

Ludovico was practised in the simulation of diplomatic faintness. This time, however, the physicians had trouble in restoring him to consciousness. When at last he regained his senses, he sighed, made the sign of the cross, and murmured:—

"Since Judas there never was a traitor like Bernardino da Corte."

And for the rest of the evening he did not utter a single word.

A few days later the Duke arrived at Innsbrück, where he was graciously received by the Emperor and lodged in the imperial palace. One evening he was walking up and down his chamber, and dictating to Bartolomeo Calco credentials for the envoys whom he was secretly despatching to the Sultan. The face of the old secretary expressed nothing but attention, and his pen travelled rapidly over the paper, as the words fell from his master's lips.

"'Firm and invariable in our good disposition towards your Highness'"—so ran the document—"'and trusting that in the task of recovering our lost dominions, we may look for aid to the magnanimity of the powerful ruler of the Ottoman Empire, we have resolved to send three different messengers by three different roads, so that at least one of them may arrive and present our letter. The Pope, who by nature is perfidious and wicked—'"

Here the pen of the dispassionate secretary stopped; he looked up, wrinkling his brows. He could not believe his ears.

"The Pope?"

"Yes, the Pope. Go on,"

The secretary looked at his work again, and the pen scratched faster than before.

"'The Pope, being by nature wicked and perfidious, has instigated the French king to carry war into Lombardy.'"

Then came the list of French victories.

"'Dismayed by these misfortunes,'" continued Il Moro frankly, "'we have judged it prudent to seek refuge at the court of the Emperor Maximilian, while awaiting the assistance of your Highness. All have betrayed us; but more than the rest, Bernardino'"—here his voice shook—"'Bernardino da Corte, a serpent warmed in our bosom, a slave whom we had heaped with favours and benefactions; a traitor like unto Judas'—Nay, 'tis vain to speak of Judas to an infidel; scratch out 'Judas.'"

He prayed the Sultan to assail Venice by sea and by land, assuring him of easy victory and the complete destruction of that secular enemy of the Ottomans, the arrogant Republic of St. Mark.

"'And we pray your Highness to remember,'" he concluded, "'that in this war, as in every other undertaking, all we have is at the disposal of your Highness, who in all Europe will find no more faithful ally than Ourselves.'"

He had approached the table and seemed desirous of adding yet another few words; but in a sudden access of discouragement he waved his hand, and threw himself on a seat. Calco carefully strewed the wet writing with sand; then he looked up and saw that the Duke had covered his face with his hands, and was weeping, his shoulders shaking with sobs.

"Lord, why hast thou permitted this? Where, where is Thine eternal justice?" he mourned. Then uncovering his distorted face, which at that moment seemed to belong to some feeble old woman, he said:—

"Bartolomeo, you know that I repose confidence in you. Tell me, on your conscience, am I acting wisely?"

"Does your Excellency refer to the embassy to the Grand Turk?"

Il Moro nodded.

The old man wrinkled his forehead and puffed his lips meditatively.

"Certes, those who hunt with wolves must howl with them; yet if we look at the matter from another point of view—in fine, if I am permitted to counsel your Excellency, I would say, wait!"

"I have waited. Now I will demonstrate that the Duke of Milan is not to be tossed aside like a mere pawn. My friend, I have been ever on the side of right, and I have been most iniquitously abused. Who shall blame me if I appeal, not only to the Grand Turk, but to the very devil himself?"

"Yet an invasion by the infidel," suggested the secretary, "might perchance be cause of grave peril to the Christian Church."

"God forbid, Bartolomeo! I have considered that. I would suffer a thousand deaths rather than bring damage to our holy Mother Church. But hark you! You do not fully understand my design."

At these words his lips took on their old rapacious smile. "We will brew these villains such a broth," he continued; "we will entangle them in such nets, that none of them shall look again on God's world! But the Grand Turk!—why, the Grand Turk is no more than a tool in my hands! When the time is ripe we will cast him aside, and then we will root out all that vile sect of Mahometans, and free the sacred sepulchre of the Lord from the unclean domination of infidel dogs!"

Calco discreetly lowered his eyes and made no answer.

"This is bad," he said to himself; "these are dreams; in all this there is no policy. He lets himself be carried too far, and he perceives not consequences."

But that night Ludovico, animated by hope in God and in the Grand Turk, prayed long before his favourite picture, by Leonardo, in which the Virgin was pourtrayed with the features and smile of Cecilia, Countess Bergamini.

III

Ten days before the surrender of the castle, the French marshal, Trivulzio, had made entry into Milan amid the pealing of bells and the acclamation of the populace. The king's entry was fixed for the 6th of October, and the citizens were preparing for his reception. The two great angels which, fifty years earlier in the days of the "Repubblica Ambrosiana," had represented the genii of popular liberty, were taken from the cathedral treasury for use in the royal procession. Long disuse had stiffened the springs by which their gilded wings were moved, and they were accordingly sent for repair to the court mechanician, Leonardo da Vinci.

Early one autumnal morning, while it was still dark, Leonardo sat at his desk, busy with his calculations and his geometrical designs. Of late he had resumed his study of aerostatics, and was constructing another flying-machine. Its skeleton was spread across the room, not, like its predecessor, resembling a bat, but rather a gigantic swallow. One of the wings was completed; slender, sharply outlined, beautiful in form and texture, it rose from floor to ceiling, and under its shadow Astro was working at the two wooden angels of the former Milanese Republic. In this latest apparatus Leonardo had determined to follow, as closely as he might, the structure of those winged creatures which nature had provided as models for a flying-machine. He still hoped to solve the problem by close observance of mechanical laws; but though apparently he knew all that could be known, there was still something which eluded his comprehension, and which perhaps lay outside these laws with which he was so familiar. As in his earlier experiments, he found himself brought up against that subtle dividing line which separates the creations of nature from the work of human hands; the structure of the living body from the structure of the lifeless machine; and he began to think he was aiming at the impossible—the irrational.

"Thank God, that is finished!" exclaimed Astro, winding up the springs of the wooden angels.

Their heavy wings moved, and in the resultant waft of air, the delicate wing of the great swallow stirred and rustled. The smith looked at it with inexpressible tenderness.

"The time I have squandered on these stupid monsters!" he exclaimed, pushing the angels away. "From this out, Master, you may say what you please, but I will not go from this room till I have finished my swallow! Give me, pr'ythee, the design for the tail."

"It is not ready, Astro. It demands further calculation."

"But, Master, you promised it to me three days ago!"

"It cannot be helped. The tail of our bird is the rudder. The smallest mistake will ruin the whole."

"You know best, I suppose! I will get on with the second wing."

"We had better wait. It may be necessary to introduce some modification."

The smith very carefully lifted the cane skeleton, overlaid with a network of bullocks' tendons; he turned it round, and contemplated it under every aspect. Then, his voice thick and trembling with excitement, he cried:—

"Master, be not wroth, but hear! If your calculations lead you to the conclusion that this machine also is useless, I swear to you that none the less *I* intend to fly. Yes, I will fly in spite of all your damnable mechanics. I have no longer patience for waiting, because—"

He stopped short. Leonardo gazed at the wide, irregular, obstinate face, impressed with a single, senseless, all-absorbing idea.

"Messere," he added, more quietly, "be so kind as to say plainly, are we going to fly, or are we not?"

Leonardo had not the heart to tell him the naked truth.

"We cannot be quite certain till we have made the experiment," he replied; "but I think we shall fly."

"That is enough; I ask no more," said the mechanic, clapping his hands. "If *you* say we shall fly, then the thing is done."

He presently burst into a great laugh.

"What the devil amuses you?" asked Leonardo.

"Ah, forgive me, Master! I am always disturbing you. But when I fall a-thinking of the poor folk of Milan, and of the French soldiers, and Il Moro, and the king, I have to laugh because I feel so sorry for them. Poor little creeping worms, poor little jumping grasshoppers! Always on the same plot of earth to which they are chained by their feet, they fight and they bite each other, and they think they are doing some very great thing! How they will stare and gape when they see men alive and flying. I misdoubt that they will believe their eyes. 'These be two gods,' they will say. Astro, a god! I doubt the whole world will be changed. I doubt wars and laws will be done with, and masters and slaves. We cannot conceive how it will be! Soaring up to heaven like the choirs of angels, all the people will shout Hosanna! O Messer Leonardo, Messer Leonardo! is it true that verily thus it will be?"

He spoke wildly, like one in delirium.

"Poor fool!" thought Leonardo; "what blind faith! What is to be done? How can I tell him the truth? He will go crazed!"

At this moment there was a great knock at the street door, then a noise of voices and steps, and then a rap at the door of the studio.

"What devil comes at this hour?" growled Astro. "A pox on him! Who is there? You won't see the Master. He has gone away from Milan."

"'Tis I, Astro—Luca Pacioli, the mathematician! Open, open, for God's sake!"

The smith opened and let the friar enter. His face was blanched with terror. Leonardo asked him hurriedly what had happened.

"To me, Messer Leonardo, nought—or leastways of that I will speak later. I come from the castle. Oh, Messer Leonardo! The Gascon bowmen—in fact the French—I saw it with my own eyes! *They are destroying your Cavallo.* Let us run! Let us run!"

"Soft!" said the painter, though he also had paled. "What shall we do by running?"

"But you cannot sit here with folded hands while your masterpiece is perishing? I have a recommendation to Monsieur de la Trémouille. We must implore him—"

"We are too late."

"No, no! there is still time! We can run by the garden, through the hedge. If we but make haste!"

Dragged along by the monk, Leonardo set forth for the castle. On the way Fra Luca told him of his own misadventure. The *lanzknechts* had plundered the cellar of the *Canonica* of San Simpliciano, where he dwelt; and being drunken, had wrought havoc through the house; and in Fra Luca's cell, having chanced on certain geometrical models made in crystal, had taken them for instruments of magic, and smashed them to atoms.

"My poor innocent crystals, which had done them no manner of wrong," mourned the friar! Reached the piazza before the castle, they saw a young French dandy attended by a numerous suite on the drawbridge.

"Maître Gilles!" cried Fra Luca overjoyed; and he explained to Leonardo that this was a considerable and authoritative personage; his title, "Whistler to the woodhens," his office, to teach the finches, magpies, parrots, and thrushes of the most Christian king their feats of singing, talking, dancing, and other performances. Rumour asserted that the "woodhens" were not the only bipeds who danced to the piping of Maître Gilles; and altogether Fra Luca had long felt that he must be presented with his books (richly bound) *De Divina Proportione* and *Summa Aritmetica*.

"Fra Luca," said Leonardo, "do not lose your opportunity—attend Maître Gilles. I can manage my own case."

"No, no," said the other, somewhat ashamed, "I can wait; or I will just fly to him for an instant and learn whither he is going, and in a trice I will be back with you—go you on towards Monsieur de la Trémouille."

And gathering up the skirts of his brown habit, his bare feet shod with clattering wooden pattens, the nimble monk ran after the "Whistler to the Woodhens"; while Leonardo crossed the drawbridge and entered the inner court of the castle.

IV

THE MORNING MISTS WERE RISING, and the watch-fires already dying down. The courtyard was crowded with cannon, ammunition, camp equipage, stable provender and refuse. All around were movable booths and cooking-spits, empty barrels serving as card-tables, hogsheads of wine, barrows of provisions; great noises of laughter, curses, quarrelings in many tongues, blasphemies, drunken shoutings and songs. At times an interval of sudden stillness when officers of rank passed. At times drums beat and brazen trumpets gave signal to the Rhenish and Suabian *lanzknechts*, or Alpine horns were blown from the walls by mercenaries from the Free Cantons of Uri and Unterwalden.

Making his way through the crowd of men and things, Leonardo reached the centre of the square and found that the Colossus, the happy labour for years of his maturest art, was still intact. The great duke, conqueror of Lombardy, Francesco Attendolo Sforza, with his bald head, in form like that of some Roman emperor, and his expression of leonine cruelty and vulpine cunning, erect as ever, still sat his huge plunging charger and trampled on his foe.

A great crowd of archers of various nationalities surrounded the statue, disputing each in his own language, and gesticulating. Leonardo gathered that a contest was imminent between a French and a German marksman, who, after drinking four tankards of wine were to shoot at a distance of fifty paces at the birthmark on the cheek of the great Sforza. The paces were measured; lots were drawn as to who should shoot first; the wine was poured out. The German drank the fill of a tankard without drawing breath, another, and another, and another. Then he took his aim, bent the bow, launched his arrow, and missed the mark. The arrow grazed the cheek, and took off the tip of the left ear, but did no further damage. It was now the turn of the Frenchman. He had brought his arbalist to his shoulder, when a commotion arose among the onlookers. The crowd divided, making space for the procession of a knight and his escort of resplendent followers. He rode past, not heeding the marksmen.

"Who is that?" inquired Leonardo.

"Monseigneur de la Trémouille."

"Then I am in time," thought the artist; "I must pursue him and make supplication."

Nevertheless he actually stood motionless where he was; oppressed by an inability, a paralysis of the will, that would have hindered the stirring of a finger had his very life been in danger. Repugnance, shame, seized him at the thought of pushing his way through the crowd that he might, like Fra Luca Pacioli, run after and pull at the skirts of a person of quality. The Gascon shot his arrow; it whizzed through the air, hit the mark, and penetrated deeply into the mole on Francesco's cheek.

"*Bigorre! Bigorre! Montjoie! Saint Denis!*" shouted the soldiers, throwing their caps into the air, "*Vive la France*!" The noisy crowd again encircled the Colossus, the jargon of many tongues broke forth anew; a fresh match was arranged, and again arrows whistled on the air and wounded the great Duke. Leonardo could not move. Inconceivable as it may seem, rooted to the spot as in some hideous dream, he watched the slow destruction of the work of the six best years of his life; of perhaps the greatest monument of the sculptor's art since the days of Phidias and Praxiteles. Under a hail of bullets, arrows, and even stones, the brittle clay was broken off in lumps or resolved into dust; the supports were laid bare. The Colossus had become an immense iron skeleton.

The sun streamed out from behind a bank of clouds. Nothing remained but the headless body of a man, the trunk of a horse, the fragment of a sceptre, and the inscription on the pedestal. "Behold a god!" Just then the commandant of the French troops, the old Marshal Gian Giacomo Trivulzio, rode up. He looked at the place of the

Colossus, stopped in sheer astonishment, looked again, shading his eyes from the sun; then turned to his attendants and asked—

"In the name of God, what has taken place?"

"*Monseigneur*," replied a lieutenant. "Captain Cockburn gave permission to his cross-bowmen—"

"The Sforza monument! the work of Leonardo da Vinci—I made a target for the archers of Gascony!" cried the marshal, and he rushed at the men, who, intent on their work of destruction, had not observed his displeasure; seized a Frenchman by the collar and flung him to the ground, rating him soundly. In his fury the old general had become quite purple.

"*Monseigneur*," stammered the soldier, struggling to his knees, shaking with fright, "*Monseigneur*, we did not know! Captain Cockburn had said—"

"To hell with your Captain Cockburn! I'll hang every man jack of you!"

He flourished his sword and would have wounded someone had not Leonardo caught his wrist with such force that the brazen sword-hilt was bent.

Trivulzio stared at the stranger in dire amazement while struggling to free himself.

"Who is this man?" he exclaimed indignantly, and the artist himself replied:—

"Leonardo da Vinci."

"And how do you dare—" began the old marshal, still beside himself, but meeting the clear unfaltering gaze of the eyes fixed upon him, he broke off. "Eh? you are Leonardo?" he said. "I pray you loose my arm—you have crushed the hilt."

"*Monseigneur*," said Leonardo, "I beseech you.—Pardon these poor fools!"

The marshal again stared in amazement; then smiled, and shook his head.

"A strange fellow! What? You entreat for them?"

"If your Excellence hangs every mother's son among them, what will it profit me? They knew not what they did."

The old man became thoughtful, then his face cleared, and his small intelligent eyes shone with good nature.

"Hark ye, Messer Leonardo! There is one thing passes me. How could you stand there stock-still, looking on? Why did you not complain to me? or to Monseigneur de la Trémouille? He must have passed by within an hour!"

Leonardo looked down and reddened. "I was not in time," he stammered, "I—I don't know Monsieur de la Trémouille."

"'Tis a misfortune," said the old man; and surveying the ruin, he exclaimed with great vehemence, "I would have given a hundred of my best troopers for your Colossus!"

On his way home, Leonardo crossed the bridge just under Bramante's loggia, the scene of his last interview with the Duke. Pages and grooms were chasing the swans which were so dear to Il Moro; and the poor creatures unable to escape from the moat, fluttered and screamed in agonies. The water was flecked with down and snowy feathers; here and there on its blackness floated a white blood-stained body. One newly-wounded bird stretched its graceful neck in the convulsions of death, uttering piercing cries and flapping its weakening wings, as if in a last vain effort for flight. Leonardo averted his eyes and hurried away.

V

Louis XII made his entry into the Lombard capital punctually on the 6th of October. Great crowds assembled to see the procession; and the newly-mended angels of the Milanese Commune waved their gilded wings to the admiration of all.

Leonardo had not touched his flying-machine since the day of the destruction of the *Cavallo*; but Astro still laboured at it indefatigably, now and then looking reproachfully at the Master with his one eye, in which blazed fires of zeal and hope.

One morning Pacioli came running with a message from the king, summoning Messer Leonardo to the castle. The artist was unwilling to leave Astro, for he had not confessed that the new apparatus was a failure, and he feared lest the enthusiast should endanger his neck in some rash experiment. However, he set forth, and presently arrived at the *Sala della Rocchetta* where Louis XII was receiving the magistrates and chief citizens of the city.

Leonardo looked at his new sovereign with attention, but discovered nothing regal in his aspect. He was lean and feeble, with narrow shoulders, a hollow chest, and a face curiously wrinkled. Evidently used to suffering, it had conferred on him neither nobility nor grace; his virtues were at best of the *bourgeois* type.

A young man, twenty years of age, dressed simply in black, stood on the first step of the throne. He wore no ornaments except a few pearls in the looping of his hat, and the gold chain of the Order of St. Michael: his face was pale, his flaxen hair was worn long, and he had dark blue eyes, soft, but singularly penetrating and observant.

"Tell me, Fra Luca," whispered Leonardo, "who is that young noble?"

"Cæsar Borgia, the son of the pope, the Duke of Valentinois," replied the monk.

Leonardo was not ignorant of the crimes imputed to this young man. There was little doubt that he had murdered his brother in order that, exchanging the cardinal's purple for the title of *Gran Gonfaloniere* of the Roman Church, he might himself have the chief place in the family honours. Further, the whisper ran, that the motive of the fratricide was not ambition only, but a monstrous rivalry between the brothers for the favour of their sister Lucrezia.

"That, at least, is impossible," thought Leonardo, looking at the calm face and clear soft eyes.

Cæsar probably felt Leonardo's scrutinising gaze, for he turned and asked his secretary some question, pointing at the artist as he spoke. The secretary, a man of venerable aspect, replied in a whisper, and Cæsar in his turn looked intently at Leonardo, while a subtle smile played upon his lips.

"Nay, it is not impossible," thought the artist, answering his own hasty judgment; "anything is possible to that face; perhaps even worse than we have heard."

The spokesman of the town syndics, having finished the reading of a long and tedious document, approached the throne and presented the parchment to the king. Louis accidentally dropped it, and before the citizen could pick it up, Cæsar had stooped dexterously and quickly, had lifted the roll, and placed it in the king's hand.

"He never loses an opportunity," grumbled someone standing near Leonardo.

"You are right," responded another; "the pope's son understands the arts of service. You should see him of a morning at the king's dressing! He warms his shirt for him! I daresay he'd be ready even to wash out the stable."

Leonardo also had observed Cæsar's too obsequious action, which seemed to him terrible rather than servile, like the caress of a wild beast; but he was no longer permitted to play the part of a spectator, for Pacioli dragged him forward and presented him to the king with a short speech made up of superlatives—"*stupendissimo! prestantissimo! invincibilissimo!*" and the like. Louis spoke at once of the *Cenacolo*, praising the figures of the Apostles, and waxing enthusiastic over the perspective of the roof. Fra Luca was quite sure his Majesty had a post ready to offer to the great artist; but unluckily at this moment a page brought in letters from France, and the king's attention was engrossed by the news that his loved wife, Anne of Brittany, had been delivered of a princess. The courtiers crowded round with their congratulations, and Leonardo and Pacioli were pushed into the background. Pacioli would again have dragged his friend forward, but Leonardo objected, and presently left the palace.

On the drawbridge he was overtaken by Messer Agapito, Borgia's secretary, who by command of his master offered him the post of "*Ingegner ducale*" (chief engineer), which he had already filled under Il Moro.

Leonardo said he would reply after a few days' reflection, and went on towards his house.

Presently he saw a crowd of people, and hurried his steps with a presentiment of disaster. The fear was well grounded; his pupils Giovanni, Marco, Salaino, and Cesare, unable to procure a litter, were carrying the unfortunate Astro on the broken wing of the new and ill-fated flying-machine, his garments blood-stained and torn, his face white as death. Leonardo guessed at once what had occurred. The smith, great in resolution and in faith, had adventured on the machine. He had fitted the apparatus to his shoulders, and leaped into the air. Then he had fallen, and would probably have been killed had not one of the wings caught in the boughs of a tree. Leonardo helped to carry the poor wretch home; with his own hands he laid him on a bed and bent over him to examine his hurts. Astro recovered from his swoon, and looking up with supplicating eyes, murmured—

"O Master! Forgive!"

VI

Louis XII celebrated the birth of his daughter with great feasts, and a solemn thanksgiving mass was performed in the cathedral. The city was quiet, and all seemed peaceful and prosperous. Having exacted an oath of fealty from his new subjects, he appointed Marshal Trivulzio his viceroy, and returned to France early in November.

The calm was, however, deceitful; Trivulzio soon made himself detested by his cruelty and greed; the adherents of the banished Ludovico took heart, and inflamed the people by liberal distribution of seditious letters. Soon those who had sent Il Moro forth with objurgations and jeers, proclaimed him the best and wisest of sovereigns.

Towards the end of January a crowd wrecked the offices of the tax-collector beside the Porta Ticinese; next day there was rioting near Pavia. The cause of the latter disturbance was an attempt made by a French soldier on the chastity of a peasant girl, who struck her assailant with a broom handle and was then threatened by him with an axe. She screamed; her father ran up with a cudgel and was killed by the soldier. Then the crowd fell upon the soldier and he was killed; after which the French drew on the populace and sacked the village.

When the news of this outrage reached Milan it acted like a spark upon gunpowder. The people poured into the squares, the streets, the market-places, shouting "Down with the king! Down with Trivulzio! Death to the foreigners! *Viva Il Moro!*"

The French troops were too few to withstand attack from the three hundred thousand inhabitants of Milan. Trivulzio placed guns upon the tower which for the present was in use as the cathedral belfry, but before giving the order to fire on the crowd he tried one more effort at pacification. He was hustled, hunted into the Palazzo del Comune, and would have perished there but for the timely intervention of the Swiss mercenaries. Then ensued burning and pillaging; torture and murder of all foreigners and their sympathisers who fell into the hands of the citizens. On the 1st of February Trivulzio fled, leaving the fortress in charge of the Captains d'Espe and Codecara. That very night Il Moro returned from Germany, and was received with great joy by the town of Como; all Milan anxiously awaited him as its saviour.

In these last days of the revolt, when the streets were being wrecked on all sides by the cannonade, Leonardo transferred his household to the ample cellars of his house, contriving living-rooms of tolerable comfort, and storing everything of value: pictures, drawings, manuscripts, scientific instruments.

He had definitely resolved to enter Cæsar Borgia's service, and was to present himself in Romagna not later than the summer of 1500; meanwhile he proposed to visit his friend, Girolamo Melzi, at his villa of Vaprio in the vicinity of Milan, living there in retirement till the disturbances were at an end. On the morning of February the 2nd, the Feast of the Purification, Fra Luca brought him the tidings that the castle had been flooded. A Milanese, Luigi da Porto, who had been in Trivulzio's service, had deserted to the rebels, first opening all the sluices which fed the moats of the fortress. The water spread over the circumjacent lands, reaching to the walls of the Rocchetta; and, making its way into the magazine and provision stores, almost forced the French to surrender, which was precisely what Messer Luigi had hoped. The flood had also overflowed the canal, had inundated the low lying suburb of Porta Vercellina, where was situated the Monastery delle Grazie. Fra Luca expressed grave fears for Leonardo's *Cenacolo* and offered to go with him and see how it fared.

The painter, feigning indifference, replied that he was too busy, and that he believed the height of the fresco would preserve it from injury. No sooner, however, was he rid of Pacioli than he hastened to the convent refectory, on the brick floor of which pools were still left, and where there was a pervading odour of miasma and stagnant water. A monk told him that the flood had risen to the fourth of a cubit.

The *Cenacolo* had not been painted in water-colours, according to the usage for fresco; such process requiring a rapidity of execution alien to Leonardo's genius.

"A painter who has no doubts will have small success," he used to say; and for his doubts, his vacillations, his experiments, corrections, and extreme slowness, only the medium of oil was suitable. It was in vain that experienced masters told him that oil paints were impossible for a damp wall standing on the verge of a marsh. His love of experiment, and of new paths and devices induced him to disregard all warnings; he mixed his paints in a special way, and prepared the wall by coating it first with clay, varnished and oiled, then with a mixture of mastic, pitch and plaster.

Having dismissed the monk, Leonardo crossed the still soaking refectory floor, and stepped close to examine his picture. The transparent and delicate colours seemed uninjured, and not even blurred; however he took a magnifying-glass and explored the surface in every part. To his dismay, there in the left-hand corner, just where the tablecloth was represented hanging in ample folds by the feet of St Bartholomew, he discovered a small crack; beside it the colours were already fading, and on the surface was a white velvety patch, scarce observable, but the beginning of mould. Sudden paleness overspread Leonardo's features; he composed himself, however, and continued his examination with minuter care. Very soon he realised what had happened. The first coating of varnished clay had bulged in consequence of the damp and had come away from the wall, raising the upper coating of plaster which carried the paint; and in the plaster tiny almost invisible cracks had formed, through which a salt sweat exuded from the porous brickwork. The *Cenacolo* was doomed. The colours might last forty or fifty years and Leonardo himself never see their decay, but it was impossible to doubt that this his greatest work must irretrievably perish. He stood looking at the face of his Christ; realising for the first time how dear to him was this, his supreme creation.

The ruin of the *Cenacolo*, the destruction of the *Cavallo*, snapped the last threads which bound him to men, which united him to friends perhaps still unborn. His soul had long been solitary; now his solitude was deeper than before. The clay of the Colossus, resolved into dust, was the sport of the winds of heaven; mould was gathering on the very countenance of the Lord, dimming its outline, blurring and fading its colours. All that had been his very life was vanishing as a shadow.

He came away, leaving the monastery without speaking to anyone; made his way to his deserted house, and descended to the place of refuge underground. He passed through the room where lay the unfortunate Astro, and stopped for a moment to speak to Giovanni who was preparing a compress for the sick man's brow.

"Fever again?" asked the Master.

"Yes; he is delirious."

Leonardo watched the bandaging, and listened for a few minutes to the rapid disconnected babble which came from the lips of the poor broken enthusiast.

"Higher! Higher! Straight to the sun—so long as the wings don't catch fire! Ha! little one! who are you? What is your name? Mechanics? That is a scurvy name! I never heard of a devil named Mechanics! What are you jeering at? Is it a joke? That's enough now; you have had your joke, and I've done with you. Ah!—Lift me! Lift me! I can bear no more! Let me just get my breath. Oh—death and damnation!" His face was anguished; cries of terror burst from his lips; he fancied himself falling into the abyss. But this passed and the rapid babbling recommenced.

"No, no! mock not! The fault was mine own. He told me they were not ready. Ay, he said so. I have betrayed the Master! I have betrayed the Master! Hush! Hush! O yes, I know him! the smallest and the heaviest of all the devils—the little one named Mechanics."

Leonardo, leaning over the bed, could not avert his gaze. He was thinking—

"Here is another man whom I have destroyed."

He laid his hand on Astro's burning forehead. It appeared to calm him, little by little he became quieter, and presently he sank into heavy sleep. Leonardo retired to his underground cell, and buried himself in his calculations. He was now studying the laws of the wind, and the aerial currents, and comparing them with the laws of the waves and currents of the sea—all still with reference to this question of flight.

"If you throw two stones of equal size into a pool, at a little distance from each other,"—he said slowly to himself—"two widening circles will be formed on the surface of the water. Then will come a moment in which the first circle will meet the second; will it enter and bisect it? or will the waves be refracted at their point of contact? I answer, taking my stand on experience: the two circles will intersect each other, remaining, however, distinct and keeping their respective centres at the points where the stones fell."

The simplicity with which nature had solved this mechanical problem filled him with enthusiasm; "How subtle is this! How beautiful!"

He made a calculation, and the result added to his conviction that the mathematical sciences, with their laws founded on the essential necessities of reason, justified the natural necessities of mechanics.

Hour after hour flew by unnoticed, and evening came on. After supper, and relaxation in talk with his pupils, he again set to work. The acumen and lucidity of his thoughts convinced him that he was on the verge of some great discovery.

"Behold how the wind, blowing across the fields, drives waves over the rye, one succeeding the other, while the stalks, though they bend, remain fixed in the ground! In like manner do the waves run over the immovable water. The ripple caused by the throwing of a stone, or by the force of the wind, should rather be called a shiver than a movement of the water. And of this you may persuade yourself by throwing a straw into the widening rings of wavelets, and watching how it rises and falls, but does not leave its place."

This experiment with the straw reminded him of a similar test which he had applied when studying the waves of sound. He mused—

"The striking of a bell will induce a slight quiver and a low resonance in a neighbouring bell; a note sounded on a lute will awake the same note in a lute by its side; and a straw laid upon the string which produces that note will show its vibration."

The soul of the student was greatly stirred; he divined some connection, a whole world of undiscovered knowledge, between the two oscillating straws; the one trembling on the surface of the waves, the other quivering on the vibrating string. And an idea, swift as lightning, flashed across his mind.

"The mechanical law is the same in the two cases! Like the waves on the water when a stone drops into it, so the waves of sound widen in the air, intersecting others, but not mingling with them, keeping their own centre in the place of their origin. What, then, of light? As an echo is the reproduction of a sound, the reflection in a mirror is an echo of light. There is but one mechanical law in all the phenomena of physical force; there is but one will; and this will is thy justice, O Prime Mover! the angle of incidence must be equal to the angle of reflection."

His face pale, his eyes burning with enthusiasm, Leonardo felt that once again, and this time more certainly than before, he was about to sound an abyss into which no man had looked before. He knew that this discovery, if confirmed by experiment, was the greatest mechanical discovery since the days of Archimedes. Two months ago, when he had heard that Vasco di Gama had doubled the Cape of Good Hope and discovered a new route to India, Leonardo had envied him, but now he had made a greater discovery than di Gama or Columbus; he had sighted more mysterious expanses, and no less than they had found a new heaven and a new earth.

But through the wall there reached his ears the groans and the ravings of the sufferer. He listened, and remembered his mechanics, the senseless destruction of the Colossus, the inevitable ruin of the *Cenacolo*, Astro's foolish and horrible fall; and asked himself:—

"Will this discovery be lost as completely, as ignominiously as all else which I have done? Will no man heed my voice? shall I ever be solitary as now? here alone in the darkness, underground, as if buried alive? I who have dreamed of wings!" After a short pause, he added; "Be it so! Darkness, and silence, and oblivion, and none to know what I have done! *I* know it!"

And indomitable pride, a sense of inalienable victory and strength filled his soul, as if the wings to which he had aspired were already lifting him above the earth.

The subterranean chamber suddenly became too strait for him; he felt stifled, and the longing was irresistible to behold the sky, and the open country. He left the house, and walked swiftly towards the cathedral.

VIII

THE NIGHT WAS MOONLIT, SERENE, and warm; from the conflagration sullen flames still glowed, and smoky spirals still rose into the sky.

The crowd increased as he drew nearer to the centre of the town. The blue rays of the moon, the scarlet glare of the torches, illuminated faces haggard with excitement, seamed with anxiety, and played on the white banner with the scarlet cross which had been used by the ancient Milanese Commune, on lantern-poles, arquebuses, pistols, clubs, halberts, scythes, pitchforks, stakes, all pressed into service against the foreigner. The people swarmed like ants, the tocsin pealed, the guns roared. From the fortress the French were firing down the street, and their boast was that they would not leave one stone upon another within the city walls. Louder than the bells, more piercing than the booming of the cannon, rose the incessant yell of the citizens; "Death to the French! Death to the foreigners! Down with the king! *Viva Il Moro!*"

To Leonardo it gave the impression of a wild and hideous dream. Near the eastern gate, a drummer from Picardy, a boy of sixteen, was being hanged, Mascarello the goldsmith playing the part of executioner. Flinging the rope round the lad's neck, and tapping him lightly on the head, he cried with ribald solemnity:—

"In the name of the Father, the Son, and the Holy Ghost, we dub this servant of God, this Frenchman, Saltamacchia, Knight of the Hempen Necklace."

"Amen!" responded the crowd.

The little drummer, ill understanding his danger, half smiling, blinking his eyes like a child about to cry, shrank into himself, twisting his neck that he might ease the noose. Then suddenly, as if awaking from a lethargy, he turned his beautiful but white and trembling face to the crowd, and would have attempted entreaty. His voice was drowned by howls and derisive laughter, and he gave up the attempt, holding his peace with the forlorn air of a resigned and innocent victim, and kissing a little cross, the gift of his mother or sister, which he had worn on a blue ribbon round his neck. Then Mascarello swung him into the void, with the jeer; "Courage, Knight of the Necklace! Show us how you dance the French *gaillard*!"

And, mid the laughter of the crowd, the child's body shuddered horribly, and was convulsed in the spasms of death, as if indeed it were dancing.

Leonardo walked on, and presently he saw a woman, dressed in rags, kneeling before a miserable half-ruined hovel, and stretching out thin bare arms to the passersby.

"Help; Help! Help!" she cried incessantly.

Corbolo the shoemaker, running up, asked what ailed her.

"My baby! My baby! He was sleeping, so pretty in his little bed! He has fallen through the floor! Perhaps he is still alive! Oh, save him! Try and save him! *Help!*"

Just then a cannon-ball, rending the air with a shriek, struck the roof of the hovel. The beams cracked, dust rose in a column, the roof fell, the walls crumbled, and the woman was forever silenced.

Again Leonardo moved on, and presently he reached the Palazzo del Comune. Here, in front of the Loggia degli Osii, an university student was haranguing the crowd, descanting on the ancient glory of the Milanese, and exhorting the people to annihilate all tyrants, and establish the reign of equality. His hearers, however, seemed hard of persuasion.

"Citizens!" he cried, brandishing the knife which on ordinary occasions served him for mending pens, slicing sausages, and cutting his sweetheart's name on the bark of trees, but which now he had christened "the Poniard of Nemesis," "Citizens! the hour has come in which we must die for Liberty! We will wash our hands in the blood of the tyrants; in their breasts we will plunge this Poniard of Nemesis. *Viva la Repubblica!*"

"Folly!" cried voices from the audience. "We know the wine of your vintage! We know the liberty you would give us, you spy, traitor, dog of a Frenchman! To the devil with you and your republic! *Viva Il Moro!* Death to all enemies of the duke!"

The orator continued to prate, enforcing his doctrine by instances from Cicero and Tacitus, but the mob overthrew his bench, knocked him down and beat him, shouting:—

"Here's for your Liberty! Here's for your Republic! Here's for inflaming fools against their legitimate ruler!"

Leonardo stood for a minute in the Piazza dell' Arengo to admire the imposing pile of the cathedral—that marble forest of pinnacles and towers, fantastic in the double light, blue rays of the moon and crimson flare of torches. In front of the archbishop's palace the press was so great that there was scarce standing-room, and from the centre of the throng came groans and ferocious howls.

"What has happened?" asked the painter of an old workman, whose gentle dignified face was blanched with horror.

"Who can understand? They themselves know neither what they want nor what they do. They are accusing Messer Jacopo Crotta of selling poisoned flour, and of being a French spy! *O Dio! Dio!* It is a lie! But they fall on the first man they meet, and listen to none! 'Tis horrible, 'tis most horrible! Lord Jesus, have mercy on us, wretched sinners!"

Just then Gorgoglio the glass-blower detached himself from the dense pack of human bodies, holding aloft a bloody human head stuck on a pole; and Farfannicchio, the madcap of the streets, danced round it, screaming and yelling.

"Down with the traitors! down with the foreigners! Death to the devils of Frenchmen!"

"*A furore populi, libera nos, Domine!*" murmured the old workman, crossing himself.

From the castle came an incessant sound of trumpets, drums, explosions of cannon, crackling of guns, cries of soldiers. The monster bombard, called by the French *Margot la Folle*, and by the Germans *die tolle Grete*, was fired; the earth shook, it seemed that the whole town must crash into ruins. The bomb fell beyond the Borgonuovo, and set fire to a house; pillars of flame rose into the quiet moonlit sky, and the piazza was lit with a crimson glare. The people hurried hither and thither, jostling, pushing, trampling each other like black shadows, like living phantoms.

Leonardo stood watching the wild scene, noting every detail, his mind preoccupied. The fiery glow, the voices of the crowd, the pealing of the bells, the boom of the guns, all brought back his discovery. Imagination pictured the waves of sound, the waves of light swelling tranquilly, circling outwards like the ripple on water where a stone has fallen, intersecting each other without mingling or confusion, each keeping its own centre in the point of its origin. Great gladness filled his soul as he thought that never at anytime could men interrupt the harmonious play of these ordered waves, nor the mechanical law which rules them, the unchanging fiat of their creator, the rule of divine justice, making the angle of incidence equal to the angle of reflection.

In his soul re-echoed—

"O wondrous justice of thee, thou Prime Mover! No force hast thou permitted to lack the order and the quality of its necessary effect!"

In the frenzied crowd, the soul of the artist preserved the eternal calm of contemplation; even as the blue rays of the moon shone with heavenly effulgence supreme over glare of torches and flames of conflagration and war.

On a certain morning in February 1500, Ludovico Sforza, Il Moro, re-entered Milan by the Porta Nuova. Leonardo had started the previous night for Vaprio, his friend Melzi's villa.

IX

Girolamo Melzi had once belonged to the court of the Sforzas, but on the death of his young wife in 1494 he had retired to his lonely villa at the foot of the Alps, a few hours' journey from Milan. Far from the noise of the world, he lived the life of a philosopher, gardening with his own hands, and devoting himself to music and to the study of the occult sciences. Some said he was an adept in black magic, accustomed to call up the shade of his lost wife from the lower world. The mathematician, Fra Luca Pacioli, and Sacrobosco, the alchemist, often visited him, and whole nights were spent in argument about Plato's ideas, and the laws of the Pythagorean numbers which governed the music of the spheres. But Melzi found his chief pleasure in the visits of Leonardo, which were not infrequent, as the works on the Martesana Canal often brought him to the vicinity.

Vaprio was situated on the left bank of the Adda; and the canal, skirting the villa garden, ran for a certain distance parallel to the river, the course of which was just here obstructed by rapids. All day the roar of the cataract made itself heard, loud as the billows of the sea surf. Free, wild, storm-tossed, untamed by man, the Adda hurled its green waves between winding precipitous banks of yellow sandstone. By its side, the same cold, green, mountain water swam noiselessly by within the straight-drawn confines of the canal; smooth as a mirror, calm, slow, submissive and subdued. The contrast delighted Leonardo, and seemed to him of pregnant meaning. Which of the two streams was the more beautiful—the Martesana, his own creation, the work of human intelligence and will, or its elder sister, the foaming Adda, savage, threatening, superb in its untrammelled freedom? He understood each, sympathised with each, and loved them with equal love.

From the upper terrace of the villa garden was a wide prospect of the immense Lombard plain, one vast and smiling garden. In the summer the fields were rank with verdure; hay scented the air; the wheat and the maize grew so tall as to overtop the vines; ears of corn kissed the pears and the apples, the cherries and the plums. The hills of Como rose dark towards the north; above them towered the first spurs of the Alps; higher still the snow-clad summits glowed in the sunset gold.

Fra Luca and Messer Galeotto Sacrobosco, whose cottage by the Porta Vercellina had been destroyed by the French, were both at the villa when Leonardo arrived; but he kept himself apart, preferring solitude. He conceived, however, a great fondness for the company of Francesco, his host's little son.

Timid and shy as a girl, the boy at first stood in great awe of the painter; one day, however, he came into his room at a moment when Leonardo, studying the laws of colour, was experimenting with coloured glass. He pleased the child by letting him look through the different pieces, yellow, blue, purple, or green, which gave a fairy aspect to familiar objects, and made the world seem now smiling, now frowning, according to the colour of the glass. Another of Leonardo's inventions proved very attractive. This was the "Camera obscura," by means of which living pictures appeared on a sheet of white paper; and Francesco saw the turning of the mill-wheel, the swallows circling round the church, the woodcutter's grey donkey with his load of faggots stepping daintily along the miry road while the poplars bowed their heads under the breeze. Still more fascinating was the weather-gauge: a copper ring, a small stick like the beam of a balance, and two little balls, the one covered with wax, the other with wadding. When the air was saturated with moisture the wadding grew heavy, and the little ball, falling down, inclined the beam till it touched one or other of the divisions marked on the copper ring. The degree of damp could thus be accurately measured, and the weather predicted for two or three days. The little boy constructed a similar apparatus for himself and was jubilant when the prophecies were fulfilled which he had deduced from its variations. Francesco went to the village school where he was taught by the old prior of the neighbour convent. The dog-eared Latin grammar and arithmetic primer were odious to him, and he learned but slackly. Leonardo's lore was of a new sort, pleasant to the child as a fairy tale. The instruments for the study of optics, acoustics, hydraulics, were to him new and magical toys, nor was he ever tired of hearing the painter's talk. Fearing ridicule or suspicion, Leonardo spoke but cautiously with adults; to Francesco he talked with the utmost frankness and simplicity. He not only taught the child, but learned of him. Paraphrasing the text of Holy Writ, he told himself—"Except ye be converted and become as little children, ye shall not enter into the kingdom of knowledge."

It was at this time that he was writing his *Book of the Stars*. On March evenings, when in the still chilly air there was a waft of spring, he would stand on the roof with Francesco, watching the tide of stars and sketching the spots on the face of the moon. Then rolling a piece of paper into an inverted cone, he bade the child look through the aperture at the end, and Francesco saw the stars robbed of their rays, and like bright, round, infinitely minute globules.

"Those globules," said Leonardo, "are of great size, many of them a hundred, nay, a thousand times larger than our earth, which, however, is not less beautiful nor more contemptible than they. The mechanical laws which obtain in our world, and which have been discovered by human sagacity, guide also those stars and suns."

"What is there beyond the stars?" murmured the child.

"More stars, Francesco; worlds which we cannot see."

"And beyond those?"

"Yet others."

"But at the end, at the very end?"

"There is no end."

"No end," cried the boy, and Leonardo felt the trembling of the little hand within his own. The child's face had grown pale.

"Then where—where," he said slowly, "where is Paradise, Messer Leonardo, and the angels, and the saints, and the Madonna, and God the Father who sits upon the throne with God the Son and the Holy Spirit?"

The teacher would have liked to answer that God was everywhere; in the grain of sand no less than in the celestial globe; in the hearts of men no less than in the outside universe. But fearing to disturb the simple faith of the little one he held his peace.

With the first budding of the trees, the painter and the child spent whole days together in the garden or in the neighbouring woods watching the reviving of life in the vegetable world. Sometimes Leonardo would draw a flower or tree, trying to seize the living likeness as in the portrait of a man; that unique particular aspect of his model which would never be repeated. He taught Francesco how the rings seen in the wood of the trunk reveal the age of the tree; and how the thickness of each ring shows the amount of moisture in the year when it was formed; how the core of the trunk is always on the southern side, which has had the most of the sun's heat. He told how in the spring-time the sap, gathering between the inner green of the trunk and the outer bark, thickens and expands and bursts the bark; how, if a branch is cut, the vital power draws an abundance of nutritive juices to the wounded place, so that the bark thickens and the wound is healed; yet its mark remains because the abundance of the nutritive juices has been too great, and has overflowed and made lumps and knots. Always he spoke of nature dryly and with apparent frigidity, seeking only scientific accuracy. With passionless exactitude he defined the tender details of the action of the spring upon the life of plants, as he would have spoken of the performance of a machine. He showed from abstract mathematics the wonderful laws which shape the needles of pine-trees and the facets of crystals. Yet for all his coldness and impartiality, the child discerned his love for all living things, for the withered leaf no less than for the mighty boughs which spread suppliant arms to their great lord, the sun. At times, in the depth of the forest, he would pause and note smilingly how under last year's withered leaves still hanging on the branches, green shoots were sprouting to oust them from their place; how the bee, weak from her winter torpor, could scarce crawl into the snowdrop's cup. In the great stillness Francesco could hear the beating of his friend's iron heart; timidly he would raise his eyes to the Master. The sun shining athwart the branches lit up his long curling hair, flowing beard, and overhanging brows, and surrounded his head with a halo: he seemed like Pan himself who listens to the growing of the grass, the murmuring of spring below the earth, the mystical forces of awakening life. To Leonardo all things lived. The world was one great body, like the body of man, who himself is a little world. In the dewdrops he saw the similitude of the watery sphere which surrounds the earth. The cataracts of the Adda near Trezzo gave him occasion to study the cascades and whirlpools of rivers which he compared to the twisting of a woman's curls. Mysterious resemblances attracted him, concords in nature's harmony like voices answering each other from distant worlds. Inquiring into the origin of the rainbow, he noted that the same prismatic colour is seen in the plumage of birds, precious stones, in the scum on stagnant water, in old dulled glass. In the patterns on frosted window-panes, he found a resemblance to living leaves and flowers, as if nature in this world of frozen crystal had seen prophetic visions of the coming spring. At times he felt himself drawing near new realms of knowledge, perhaps to be entered only by men of ages to come. He used to say about the attractive powers of amber:—

"I see not the mode by which the human mind shall apprehend the mystery. These powers of the magnet and the amber are among those occult forces which are as yet unrevealed."

And further—

"The world is full of countless possibilities of which yet there has been no experience."

One day, a certain Messer Guidotto Prestinari, a poet from Bergamo, came to the villa. Offended with Leonardo, who did not sufficiently praise his verses, he began a discussion on the comparative excellence of poetry and painting. Leonardo spoke little, but the fury with which Messer Guidotto assailed his art at last amused him and he said, half jesting:—

"Painting is higher than poetry, inasmuch as it reproduces the eternal works of God and not human inventions, to which the poets, at least of our day, are too apt to confine themselves. They depict not, but describe, borrowing all they have and trading with each other's wares. They but put together and combine the refuse of knowledge. They may be compared to the receivers of stolen goods. . ."

Fra Luca, Messer Galeotto, and Melzi himself cried out; but Leonardo had now warmed to the subject and cried:—

"The eye gives a more complete knowledge of nature than the ear! Things seen are less to be doubted than things heard. Painting, which is silent poetry, comes nearer to positive science than poetry, which is invisible painting. Words give but a series of isolated images following one another; but in a picture, all the forms, all the colours appear synchronously, and are blended into a whole, like the notes of a chord in music; and thus both to painting and to music a more complex harmony is possible than to poetry. And the richer the harmony, the richer is that delight which is the aim and the enchantment of art. Question, say, any lover, whether he would not rather have a portrait of his loved one than a description in words of her countenance, though it were composed by the greatest of poets?"

This argument provoked a smile, and presently Leonardo continued:—

"Hear a narrative from my own experience. A certain Florentine youth fell into such a longing for the face of a woman whom I had painted in one of my sacred pictures, that, having bought it, he cancelled all the signs of its religious character, so that he might kiss his adored one without fear or scruple. But soon the voice of conscience overcame the passion of love, nor could he recover his tranquillity of mind till he had removed the picture from his dwelling. Think ye, O poets, that with your words you could rouse a man to like vehemence of desire? Believe me, Messeri, I speak not of myself, for I know how greatly I fall short, but of that painter who attains to the perfection of his art. He is no longer a man; rapt in the contemplation of divine and eternal beauty, or turned to the study of monstrous forms, grotesque, pathetic, terrible, he can comprehend and give shape to all; he is a sovereign—a god."

Many such ideas Leonardo had inscribed in his note-books; and Fra Luca urged him to order his manuscripts and give them to the public. He even offered to find him an editor. Leonardo, however, refused, and remained firm in his resolution that he would publish nothing. Yet all his writings were couched in the form of address to a reader; and at the commencement of one of his diaries he apologised in these words for the disconnected style and frequent repetitions:—

"Blame me not, O reader, for the subjects are numberless and my memory is weak, and I write at long intervals in different years."

XI

In the last days of March disquieting tidings reached the Villa Melzi. The French army, led by Monsieur de la Trémouille, had crossed the Alps and was descending for the reconquest of Milan. Il Moro, suspicious of all, and oppressed by superstitious fears, dared not meet the enemy in the open field, and daily showed himself *più pauroso d'una donniccuola*, "more panic-stricken than a silly girl."

But at the villa news of the great world seemed but a faint and far off hum. Careless of duke and king, Leonardo roamed the neighbouring hills and glens and woods, accompanied only by the little Francesco. Sometimes they ascended the river to its source among the pine-clad mountains; and there they hired workmen and made excavations, seeking fossil shells and plants.

One evening, wearied by a long day's march, they rested under an old lime-tree, overhanging the steep bank of the Adda. The unbounded plain, with its long rows of wayside poplars, lay stretched at their feet. The white houses of Bergamo shone in the evening sunlight: the snowy mountain-tops seemed to float in the air. All the sky was clear, save that in the far distance, almost on the horizon, between Treviglio, Brignano, and Castel Rozzone, there suddenly appeared a light cloud of smoke.

"What is it?" asked Francesco.

"I know not. It may be a battle. I see what may be fire, and think I hear the sound of cannon. It may be a skirmish between our folk and the French."

Latterly, such chance encounters had not been infrequent. They watched the cloud silently for a few minutes, then turned their attention to the fruit of their day's digging. The master picked up a large bone, sharp as a needle, the fin of some primeval fish.

"How many kings, how many nations has not time destroyed since this creature fell on its sleep in that great cavern, where today we have found it? How many thousands of years has the world seen, what changes have taken place, while it was lying hid, concealed from all eyes, supporting heavy masses of earth with its bare skeleton?"

He made a large gesture with his hand, as if to embrace the verdant plain stretched at their feet; then continued:—

"All that you see, Francesco, was once the bed of an ocean which covered the chief parts of Europe, Africa, and Asia; the summits of the Apennines were islands in a great sea, and fishes swam in these fields of singing birds."

He interrupted himself, and they looked once more at the distant smoke-drift, and the flashes of fire from the cannon, so insignificant in the boundless expanse, which lay all peaceful and rose-tinted in the sunset glow. It was hard to believe that a fight was taking place, and that men were killing each other almost within range of their eyesight. More vivid to Francesco were the birds flying to roost, the fish of that forgotten sea. Neither spoke, but at that moment the painter and the child had the same thought:—

"'Tis a small matter whether the Lombards prevail or the Frenchmen; Ludovico the duke, or Louis the foreign king; our own people or the strangers. Country, glory, war, the strife of policy, the fall of thrones, the upheaval of nations, all that to man seems great or terrible—all are no more than yonder little cloud of smoke, melting into the peaceful twilight, dissolving in the immutable serenity of Nature."

XII

It was at Vaprio that Leonardo finished a picture begun long ago at Florence. In a cavern, surrounded by great rocks, the Mother of God was folding one arm round the infant John the Baptist, with the other clasping her Son, as if she desired to unite the Human and the Divine in the indissoluble embrace of a single love. John, devoutly joining his little hands, bent his knee before Jesus, who blessed him with two fingers raised. The attitude of the infant Saviour, sitting naked on the naked earth, one plump dimpled leg tucked under the other, while he leaned on a plump hand, all its fingers outspread upon the sand—suggested the baby still unable to walk; yet already on his face, perfect wisdom was blent with the simplicity of infancy. A kneeling angel supporting the little Jesus, and pointing at the Precursor, turned to the spectator a face instinct with mournful foreboding, yet illumined by a strange and tender smile. Behind the rocks a pale sun shone through drizzling rain, and blue mountains rose into the sky, their sharp peaks weird and unearthly; the rocks, smoothed and polished as if by the action of salt water, suggested some dried-up ocean bed; and in the cavern was most profound shadow, almost concealing a bubbling spring, leaves of water-plants, pale dim cups of purple iris-flowers. One could fancy slow tricklings and droppings from the overhanging arch of black dolomite; and the creeping weeds and grasses were heavy with the continuous ooze of the ground and the damp saturation of the air. The face of the Madonna alone shone with the delicate brilliance of alabaster within which glows a light. Queen of Heaven, she was shown to men in the gloom of twilight, in a subterranean cavern, in the most secret of the recesses of nature, perhaps the last refuge of ancient Pan and the wood nymphs—she, the mystery of mysteries, the mother of the God-man, in the very bosom of mother earth.

It was the creation at once of a great artist and of a great student; the play of light and of shadow, the laws of vegetable life, the anatomy of the human body, the science of drapery, the spirals of a woman's curls (which he had compared to the circling of a whirlpool), all that the natural philosopher had searched into with "unrelenting severity," had measured with mathematical accuracy, had dissected as one dissects a corpse—all this the artist had recombined into a new creation, living beauty, a silent melody; into a mystic hymn to the Holy Virgin, the Mother of God. With knowledge equalled by love he had depicted the veins in the iris petals, the dimples in the baby's elbow, the ancient cleft in the dolomite rock, the quiver of the water in the secret spring; the quiver of infinite grief in the angel's smile. He knew all and loved all. Great love is the daughter of great knowledge.

XIII

One day the alchemist, Messer Galeotto Sacrobosco, undertook to experiment with the "Rod of Mercury," under which name were known all those staves of myrtle, almond, tamarind, or other "astrological" woods, which were supposed to have a kinship with metals, and the property of discovering veins of gold, silver, and copper in the rocks. Accompanied by Messer Gerolamo, he went to the east side of the lake of Lecco, known to be rich in ores; and Leonardo joined the company, though he had no faith in the "Rod of Mercury," and mocked at it no less than at the other delusions of the alchemists.

Near the village of Mandello, at the foot of Monte Campione, there was an abandoned iron mine. Some years before the ground had fallen in and buried a number of the miners; and it was reported that sulphurous exhalations rose from a rent in the lowest depths of the mine, into which, if a stone were thrown, it fell, and fell, and fell, but was never heard to strike the bottom, for the sufficient reason that the pit was bottomless. Leonardo's curiosity was excited by these tales, and he determined to explore the mine while his companions were busied with the magic rod. Not without difficulty, for the peasants believed the mine to be the dwelling-place of a devil, he obtained the services of an old man as guide. A subterranean passage, very steep and dark, and with broken and slippery stairs, led to the central shaft. The guide walked stolidly in front with a lantern, and Leonardo followed, carrying Francesco, who had insisted on accompanying his friend. They descended more than two hundred steps, and were still going down, the passage becoming ever narrower and more steep. A stifling smell of subterranean damp assailed the nostrils. Leonardo struck the wall with a spade, listened to the sound it made, and examined the piece of rock he had detached, the nature and layers of the soil, and the bright mica sparkling in the veins of granite.

He felt the child clinging to him very tightly, and he asked with a smile whether his little comrade were afraid.

"With you, I am never afraid," said Francesco; presently he added shyly, "is it true what my *babbo* says, that you are going to leave us?"

"Yes, Francesco."

"Where are you going?"

"To Romagna; to the Duke Valentino."

"Is it very far?"

"Several days' journey."

"Several days!" sighed Francesco; "then shall we never see you again?"

"Why not? The first minute I can, I will come and see you."

The boy became thoughtful. Squeezing Leonardo's neck tightly with his two arms, he cried:—

"Take me with you! Oh, Messer Leonardo, take me with you."

"Alack, my child! How is it possible? There is war there."

"I don't care for the war. Have I not said that with you I am never afraid? Even if it be more fearsome than it is in this place where we are now, I shall not be afraid. I will be your servant, brush your clothes, carry hay to your horses; and I will seek shells for you, and make you drawings of leaves. Did you not say to me I drew them well? I will do everything like a man. I will obey you in whatever you command. Take me with you, Messer Leonardo!"

"And how about Messer Gerolamo? Would he consent?"

"He will consent if I cry for it. And if he doesn't consent, then I will run away. Say you will take me with you! Say it!"

"No, Francesco; it is idle talk. I know thou would'st not leave thy father. He grows old, and thou must have a fondness for him."

"Of a surety I have a fondness for him. But for you, too, Messer Leonardo! You think me very little, but truly I comprehend everything. Aunt Bona says you are a sorcerer, and Don Lorenzo, my schoolmaster, says it likewise, and that you are wicked, and that with you I shall lose my soul. But when he speaks ill of you, I answer him in such wise that he comes near beating me."

Suddenly Francesco's eyes filled and the corners of his lips drooped.

"I understand," he said; "I understand why you don't want me. You don't love me. And I—." He burst into tears.

"Hush! hush! Thou should'st cry shame to weep! Hearken to what I tell thee. In a few years, when thou art grown, then I will take thee for my disciple, and keep thee always at my side."

The child raised his eyes, tears still trembling on their long lashes.

"But do you mean it? or is it said to comfort me, and afterwards will you forget?"

"No, Francesco, I promise."

"You promise? And how long must I wait?"

"Eight or nine years; till thou art at the least fifteen."

"Eight years," sighed the child, reckoning on his fingers "and I shall be always with you?"

"Unless we die."

"Eight years! Well, if you say it, it is certain."

Francesco smiled, and rubbed his cheek against Leonardo's with a pretty gesture peculiar to himself.

"Messer Leonardo, once I dreamed I was in the dark, going down a long, long stair like this one, only it had no beginning and no end. But I was not frightened, for someone was carrying me. I thought it was my mother, who died ere ever I saw her; but now I know it was you. I am as happy with you as if I was with her."

Leonardo looked at the child with inexpressible tenderness. The innocent eyes shone; he put out his bright lips as confidingly as to a mother, and when Leonardo kissed them he felt the child was giving him his soul. Thus, with the little heart beating against his own, he descended with firm steps into the subterranean night.

XIV

Upon their return to Vaprio they found alarm in the villa; the French were approaching. Louis, furious at the revolt of the Milanese, had given their city over to pillage. Many of the inhabitants fled to the mountains. Along the road was an endless procession of carts laden with household stuff, and of weeping women dragging children by the hand. At night, from the top windows of the villa, flames were still seen citywards. At Novara a battle was daily expected which should decide the fate of Lombardy.

At last Fra Luca brought news of the sad event which had ended the war. The battle was ordered on the 10th of April, but when the duke was reviewing his forces, prior to its commencement, the Swiss mercenaries refused to advance, for they had been secretly bought by Trivulzio. In vain Il Moro conjured them with tears not to bring him to ruin, and promised them extravagant reward in recompense for fidelity. They remained obdurate.

Then Ludovico, disguised as a monk, sought to flee; but a Swiss named Schattenhalb betrayed him to the French captains. He was seized and carried before the marshal, who rewarded the Swiss with thirty pieces of silver.

The Sire de la Trémouille had charge of the prisoner to escort him to France. He, who, in the words of the court poet, "first after God had guided the wheel of Fortune," was placed in a barred cage and carried in a cart, like a trapped wild beast. The duke asked one favour of his captors, that he might carry a copy of the *Divina Commedia* with him into his exile, "*per istudiari*."

Life at the Villa Melzi became daily more perilous. The French had sacked Lomellina. The Venetians had destroyed the Martesana. Robbers roamed in the neighbourhood of Vaprio; already Messer Gerolamo Melzi was preparing to carry Francesco and Aunt Bona into refuge at Chiavenna.

Leonardo's last night came; he inscribed in his diary the thoughts of the day:—

"A bird having little tail but broad wings, flaps them with great violence, and turns *so that the wind may blow under them* and raise her *aloft*. This I observed watching a young hawk above the canonry of Vaprio, on the road to Bergamo, today, April 14th."

And in the margin he added incidentally; "Il Moro has lost his state, his goods, and his liberty; not one of his undertakings will be achieved by himself."

The overthrow of the great house of Sforza, the ruin of the man he had served for sixteen years, were to him of far less interest than the flight of a bird of prey.

Book XI

There Shall Be Wings—1500

"Piglierà il prima volo il grande ucello sopra del dosso del suo magno Cecero, empiendo l'universo del stupore, empiendo di sua fama tutte le scritture, e gloria eterna al nido dove nacque."

—Leonardo Da Vinci

(The human bird shall take his first flight, filling the world with amazement, all writings with his fame, and bringing eternal glory to the nest whence he sprang.)

I

The little town of Vinci, Leonardo's native place, lay on the western slope of Monte Albano, in Tuscany, between Florence and Pisa, and not far from Empoli. There he had an uncle, Ser Francesco da Vinci, who had amassed wealth in the silk industry, and who, unlike the rest of the family, was friendly to his nephew. Before journeying to Romagna the painter proposed to visit Ser Francesco, and if possible to leave Astro in his charge, the unfortunate smith not yet having recovered from the effects of his fall. Leonardo hoped that the mountain air, with quiet and rest, might accomplish more for him than the drugs and experimental surgery of ignorant physicians. The artist, who had been in Florence for a few days, journeyed to Vinci alone, riding a mule. He left the town by the Porta a Prato, and took his way along the banks of the Arno; at Empoli he left the high road and followed a narrow and winding mountain path. The day had been clouded and cool; at evening the sun set in a bank of mist which foreboded a north wind. The prospect on either side continually widened; the hills became higher; and though their undulations were still gentle, they gave promise of higher mountains behind. The ground was carpeted with scanty herbage of a dull green; and the fields, with fallow stripes of brown earth, the stone walls, the grey olives were all dull and whitish in tone, suggestive of the calm, the simplicity, the poverty of the north. Here and there in the distance, beside some solitary chapel or farmhouse with yellow walls and barred windows, dark pointed cypresses, such as may be seen in the pictures by early Florentine masters, rose against quiet hills and an even background of clear, delicately gradated sky.

The path became gradually steeper, the air fresher and more invigorating. Sant' Ausano, Calistri, Lucardi, and the Chapel of San Giovanni were already past. Now the day closed, and one by one the stars came out in the blue sky, from which the clouds had disappeared. The wind freshened; the *tramontana*, that piercing wind from the Alps, was beginning to blow. Every appearance of the lowlands had vanished; as the plain had passed into hills, so now the hills passed into mountains. Quite suddenly, at a turn of the road, Vinci came in sight, a little, crowded, stone-built town, clustering round the black tower of its ancient castle, clinging to the rock, crowning the peaked summit of a low but sharply precipitous hill. Lights were gleaming in the windows of the houses.

At the cross-roads near the foot of the hill there was a little shrine known to Leonardo from his earliest childhood; a clay image of the Virgin glazed in blue and white, before which a lamp burned continually. As he passed he saw a woman kneeling, bowed together dejectedly, covering her face with her hands, a poor peasant woman, in a thin dark dress, torn and weather-stained.

"Caterina!" murmured Leonardo. It was his mother's name; she too had prayed here, a poor peasant.

After crossing the swift mountain stream, the path turned to the right between garden walls overgrown with weeds. Here it was quite dark, and the traveller did not see the rose-branch which kissed his face as he passed, and scented the air with balm. He dismounted at an ancient wooden door let into the wall, and knocked with a stone on the iron cramp. It was the house which had belonged to Leonardo's grandfather, and from him had passed to Ser Francesco. The painter himself had spent his childhood within its walls. No one answered the knock, nor was there for a long time any sound but the rushing of the mill-stream, and presently the quavering bark of an old watch-dog.

An old man came out, very much bowed and wrinkled, with silvery hair. He carried a lantern, and was very deaf and rather stupid, so that it took him time to understand who Leonardo was.

However, when at last he recognised him whom he had carried in his arms forty years earlier, he burst into tears of joy, dropped his lantern, and, stooping over the painter's hand, mumbled it with his lips, sobbing out:—

"*O Signore! Signore! Leonardo mio!*"—while the dog wagged his tail to please the old gardener, pretending that he clearly comprehended what was taking place. Gian Battista, the old man, explained that Ser Francesco was away at Marcigliano, where a monk of his acquaintance had promised a drug to cure him of the stomach-ache; he would not be home for two days. Leonardo determined, however, to wait for him; more especially because next day Boltraffio was to bring up Zoroastro from Florence.

The old man ushered the visitor into the house, and bade his granddaughter, a pretty fair-haired girl of sixteen, to prepare supper. Leonardo declined anything but bread, home-grown wine, and iron-water from the spring on the property. Ser Francesco, though well-to-do, continued the hardy, simple style of living which had been a necessity to his forefathers, and his house was anything but luxurious.

Leonardo entered the familiar apartment, at once kitchen and parlour, where the few clumsy chairs, settles, and chests had become smooth and polished with age; a dresser carried heavy pewter dinner-plates, and medicinal herbs were hanging from the beams of the raftered ceiling. The walls were whitewashed, and quite bare; there was a brick floor, and an immense fireplace begrimed with soot.

All this was as Leonardo remembered it, but there was one innovation; thick dull green glass had been inserted in the window-panes, formerly covered only with oiled cloth, causing twilight in the room on the brightest day. Upstairs, in the sleeping rooms, the windows were protected by wooden shutters, which did not fit close enough to keep out the cold.

The gardener made a fire of fragrant juniper and mountain heather, and lit a hanging earthenware lamp, in shape much like the lamps found in Etruscan tombs. In this remote corner of Tuscany the furniture, the customs, even the language had preserved traces of immemorial antiquity. While the young girl was preparing the supper of wine, bread, and a lettuce salad, Leonardo mounted to the upper rooms, where little had been changed since his last visit. He saw the same immense four-poster bed, in which his grandmother had sometimes permitted him to sleep, and which had now passed, with the other heirlooms, to his uncle Francesco. On the wall hung the well-remembered crucifix, the image of the Madonna, the shell for holy water, a bunch of dried grass, called *nebbia*, and a book of Latin prayers in cursive script, written on paper deeply yellowed by time.

Returning to the parlour, he sat in the chimney-corner, drank from a wooden cup with a pleasant scent of olive-wood, and remaining in the room alone, after Gian and his grand-daughter had gone to bed, abandoned himself to happy recollections.

II

He thought of his father, Ser Piero da Vinci, the notary of the Florentine Commune, a man of seventy, white-haired, but still vigorous, whom he had seen a few days ago at Florence, in his house in the Via Ghibellina. No one had ever loved life better than Ser Piero, with a love simple and unabashed. He had cherished a great tenderness for his first-born, but his legitimate sons, Antonio and Giuliano, fearing lest their father should alienate part of his patrimony in favour of the bastard, had done all in their power to induce bad blood between them.

Leonardo now felt himself a stranger in his father's house. His youngest half-brother, Antonio, was more especially prejudiced against him on account of his supposed atheism, for Antonio was one of the Piagnoni, a zealous and rigid follower of Savonarola, and also a conventional, virtuous, and money-loving trader of the guild of the woolstaplers. Antonio often addressed his half-brother on the subject of the Christian faith, the need for repentance, the heresies of the philosophical thinkers of the day, and he had given him a book compiled by himself, a *Manual of the Art of Saving the Soul*. Leonardo carried this book in his pocket, and now, seated in his uncle's chimney-corner, he drew it forth. It was a little volume, written in the small laborious hand which befitted a merchant's office.

"The book of confession compiled by me, Antonio di Ser Pietro da Vinci, a Florentine, sent to Nanna, my sister-in-law; most useful to all who desire to confess their sins."

For Leonardo, his brother's book breathed the air of conventional and bourgeois piety, which had weighed upon his childhood, and had been an inheritance in his family. A century before his birth the founders of the house of Vinci were just as prudent, just as avaricious, just as pious servants of the Florentine Commune as was now Ser Pietro, his father. Their name appeared first in a writing of 1339, where mention was made of one Michele da Vinci, a notary. Leonardo imagined him like Antonio, his well-remembered grandfather. Antonio instructed his sons to aspire to nothing over high, not to fame, nor to honours, nor to public office, civil or military, nor to exceptional wealth, nor to exceptional learning.

"*Starsi mezzanamente è cosa più sicura*," "'Tis safest to keep the mean," was his constant saw; and Leonardo remembered the gravity and calm assurance with which he enunciated this infallible rule.

After thirty years' absence, sitting under the roof of his grandfather's house, listening to the moaning wind and watching the logs burning in the fireplace, Leonardo thought how his own life had been one long breach of this "ant and spider" policy; had been an exuberant blossoming which, according to his brother Antonio, temperance should have measured with compasses and shorn away with iron shears.

III

Next morning, before the old gardener was awake, Leonardo left the house, and having traversed the poor little town of Vinci ascended to Anchiano, the neighbouring hamlet. The path was steep, and as on the previous day, the sun colourless and wintry. At the verge of the horizon, the cold cloudless blue of the sky melted into a dull purple. The *tramontana* blew steadily from the north, whistling monotonously in the ears. The vegetation was still colourless and poor; little meagre vineyards in semicircles, sparse dull grasses, mingled with fluttering poppies; on all sides dusty grey olives, with knotted, blackened, and twisted trunks of great antiquity. Entering Anchiano, Leonardo halted, for he did not recognise the place. Where had been the Castello degli Adimari with a wine-shop in its only unruined tower, there was now a vineyard and a new house, with smoothly whitewashed walls. A husbandman digging trenches among the vines, explained that mine host of the tavern having died, the land had been sold to a sheepbreeder from Orbignano, who had cleared away the ruins, and made a vineyard and an olive-grove on their site.

Leonardo had good reason to ask after that little tavern, for it was there he had been born.

Fifty years earlier, the village wine-shop had been lively enough. It stood a little back from the road, its signboard swinging merrily. The inhabitants of the surrounding hamlets on their way to the fairs of San Miniato or Fucecchio, chamois-hunters, mule-drivers, custom-house officers, and other persons who were not too exclusive in their taste for company—all met here. The maid of the tavern was a girl of sixteen, an orphan, a *contadina* from Vinci; her name Caterina.

One day, in the spring-time of 1451, Piero di Ser Antonio da Vinci, a young notary from Florence, was called to Anchiano to draw up an agreement for the lease of the sixth part of a certain oil-press. Business concluded, the peasants invited the notary to drink at the tavern in the old tower of the Adimari. Ser Piero, always affable, even among simple folk, accepted the invitation. The party was served by Caterina, and the young notary, as he afterwards confessed, became enamoured at first sight. Under pretext of quail-shooting, he delayed his return to Florence; he haunted the tavern, and laid siege to Caterina. Ser Piero was already celebrated as a conqueror of women; he was four-and-twenty, handsome, strong, something of a coxcomb. He possessed that self-confident eloquence which in a lover is irresistible. Caterina hesitated, prayed to the Virgin for assistance, finally succumbed. At the time when the quails took their flight from the Val di Nievole, she was with child.

Ser Antonio da Vinci soon learned that his son had entangled himself with the maid-servant at a village hostelry. He despatched him to Florence and wedded him as quickly as possible to Madonna Albiera di Ser Giovanni Amadori, who was neither very young nor very fair, but had a substantial dowry. Caterina he mated also with a peasant named Accattabrighe di Piero del Vacca, who was said to have beaten his first wife to death in a drunken fit. The girl resigned herself without protest, but with inward grief which threw her into a fever when she was brought to bed. She was unable to suckle her child, and the little Leonardo was wet-nursed by a goat from Monte Albano. Piero, however, begged his father to take Caterina's child to be bred in his house. In those times no one was ashamed of bastards, and they were frequently educated on the same footing as their legitimate brethren, and even preferred to them. Leonardo accordingly entered the virtuous and pious family of da Vinci, and was entrusted to the care of his grandmother, Lena di Piero da Baccareto.

As the vision of a dream, Leonardo remembered his mother; more especially her smile, so delicate, so fleeting, full of mystery, and gently malicious; singularly in contrast with the habitual expression of her beautiful but melancholy face, which to some seemed even harshly severe. Once he found that smile again, on the face of a small antique bronze statue of Cybele, the immemorially ancient goddess of the earth; the same subtle smile which he remembered as the characteristic of the young peasant woman of Vinci—his mother.

He thought:—

"Ah, how the mountain women, dressed in poor coarse raiment, excel in beauty those who are adorned!"

It was said by persons who had known Caterina that her son resembled her; his long and slender hands, his golden hair, his smile, were inherited from her. From his father he had a powerful frame, health, zest of life; from his mother that almost feminine charm. Brought up in the paternal house, Leonardo had never been entirely separated from his mother. Her cottage was not far from Ser Antonio's villa; and at mid-day when Accattabrighe had gone forth with the oxen, the boy would make his way through the vineyard, climb the wall, and run to his mother. She was awaiting him on the threshold, distaff in hand; she stretched out her arms, and when he came she covered his eyes, his lips, his hair with her kisses. Or at night when Accattabrighe would be at the tavern, dicing and swilling, the child would escape from his bed, crawl through the window and down the fig-tree, and run to Caterina's home. Sweet to him was the cool of the dewy grass, the cry of the night-jar, the very nettles and stones which wounded his feet; the glow of the far-off stars, and the very anxiety lest his grandam should awake and miss him.

Yet Monna Lena likewise loved and pampered her grandson, and he remembered her well, her one vesture of dark brown, her white kerchief, her dark, wrinkled, kind old face, her lullabies, and the appetising odour of the "berlingozzi" which she baked after the ancient Tuscan recipe. With his grandfather, he had not agreed so well. At first Ser Antonio had taught him personally; but Leonardo was an unwilling pupil, and at seven he was sent to school at the Oratory of Santa Petronilla. But neither was the Latin grammar to his liking. He played truant, wandering to a wild ravine behind the town where he would lie on his back watching the flight of the cranes with torturing envy; or unfolding the cups of flowers, wondering at their coloured petals and pollen-covered stamens, moist with honey. Sometimes during his grandfather's absence the little Nardo would escape for whole days into the mountains, making his way by the tracks of goats and along the edges of precipices to the summit of Monte Albano. Thence he could see a boundless expanse of meadows, pastures, groves, and forests; the marshes of Fucecchio; and Prato,

Pistoia, Florence, and the snowy peaks of the Alps; when the sky was clear, the misty blue of the Mediterranean Sea. At last he would return home, dusty, sunburnt, his hands scratched, his garments torn; but his grandam, seeing his happiness, had not the heart to punish him, or to betray him to Ser Antonio. The boy lived alone; his father and his uncle Francesco he saw but seldom, for they were away in Florence; with his schoolmates he did not associate. Their sports displeased him; on one occasion when they tore the wings from a butterfly and laughed at its writhings, he frowned, turned pale, and went away. Complaints of his surliness were in consequence made to Ser Antonio; great displeasure followed, threats of flogging, and an actual imprisonment for three days in a cupboard under the staircase.

Later, recalling this link in a long chain of injustice, he wrote in his diary:—

"If as a child you were put in prison for doing your duty, what will they do to you as a man?"

IV

Not far from Vinci a large villa was in course of construction by the Florentine architect, Biagio da Ravenna, a pupil of Alberti. Leonardo watched the raising of the walls, the levelling of the stonework, the elevation of huge blocks by machinery. One day Ser Biagio talked with the lad, and was astonished by the understanding which he showed. At first in jest, then seriously, he taught him the first principles of arithmetic, algebra, geometry, and mechanics. The teacher marvelled at the facility with which the boy caught each idea as it were on the wing, and made it his own; it seemed as though he were not learning but remembering. The grandfather looked askance at what he called "caprices," and he thought it a bad omen that the boy used preferably his left hand when he wrote; for sorcerers, necromancers, and those who make compacts with the devil are, of course, always born left-handed! His suspicion of the lad increased when a neighbour from Fortuniano assured him that the old woman of the village on Monte Albano who had provided the black goat for the suckling of the babe was an undoubted witch.

"Do what you will," thought the old notary, "but if you bring up a wolf he will always have his eye on the forest. Well, well! Submit to the will of Heaven! There's no family without *one* abortion."

And he waited with desperate anxiety for the birth of a legitimate heir to Piero, his favourite son; since Nardo, the product of illicit love, was showing himself thus clearly "ill-born" into this eminently respectable family. 'Twas a tale of Monte Albano, which indeed accounted for its name, that many plants and animals there mysteriously changed their natural colour into white; so that the traveller, roaming its woods and meadows, would chance upon white violets, white strawberries, white sparrows, white nestlings in a brood of blackbirds. In like manner the little Nardo was one of the wonders of the White Mountain; a changeling in the virtuous and commonplace family of the Florentine notary; a big white cuckoo in a nest of blackbirds.

V

When the boy had reached the age of thirteen, his father removed him from Vinci to his house. Florence; since then he had rarely visited his birthplace. But long after, in one of his note-books of the year 1494, when he was in the service of the Duke of Milan, he wrote, "Caterina, came in July last year." It might signify the beginning of somc kitchen wench's service; in reality it referred to his mother. Her husband had died, and feeling that her own time might be short, she desired to see her son at least once again. She joined a party of pilgrims on their way to Milan for adoration of the Holy Nail; journeyed from Tuscany, and presented herself at Leonardo's house. He received her with pious affection; for her he was ever the little Nardo, who had come secretly by night with bare feet and nestled at her side.

She would have returned to Anchiano, but her son would not permit it. He placed her in a quiet and commodiously-fitted cell of the Convent of Santa Chiara, near the Porta Vercellina. Later she fell ill, and at her own request was taken to the *Ospedale Maggiore*, built by Francesco Sforza and the finest hospital in Milan. Here he visited her for months everyday, at the last scarcely leaving her for an hour. Yet he had told none of his friends nor even his pupils of her presence in Milan.

But when for the last time he had pressed his lips on the cold hand of this peasant woman who had been his mother, it seemed to him that to her he owed everything. He honoured her with a sumptuous funeral.

Six years later, after the fall of Ludovico Sforza, when he was leaving Milan, he found a small carefully wrapped bundle in one of his chests. It contained a couple of coarse canvas shirts and three pair of goats'-hair stockings, all made by Caterina's hand, and brought to him from Vinci. He had never worn them, but now coming upon the poor things among his scientific books and mechanical apparatus, and the garments of fine linen to which he had habituated himself, he felt inexpressibly touched. Nor in the years which followed, when he was a solitary and weary wanderer from country to country, from town to town, did he ever omit to take this poor little parcel with him, packed among the dearest of his treasures.

VI

Such were Leonardo's recollections as he climbed the slopes of Monte Albano, familiar to him in his childhood. He sat down under the shelter of a rock and surveyed the well-remembered landscape. Dwarfed and gnarled oak-trees surrounded him still hung with withered leaves, perfumed juniper, which the peasants called *scopa* (besom), pale shy violets, and low bushes of dried mountain heather, exhaled that intangible freshness which is the odour of spring. Far away the valley of the Arno met the sky; but to the right rose bare lofty mountains with undulating shadows, twisted hollows like gigantic serpents, and wide ravines, delicate purple in colour. At his feet was Anchiano, white and shining in the sunlight; further away, Vinci clung to its little conical hill like a wasp's nest; the castle tower distinct and black as the two cypresses by the side of the Anchiano road.

Nothing was changed since the day when he had first climbed these paths. Forty years before the *scopa* had grown as luxuriantly, the violets and thyme had scented the air, the oaks had rustled their withered leaves; as now, Monte Albano had seemed colourless, bare, northern. Etruria of the ancients, now Tuscany, land of perpetual spring, land of unfailing renaissance—to Leonardo it wore that subtle and tender smile brightening a beauty otherwise too austere, which he had first seen on the countenance of Caterina his peasant mother.

He rose and pursued his way, the path growing more rugged, the wind colder, sharper, more northerly. Memories of his youth crowded upon his soul.

VII

Ser Piero da Vinci had prospered. Skilful and good-hearted, his life ran upon greased wheels. Live and let live, was his maxim, and he stood well with all, more especially with the clerical party. Procurator of the monastery of the Santissima Annunziata, and of many other rich foundations, he acquired wealth in abundance, adding largely to his property, but never changing the modest fashion of life which he had learned from Ser Antonio. His wife died when he was eight-and-thirty, but he soon married a young and beautiful girl, Madonna Francesca di Ser Giovanni Lanfredini. She, like her predecessor, was childless; and Leonardo, the bastard, lived with his father, and had every prospect of becoming his heir.

At that time Paola dal Pozzo Toscanelli, a famous astronomer and mathematician, lived at Florence. He had written a letter to Christopher Columbus, assuring him on the authority of his calculations that the route to India by the Antipodes was neither so long nor so arduous as had been supposed, encouraging him to make the adventure, and prophesying its success. Columbus therefore carried out what had been conceived in the lonely cell of the Florentine scholar, and was, as it were, the instrument played by the hand of a skilled musician. Toscanelli was said by his contemporaries to "live like a saint"; reserved, frugal, chaste, he frequented neither the brilliant Medicean court, nor the vain assemblies of the Neo-Platonist imitators of antiquity. His face was curiously ugly, but redeemed by eyes of great brilliance.

One evening a lad, scarcely more than a child, knocked at his door and was coldly received, being suspected of mere idle curiosity. But short conversation with the young Leonardo—for it was he—convinced the astronomer, as before it had convinced Biagio da Ravenna, of his wonderful aptitude for mathematics. Ser Paola became his teacher; on summer nights they went together to Poggio del Pino, one of those fragrant, pine-clad, heather-carpeted hills, girdling the City of Flowers; there Toscanelli had built his observatory. He taught the boy all he himself knew of the laws of the universe. It was from these lessons that Leonardo dated his faith in the experimental study of nature, as yet too much neglected by the philosophers.

Ser Piero da Vinci, though he put no difficulties in the way of his son's studies, advised him to choose some more lucrative occupation;

having noticed his bent towards modelling and drawing, he showed some of the boy's work to Andrea Verrocchio, the painter and goldsmith; and shortly afterwards Leonardo was formally entered as one of this artist's pupils.

VIII

VERROCCHIO, THE SON OF A poor furnace-stoker, was seventeen years the senior of Leonardo. His face was placid, flat, and pale, with a double chin. Only in his tight shut lips and piercing eyes was there evidence of singular intelligence. Spectacles on nose, magnifier in hand, he sat in his dark *bottega* near the Ponte Vecchio, looking more like a small shopkeeper than a great artist. A disciple of Paolo Uccello, he, like his master, affirmed that Perspective must be based on science. "Geometry," he said, "being a part of mathematics, mother of all knowledge, is also the mother of drawing, which is the father of all the arts." Complete knowledge and complete enjoyment of beauty were to him identical. Unlike Botticelli, and others of his kidney, Verrocchio was neither ravished by extraordinary beauty nor repelled by unusual deformity. In both he found occasion for study. He was also the first master who made anatomical models. If Botticelli had found the fascination of art in the miraculous, in the fabulous, in that mystic haze which confounds Olympus with Golgotha—for Verrocchio it lay in patient investigation and a firm grasp of the verities of nature. The miraculous was not true for him. Truth was the miracle.

This was the man to whom Ser Piero brought his seventeen-year-old son; he became Leonardo's teacher; further, he became his disciple. The monks of Vallombrosa had commissioned Ser Andrea to paint them a Baptism of Christ, and the master set his pupil to execute the kneeling angel which formed part of the composition. The result showed Verrocchio that his scholar knew intuitively and clearly all that he himself had dimly guessed and sought for gropingly, slowly and laboriously, through a fog.

Later it was said that Verrocchio gave up painting because jealous of the young man's superiority; in reality there was never anything but harmony between the two. Each supplied the deficiency of the other. The pupil had lightness and precision of touch; Verrocchio, perseverance and concentrated attention. They worked together without envy, without rivalry, scarce knowing how much they owed each other.

At that time Verrocchio executed the bronze group for Orsanmichele, which was known as the "Incredulity of St. Thomas." It was altogether unlike the celestial dreams of the Beato Angelico or the delirious idealism of Sandro Botticelli. In St. Thomas's mysterious smile, as he put his fingers into the print of the nails, was exhibited for the first time the boldness of man before his God; Reason face to face with Miracle.

IX

Leonardo's first independent work was a cartoon for a curtain of Flanders tissue, a gift from the Florentines to the King of Portugal. The subject was the Fall of Man; and such was the accuracy with which the palm branches, the flowers, and the animals of Paradise were drawn, that Vasari the critic was stupefied at so great patience.

Eve, stretching out her hand to the Tree of Knowledge, wore the same smile of bold curiosity which Verrocchio had given to St. Thomas.

A little later Ser Piero employed his son to paint one of those round wooden shields called *rotelle*, which were used as ornaments for houses, and which generally carried some allegorical design. Leonardo painted an animal, terrible as the face of Medusa. He had collected lizards, snakes, crickets, spiders, centipedes, moths, scorpions, bats, every sort of noxious creature, and had studied their characteristics. By a process of selection and exaggeration of their individual truth, he had put together a monster, such as had never existed, yet which might have been possible, deducing what is not from what is with the precision of an Euclid or a Pythagoras. The beast was issuing from its den in the rock; grating its black and shining scales upon the gravel. Fetor exhaled from its gaping jaws, smoke from its nostrils; its eyes were flame. Horrible as was the monster, the wonder of it lay less in its deformity than in its charm, which was no less powerful than the charm of beauty.

Day and night Leonardo had studied and painted in the stifling room empoisoned by the stench from the dead reptiles; at last the picture was finished, and he summoned his father to see it. He had placed it on a wooden stand surrounded by black cloth, the light being so disposed that only the monster was illuminated. Ser Piero came in, saw the beast, and involuntarily drew back. Recovering himself, he looked again, and his expression changed from great fear to great pleasure.

"The *rotella* is ready," said Leonardo; "it produces the effect at which I have aimed. You may take it away."

Next he received an order for an "Adoration of the Magi" from the monks of San Donato a Scopeto. In the sketch for this picture he exhibited a knowledge of anatomy and of the outward expression of the emotions, surpassing that of any previous painter. Against a background almost Hellenic in its beauty, he showed the Mother of God with the divine Infant, who, smiling shyly, seemed to marvel at the precious gifts brought by the strangers. They, wearied and bowed down by the load of ancient and earthly wisdom, bending their heads, shading their eyes, were absorbed in contemplation of that miracle of miracles, the Epiphany of God in man.

In his picture of the Fall, Leonardo had realised the boldness of reason—the wisdom of the serpent; in this of the Adoration he had shown the innocence of the dove, the humility of faith. One picture the complement of the other; the two exhibited the full circle of his philosophy.

But the second picture was never finished. In the quest for perfection he made difficulties for himself which his brush could not overcome. In the words of Petrarch, "*al dissetamento era d'ostacolo l'eccessiva brama*"—"excessive thirst hindered its own quenching."

Meanwhile, Ser Piero married his third wife, Margherita, who brought him two sons, Antonio and Giuliano. The step-mother hated Leonardo, and accused her husband of wasting the inheritance of his lawful children upon a bastard, foster-child of a witch's goat. The young painter had enemies also among his fellow-students; and it was one of them who brought against him and against Verrocchio the accusation of which Cesare da Sesto had told Giovanni Boltraffio. The calumny had acquired some verisimilitude from the exceptional friendship between master and scholar, and from the fact that Leonardo, though the handsomest man of young Florence—("in his exterior, says a contemporary, there was such radiance of beauty that at sight of him sad hearts were gladdened")—eschewed the society of women. The accusation came to nothing, but he left Verrocchio, and henceforth painted independently.

Reports now got about touching his heresies and atheism, and it became increasingly difficult for him to remain in Florence. Ser Piero introduced him to Lorenzo de' Medici; uselessly, however, for *Il Magnifico* disapproved spirits too daring and unconventional, and demanded a constant and servile adulation which Leonardo was ill fitted to supply. The tedium of inaction oppressed him. He entered into negotiations with the Egyptian ambassador for the purpose of obtaining the post of chief architect to the "diodario" of Syria, though he knew that it would require his embracing the Mahometan faith. His one desire was to escape from Florence. Chance favoured him. He made a many-stringed silver lute in the form of a horse's head, which took Lorenzo de' Medici's fancy. Lorenzo sent it by the hand of the inventor to Milan, as a gift to Ludovico Sforza.

Leonardo was received at the Lombard court not as a man of science, not as a painter, but as the *sonatore di lira*—the "player of the lyre."

But before starting he had written a long letter to the duke, setting forth how useful he might be to him.

"Most Illustrious Lord,—Having studied and estimated the works of the present inventors of warlike engines, I have found that in them there is nothing novel to distinguish them. I therefore force myself to address your Excellency that I may disclose to him the secrets of my art.

"1st. I have a method for bridges, very light and very strong; easy of transport and incombustible.

"2nd. New means of destroying any fortress or castle (which hath not foundations hewn of solid rock) without the employment of bombards.

"3rd. Of making mines and passages, immediately and noiselessly, under ditches and streams.

"4th. I have designed irresistible protected chariots for the carrying of artillery against the enemy.

"5th. I can construct bombards, cannon, mortars, "passavolanti": all new and very beautiful.

"6th. Likewise battering rams, machines for the casting of projectiles, and other astounding engines.

"7th. For sea-combats I have contrivances both offensive and defensive; ships whose sides would repel stone and iron balls, and explosives, unknown to any soul.

"8th. In days of peace, I should hope to satisfy your Excellency in architecture, in the erection of public and private buildings, in the construction of canals and aqueducts. I am acquainted with the arts of sculpture and painting, and can execute orders in marble, metal, clay, or in painting with oil, as well as any artist. And I can undertake that equestrian statue cast in bronze, which shall eternally glorify the blessed memory of your lordship's father and of the illustrious house of Sforza.

"And if any of the above seem extravagant or beyond the reach of possibility, I offer myself prepared to make experiment in your park; or in whatsoever place it may please your Excellency to appoint; to whose gracious attention I most humbly recommend myself. LEONARDO DA VINCI."

When he caught his first glimpse of the snow-clad Alps shining above the green plain of Lombardy, he felt himself entering upon a new life, in a strange land which was to become his true country.

X

SUCH WAS THE HALF CENTURY of life upon which Leonardo looked back as he ascended Monte Albano. The path had become direct, vegetation was left below, the mountains were bare, solitary, and terrible, as belonging to another planet. He was blinded by fierce gusts of icy wind. Stones breaking away from his feet fell noisily into the ravine. He was still ascending, and at every step the prospect widened. He found exhilaration in the effort of climbing, gradually conquering the great mountains and compelling them to give up their treasures. Florence was out of sight, but the spacious district of Empoli was spread at his feet; first the mountains, cold dull purple with broad shadows; then the unnumbered billowy hills from Livorno to San Geminiano. Everywhere was air, emptiness, space. The narrow footpath seemed to vanish; he fancied himself flying over this boundless expanse on gigantic wings. The realisation that he had no such equipment produced in his mind the wondering alarm felt by a man who is suddenly deprived of his legs. He remembered how in boyhood he used to watch the flight of cranes; and how, hearing their cry, he had fancied it a summons to himself, and had wept for disappointment that he could not obey. He remembered releasing his grandfather's cage-birds, and joying in the wild swoops of their recovered liberty. He remembered listening to the tale of Icarus, who had thought to fly on waxen wings, but had fallen and perished; and how, when bidden by his teacher to name the greatest of ancient heroes, he had answered without a moment's hesitation "Icarus, son of Dædalus." He remembered, too, his pleasure in finding a clumsy representation of his hero among the bas-reliefs of Giotto's campanile in Florence. He retained one other memory of his childhood which, however absurd it might have seemed to another, had for him a prophetic meaning. He wrote of it:—

"I remember that once in infancy, lying in my cradle, I fancied that a kite flew to me and opened my lips, and rubbed his feathers over them. It would seem to be my destiny all my life to talk about wings."

The question of human flight had indeed become the preoccupation of his whole life. Now, even as forty years before, standing again on the slope of the White Mountain it seemed to him an intolerable injury, even an impossibility, that men should remain wingless.

"He who knows all can do all," thought Leonardo. "I have only to *know*; and there shall be wings."

XI

On one of the final zigzags of the path he felt himself touched from behind, and turning saw Giovanni Boltraffio who, hat in hand, eyes half shut, head bent, was battling with the wind, and had evidently been calling for sometime unheard. When he saw the Master with long hair streaming on the blast, and look of indomitable will, his thoughtful eyes, deep lines on his forehead, and overhanging brows contracted in a frown, seemed to the disciple so strange and terrible as to be barely recognisable. Even the broad folds of his red cloak bellying in the wind were like the pinions of some strange bird.

Giovanni shouted as loud as he could, but he was so much out of breath he could only articulate broken phrases.

"Just come—from Florence. Letter—important—told to give it into your hands at once!"

Leonardo guessed at a communication from Cæsar Borgia, and quickly recognised the writing of Messer Agapito his secretary.

"Go down at once," said Leonardo, seeing Giovanni blue with cold. "I will follow you immediately." And he watched Boltraffio as he fought his way through the storm, clinging to frail boughs of low-growing shrubs, crawling over rocks, bending double, absurdly small and weak in comparison with his surroundings and the fury of the elements. He appeared an epitome of all human weakness; and, watching him, Leonardo was reminded of the curse of some grave impotence which seemed to have lain upon his whole life, which had, he feared, condemned him to eternal sterility, besides depriving him of the sympathy of his fellows.

"My Wings!" he thought, "Ah! will not they fail like everything else?"

And he remembered the words spoken by Astro in his delirium, the answer of the Son of Man when the devil would have seduced him by the terror of the abyss, by the fascination of flight; "Thou shalt not tempt the Lord thy God!"

He raised his head, set his teeth, and again addressed himself to the ascent, conquering the mountain and the storm. The path had disappeared. He guided himself over the bare rocks where, perhaps, none had trodden before. Suddenly he found himself upon the edge of a precipice, till now unseen; misty dull purple filled with air and yawned beneath his feet as if the void and endless heaven were below no less than above. The wind had become a hurricane, and howled and roared like continuous thunder. Leonardo could have fancied that unseen evil birds—flock after flock—were sweeping past him on gigantic wings. No further advance was possible; never had the long familiar idea appealed to him with such force; never had he been so impressed by the logic, by the necessity, of the power of flight.

"*There shall be wings!*" he cried, "if the accomplishment be not for me, 'tis for someother. It shall be done. The spirit cannot lie; and Man, who shall know all and who shall have wings, shall indeed be as a god."

And he pictured to himself the King of the Air, Him who can pass all bounds and supersede all the laws which limit human intelligence, the Son of Man coming in his glory and power, the *Magno Cecero*, "the Great Swan," borne on wings immense, white, shining as light itself, in the blue of heaven.

And his soul was filled with a joy akin to terror.

XII

As he descended from Monte Albano the sun was setting. The pointed cypresses were black against the golden sky; the receding mountains tender and translucent as amethyst. The wind had subsided. He was approaching Anchiano, and the hill town of Vinci was already in sight.

He stopped, and murmured:—

"From the mountain which takes its name from the conqueror (Vinci—Vincere) Man shall take his first flight!"

And gazing at his birthplace, there at the foot of the White Mountain, he repeated; "Eternal glory to the nest from whence he sprang!"

The letter from Messer Agapito announced the approaching siege of Faenza, and demanded the immediate presence of the new engineer and architect in Cæsar Borgia's camp.

Two days later Leonardo left Florence for Romagna.

Book XII

"Aut Cæsar Aut Nihil"

Cæsar Borgia
1500–1503

"A prince must be a beast as well as a man."

—Niccolò Machiavelli—*Il Principe*

I

"We, Cæsar Borgia of France, by the Grace of God, Duke of Romagna, Lord of Piombino, Gonfaloniere of the Holy Roman Church, and Captain-General;

"To all our lieutenants, castellans, captains, condottieri, officers, and subjects;

"We commend unto you the most famous and well-beloved Leonardo Vinci, our architect and chief war-engineer, and command that ye give him everywhere unhindered passage, permitting him to examine, measure, and judge of everything he may desire to see in our fortresses, and affording him all co-operation, and as many men as he may need to help him. And we bid our other contractors to enter into accord in all matters with the will of the above-mentioned Leonardo, to whom we entrust the oversight of all the fortresses and castles in our dominions.

"Given at Pavia on August 18th, in the year of our Lord, 1502, and the second of our reign in Romagna.

Cæsar, dux Romandiolæ

So ran Leonardo's new credentials.

These were the years in which Cæsar Borgia was gradually recovering for Alexander VI the ancient States of the Church, said to have been conferred on the papacy by Constantine the Great. He had taken the town of Faenza from the eighteen-year-old Astorre Manfredi; and

Forlì from Caterina Sforza. The lad and the woman had been confided to his protection. He threw them both into the Castle of St. Angelo. He concluded a fraudulent treaty with the Duke of Urbino, and in 1502 planned a campaign against Bologna. He was intent upon making himself sole and absolute ruler of Italy. In September his enemies, including the dukes of Perugia and Siena, as well as other important personages, assembled at Mugione, and concluded a secret alliance against him. Vitellozzo Vitelli swore the oath of Hannibal, that within a year he would slay, imprison, or exile the common foe. Report of this alliance having been bruited abroad, it was joined by some of the greater princes. Urbino rose in revolt; Cæsar's own troops mutinied; the King of France was slow in coming to his help; he seemed on the verge of ruin. Nevertheless he still had resources, and his enemies were dilatory. The opportunity was let slip, and presently these, his allied enemies, entered into negotiations with the usurper. He overreached them, contriving to set them at variance with each other; by profound dissimulation and courteous manners converted them to a more or less favourable attitude; and presently made an urgent appointment to meet his foes in parley at the newly-conquered town of Sinigaglia.

Leonardo had quickly become a prominent personage at Cæsar's court. The duke employed him in adorning the various towns with palaces, libraries, schools, barracks, and canals. He constructed engines of war, made military maps, and was present at all Cæsar's bloodiest exploits.

Leonardo did not wish to see too clearly, or to know too accurately, what was taking place around him. He eschewed politics. He confined himself almost entirely to observations on physical and social phenomena: the manner of planting orchards, the machinery for ringing the bells at Siena Cathedral, the low music of the falling water in the fountain of Rimini, the dove-cot in the Castle of Urbino. He noted how the shepherds at the foot of the Apennines placed their horns in the narrow openings of deep hollows, so that echo should increase the volume of their sound. For whole days he stood on the desolate shore of Piombino, watching the falling of the waves; and while all around him the laws of human justice were being broken, mused on the invariability of nature, and found deep-seated joy in the eternal justice of the Prime Mover.

On a day in June the corpses of the young Astorre and his brother were found in the Tiber, stones tied round their necks. The crime was universally attributed to Cæsar. But that day Leonardo noted—

"In Romagna four-wheeled carts are used, the front wheels small, the back large: the construction is faulty, for all the weight rests on the front."

II

In the latter half of December 1503 the Duke of Valentinois, with his whole court, moved from Cesena to Fano, on the shores of the Adriatic, twenty miles from Sinigaglia, where the meeting was appointed with his former enemies, Oliverotto da Fermo, Vitellozzo Vitelli, and Gian Paolo Baglioni. A few days later Leonardo came from Pesaro to join his patron.

On the way he was overtaken by a storm. The mountains were covered with impassable snow-drifts, the mules slipped on the ice; great waves were heard breaking on the seashore at the foot of the precipice. As darkness came on the travellers lost the path, and, dropping the reins, they trusted themselves to the instinct of their beasts. The mule Leonardo was riding suddenly stopped and grew restive, scenting the corpse of a man who had been hanged, which still dangled from the branch of a solitary tree.

At last they saw a distant light, and the guide recognised the inn at Novilara, a mountain town half way between Pesaro and Fano. The travellers quickened their steps, and presently were knocking at the massive entrance door, studded with nails like the gate of a fortress. A sleepy ostler came first; then the landlord, who declined to receive the new arrivals. All his rooms, all his stables were overfilled; there was not a bed in which three or four were not sleeping—all persons of quality, soldiers and courtiers of the duke's suite.

Leonardo told his name and exhibited his credentials, sealed with the duke's seal. The host poured forth a torrent of apology, and made offer of his own chamber, which at present contained only three French captains, all passably drunk and sound asleep.

Leonardo entered the kitchen, which according to the wont of the Romagna inns served also as a parlour. It was very dirty, with patches of damp on the bare walls; guinea-fowl were sleeping on their perches, and baby porkers squeaking round the door; onions, gherkins, and sausages were suspended from the ceiling. A whole pig was roasting before the immense glowing fire. Guests crowded at long tables, drinking and quarrelling over cards.

Leonardo sat down by the stove, and presently, at a square board close by, he saw Baldassarre Scipioni, an old man, formerly captain of the duke's Lancers; Alessandro Spanocchia, the treasurer; Pandolfo Collenuccio, legate from Ferrara, and a fourth gentleman, a stranger, who was gesticulating forcibly, and crying in a thin squeaky voice:—

"I can prove this also, *Messeri*! I can prove this by instances from ancient and from modern history! Call to mind the states which have acquired military glory—Romans, Spartans, Athenians, Ætolians, and the trans-Alpine hordes. All the great commanders collected their armies from the citizens of their own country. Ninus from the Assyrians, Cyrus from the Persians, Alexander from the Macedonians. I grant you that Pyrrhus and Hannibal won victories by means of mercenaries, but these were generals of exceptional genius. Nor must ye forget my main proposition—the very corner-stone of military science—viz., that in infantry, and infantry alone, lies the strength of an army. Not in cavalry, not in fire-arms and powder, ridiculous toy inventions of modern times."

"You go too far, Messer Niccolò," replied the captain of lancers with a smile; "fire-arms are becoming of some importance. Whatever you say about the Romans and the Spartans, I venture to think our troops are much better equipped. A squadron of our French soldiers, or a battery of thirty bombards, would have made short work of your ancient Romans."

"Sophisms! Sophisms!" retorted Messer Niccolò with increasing excitement. "I perceive in your words fearfully perilous error! Some day the Italians will be taught, by a rude lesson, the weakness of mercenary armies, and the pitiful powerlessness of cavalry and artillery. Remember how the handfuls of Lucullus routed 150,000 horsemen, among whom were cohorts of mounted men exactly similar to the squadrons of the present French cavalry!"

Leonardo looked curiously at this man who spoke like an eye-witness of the victories of Lucullus. The stranger wore a long garment of dark red cloth, falling in straight folds; it resembled that worn by the statesmen of the Florentine Republic and the secretaries of the embassies. It was, however, old and stained. The sleeves were threadbare, and such linen as was to be seen was frayed and soiled. The man had great bony hands, copiously dyed with ink, and a wart on one finger. There was little dignity in his air; he was lean and narrow shouldered, about forty years of age, and with sharp irregular features. Sometimes when he was speaking he would look over the head of his interlocutor, as if peering into space like some long-sighted rapacious bird. In his restless movements, in the feverish flush of his swarthy cheeks, above all, in the intentness of his large grey eyes, there was evidence of smouldering fire within. The eyes themselves were malicious; yet at times, in their sardonic smile, in their cold displeasure, there was an expression of weakness almost pathetic.

Messer Niccolò continued to pour forth his notions; and Leonardo marvelled at the strange mixture of truth and error in his talk, at his audacity, and his slavish appeal to the authority of the ancients. He approved him when he spoke of the scientific difficulty in using guns of large calibre, owing to the inaccuracy of their range; but the next minute he asserted that fortresses were useless, because the Spartans and the Romans built none. He appeared to regard the opinions of the Greeks and Romans much as Leonardo regarded mathematical axioms. The latter, however, did not hear the conclusion of the dispute, as the landlord called him to the bedchamber reserved for him upstairs.

III

It snowed all night, and in the morning the guide refused to continue the journey, the weather being in his opinion not fit even for a dog to go out in. Leonardo was forced to remain at the inn. He amused himself trying a self-turning roasting-spit which he had invented.

"With this mechanism," he expounded to the astonished onlookers, "the cook need have no fear of burning the meat, for the action of the fire remains even. With increase of heat it turns faster, that is all."

It would seem that the success of his flying-machine could hardly have afforded him greater pleasure than the perfection of this cooking engine.

In the same room Messer Niccolò was explaining to certain young artillery sergeants an infallible system, based on abstract mathematics, for winning at dice—"circumventing," as he called it, "the caprices of the strumpet Fortune." Everytime he tried to give a practical illustration of its value, he lost, greatly to his own astonishment and to the amusement of his audience. The conclusion of the game was unexpected and not entirely to Messer Niccolò's glory. It revealed that his pouch was empty, and that he could not meet his losses.

Late that evening there arrived another guest, with a great array of servants, pages, grooms, jesters, negroes, animals, boxes, and chests. It was the elegant Venetian courtesan, the *magnifica meretrice*, Lena Griffi, who had been so nearly despoiled by Savonarola's "youthful inquisitors." Two years ago, following the example of many of her sisterhood, the repentant Magdalen had cut her hair and shut herself up in a convent. This was, however, merely an artifice to raise her price in the city tariff of courtesans, drawn up for the use of strangers. From the monastic chrysalis she had emerged like a butterfly awakened to a new and more splendid life. Very soon the *mammola veneziana* had risen to great celebrity, and had fashioned for herself, according to the usage of the principal courtesans, a fine genealogical-tree, by which it appeared that she was the daughter of Cardinal Ascanio Sforza, brother of Ludovico, Duke of Milan. She became the mistress of an old and doting cardinal, whose infirmities were palliated by his wealth, and was now journeying to Fano, where her elderly lover was attached to Cæsar Borgia's camp. The host could not refuse admission to so exalted a personage. He accommodated her suite by turning out certain Ancona merchants from a fair-sized bedroom, housing them in the forge, and promising them a reduction in their bill. Similar treatment he proposed for Messer Niccolò and his room-mates, the French captains, in order to provide a chamber for the lady herself.

Messer Niccolò, however, protested, and grew very angry, asking the landlord if he had lost his reason, if he knew with whom he was speaking? if it were not unheard-of insolence to insult respectable people for the pleasing of the first jade tumbled in out of the street? Here intervened the hostess, a masterful lady who, in the words of the proverb, had not "pawned her tongue to a Jew"; she suggested that before making so much noise he had better pay the bill for himself, his servant, and his three horses; and also return the four ducats lent him last Friday by her husband. And she added, in a stage whisper, that she wished a bad Easter to all the adventurers and beggars who swarmed on the high roads, and, pretending to be great ones, lived at free quarters and mocked at honest people. No doubt there was some applicability in all this, for Messer Niccolò was reduced to silence, and seemed considering how he could retire with the best grace from his position. Meantime servants were already removing his goods, and Madonna Lena's monkey was grimacing at him, and jumping over the table among his papers and great leather books, the *Decades* of Livy and Plutarch's *Lives*.

Leonardo now approached and said, raising his berretto:—

"Messere, if it would please you to share my room, I shall account it an honour, if your worship will permit me to render so slight a service."

Niccolò seemed astonished, and even confused; recovering himself, however, he accepted the offer with suitable thanks. Leonardo took him to his room, and assigned him the best place. The more he looked at this strange man the more attractive and interesting did he seem to him. He presently learned his name: He was Machiavelli, secretary to the Council of Ten in the Florentine Republic.

Three months earlier the astute and vigilant Signoria had sent Machiavelli to make a treaty with Cæsar Borgia. The latter had proposed a defensive alliance against their common enemies, Bentivoglio, the Vitelli, and the Orsini; but the Florentines, fearing the duke too much to desire either his friendship or his enmity, had commanded their envoy to meet his propositions merely with diplomatic and ambiguous expressions of goodwill, and secretly to obtain free passage for their traders through the duke's territory along the shores of the Adriatic, a matter of no small importance to their commerce.

Leonardo also disclosed his name and rank; and soon he and his new friend were conversing with that ease and mutual confidence occasionally natural to persons of opposite character, and habitually solitary and meditative.

"Messere," burst out Niccolò, and his candour was not unattractive, "I know you by repute as a great painter; but I warn you I have no knowledge of painting, nor am I even fond of it. Of course you may respond, as did Dante to the street mocker who offered him a fig, 'I wouldn't change one of mine for twenty of yours!' but I confess I am more interested in having learnt from the duke that you are an expert in military science. How important that is! Civil greatness is founded upon war, and depends on the regular army. I am writing a book on monarchies and republics, wherein I shall discuss the natural laws which govern the life, growth, decline, and death of every state, just like a mathematician discussing the laws of number, or a natural philosopher physics. Hitherto, sir, all who have written about the state—"

Here he stopped, and chid himself with a good-humoured smile.

"Forgive me, Messere, I am taking a mean advantage. It may be that policy interests you as little as painting interests me?"

"Not so," said Leonardo. "I tell you candidly I don't affect statecraft, because such talk is apt to be idle. But your opinions are so new and surprising, that, believe me, I am thrice happy to learn."

"Beware, Messer Leonardo," said the other; "these matters are my hobby-horse. I will go without bread, if I may but talk upon politics with a man of understanding. The mischief is, to find the man of understanding! Our great ones think of naught but the price of wool and of silk, while I" (he smiled bitterly) "am made of neither."

Leonardo reassured him, and added, in order to keep the conversation going:—

"You have said, Messere, that politics should be an exact science founded upon mathematics, like mechanics, which finds its certainty in the observation and experience of nature. Did I understand you aright?"

"Perfectly!" cried Machiavelli, frowning, and looking into space beyond his companion's head, with that air of a far-sighted bird habitual to him. "I desire to reveal a new thing to men about human affairs. The Laws of nature, which are outside man's will, outside good and evil, are the laws which guide the life of every society. All former writers on this subject have dealt with the good and the bad, the noble and the base. I do not concern myself with governments which ought to be, nor with what seems to be, but with that which really is. I inquire into the nature of the great bodies, known as republics and monarchies, and I commit myself neither to praise nor to blame, like a mathematician or an anatomist. I will tell men the truth, even if they burn me for it, as they burned Fra Girolamo. For the task is dangerous."

Leonardo smiled, observing Machiavelli's excitement, and thought; "With what passion he praises dispassionateness!"

"Messer Niccolò," he said aloud, "if you succeed according to your intentions, you will have done more than Euclid or Archimedes."

Leonardo was struck by the unconventionality of what he had heard. He remembered how, thirteen years earlier, he had himself written on the margin of certain anatomical sketches:—

"May the Most High assist me to study the nature of human beings, their temperaments and habits, even as here I have studied their internal organs!"

IV

Suddenly Machiavelli exclaimed, his eyes sparkling merrily; "The more I listen to you, Messer Leonardo, the more I am astounded that we should have met. Some most rare combination of the stars! The minds of men are, I protest, of three qualities. First, those who see of themselves; secondly, those who see when they are shown; thirdly, those who see not of themselves, neither see when they are shown. Your worship, and I myself (for I would not be guilty of false modesty) belong to the first category. But you laugh? Ah! such a meeting will not easily come to me again on this side the grave, for on earth the elect are few. Permit me to read you a most beautiful piece of Livy."

He took a book from the table, adjusted the tallow candle, put on iron spectacles (broken and tied up with string), the large round glasses of which gave him a grave and devout expression, as if he were addressing himself to some act of worship. But no sooner had he found his passage, and opened his lips, than the door opened, and a little wrinkled old woman came in, curtseying and bowing.

"I crave your pardon, gentlemen, for this annoyance," she mumbled, "but my illustrious lady, Madonna Lena Griffi, has lost her favourite animal—a rabbit with a blue ribbon round its neck. We have searched two hours for it, but vainly."

"There are no rabbits here," said Messer Niccolò, angrily; "go to the devil!" And he was about to eject her, but suddenly checked himself, and having looked at her narrowly, both with and without his spectacles, he cried:—

"Monna Alvigia! Is it really you, you old witch? I thought the devil had long ago roasted your old carcase!"

The woman blinked and cowered, answering his polite greeting with a sorry smile.

"Oh, Messer Niccolò! how many years, how many winters since we have seen each other! I had never expected God would give us this pleasure again!"

Machiavelli invited the old woman to follow him to the kitchen for a crack; but Leonardo, providing himself with a book and seating himself in a corner, begged them to remain. Then Messer Niccolò sent for wine with a lordly air, as if he were the most honoured guest in the inn.

"Hark ye, friend," he said to the servant who took his order, "bid that skinflint, your master, beware how he serve us that acid stuff we had yesterday, for Monna Alvigia and I are like Arlotto the priest, who would not kneel if the wine were bad."

Monna Alvigia forgot her rabbit and Niccolò his Livy; over their pitcher of wine they gossiped like old friends. Alvigia told tales of her youth when she had been fair to see and much courted, and she had done what she wished and it had not mattered what she did. Had she not once in Padua lifted the mitre from the head of the bishop and placed it upon her own? But years passed by, and her beauty faded, and her lovers abandoned her, and she had to support herself by hiring rooms and by taking in washing. Then she fell ill, and she thought of sitting among the beggars at the church door, and even of ending herself by poison. But the Holy Virgin came to her aid and rescued her from death. With the aid of an old abbot, who was in love with the young wife of a blacksmith, she entered upon a trade far more profitable than that of a laundress.

The story was interrupted by a summons from Madonna Lena, who required pomade for her monkey's wounded paw, and Boccaccio's *Decameron*, which she always kept under her pillow beside her prayer-book.

The old woman gone, Messer Niccolò mended a pen, took paper, and began his report to the Magnificent Signori of Florence, on the dispositions and actions of the Duke of Valentinois, a piece of profound statesmanship, written in easy, almost jocular style.

"Messere" he exclaimed, raising his eyes to Leonardo, "confess I surprised you by my sudden passage from discussion of the virtue of ancient Sparta to vain gossip about women with that old hag! Judge me not too harshly! We must imitate nature. Are we not men? Is it not legended that Aristotle, in the very presence of Alexander his pupil, permitted the leman whom he loved to ride on his back while he caracoled on all fours? Shall simple sinners be more discreet?"

By this time the household slept. All was silent save for the chirp of the cricket, the muttering of Monna Alvigia, and the growling of the monkey as she anointed its paw. Leonardo had gone to bed, but lay watching his quaint companion, who still gnawed his pen and stooped over his writing. The candle flame threw on the wall a vast shadow of his head with its sharp-cut angles, its protruding lower lip, its thin neck and long beak-like nose. Having finished his report he sealed it up, and wrote the words usual on despatches; "*Cito, citissime, celerrime*." Then he opened his Livy and pursued his occupation of many years, the compiling of notes for the *Decades*.

The shadow on the wall danced and wavered and grimaced as the candle flickered and burned low; but the face of the Florentine secretary preserved its stern and dignified calm; the reflection of the greatness of ancient Rome. Only in the depth of his eyes, in the corners of his lips there showed sometimes a two-faced cunning, a mocking cynicism.

V

Next day the storm was over. The sun sparkled on the frozen windows; the snowy fields and hills, soft as down, shone dazzlingly white under the azure sky. His companion was no longer in the room when Leonardo awoke. He dressed and descended to the kitchen where, to the joy of the cook, a joint was roasting on the automatic spit.

He ordered his mule and sat down to breakfast. Beside him was Messer Niccolò talking excitedly to a couple of newcomers. One of these was a faultlessly fashionable youth with an undistinguished face, a certain Messer Lucio, related to Francesco Vettori. This Vettori was a man of note in Florence, intimately connected with Piero Soderini the *Gonfaloniere*, and very favourably disposed to Machiavelli. He had sent Lucio with letters to Messer Niccolò from his friends.

"Be not disquieted about the money," Lucio was saying; "my uncle assures me that last Thursday the Signori promised—"

"But, my dear sir," interrupted Machiavelli, "can two servants and three horses be fed with promises? At Imola I received sixty ducats and paid debts of seventy. If it were not for the compassion of the benevolent, the secretary of the Florentine Republic would starve. It is vain for the Signori to talk of the honour of their town if they force the man whom they send to a strange court to beg for his sheer necessities."

Messer Niccolò knew these complaints were useless, but it solaced him to make them. The kitchen being nearly empty, he spoke without reserve.

"Here is our fellow-citizen, Messer Leonardo da Vinci—the *Gonfaloniere* must know him," resumed Machiavelli, indicating the painter, to whom Lucio bowed courteously. "Messer Leonardo was witness only last night of the humiliations to which I am daily subjected. I demand—hear you?—I do not ask, but I demand leave to resign my office," he concluded, his anger still waxing, and addressing the young Florentine as if he saw in him the whole Magnificent Signoria. "I am a poor man, sir, and my affairs go from bad to worse, and my health likewise. If matters continue as they are I shall return home in my coffin. Moreover I have done all which is possible to do, with the poor powers accorded me. To drag out the negotiation, to go around and about, one step forward and two steps back, 'I will' and 'I won't'—that is not work for me! The duke is too clever for such childishness! Well, I have written to your uncle—"

"My uncle," interrupted Lucio, "will doubtless do all he can for you, Messer Niccolò; but the Magnificent Ten, to tell truth, consider your reports so essential to the weal of the republic that they will not permit you to retire. 'Who is there,' they say, 'able to take his place? He is a man of gold; he is the ear and the eye of our commonwealth!' I swear to you, Messere, that your letters have so great a success in Florence that you could not desire a greater. All are bewitched by the incomparable felicity of your style. My uncle informed me that at a late meeting in the council chamber, upon the reading of one of your merry letters, the Signori burst themselves with laughter—"

"Oh, that's it, is it?" exclaimed Machiavelli, his face contorted with rage. "Ah, now I understand! My letters are amusing to the Magnificent Signori; they burst themselves with laughter, and they admire my diction. Thank God, Niccolò Machiavelli is capable of something! Yet I live here like a dog, I freeze and go hungry, I shake with fever, and am insulted by landlords, all for the good of the republic. The devil take the republic, and the *Gonfaloniere* too, snivelling old woman! May you all be buried unshriven and uncoffined!" And he burst into the vulgar vituperation of the market-place, helplessly furious at the thought of these chiefs of the people, so utterly despicable, and yet his masters. To divert his thoughts Lucio handed him a letter from his young wife, Marietta; a few lines written in a round childish hand on coarse grey paper.

> "*Carissimo Niccolò mio*," so she wrote, "I am told that in those parts, where you are now, fevers and other sicknesses abound. You may fancy my care for you. My thoughts give me no peace day nor night. The boy, thank God, is well. He grows apace, and is like you. His little face is white as the snowdrift, but his head, with its thick black curls, is like yours. He seems beautiful to me because he is like you. He is lively and merry as though he were a year old. Believe me, directly he was born he opened his eyes and he shouted with a voice which filled the house. I pray you, forget us not. I entreat, return to us at the earliest moment, for to wait longer passeth my endurance. And, meanwhile, may the Lord protect

you, and the blessed Virgin! I send you two shirts and two handkerchiefs and a towel."

Your,
MARIETTA in Florence

Leonardo observed that Machiavelli reading this letter seemed another man. His face lit up with a tender smile not to be expected on his harsh features. The smile, however, quickly disappeared. He shrugged his shoulders, crumpled the letter and stuffed it into his pouch, then said savagely—

"Who told her I was ill?"

"Messer Niccolò," replied Lucio, "everyday Monna Marietta has been to the members of the council asking for you, and inquiring where you are and how you fare."

"I know! I know! 'Twas like to be so. Affairs of state should be reserved for celibates. One of the two—politics or a wife—not both." Then he turned abruptly and said, "And you yourself, good youth; you are perhaps thinking of wedding?"

"Not at present, Messer Niccolò," replied Lucio.

"Never commit that folly; unless you have the shoulders of Atlas. Eh! Messer Leonardo?"

The painter understood that Messer Niccolò loved Marietta passionately, but was ashamed to admit the fact.

The inn was now emptying fast; Leonardo prepared for his start and invited Machiavelli to ride with him. But Messer Niccolò shook his head, saying he must wait for money from Florence before he could pay his bill. He spoke sadly, his assumed levity having suddenly collapsed. He looked ill and wretched. Inaction, long stay in one place was misery to him. Not without cause had the Council of Ten complained of his frequent, causeless, and unexpected removals, which were great embarrassment to their affairs.

Leonardo took him aside and offered to lend the requisite money. Machiavelli declined.

"You hurt me, my friend," said the painter; "remember this rare conjunction of the stars! You would confer a benefit upon me."

There was so much kindness in Leonardo's voice that Messer Niccolò had not the courage to persist in his refusal. He took twenty ducats which he promised to return on receipt of his money from Florence; then immediately paid his score, with the lavishness of a great noble.

VI

THEY STARTED. THE MORNING WAS calm and exquisite; the air, still freezing in the shade, was in the sunshine almost spring-like in its warmth. The deep blue-shadowed snow crackled under the feet of the beasts. Between the white hills shone the pale green of the winter sea, and yellow lateen sails glanced here and there like poised butterflies.

Niccolò talked, jested, and laughed. Every trifle excited him to some amusing or cynical reflection.

Passing a fishing village the travellers saw a group of fat and jolly friars on the church steps selling rosaries to the women, whose husbands and brothers stood aloof staring stupidly.

"Fools!" shouted Messer Niccolò, "know you not that fat easily goes aflame; and that holy fathers like pretty women not only to call them fathers but to make them so?"

Leonardo asked him what he had thought of Savonarola. Niccolò replied that at one time he had been Fra Girolamo's zealous partisan, hoping to find him the saviour of his country; but too soon he had begun to see the weakness of the prophet.

"The whole splenetic gang became nauseous to me," he mused. "I detest even to think of it. The devil take them!" he added energetically.

VII

ABOUT NOON THEY RODE IN at the gates of Fano. The houses were alive with Cæsar's courtiers, captains, and troopers. Two rooms in the best situation had been assigned to the ducal engineer; he offered one of them to his travelling companion, who in such a crowd might have had difficulty in procuring a lodging.

Machiavelli presented himself at once at the palace, and when he returned he brought important news.

Don Ramiro de Lorqua, who had been governing in the duke's name, had been executed. On Christmas day the people had found the headless corpse wallowing on the ground in a pool of blood, an axe beside it, the ghastly head stuck on a spear.

"The cause of the execution is unknown," said Messer Niccolò, "but 'tis the talk of the whole town. Let us go together and listen to the conjectures of the rabble. 'Tis an opportunity to study the natural laws of politics."

Before the old cathedral of San Fortunato a crowd was expecting the coming forth of the duke, who was about to review his troops. Leonardo and Machiavelli joined the throng in which but one subject was being discussed.

"I can make nothing of it," said a young workman with a dull, good-natured face. "I thought Don Ramiro had been loved and enriched above all the court."

"The very reason of his chastisement," replied a respectable shopkeeper, dressed in a squirrel pelisse; "Don Ramiro has been deceiving our duke. He has oppressed, imprisoned, plundered the people. Before his lord he wore sheep's clothing; he fancied things hid were not things forbid. But his hour came; the sovereign's patience was exhausted, and for the good of the people he did not spare his friend; he cut off his head without trial, without hesitation, without delay, as a warning to others. Now they see how terrible is the duke's wrath, how impartial his justice. He puts down the mighty from their seats and exalteth them of low degree."

"*Reges eos in virga ferrea*," declaimed a monk. "Thou rulest them with a rod of iron."

"Ay, ay! They need an iron rod, the sons of dogs, the oppressors of the people!"

"He knows when to pardon, and when to strike."

"We want no better sovereign."

"Truly," said a peasant, "the Lord has at last had pity on Romagna. Before, there was flaying both of the living and of the dead and the taxes were our starvation. The last pair of oxen in our stalls had to go! But since the Duke Valentino came we have been able to breathe. May the Lord keep him in health!"

"And the judges!" said the shopkeeper; "their delay used to eat one's very heart! 'Tis different now."

"He has protected the orphan and consoled the widow," put in the monk.

"He is merciful. 'Tis not to be denied he is merciful to the people."

"He gives offence to none."

"O Santo Iddio!" murmured a feeble old woman, beside herself with admiration; "may the Blessed Virgin preserve to us our father, our benefactor, our bright sun!"

"Do you hear them?" whispered Machiavelli. "*Vox populi vox dei.* I have always said one must be in the plains to see the mountains; one must be among the people to know the sovereign. I'd like to get them here, those folk who call the duke a tyrant! These things are hid from the wise and prudent, but revealed unto the simple."

Martial music was heard and the crowd was astir.

"He comes! Look!"

They stood on tiptoe and craned their necks, curious heads were thrust from windows, women and girls, their eyes full of love, ran out on the balconies and *loggie* to see their hero, *Cesare bello e biondo*—"Cæsar, the blond and beautiful." It was rare good luck, for he hardly ever showed himself to the people.

The musicians walked first, making a deafening clatter of kettledrums in time with the heavy tread of the soldiers. Next came the duke's Romagnole guard, all picked and handsome men, carrying halberts three cubits long. They wore cuirasses, and helmets of steel, and their garments were parti-coloured, the right side yellow, the left red. Niccolò could not admire enough this truly Roman array. After the guard came equerries and pages, in clothes of unsurpassed splendour; camisoles of gold brocade, mantles of pounce velvet with gold-embroidered slashings, their scabbards and belts of snakes' scales, with knobs representing the seven heads of the viper vomiting poison—the cognisance of the Borgias. Embroidered on their breasts was the word, "Cæsar." They were followed by the bodyguard, Albanian *stradiotes*, with curved yataghans. Then Bartolomeo Capranica, the *Maestro del Campo*, carried the naked sword of the Gonfaloniere of the Roman Church. After him came the ruler of Romagna himself, Cæsar Borgia, Duke of Valentinois. He was mounted on a black Barbary stallion, with a diamond sun on its headband: he wore a pale blue silk mantle with the white lilies of France embroidered in pearls, and a corselet wrought into the gaping mouth of a lion. His helmet was a dragon, with scales, wings, and fins of wrought brass, resounding at every movement.

At this time Cæsar Borgia was six and twenty; his face had grown thin and worn since Leonardo had seen him at Louis XII's court at Milan. His features were sharper, and his eyes, with their glow like polished steel, were graver and more impenetrable. His hair and pointed beard had darkened; his long nose seemed more aquiline. Complete serenity still reigned upon his impassive face; only now there was a look of still more strenuous daring, of terrifying keenness, like the edge of a bared and sharpened sword.

The duke was followed by his artillery, the best in Italy. Brass culverins, falconets, iron mortars firing stones—drawn by oxen, their heavy chariots rolling along with a dull roar and mixing with the voices of the trumpets and kettledrums. In the glow of the setting sun, cannon, cuirasses, helmets, spears, flashed lightning; Cæsar was riding in the imperial purple of a conqueror, straight towards the immense blood-red sun.

The crowd gazed at the hero in silence, holding its breath, wishing, yet fearing, to greet him with applause, in an ecstasy of admiration akin to terror. Tears flowed down the cheeks of the old beggar woman, and she murmured:—

"Holy saints! Holy mother! The Lord has permitted me to see his face! O, our beauteous sun!"

The flashing sword entrusted to Cæsar by the pope was the fiery glaive of the archangel Michael himself.

Leonardo smiled, seeing on Machiavelli's face the very same look of artless enthusiasm.

VIII

On reaching home Leonardo found a letter from Messer Agapito, bidding him wait on his Excellency the next day. A little later, Lucio, who was passing through Fano on his way to Ancona, came in for a visit, and Machiavelli spoke to him of the execution of Don Ramiro de Lorqua.

"To divine the real reasons for the actions of a ruler like Cæsar Borgia, is almost impossible," he said, "but as you ask me what I think of this deed, I will tell you. Till its conquest by the duke, Romagna was under the yoke of a number of petty tyrants, and full of disorder, plundering and violence. To end this state of turbulence Cæsar appointed his astute and faithful servant, Don Ramiro, as his lieutenant. This man accomplished his task; he inspired the people with a salutary terror, and established perfect tranquillity throughout the country, but he did it by a long series of cruel punishments. When the prince saw that his object was gained he determined to destroy the instrument of his severity. Don Ramiro has been seized, on the ground of extortion, and executed; his dead body lies exposed to public view. This terrible spectacle has at once gratified and awed the people. The duke's action has been wise, for he has reaped three clear advantages. First, he has slain the tyrants; secondly, by condemning Ramiro he has disassociated himself from his lieutenant's ferocity and so has gained a character for gentleness; thirdly, by sacrificing his favourite servant he has set an example of incorruptible equity."

Machiavelli spoke in a low dry voice, with expressionless countenance, as if stating his reasoning on some theorem.

"From your own words, Messer Niccolò," cried Lucio, "I perceive that this supposed equity is the excess of villainy!"

Sparks of fire appeared in the secretary's eyes, but he looked away and spoke as coldly as before.

"It may be so," he assented, "but what of it?"

"What of it? Would you approve such scoundrelly statecraft?"

"Young man, you speak with the inexperience of youth. In politics, the difference between the way men should and the way they do act, is so great, that to forget it means to expose yourself to certain ruin. For all men are by nature evil and vicious; they are virtuous only for advantage or through fear. A prince who would avoid ruin, must at all hazards learn the art of appearing virtuous; and he must be or not be virtuous as the case may require. He must disregard all uneasiness of conscience as to those secret measures without which the preservation of power is impossible; for upon accurate knowledge of the nature of good and evil, it is clear that the power of a prince will often be undermined by his virtuous actions and augmented by his crimes."

Lucio again protested. "Reasoning thus," he cried, "anything would be permissible, and there is no wickedness which you could not justify!"

"That is so," replied Machiavelli with perfect serenity, and, as if insisting upon the significance of his words, he raised his hand and added solemnly; "All is permissible to the man who knows how to rule." Then he resumed in his former dry tone of ratiocination, "Therefore, I conclude that the severity of the Duke of Valentinois, who has put an end to pillage and violence throughout Romagna, has been more rational and no less merciful than the leniency of our Florentines, who have permitted continued revolts and have fomented disorder in all the provinces under their sway. For it is better to strike down a few than bring a whole state to ruin as result of its licence."

"But," said Lucio, somewhat overwhelmed, "have there been no rulers that were strangers to this cruelty? Think of Antoninus and Marcus Aurelius."

"Do not forget, Messere, that I am discussing the government of conquered, not of hereditary principalities; and the acquisition, not the maintenance, of authority. The emperors you have named could afford clemency, because in the preceding years there had been sufficiency of bloody deeds. The founder of Rome slew his brother—a horrid crime—but this fratricide was necessary to the establishment of a sole authority, without which Rome would have perished from the weakness consequent on domestic strife. Who shall be able certainly to balance a single fratricide against all the virtue and wisdom of the Eternal City? Doubtless we ought to prefer the most humble fortune to greatness founded upon evil deeds; but he who has once abandoned the path of abstract righteousness, must, if he would not perish, walk resolutely in the path of evil and follow it to the end: for men revenge themselves only for small offences, great offences depriving them of the power of revenge. Therefore, a prince must inflict only serious injuries on his subjects, and must refrain from minor injustices. Yet the generality persist in choosing the middle course between wrong and right, which is the most perilous. They recoil from crimes which demand great courage, and commit only vulgar baseness which profits them not."

"Your words make my hair stand on end, Messer Niccolò," said Lucio, much shocked, but thinking a jest the most courteous form of reply; "You may speak the truth, but I shall flatly refuse to believe these your real opinions."

"Truths always seem improbable," said Machiavelli dryly.

Leonardo, who was listening, had already observed that Messer Niccolò, while pretending indifference, was casting sly glances at Lucio as if to gauge the effect his words were producing. It was evident that Machiavelli had little self-command, was not possessed of calm and conquering strength. Unwilling to think like other men, hating the commonplace, he had fallen into the opposite error, into exaggeration, into the affectation of views rare and startling, but incomplete and paradoxical. He played with such words as *virtue* and *ferocity*, much as a juggler plays with naked swords. He had a whole armoury of these polished, shining, tempting and dangerous weapons, ready for the disabling of men like Messer Lucio; men of the herd, respectable, sensible, conventional. He punished them for their triumphant mediocrity, and for his own disregarded superiority; he cut and scratched them; but did not kill or even seriously wound them. Leonardo remembered the monster which he had once painted on the wooden "rotello" for Ser Piero da Vinci; an animal put together from the different parts of a variety of repulsive reptiles. Had not Messer Niccolò put together as useless and impossible a monstrosity in his superhumanly astute and conscienceless prince? A being contrary to nature, fascinating as Medusa, invented for the terrifying of the vulgar? Yet under this wantonness of imagination, this artistic dispassionateness, Leonardo perceived great suffering in the soul of Messer Niccolò, as if a juggler, playing with swords, were himself cut to the quick.

"Is he not one of those unhappy sick men," thought the painter, "who seek relief from pain in envenoming their wounds?" He did not know the last secret of this dark spirit, so like, and yet so unlike, his own.

Messer Lucio, like a man in a nightmare, was struggling with the Medusa head evoked by Messer Niccolò.

"Well, well!" he said, "I will not dispute with you. Severity may have been necessary to princes in the past. We can pardon them a good deal for the sake of their heroic virtues and exploits. But, pardon me, what has this to do with the Duke of Romagna? *Quod licet Jovi non licet bovi.* What is permitted to Alexander the Great or to Julius Cæsar, may be unpardonable in Alexander the pope or in Cæsar Borgia, of whom we cannot yet say whether he be Cæsar or nothing. I at least think, and all will agree with me—"

"Oh, of course, all will agree with you," interrupted Niccolò, out of patience, "but that is no proof, Messer Lucio. The truth does not lie on the high road where all men pass. But to conclude the discussion, here is my last word. As I observe the acts of Cæsar, I find them perfect; and I would suggest him as a model to all who would obtain power by force of arms and by successful adventure. He combines cruelty so well with virtue, he knows so accurately when to caress and when to crush, the foundations of his power are so firmly though so quickly laid, that already he is an autocrat, the only one in Italy, perhaps the only one in Europe. It is hard to imagine what may not lie before him in the future." Machiavelli's eyes burned, his voice shook, and red spots glowed on his sunken cheeks; he seemed like a seer. From the mask of a cynic looked out the face of the former disciple of Savonarola, the fanatic.

But Lucio, weary of the discussion, had no sooner suggested sealing a truce with two or three bottles from the neighbouring cellar than the visionary disappeared.

"Nay," cried Messer Niccolò eagerly, "let us go to a different tavern. I have a good scent in such matters, I know where we shall find handsome women."

"What, in this scurvy little town?" said Lucio.

"Listen, my lad," said the dignified secretary of the Florentine Republic, "never you despise these same small towns. In their vile alleys you can sometimes find what will make you lick your fingers for delight."

At these words Lucio slapped Messer Niccolò on the back, and called him a sly dog.

"We will take lanterns," continued Niccolò, "we will wear cloaks and vizards. On such expeditions mystery is half the pleasure. Messer Leonardo, you accompany us?"

The artist excused himself.

He did not enjoy the customary gross talk about women, and avoided it with instinctive repulsion. This man of fifty, the intrepid student of the secrets of nature who could accompany criminals to their execution that he might see the last look of terror in their eyes, was often put out of countenance by a jest, did not know which way to look, and blushed like a schoolboy.

Niccolò, without more ado, carried off Messer Lucio.

IX

Early next day a chamberlain came to inquire whether the ducal engineer were satisfied with his quarters, and to bring him a present from Cæsar. According to the hospitable custom of the time it consisted of provisions, a sack of flour, a cask of wine, a sheep, a dozen fat capons; and also two large torches, three packets of wax candles, and two boxes of *confetti*. Impressed by these compliments, Machiavelli begged Leonardo to say a word for him to the duke, and obtain him the favour of an interview. At eleven in the evening, Cæsar's customary reception-hour, they went together to the palace.

The duke's manner of life was strange enough. Summer and winter he went to bed at four or five in the morning, so that for him it was dawn at three in the afternoon, sunrise at four; at five he began to dress and to dine and to conduct his business affairs all simultaneously. He surrounded his doings with mystery, not only out of natural secretiveness, but by studied calculation; he seldom left his palace, and always masked. Only on great festivals did he show himself to the people, and to the troops only in moments of extreme danger. He liked to astonish; his appearances were always dramatic, like those of a demi-god.

Scarce credible reports were current as to his profuseness. All the gold continually flowing into the treasury of St. Peter's did not suffice for the expenditure of the *Gonfaloniere* of the Church. Envoys reported that he spent not less than eighteen hundred ducats daily; and that when he rode through the streets crowds followed him to pick up the easily dropped silver shoes, with which his horses were shod, solely as largesse to the people. Wonders were told also as to his physical strength. He could bend horse-shoes in his fingers (thin and delicate as a woman's), twist iron rods, break the cables of ships. At a bull-fight in Rome some years ago, when he had been Cardinal of Valenza, the youthful Cæsar had cut a bull in half with a single stroke of his sword. Inaccessible to his courtiers and to the ambassadors of great potentates, he was often to be seen on the hills round Cesena watching the boxing matches of the wild Romagna herdsmen, and sometimes taking part in the sport.

At the same time he was the ideal of a cavalier and the paragon of fashion. On the day of his sister Lucrezia's marriage with Alfonso d'Este, he left the siege of a fortress and rode from the camp to the wedding, unrecognised, and clad in black velvet with a black mask. He passed through the crowd of guests, bowed, and when all drew back in surprise, danced to the strains of the music with such grace that at once the cry was raised, "*Cesare! Cesare! L'unico Cesare!*"

Heeding neither guests nor bridegroom, he drew Lucrezia aside and whispered in her ear. Her eyes fell, she flushed, then grew white, to the enhancement of her dainty pearl-like beauty. It might be she was innocent; there was no question that she was frail; report added submissive, perhaps even criminally submissive, to the terrible will of this her brother.

He, it seemed, cared for one point only, that there should be no proofs. Fame probably exaggerated his sins; but possibly the reality was more terrible than fame. At any rate he knew how to conceal his actions, and to wipe out every trace of them.

X

The old Gothic municipal palace of Fano served as the duke's residence. Leonardo and Machiavelli crossed the dreary hall where less important visitors were received, and entered an inner apartment, once a chapel. There was stained glass in the lancet windows; and the Apostles and Fathers of the Church were carved in oak on the high stalls of the choir. On the ceiling was a faded fresco of the Holy Dove hovering over clouds and angels. The courtiers were standing and talking in undertones, for the near presence of the sovereign was felt even through the walls. The ill-starred envoy from Rimini, a bald and feeble old man who had been waiting three months for his audience of the duke, clearly worn out by many sleepless nights, had fallen into a doze. Now and then the door opened, and the secretary Agapito, with an anxious air, spectacles on nose and pen behind his ear, looked in, and summoned to his Highness one or other of those waiting. Each time, the bald old man from Rimini shuddered, started up, saw it was not his turn, sighed heavily, and again sank into his doze. His slumbers were soothed by the sound of an apothecary's pestle beating in a mortar; for, a suitable room being lacking, this chapel was used not only as the ante-chamber to the presence but also as the surgery. Where the altar had stood was a table crowded with the bottles, gallipots, and retorts of a physician's laboratory, and behind it Gaspare Torella, the bishop of Santa Giusta, and the chief physician to the Duke of Valentinois, was preparing a fashionable medicine, a decoction of "*guaiaco*," or, as it was commonly called, "Holy tree," brought from the new islands discovered by Columbus. The bishop-doctor, while he rubbed the yellow lumps in his shapely hands, was discoursing on the nature of this healing tree; and the oaken saints on the stalls seemed listening in amazement to the strange talk of these new shepherds of the Lord's flock. The chapel was lighted only by the physician's blinking lamp; the air was choked by the pungent smell of the medicine, mingled with faint perfume of the incense of earlier years; one might have fancied this an assembly of prelates engaged in the performance of some strange mystic rite. Meantime the Florentine secretary was taking now one, now another of the courtiers aside, and adroitly questioning them as to Cæsar's policy. Presently he approached Leonardo and whispered to him very mysteriously.

"I shall eat the artichoke; I shall eat the artichoke!"

"What artichoke?" asked the painter, bewildered.

"Precisely; what artichoke? It seems the duke propounded a riddle to Messer Pandolfo Collenuccio, the Ambassador from Ferrara. He said, 'I shall eat the artichoke, leaf by leaf.' It may signify the league of his enemies whom he means to separate, and so destroy one by one. I have puzzled my brains over it for an hour." Speaking still lower, he continued, "Here all is riddle and trap. They chatter about every kind of nonsense, but directly you speak of affairs they become dumb as monks at dinner. But they shall not deceive me; I know very well there is something in the air. I' faith, sir, I would sell my soul to know what."

And his eyes glowed like a desperate gamester's. Before Leonardo could reply, he was summoned by Messer Agapito. Through a long gloomy passage guarded by the Stradiotes, Leonardo arrived at the duke's bedchamber, a spacious room hung with tapestry and silk. On the ceiling were painted the amours of Pasiphae and the bull. The bull, the heraldic emblem of the Borgias, was repeated on all the ornaments of the room, together with the triple tiara and the keys of St. Peter. The room was warm and scented. A fire of juniper burned on the marble hearth, and the lamp oil was perfumed with violets. Cæsar, elegantly dressed, lay on a flat couch in the middle of the room; he cared for two postures only, reclining, or sitting on horseback. Apparently indifferent to everything, he leaned his elbow on a pillow, listened to a report from a secretary, and watched a game of chess which two of his attendants were playing on a jasper table by his side. He had the faculty of divided attention. With a slow, uniform, mechanical movement he passed backwards and forwards from one hand to the other a golden ball filled with scent, which he carried as religiously as his Damascene dagger.

XI

He received Leonardo with a peculiar and charming courtesy. Not permitting him to kneel, he held his hand and made him sit in an armchair by his side. The duke wished to consult him about plans tendered by Bramante for a new monastery at the town of Imola, which was to be called Valentino, and to have a superb chapel, a hospital, and a refuge for pilgrims. By such munificent works of charity he wished to erect a monument to his own Christian beneficence. After Bramante's designs, he exhibited letters just cut for Girolamo Soncino's new printing-press at Fano, being zealous in the encouragement of the arts and sciences in his dominions. Agapito then gave his master a collection of eulogistic odes by Franceso Uberti the court poet; these Cæsar received graciously, commanding a liberal reward for the author. Then, as he insisted upon seeing satires no less than eulogies, the secretary handed him a poem by Mancioni the Neapolitan, who had been seized and confined in the Castle of St. Angelo in Rome. This sonnet was full of savage abuse; in it Cæsar was called a mule, the mongrel offspring of a harlot and a pope, sitting on a throne, once Christ's now Satan's; a circumcised Turk, a disfrocked cardinal, incestuous, apostate, fratricidal.

"Why, O God, waitest Thou?" cried the poet; "carest thou not that Holy Church has become a stall for mules, a den of orgies?"

"How does your Excellency wish the villain to be dealt with?" asked Agapito.

"Leave him till my return," replied the duke quietly, "I will deal with him myself. I shall know how to teach these scribblers manners!" he added, in a low voice.

Cæsar's method of teaching manners was not unknown. For less serious affronts he had cut off hands, and seared tongues with red hot irons. His report finished, the secretary withdrew. Then audience was given to Valguglio, the astrologer, who had drawn a new horoscope. The duke listened attentively, for he was a believer in the influences of the stars. Valguglio explained that Cæsar's late illness was due to the entrance of Mars into the sign of the Scorpion; the complaint would pass when Venus had reached her rising in Taurus. Had the duke any matter of importance in hand, let him choose for its date the afternoon of the 31st of December, as the conjunction of stars that day was propitious; and bending toward the duke's ear and raising his finger impressively, the astrologer repeated thrice in a mysterious whisper—

"*Fatilo*, *Fatilo*, *Fatilo*"—"Do it. Do it. Do it!"

Cæsar made no reply, but it seemed to Leonardo that a shadow passed over his face. Then he dismissed the seer and turned again to the *Ingegnere Ducale*.

Leonardo unfolded military plans and maps. Not merely scientific, showing the nature of the soil, the direction of the watersheds, the mountains, the windings of the rivers—they were also artistic bird's-eye pictures of the localities, coloured after Nature, and with every detail executed in perfection. Squares, streets and towers of the towns could be recognised; the spectator felt as if flying over the earth, and seeing at his feet an infinite expanse. Cæsar examined with great attention the topography of the district bounded on the south by the lake of Bolsena, on the north by the Val d'Ema, on the east by Arezzo and Perugia, on the west by Siena and the littoral. This was the heart of Italy, Leonardo's home, the territory of Florence, long coveted by the duke. Immersed in thought, enjoying this fancied flight, Cæsar gazed long at Leonardo's drawing, and felt as if he and the great inventor were in such sort engaged in the same work. He raised his eyes to the artist and cordially pressed his hand.

"I thank you, my Leonardo. Continue to serve me thus and I shall know how to reward you. Are you comfortable among us?" he continued solicitously; "are you satisfied with your salary? Have you any request to make? You know my pleasure in gratifying you."

Leonardo, profiting by the opportunity, asked an audience for Messer Niccolò. Cæsar shrugged his shoulders with a good-humoured smile.

"He is a strange man, your Messer Niccolò. He demands audience, and, when I receive him, talks about nothing at all. Why did they send me such a mysterious person?" Presently he asked Leonardo's opinion of the man.

"I find him, Excellence, one of the most astute and most clear-sighted persons I have met in my whole life."

"He is certainly intelligent," said the duke, "and I doubt not he has understanding of affairs. And yet—he is unreliable. He knows no mean in anything. However—I wish him well, especially since he has your good word. He is guileless, though he thinks himself the most cunning of men, and would deceive me, whom he considers the enemy of your Republic. I pardon him, understanding that he loves his country better than his soul. Well, I will receive him; tell him so. By the way, have I not heard he is compiling a book on Statecraft and the Art of War?"

Cæsar laughed his low pleasant laugh, as if reminded of something which had tickled him.

"Have you heard about the Macedonian phalanx? No? Then listen. Once, Messer Niccolò explained from this very book on war to my Master of the Camp, Bartolomeo Capranica, and other captains, the laws of ranging troops after the manner of the phalanx. He spoke with such eloquence that all desired to see the phalanx in actual fact. We went to a suitable field and Niccolò was to give orders. Well, he wrestled with two thousand soldiers for nearly three hours exposing them to the cold, the wind, the rain, but he could not form his own phalanx. At last Bartolomeo lost patience; he had never read a military book in his life, but he took the troop in hand, and in the twinkling of an eye he had drawn up the infantry in the desired order. There we see the difference between practice and theory. But take care how you allude to it! Messer Niccolò does not like to be reminded of anything Macedonian!"

By this time it was three o'clock and the duke's supper was brought, a dish of fruit, trout, and some white wine; like a true Spaniard he ate and drank most sparingly. Leonardo was dismissed, but not before Cæsar had again thanked him for the maps. Three pages carrying torches were detailed to escort him to his lodging.

The painter told Machiavelli about his interview with the duke. When he spoke of the maps of the Florentine territory Messer Niccolò grew thoughtful.

"What? You? A citizen of our republic, for our bitterest enemy? Do you know, sir, that for this you may be accused of treason?"

"Really?" said Leonardo, astonished; "I don't wish to think so, Niccolò. I am no politician, but obey like a blind man."

Silently they looked into each other's eyes; and each recognised the profound difference between them. The one might be said to have no country: the other loved his country, in Cæsar's phrase, "above his own soul."

XII

That night Niccolò went away, leaving no word as to the Whither and the Why.

He returned next day, weary and frozen, entered Leonardo's room, bolted the door, and announced that he wished to speak on a matter of profoundest secrecy. Then he began a narrative.

Three years ago, one winter evening, in a deserted corner of Romagna between Cervia and Porto Cesenatico, a body of cavalry was escorting Madonna Dorotea, wife of Battista Caracciolo, captain of infantry in the service of the *Serenissima Signoria* of Venice, and her cousin, Maria, a fifteen year old novice in an Urbino convent, from Urbino to Venice. Horsemen armed and masked fell on the party, seized the ladies, put them on horses, and carried them off. From that day they had not been heard of. The Council and Senate of Venice, considering themselves outraged in the person of their captain, appealed to Louis XII, to the King of Spain, and to the pope, openly accusing the Duke of Romagna of the abduction of Dorotea. However, they could not prove their case, and Cæsar replied mockingly that, having no lack of women, he had not occasion to steal them by highway robbery. Reports began to be current, moreover, that Dorotea had quickly consoled herself, and that, having forgotten her husband, she followed the duke in all his campaigns.

Maria, however, had a brother, Messer Dionigi, a young captain in the service of Florence. When all the complaints of the Florentine

Signoria, before whom he had laid the matter, proved as vain as the representations of the Venetians, Dionigi determined to act on his own authority. He presented himself before the duke under a feigned name, gained his confidence, obtained admission to the dungeon of the Castle of Cesena, found his sister, disguised her as a boy, and made his escape with her. But at the Perugian frontier the fugitives were overtaken, Dionigi was killed, and Maria haled back to her prison.

Machiavelli, as Secretary of the Florentine Republic, was interested in the event. He had been in Dionigi's confidence, and had learned from him not only the plan of rescue, but the accounts which the brother had acquired of his sister's ill-fortune, and of her reputation as a miracle-working saint, bearing the "stigmata" like St. Catharine of Siena.

Cæsar, tired of Dorotea, had cast his eyes on Maria, and having never experienced difficulty with women, not even with the most discreet, counted on an easy conquest. He was mistaken. The girl met him with a resistance which he could not overcome. Report said that of late the duke had constantly visited her in her cell, staying for long periods alone with her. But what passed at these interviews no one knew.

Machiavelli ended his recital with expression of a fixed determination to rescue Maria.

"If you, Messer Leonardo, will consent to help me, I will so arrange the matter that none shall know of your share in it. First I shall require of you information as to the internal construction and arrangement of the Castle of San Michele, where Maria is kept in durance. You, as the court engineer, will find it easy to obtain entrance and to discover all we need to know."

Leonardo for all reply gazed at his friend in amazement, and presently Messer Niccolò broke into a forced and somewhat angry laugh.

"I hope," he said, "you do not honour me by thinking me over sentimental, too chivalrously generous? Whether Cæsar seduce this minx or no is nothing to me. Would you know why I concern myself in the affair? First, to show the illustrious Signoria that I am good for something besides foolery; but secondly and chiefly, because I require amusement. If a man commit no follies he loses his wits through weariness. I am sick of chattering, playing dice, going to bawdy houses, and making vain reports to the Florentine Wool-staplers. So

I have devised this adventure: action I assure you, not mere talk. The opportunity must not be wasted. My whole plan is ready and I have taken all necessary precautions."

He spoke hurriedly as if excusing himself. Leonardo, however, understood that he was ashamed of genuine kind-heartedness, and was trying to conceal it under a mask of cynicism.

"Messere," said the artist, "I pray you to rely on me in this matter as on yourself. But on one condition, that if we fail, I shall share your responsibility."

Niccolò, visibly touched, clasped his hand, and at once set forth his design. Leonardo made no criticism, though in his heart he doubted whether it would prove practical. The liberation of the captive was fixed for the 30th of December.

Two days before the date agreed upon, one of Maria's gaolers, who was in Niccolò's pay, came running to inform him that Cæsar knew all. Machiavelli being absent, Leonardo went in search of him to give him this news. He found the Florentine Secretary in a tavern, where a troop of gamesters, chiefly Spanish soldiers, were fleecing inexpert players at dice or cards. Surrounded by a merry group of young libertines, Machiavelli was expounding that famous sonnet of Petrarch's on Laura, which ends:—

"E lei vid" io ferita in mezzo "l core"

and discovering some obscene allusion in every line, while his hearers were convulsed with laughter.

Suddenly an uproar arose in the next room; women screamed, tables were overthrown, swords clashed, coins and broken bottles were dashed against the walls and floor. One of the players had been detected cheating. Niccolò's audience ran to join the fray, and Leonardo whispered his news to his friend, and led him home.

It was a still, star-lit night. New fallen snow creaked under their feet; the fragrance of the air was delicious after the stifling tavern. When Messer Niccolò heard that their plot for the rescue of the girl Maria had come to the knowledge of the duke, he replied coolly that for the moment there was no occasion for alarm. Then he continued with voluble apology.

"You were surprised to find me acting cheap jack to that Spanish rabble? What of it? 'Tis law of necessity. Necessity jumps, Necessity dances, Necessity trolls catches. They may be rascals, but they are more generous than the magnificent Signoria of Florence."

There was so much bitterness and self-accusation in his tone that Leonardo could not bear it.

"You are wrong, Messer Niccolò," he said, "to speak thus with me. I am your friend and shall not judge like the vulgar."

Machiavelli turned away—and answered in a low voice, "I know it—judge me not harshly, Leonardo. Often I jest and laugh lest my heart's grief should set me weeping. Such is my lot! I was born under a luckless star. While my fellows, men of no intelligence, succeed in everything, live in honour and luxury, acquire power and wealth, I remain behind them all, out-jostled by fools. They think me a buffoon, perchance they be right. Yet I fear neither great labours nor certain perils; but what I cannot suffer is that my life should be consumed in the pitiful effort to make two ends meet, to tremble over every groat, to endure paltry affronts daily from my inferiors! 'Tis an accursed life! If God do not come to my aid, I shall end by abandoning my work, my Marietta, and my son. What am I but a burden to them and to all? Let them think what they will: let them imagine me dead. I will hide me in some distant hamlet, some corner of the earth where none shall know me; where I shall be clerk to the *podestà*, or teacher of the alphabet in a village school, that I may not die of starvation so long as I retain my senses. My friend, there is naught more terrible than to feel in yourself the power to do something, and to know that you will perish and die without ever having accomplished anything whatsoever."

XIII

As THE DAY FOR THE adventure approached, Leonardo perceived that Machiavelli, notwithstanding his anticipations of success, was losing his coolness, and becoming inclined either to undue caution or to over precipitancy. The artist knew well this state of mind: the result, not of cowardice nor of pusillanimity, but of that treachery of the will, that fatal irresolution when the moment for striking has arrived, which is inherent in men made for contemplation rather than for action.

On the eve of the eventful day Niccolò went to a little place near the Torre di San Michele, to make the final preparations. Leonardo was to join him early in the morning. Left alone, the latter momentarily expected disastrous news; he felt very little doubt that the affair would end in some stupid failure, on a par with the prank of a schoolboy.

The dull winter morning was dawning, and he was about to make his start when Niccolò returned. Pale and woe-begone, he sank half-fainting on a chair.

"'Tis at an end," he said shortly.

"I expected as much!" cried Leonardo. "I guessed we should fail."

"We have not failed, but we are too late; the bird has flown."

"How has she flown?"

"This morning, before the dawn, Maria was found on the prison floor with her throat cut."

"And the murderer is—?"

"The murderer is unknown, but it is not the duke. Cæsar and his executioners are no bunglers, and this poor child has been hacked—They say she has died a maid. My notion is that she herself—"

"Impossible! She would not have done it. She was a saint—"

"Anything is possible. You don't know this crew yet. And that infamous assassin—I tell you that infamous assassin is capable of anything! He could force even a saint to lay hands on herself! Ah! I saw her twice in the beginning of her martyrdom, when she was not so closely watched. She was fragile, with an innocent face like a child's. Her hair was thin and of pale gold, like Lippo Lippi's Madonna in the Badia. There was no special beauty about her. Oh, Messer Leonardo, you cannot know what a sweet, helpless child she was!"

He turned away, tears glistening on his eyelashes. But he continued in a sharp, forced voice:—

"I have always said it! An honourable man in this court is like a fish in a frying-pan. I have had enough of it! I was not made to be a slave. The Signoria must transfer me. I won't stay here."

Leonardo was sincerely grieved for Maria, and he would have done his utmost on her behalf. Nevertheless it was a relief both to him and to Messer Niccolò that there was no longer any demand upon them for decisive action.

XIV

The larger part of Cæsar's army marched out of Fano at dawn on the 30th of December, and encamped outside Sinigaglia. Next day (the date recommended by the astrologer), the duke himself was to arrive.

Sinigaglia had been besieged by the confederates of Mugione, who had come to terms with Cæsar, and were now acting for him. The town had surrendered, but the commandant of the castle swore he would open his gates only to Cæsar in person. Accordingly the duke had sent word that he was coming, and he had invited the repentant confederates to meet him on the banks of the Metauro, where his camp lay, that they might hold a council of war. These men, his former enemies, now his allies, had perhaps a presentiment of evil, and would have declined to meet him. However, he reassured them, "bewitching them," as Machiavelli afterwards wrote, "like the basilisk which entices its victims by the sweetness of its singing."

Machiavelli left Fano with the duke. Leonardo followed alone some hours later.

The road led southwards along the seashore. On the right, mountains descended sheer to the sea, scarcely allowing room for the narrow road at their base. It was a grey day, very still; the water was grey and unruffled as the sky. The drowsy air, the chirping of the birds, black spots and holes in the surface of the snow, all portended a thaw.

At last the brick towers of Sinigaglia came in sight; the town lay like a trap between the mountains and the sea, not a mile from the Adriatic, not a cross-bow shot from the foot of the Apennines. Upon meeting the stream of the Misa, the road turned sharply to the left; here was a bridge slanting across the little river, and behind it the gates of the town frowned across a square with low buildings, chiefly storehouses belonging to Venetian merchants. At that time Sinigaglia was a large semi-Oriental bazaar, where Italian traders exchanged their wares with Turks, Armenians, Greeks, Persians, and Slavs from Montenegro and Albania. At this moment, however, even the busiest streets were empty. Leonardo met only soldiers. Here and there in the long arcades, which extended monotonously along each side of the street, in the shops, the warehouses, the *fondachi*, he saw traces of plunder—broken glass, forced locks, severed bolts and bars, doors thrown open, and wares and bales ruthlessly exposed. There was a smell of fire, and some half-consumed houses were still smoking; corpses hung from the iron lamp-stanchions at the corners of the palace.

It was growing dark when, in the principal piazza near the palace, Leonardo saw Cæsar Borgia surrounded by his guards. He was punishing the soldiers who had pillaged the town. Messer Agapito was in the act of reading their sentences; then at a sign from the duke the condemned were conducted to the gallows. At this moment Leonardo was joined by Machiavelli.

"What do you think of it?" asked Messer Niccolò eagerly, "if indeed you have heard—"

"I have heard nothing, and am glad to meet you. Pray tell me."

Machiavelli took him into the next street, then through several narrow lanes, choked with snow, to a deserted district by the shore. Here in a lonely tumble-down hovel, belonging to the widow of a shipbuilder, he had succeeded in finding the only vacant quarters in the town, two diminutive rooms for himself and his friend. He lit a candle, drew a bottle of wine from his pocket, broke its neck against the wall, and seated himself opposite Leonardo, gazing at him with glowing eyes.

"You have not heard?" he said gravely. "A rare and memorable thing has been done. Cæsar has revenged himself on his enemies. The conspirators have been seized; Oliverotto, Orsini, and Vitelli are awaiting sentence of death." He threw himself back in his chair, watching Leonardo, and enjoying his astonishment. Then making an effort to appear calm and dispassionate, he told the story of the trap of Sinigaglia.

Arrived early at the camp on the Metauro, Cæsar sent forward two hundred horsemen, set the infantry in motion, and followed them himself with the rest of the cavalry. He knew that the allied generals would come to meet him, and that their forces had been distributed in the forts surrounding the town, so as to make room for the new troops. Outside the gates where the road curved, following the bank of the Misa, he drew up his cavalry in two lines, leaving space between them for the passage of the infantry, which, without a halt, crossed the bridge and entered the gates of the town.

The allies, Orsini, Gravina, and Vitellozzo, rode out to meet the duke, escorted by a few horsemen. As if presaging disaster, Vitellozzo was so gloomy and abstracted that those about him who knew his customary phlegm were astounded; it was known that he had taken leave of his family as if going to his death. The generals dismounted from their mules and saluted the duke. He also left his horse, gave his hand to each, and then embraced and kissed them, calling them his "beloved brothers," with many demonstrations of courtesy. According to a preconcerted arrangement, Cæsar's captains surrounded the generals in such a way that each was the centre of a group of Borgia's adherents; meantime the duke, observing the absence of Oliverotto, signed to

Don Michele Corella, his captain, who rode off, and having found Oliverotto with his troops, made a pretext for bringing him also to Cæsar's presence. Then, conversing amicably on military matters and future tactics, they went all together to the palace, which stood just in front of the fortress.

At the entrance the generals would have taken their leave, but the duke, with the same urbanity as before, invited them into the palace.

Scarcely had they set foot in the first chamber, when the doors were secured, armed men rushed on the four generals, seized, disarmed, and bound them. Such was their astonishment that they scarce offered any resistance. The duke intended to disembarrass himself of his victims that very night by strangling them in a secluded part of the palace.

"Truly, Messer Leonardo," cried Machiavelli, "I would you had seen how he embraced them and kissed them! One mistrustful glance, one suspicious gesture might have betrayed him; but there was such sincerity in his voice, on his countenance, that till the final moment I guessed naught, nor could have believed he was acting a part. Of all stratagems since politics began, this must be the finest!"

Leonardo smiled. "Doubtless," he said, "his Excellency has exhibited audacity and craft; but I comprehend not what in this betrayal so moves your admiration."

"Betrayal? Nay, sir, when it is a question of saving your country, there can be no question of betrayal or of loyalty, of good or evil, of clemency or cruelty. All means are alike, provided the object is gained."

"Is this a question of saving his country? Methinks the duke has studied but his own advantage."

"Can it be that even you do not understand? Cæsar is the future autocrat of an united Italy. Never was a time more favourable for the advent of a hero. If Israel had to serve in bondage in order that Moses should arise; if the Persians had to lie under the yoke of the Medes that Cyrus might be exalted; if the Athenians had to waste themselves in internecine strife that Theseus might have eternal glory, then it is necessary also, in this our own day, that Italy be shamed, and enslaved, bound, and divided, without a head, without a leader, without a guide; devastated, trampled on, crushed by all the woes which a nation can endure, in order that a new hero shall rise to be the saviour of his land. Many times men have appeared whom she has fancied the destined one, and have died leaving the great deed undone. Half-dead, scarce breathing, she still awaits her deliverer, who shall heal her wounds, put an end to disorder in Lombardy, plunder in Tuscany, extortion and murder in Naples. Day and night Italy cries to her God, if, perchance, He will send her a saviour!"

His voice rang like a chord too tightly stretched, and broke. He was white and shaking, and his eyes glowed. In his excitement was something convulsive, powerless, akin to epilepsy.

Leonardo remembered how, speaking of Maria's suicide, he had called the Duke of Valentinois a monster of crime. He did not point out the inconsistency, knowing that Messer Niccolò, in his exaltation, would repudiate his softer mood.

"Who lives long, sees much, *Niccolò mio*. But permit me one question. Why is it *today* that you have assured yourself of Cæsar's divine election? Has the *inganno di Sinigaglia* proved his heroism?"

"Yes," replied Machiavelli, recovering his impartial air; "the violence of his action has shown that he has the rare combination of great qualities and their opposites. I do not blame. I do not praise. I simply examine. Here is my reasoning on the matter: there are two ways open to him who would arrive at a particular end. The first is law, the second violence. The first belongs to men—the second to beasts. He who wishes to rule must tread both ways, must know how to be either beast or man. Such is the inner meaning of the old legends of Achilles and other heroes nurtured by Chiron, the centaur, half-god, half-beast. The major part of men cannot support the weight of liberty, and fear it more than death. When they have committed a crime they are crushed under the burden of repentance. 'Tis only the hero, the man of destiny, who has the strength to support liberty, who breaks laws without fear, without remorse, who remains innocent even in evil, as do beasts and gods. Today, for the first time, I have seen in Cæsar the infallible sign that he is elect of God!"

"Yes, yes, I understand," said Leonardo moodily; "but to my thinking that man is not free who, like Cæsar, dares all because he knows naught and loves naught. *I call him free who dares all because he knows all and loves all.* That is the liberty whereby men shall conquer both good and evil, the height and the abyss, the bounds of earth, its obstacles and burdens; shall become as gods, and fly."

"Fly?" said Machiavelli bewildered.

"When they have perfect knowledge they will make themselves wings. 'Tis a subject upon which I have thought much. Perhaps nothing will come of it. I care not; if it be not I, 'twill be another. The day will come when there shall be wings."

"Well, let us congratulate each other. Our talk has led us to a new creation. My prince is to be half-god, half-beast; and you have given him wings."

But the striking of a clock in the neighbouring tower drove Messer Niccolò forth; he had to hasten to the palace that he might learn of the impending execution of the generals.

Isabella Gonzaga, Marchesa of Mantua, by way of congratulation, sent Cesare a carnival gift of a hundred pretty masks in coloured silk.

XV

Cæsar returned to Rome in the beginning of March 1503. The Pope proposed to reward the hero with the Golden Rose, the highest distinction which the Church could confer on her champions. The cardinals assented, and two days later the ceremony of investiture took place. The Roman Curia and the envoys of the great powers assembled in the Sala de' Pontefici, which looks out on the Cortile del Belvedere. Alexander VI, seventy years of age and corpulent, but still vigorous and majestic, ascended the dais, wearing the begemmed mantle and triple crown, the ostrich fans waving over his head.

Trumpets blared, and at a signal from Johann Burckhardt, Master of Ceremonies, the armour-bearers, pages, couriers, and guards of the Duke of Romagna, entered the hall, accompanied by Bartolomeo Capranica, his Master of the Camp, bearing the naked sword of the *Gonfaloniere* of the Roman Church. The sword was gilded and damascened with delicate designs. First, the Goddess of Fidelity seated on a throne, with the legend, "Fidelity is stronger than Arms." Secondly, Julius Cæsar in his triumphal car, with the legend, "*Aut Cæsar aut Nihil*." Thirdly, the passage of the Rubicon with the legend, "The die is cast." Lastly, a sacrifice to the Bull of the House of Borgia—naked priestesses burning incense over a human victim, and on the altar the inscription "*Deo optimo maximo Hostia*," and lower, "*In nomine Cæsaris omen*." The human sacrifice to the beast acquired a more terrible meaning from the fact that these engravings and mottos had been ordered at the moment when Cæsar was contemplating the murder of his brother Giovanni, in order to take from him this sword of the standard-bearer of the Church.

Following the insignia of his office came the hero himself, crowned with the lofty ducal *berretto*, embroidered in pearls with the Holy Dove. He approached the Pope, removed the *berretto*, knelt and kissed the ruby cross on the shoe of the Pontifex Maximus. Cardinal Monreale handed the Golden Rose to His Holiness. It was a marvel of the jeweller's art; from a phial concealed under the gold filigree petals exhaled the perfume of innumerable roses. The Pope stood, and in a voice quivering with emotion uttered the words:—

"Receive, most beloved son, this rose, symbol of the joy of the two Jerusalems, earthly and heavenly, of the two churches, militant and triumphant; the incorruptible flower, the delight of the saints, the beauty of imperishable crowns. May thy virtue flower in Christ as this rose, which blossoms on the shore of many waters! Amen."

Cæsar received the mystic rose from the paternal hands.

It was more than the old man could bear. To the disgust of Burckhardt, the stolid German master of the ceremonies, he broke through the prescribed ceremonial; bending over his son he stretched out his trembling hands, his face contracting and his shoulders shaking as he murmured:—

"Cesare! Cesare! *figlio mio!*"

The duke handed the rose to the Cardinal di San Clemente, and the Pope embraced him in a frenzy of joy, laughing and weeping.

Again the trumpets blared, the great bell of St. Peter's pealed, and was answered by the bells of all the churches in the city, and by salvos of artillery from the Castle of St. Angelo. In the Cortile del Belvedere the Romagnole guard shouted:—

"*Viva Cesare! Viva Cesare!*"

And the duke came out on the balcony to greet his troops. Under the blue sky, in the brilliance of the morning sun, his vesture gold and purple, the Dove of the Holy Spirit on his head, the mystic rose in his hand, to the people he was not a man, but a god.

XVI

That night there was a splendid masked procession; the triumph of Julius Cæsar as it was shown on the sword of the Duke of Valentinois and Romagna. He himself took his seat in the chariot bearing the inscription "Cæsar the divine"; his head was crowned with laurel, and he carried a palm-branch in his hand. The chariot was surrounded by his soldiers, dressed as Roman legionaries, with eagles and javelins. All was correctly ordered in accordance with descriptions on books and representations in monuments and medals.

Before the chariot walked a man in the long white robe of an Egyptian hierophant, carrying a banner with the Borgia Bull, purple and gilded; the bloody Apis, protecting god of Alexander VI. Boys in cloth of silver sang to the clashing of timbrels:—

"*Vive diu Bos! Vive diu Bos! Borgia vive!* Glory to the Bull! Glory to the Bull! Glory to Borgia!" And high above the crowd, lighted by the flare of torches, swung the image of the beast, fiery as the rising sun.

In the crowd was Leonardo's pupil, Giovanni Boltraffio, who had newly arrived from Florence. Looking at the purple beast he remembered the words in the Apocalypse:—

"And they worshipped the Beast, saying, Who is like unto the Beast? who is able to make war with him?

"And I saw a woman sit upon a scarlet-coloured beast, full of names of blasphemy, having seven heads and ten horns. And upon her forehead was a name written—'MYSTERY, BABYLON THE GREAT, THE MOTHER OF HARLOTS AND ABOMINATIONS OF THE EARTH.'"

Like the Seer of Patmos, Giovanni "wondered with a great wonder."

Book XIII

The Purple Beast—1503

"The beast that ascendeth out of the bottomless pit."

—Rev. xi. 7

I

Leonardo was threatened with a lawsuit touching his vineyard at Fiesole, a slice of which was coveted by the neighbouring *contadino*. He had entrusted the matter to Giovanni Boltraffio; and wishing to speak to him, had sent for him to Rome. On his way, Giovanni visited Orvieto to see the famous frescoes lately painted by Luca Signorelli in the Cappella Nuova of the cathedral. One of these frescoes showed the coming of Antichrist.

Giovanni was greatly impressed by the countenance of the enemy of God. It was not evil; it was only a face of infinite grief. In the clear eyes, with their troubled gentleness, was reflected the final remorse of the wisdom which has renounced its God. The figure was beautiful, notwithstanding the satyr ears, the claw-like fingers. And, as occurs sometimes in delirium, Giovanni saw behind this face Another terribly like it, a divine face, which he dared not own he recognised.

In the same picture, at the left, was seen the fall of Antichrist. Soaring upward on invisible wings, assuming the character of the Son of Man coming in the clouds to judge the quick and the dead, he was hurled back, down to the pit by the Archangel. These human wings, this failing flight reawakened in Giovanni the old appalling doubts about Leonardo, his master.

There were two other persons in the chapel with Giovanni also looking at the frescoes; a stout monk, and a long lean man of uncertain age with a keen hungry face, in the garb of a "goliard," as the itinerant scholars of the middle ages were called. They made friends with Giovanni, and the three continued their journey in company. The monk was a German, Tomaso Schweinitz, the librarian of an Augustinian monastery at Nuremberg; he was going to Rome about certain disputed benefices. His companion was also German, Hans Platter, from Salzburg; he was acting partly as Schweinitz's secretary, partly as his jester, partly as his groom. On the journey the three discussed ecclesiastical affairs. Calmly and with scientific acumen, Schweinitz demonstrated the absurdity of imputing infallibility to the Pope, and prophesied that within twenty years Germany would shake off the intolerable yoke of the Romish church.

"This man will never die for his creed," thought Giovanni, looking at the full-fed round face of the Nuremberg monk; "he will not face the fire like Savonarola; yet, who knows? he may be more dangerous to the church."

One evening soon after their arrival in Rome, Giovanni met Hans Platter in the square of St. Peter's, and the German took him to the neighbouring Vicolo de' Sinibaldi, where among a number of foreign taverns was a small wine-cellar with the sign of the Silver Hedgehog. Its host was a Czech of the Hussite heresy, Yan Khromy, who entertained with his choicest wines all free-thinkers or enemies of the papacy—such were indeed daily increasing, and preparing the way for the great reformation of the church.

In an inner room, where only the elect were admitted, was a fairly numerous company; and at the head of the table sat Schweinitz, leaning back against a cask, his fat hands resting on his paunch, his face bloated and stupid. Now and then he raised his glass level with the candle-flame admiring the pale gold of the Rhenish; apparently he had already drunk more than enough.

Fra Martino, a violent little monk, was pouring out vials of wrath against the extortions of the Curia Romana.

"Better to fall into the hands of brigands than of the prelates here! Daily pillage! Give to the Penitenziere, to the Protonotary, to the Cubiculary, to the door-keeper, to the groom, to the cook, to the man who empties the slops of her reverence, the cardinal's concubine; Lord, forgive us! 'Tis like the song:—

'New Pharisees they,
The Lord they betray!'"

Then Hans Platter rose, his face grave, his voice drawling, and said:—

"The cardinals went to their lord the Pope and inquired—'What shall we do to be saved?' And Alexander answered: 'Why do ye ask of me? Is it not written in the Law? "Love silver and gold with all thine heart and with all thy mind and with all thy strength, and love thy rich neighbour as thyself. Do this and ye shall live."' And the Pope took his seat upon his throne and said: 'Blessed are they who have, for they shall see my face. Blessed are they who bring offerings, for they shall be called my sons. Blessed are they who come in the name of gold and silver, for of them is the Curia Romana. But woe unto you, ye who present yourselves with empty hands! It were better that a millstone were hanged about your necks and ye were cast into the depth of the sea.' And the cardinals answered: 'All that thou sayest we will do.' And the Pope said: 'Lo, I set before you an example, that ye may spoil the people, even as I have spoiled the living and the dead.'"

This sally provoked great mirth. Next Otto Marburg the organ-master, a handsome old man, with a boyish smile, read a satire just printed and already handed about all over the city. It was in the form of an anonymous letter to Paolo Savelli, a rich noble who had fled to the emperor from the persecutions of the Church. A long catalogue was set forth of the crimes and abominations in the house of the pontiff, beginning with simony, and ending with Cæsar's fratricide and the pope's criminal amours with his own daughter. The epistle concluded with a passionate appeal to all princes and rulers in Europe, calling on them to unite and destroy this nest of assassins, these filthy reptiles disguised in the semblance of men; and asseverated that the reign of Antichrist had commenced, for of a truth the faith of the church of God had never had such foes as Pope Alexander VI and Cæsar his son.

A discussion now arose as to whether, in very truth, the Pope were Antichrist. Otto Marburg said No; not he but Cæsar, who, it was clear, intended to be Alexander's successor. Fra Martino argued that Antichrist would be an incorporeal phantom; for, as said St. Cyril of Alexandria, "The Son of Perdition, called Antichrist, is none other than Satan himself."

Schweinitz shook his head and quoted St. John Chrysostom, who said, "Who is this? Is he Satan? By no means, but a man who shall have inherited Satan's power, for there are two beings in him: one human, the other devilish. And he shall be the son of a virgin, which could never have been said of Alexander or of Cæsar."

But Schweinitz further quoted from Ephraim of Syria; "The devil shall seduce a virgin of the tribe of Dan, and she shall conceive and bring forth."

All crowded round him with questions and doubts; but imposing silence with his finger, and quoting from Jerome, Cyprian, Irenæus, and other of the fathers, he spoke further of the coming of Antichrist.

His face shall be as the face of a were-wolf, yet to many it shall seem like the face of Christ. And he shall do marvellous things. He shall bid the sea be still, and the sun turn into darkness; and the mountains remove, and the stones become bread. And he shall feed the hungry, and heal the sick, and the deaf, and the blind, and the feeble-kneed.

"Ah, the abominable dog!" cried Fra Martino beside himself, and thumping his fist on the table; "but who will believe in him? Fra Tomaso, I think that not even babes could be taken by his deceits!"

"They will believe. Many will believe," said Schweinitz shaking his head. "He shall lead them astray by the mask of sanctity. For he shall mortify his flesh, live chastely, contemning the love of women; he shall taste no meat, and shall be loving not only to men but to all living creatures which have breath. And like the wild partridge he shall utter a strange call and shall deceive with his voice; 'Come unto me,' he shall say, 'all ye that labour and are heavy laden and I will give you rest.'"

"Then," interrupted Giovanni with bated breath, "who shall recognise, who unmask him?"

The monk fixed on the youth a profound and scrutinising regard and answered; "It will be impossible for men, but not for God. Even the saints shall not know to distinguish the light from the darkness. And there shall be weariness unto all nations, and confounding such as there was not from the beginning of the world. And they shall say to the mountains, 'Fall on us, and to the hills, cover us,' and shall faint for fear and for expectation of the woes which are coming on the earth, for the powers of heaven shall be shaken. Then he who impiously sitteth on the throne, in the very Temple of the Most High, shall say, 'O faithless generation! Ye ask for a sign and a sign shall be given unto you. Ye shall behold me, the Son of Man, coming in the clouds to judge both the quick and the dead.' And he shall take great wings, formed by devilish cunning, and shall soar into the sky amid thunders and lightnings, surrounded by his disciples in the semblance of angels."

Giovanni listened, pale as death, his eyes terror-struck; he remembered the broad folds of the raiment of Antichrist in Luca Signorelli's fresco; and he remembered also the folds flapping in the wind on Leonardo's shoulders as he stood upon the precipice edge on the lonely summit of Monte Albano.

At this moment, from the larger room, whither Hans Platter had fled from the too serious discussion, came cries and the laughter of girls, the sound of running to and fro, the noise of overturned chairs and broken glasses—evidently Hans romping with the servant-maids. Presently to the jangling of strings rang out the old song:—

"Virgin of the wine-cellar,
Sweet and fragrant Rosa,
'Ave! Ave!' I must sing
Virgo gloriosa.
A sober knave is he our host
With his fox's mask, Sir.
More than Holy Church, I boast,
Do I love his cask, Sir!
From the wiles of Cypris fair
And from Cupid's darts, oh!
Cowls nor tonsures can avail
To defend our hearts, oh!
For a solitary kiss
I'd go to the block, Sir;
Fill me full of wine, Monk,
Or I'll thee unfrock, Sir!
Holy fathers fear I not—
It is troth they say, Sir,
Gold in Rome has but to chink
And the laws give way, Sir.
Rome! the robbers' shrine is,
Thorny road to Hades—
And the Bishop's wine is
Made to toast the ladies!
Come then, wench, and kiss us.
Dum vinum potamus,
To Bacchus on Ilissus—
Te Deum Laudamus."

Thomas Schweinitz listened, and his fat visage expanded in a beatific grin.

II

At the hospital of San Spirito in Rome Leonardo had returned to his anatomical studies, assisted by Giovanni.

Noticing his pupil's low spirits, and wishing to divert him, the Master one day proposed to take him to the Vatican. The Pope had convened an assembly of learned men to discuss the boundaries of Spanish and Portuguese territory in the new world, with regard to which decision had been requested from the head of the church. Curiosity prompted Giovanni to accept the invitation. Accordingly the two set out for the Vatican.

Passing through the Hall of the Popes, where Alexander had invested Cæsar with the Golden Rose, they entered the inner chambers (now called the Apartamenti Borgia). The arches and vaulting, and the mural spaces between the arches had all been decorated by Pinturicchio with brilliant frescoes—scenes from the New Testament, from the lives of the saints; scenes also from the pagan mysteries. Osiris was seen at his espousals with Isis, teaching men to till the ground, to gather fruits, to plant the vine; he was shown slain of men, rising again, leaving the earth, reappearing as the White Bull, the blameless Apis. However strange this deification of the Bull of the House of Borgia might seem in the chambers of the High Priest of Christendom, the all-pervading joy of life harmonised the two sets of subjects, the sacred and profane, the Christian and the pagan mysteries, the son of Jupiter and the Son of Jehovah. In each picture slender cypresses bent before the breeze, among the broad hills proper to the painter's native Umbria; birds played at the vernal sports of love; St. Elizabeth embracing the Virgin cried, "Blessed is the fruit of thy womb"; by her side a boy was teaching a dog to stand on his hind legs; in the Espousals of Osiris and Isis just such another boy was riding naked on a sacred goose. The same spirit of delight breathed everywhere; in the rich saloons, flower-garlanded; in the angels, with their censers and crosses; in the dancing, goat footed fauns carrying thyrsi and baskets of fruit; in the mystic Bull, the purple Beast, who, radiant as the morning sun, seemed to pour forth the joy of living.

"What is this?" questioned Giovanni of himself, "is it blasphemy, or a childlike artlessness? Is not the sacred emotion on the face of Elizabeth the same as that on the face of Isis? Is there not the same prayerful ecstasy on the face of Pope Alexander, bending the knee before the rising Lord, and on the countenance of the Egyptian priest receiving the sun-god slain of men and risen again in the shape of Apis? And this god before whom the people bow, singing hymns of praise and burning incense on his altar, this heraldic Bull of the Borgias, transformed into a Golden Calf—is nothing else than the Roman pontiff himself, whom the servile poets have called a god."

Cæsare magna fuit, nunc Roma est maxima · Sextus
Regnat Alexander, ille vir, iste Deus.

This identification of the God and the Beast seemed to Giovanni absurd, yet awful.

As he examined the magnificent paintings with which the walls were adorned, he listened to the talk of the prelates and great men who filled the saloons, and waited for the Pope.

"Whence come you, Messer Bertrando?" asked Cardinal d'Arborea of the envoy from the court of Ferrara.

"From the cathedral, Monsignore."

"How is His Holiness? Tired?"

"Not at all. He chanted as well as could possibly be. There is in his voice something so holy, so majestic, so angelic, that I could have imagined myself in heaven. When he lifted the cup, not I only, but many, could scarce restrain their tears."

"Of what disorder did Cardinal Miquele die?" asked the French ambassador abruptly.

"Of drinking something disagreeable," answered Don Juan Lopez dryly. The majority at Alexander's court were Spaniards like himself.

"They say," observed Bertrando, "that on the day after the cardinal's death His Holiness declined to receive the Spanish ambassador on account of his grief."

All exchanged glances. There were covert meanings in these remarks. The Pope's grief had been connected with counting the dead man's money which proved less than he had expected; and the unwholesome drink was the Borgia poison, a sweet white powder which killed slowly. Alexander had invented this easy method of acquiring money. He knew the incomes of all the cardinals, and when he wanted money would despatch the wealthiest of them to the other world, and declare himself the heir. He fattened them for the table. The German, Johann Burckhardt, master of the ceremonies, frequently noted deaths of prelates in his diary, adding the pregnant laconicism, *Biberat calicem*—"He had drunk of the cup."

"Is it true, Monsignore," asked Don Pedro Carranca, a chamberlain, "that Cardinal Monreale is taken ill?"

"Really? What ails him?" cried d'Arborea alarmed.

"Vomiting."

"*Dio mio! Dio mio!* the fourth!" sighed the poor cardinal. "Orsini, Ferrari, Miquele, and now Monreale!"

"The waters of Tiber must be bad for your Eminences," said Messer Bertrando slyly.

"One after the other! one after the other!" sighed d'Arborea; "today strong and well, tomorrow—"

All became silent. From the next room entered a fresh crowd of courtiers marshalled by Don Rodriguez Borgia, the Pope's nephew. A murmur ran through the room.

"The Holy Father! The Holy Father!"

The crowd parted, the doors were thrown open, and into the audience-chamber came Pope Alexander VI.

III

He had been singularly handsome in his youth. It was said then that he had only to look at a woman to inspire her with the wildest passion, as if in his eyes a force was concentred which drew women like a magnet. Even now his features, though blunted and coarsened by age and fat, retained an imposing beauty of line. His skin was bronzed, his head bald, with a few tufts of grey hair at the nape. The nose was large and aquiline, the chin receding, the eyes vivacious. The full protruding lips showed sensuality, yet had something simple and naïve in their expression.

Giovanni could see nothing terrible or cruel in his face. Alexander Borgia possessed in the highest degree the gift of taste; he had that attractive exterior which made whatever he said or did appear said or done in the only right way.

"The Pope is seventy," said the ambassadors, "but he grows daily younger. His heaviest cares last but twenty-four hours. His temperament is cheerful; everything to which he puts his hand turns out well. He thinks of nothing but the reputation and the happiness of his children."

The Borgias were descended from Moors of Castile; it was, indeed, not difficult to recognise in the Pope the bronze skin, the full scarlet lips, the flashing eyes of the African Arab.

"He could not have a more appropriate background," thought Giovanni, "than these pictures of the joys and triumphs of Apis, the ancient Egyptian Bull."

Indeed the septuagenarian Pope seemed, in the vigour of his health, like enough to his own heraldic Beast, the sun-god, the god of merriment, lubricity, and generation.

As he entered, he was in conversation with a Jew, the goldsmith Salomone da Sessa, who had engraved the Triumph of Cæsar on the sword of the *gonfaloniere*. He had also pleased the Pope by so exquisitely cutting an emerald with a figure of Venus that Alexander had had it set on the cross which he used when blessing the people on solemn festivals, so that when he kissed the crucifix he should kiss also the Goddess of Love. In spite of his crimes, Alexander was not impious; he was really devout, particularly reverential of the Blessed Virgin, whom he considered his gracious Mediatress at the throne of the Most High. He was ordering a lamp now of Salomone, an offering he had vowed to St. Maria del Popolo, in gratitude for the recovery from illness of Madonna Lucrezia his daughter.

Seating himself at the window, the Pope inspected some precious stones; he was passionately fond of jewels. With long shapely fingers he touched the crystals gently, his thick lips parted in a smile; especially he admired a large chrysoprase—darker than an emerald, with mysterious sparkles of gold, green, and purple. Then he called for a casket of pearls from his treasure-chest. Whenever he opened this casket he thought of his beloved daughter, who was herself like a pearl. He called the envoy from Ferrara, whose duke, Alfonso d'Este, was his son-in-law.

"Take heed, Bertrando, that you do not leave Rome till I have given you a present for Madonna Lucrezia. You mustn't leave the old uncle with empty hands." (He had sufficient care for appearances sometimes to call Lucrezia his niece.)

Taking a priceless pink Indian pearl, the size of a hazelnut, from the casket, he held it up to the light and gloated over it. He pictured it on Lucrezia's white bosom; he hesitated whether he should give it to her or to the Blessed Virgin. But reminding himself that it was sinful to take away what had been vowed to Heaven, he handed the pearl to Salomone, and bade him set it in a lamp between the chrysoprase and the carbuncle, gift from the Sultan.

"Bertrando," he turned again to the ambassador, "when you see the duchess, tell her from me to keep well, and to pray earnestly to the Queen of Heaven. Tell her we are in the best of health, and give her our apostolic blessing. This evening I will send you the little gift for her."

The Spanish ambassador exclaimed, drawing nearer:—

"Of a truth, I have never seen such richness of pearls!"

"Yes," said the Pope complacently, "I have a fine collection. I have been making it for twenty years. My daughter is very fond of pearls." He laughed. "She knows what suits her, the little rogue!"

Then after a pause he added solemnly, "When I die, Lucrezia shall have the best pearls in Italy!"

And plunging his hands in them he let them trickle through his fingers, delighting in their soft pale splendour and smooth, satin-like texture.

"All for her! All for her, our delicious daughter," he repeated in a low hoarse voice.

And suddenly a fire sparkled in his eyes; and Giovanni, remembering whispers of the monstrous passion of the aged Borgia for this Lucrezia, froze at heart with horror and shame.

IV

Just then a page announced that, according to His Holiness's order, Cæsar was waiting in the next saloon. Alexander had summoned him on a matter of urgent importance: the French king had expressed disapproval of Valentinois' designs against Florence, and had charged the Pope with countenancing them.

After listening to the page's announcement, Alexander glanced at the French ambassador, drew him adroitly aside, left him (accidentally, apparently) by the door of the room where Cæsar was waiting, and passing through the door, left it (accidentally again) slightly ajar, so that the ambassador and those about him should hear all that passed between father and son.

Soon vehement reproaches were audible. Cæsar spoke calmly and respectfully, but the old man, stamping his foot, cried furiously:—

"Out of my sight! Choke, son of a cur! son of a harlot!"

"*Dio mio*, do you hear?" whispered the Frenchman to Messer Antonio Giustiniani, the Venetian ambassador, "he will strike him!"

The Venetian shrugged his shoulders. If it came to blows, he thought the son more likely to stab the father, than the father the son. Since the murder of the Duke of Candia, the Pope had feared Cæsar; his paternal pride and doting fondness had become mixed with a superstitious terror. All remembered how Perotto, the youngest of the chamberlains, had taken refuge from Cæsar under the folds of the papal mantle, and Cæsar had poniarded him on the pontiff's breast, splashing Alexander with his blood. Giustiniani guessed also that the present dispute was a feint, got up for the Frenchman's benefit, to persuade him that if the duke had designs against Florence the Pope was innocent of them. Giustiniani believed that the two always supported each other; the father never doing what he said, the son never saying what he did.

Having threatened, cursed, and all but excommunicated his son, the Pope returned to the hall of audience still trembling, panting, and wiping the perspiration from his empurpled face. Nevertheless, in his eyes shone a gleam of amusement. Again he called the Frenchman, and this time drew him towards the Cortile del Belvedere.

"Your Holiness knows," began the envoy, much distressed, "I had no desire to breed discord—"

"What? did you hear?" cried the Pope, seeming much astonished. And without giving him time to think, he took him familiarly by the chin with finger and thumb (a sign of great amity), and spoke impetuously of his devotion to the Most Christian King, and of the extraordinary purity of Cæsar's motives. The Frenchman was bewildered, and though he had irrefragable proof of the deception, felt disposed rather to deny the evidence of his own eyes than to disbelieve that voice, those eyes, those lips. Indeed, Alexander always lied like one inspired. He never pre-arranged what he was going to say, but lied as artlessly, as innocently as a woman in love. He had practised this art so long that he had attained perfection in it; he was an artist carried away by his imagination.

V

At this moment his secret body-servant approached the pope and whispered to him. Alexander with an anxious air passed into the next room, and thence through a concealed door into a narrow vaulted passage where Cardinal Monreale's cook was awaiting him.

He brought news that the quantity of poison had been insufficient and the cardinal was recovering. However, after minutely catechising the cook, the Pope convinced himself that his victim would die in two or three months' time, which would be all the better as averting suspicion.

"It seems a pity, too!" thought Alexander. "The poor old man was amusing and a good Christian."

Wishing he could have got the money in someother way, he sighed and returned to the audience hall. In the adjoining chamber, sometimes used as a refectory, he saw a table laid and felt hungry. Deferring the business matters, he invited the company to dinner. The table was ornamented with white lilies, the flower of the Annunciation, a favourite with the pope, who said it reminded him of Madonna Lucrezia. The dishes were not numerous, for the pope was plain and sparing in his diet. Giovanni listened to the talk among the chamberlains.

Don Juan Lopez, the "laterculensis," spoke of the late dispute between father and son, and defended Cæsar as if he had no suspicion that the whole affair had been a comedy. The rest agreed with him and lauded Cæsar to the skies.

"Ah no," said the Pope shaking his head with reproachful tenderness, "you don't know what he is. A day never passes in which I am not in terror about him lest he should commit some new imprudence. He will end by breaking his neck and bringing us all to ruin."

His eyes sparkled with paternal pride.

"But what makes Cæsar like this?" he went on; "whom does he take after? You know me, a simple and guileless old man; what I have in my heart, that comes from my tongue! But Cæsar, Lord knows, keeps counsel; always hiding something. Believe me, sirs, sometimes I reprove and scold at him, and at the same time I have terror in my soul. That's it. I am afraid of my own son! He is polite—ay, too polite; and then of a sudden he looks me a look like a dagger in my heart."

The guests, however, defended Cæsar still more warmly.

"Oh, I know! I know!" said the Pope, "you love him like your own, and won't let us abuse him."

The room was suffocatingly hot, and Alexander's head swam, not from wine, but from the intoxication of his son's glory. They all rose and went forth on the balcony which gave on the Cortile del Belvedere. The air was pure and delicious; below, the grooms were bringing fiery mares and ardent stallions out of the stables.

Surrounded by the cardinals and dignitaries, the Pope stood watching the horses, long silent. Gradually his face clouded, for he remembered Lucrezia. Her image rose before him; her blue eyes, the pale gold of her hair, her rosy lips a little full like his own; pure and dainty as a pearl; docile and gentle; in the midst of evil, knowing it not; passionless and unsullied. Why had he consented to her marriage with Alfonso d'Este, the Duke of Ferrara?

Sighing heavily, with drooping head, as if for the first time the burden of age had fallen on his shoulders, he led the company back to the Hall of Audience.

VI

Globes, maps, compasses were there lying ready for the marking out of the meridian, which was to pass over a point three hundred and seventy Portuguese leagues to the south of the Azores and the island of Cape de Verde. This point was chosen because, according to Columbus, the "navel of the earth" was there; the pear-like projection, the mountain reaching to the lunar sphere, which he had postulated on account of the deviation in his compass.

From the extreme western point of Portugal on the one side and the coasts of Brazil on the other, even distances were to be measured to the proposed line. Then shipmasters and astronomers were bidden to calculate how many days of sailing were equal to these distances. The Pope offered prayer, blessed the globe, and dipping a brush in red ink, drew across the Atlantic from the North Pole to the South the broad line which was to secure peace. All islands and lands to the east of this line were to belong to Spain, all to the west, to Portugal. Thus by one motion of his hand he parted the globe in halves and divided it between the Christian nations. At this moment Alexander seemed grand and majestic to Giovanni; full of the consciousness of his power, the world-swaying Cæsar-Pope, centre of two kingdoms—the earthly and the heavenly.

That same evening in his apartments in the Vatican, Cæsar Borgia gave a feast to His Holiness and the Sacred College of Cardinals, at which were present "fifty of the fairest and most famous of the Roman *cortigiane oneste*"; called officially "*meretrices honestæ nuncupatæ*."

THUS WAS CELEBRATED THAT MEMORABLE day in the annals of the Church, which had been marked by the partition of the globe.

Leonardo was present at the supper and witnessed everything. Invitations to such feasts were great favours, and could not be declined. On returning home he said to Giovanni:—

"In every man there is a god and a beast, coupled."

Going on with his anatomical drawing, he added—

"Persons with base minds and unworthy passions do not merit so complex and beautiful a physical structure as others, of high intelligence and lofty thoughts. 'Twere enough if they had a bag with two openings, one to receive, the other to eject food; for, in plain fact, they be no more than a passage for nourishment."

Next morning Giovanni found the Master at work on his painting "*San Gerolamo nel deserto*." In a savage den, the recluse, kneeling and gazing at the Crucified, beats his breast so vehemently that the lion at his feet looks into his eyes, and has opened his jaws in a long and pitiful moan, as if in compassion for his master.

Boltraffio remembered that other picture, white Leda embraced by the swan, the Goddess consumed by the flames of Savonarola's pyre. And as so often before, he asked himself again which of these opposed conceptions was dearest to the heart of the master? or could the two be equally dear?

VII

SUMMER CAME. PUTRID FEVER OF the Pontine marshes, the "malaria," began to rage in the city; at the end of July there were daily deaths among those about the Pope. He himself appeared troubled and sad; but it was less the fear of death which was oppressing him, than the absence of his idolised Lucrezia. He had before now had several attacks of fierce desire, blind and dumb, like madness, terrifying even to himself; he fancied that if he did not satisfy them at once they would suffocate him. He wrote begging her to come for a few days; she replied that her husband would not permit her to leave him. The aged Borgia would have shrunk from no crime to rid himself of this detested son-in-law as he had rid himself of Lucrezia's earlier husbands. But there was no jesting with the Duke of Ferrara, for he had the finest artillery in Italy.

At the beginning of August Alexander went to the villa of Cardinal Adrian of Corneto. At supper he ate more heartily than usual, and drank heavy Sicilian wines; afterwards he sat long on the terrace, enjoying the insidious freshness of the Roman night. Next morning he felt himself indisposed. It was told afterwards that having approached the window he saw two funerals, that of his favourite chamberlain, and that of Messer Guglielmo Raimondi, both men heavy in figure like himself.

"The season is dangerous for us fat folk," he murmured forebodingly. The words were no sooner uttered than a dove flew in at the window, dashed itself against the wall, and fell stunned at the feet of His Holiness.

"Another omen," he muttered, turning pale; and at once he went to his apartment and lay down. In the night he was seized with violent vomiting. The physicians had different opinions about his malady; some called it a tertian fever; others apoplexy, others inflammation of the gall bladder. In the town it was said that he was poisoned.

Every hour his strength declined. Ten days later they had recourse to their extreme measure, and gave him a decoction of precious stones reduced to powder. Still he grew worse.

One night, awaking from delirium, he fumbled anxiously in his breast for a small gold reliquary worn by him for many years and containing minute particles of the body and blood of the Lord. The astrologers had told him his life was safe so long as he carried it. But now, whether it had been lost or stolen, it could nowhere be found, and he closed his eyes in the calm of despair, saying—

"It means I am to go: all is ended."

Next morning, feeling the weakness of death coming over him, he required all to leave him except his favourite physician, the Bishop of Venosa. Him he reminded of the remedy employed by a Hebrew doctor on his predecessor, Innocent VIII, namely, the injection into the veins of the dying Pope of the blood of three children newly slain.

"Does your Holiness know how it ended?" asked the bishop.

"I know! I know!" said Alexander faintly. "But the children were seven years old and they should have been unweaned."

The bishop made no reply; already the sick man's eyes were clouding, and he fell back into delirium.

"Yes; quite young: little white ones! They whose blood is pure and scarlet. I love children! Let them come to me. *Sinite parvulos ad me venire!* Suffer little children to come unto me!" . . .

At these ravings, even the imperturbable bishop, long inured to the horrors of the court, could not repress a shudder. With monotonous convulsive movements, the Pope still fumbled and groped in his bosom for the vanished reliquary.

During his illness he had never once mentioned his children. They told him that Cæsar, like himself, lay at death's door, but he remained unmoved. Now they asked him if he desired any last message to his son or his daughter, but he turned away his head and said no word. It seemed as if those, whom in his lifetime he had so passionately loved, no longer had any existence for him.

On the 18th, Friday, he confessed to his chaplain, and made his communion. At the hour of vespers they read the prayers for the dying. Several times he made an effort to speak, and Cardinal Ilerda, bending down, at last caught the faint sounds coming from his cold lips:—

"Quick! quick! The Stabat Mater! the hymn to my Mediatress!" he whispered.

The hymn is not included in the office for the dying, but Ilerda repeated it:—

"Stabat Mater dolorosa
Juxta Crucem lacrimosa
Dum pendebat Filius. . ."

An ineffable comfort shone in the dying eyes, as if he saw heaven opened and his Mediatress waiting. He stretched out his hands, shuddered, raised himself, and murmured:—

"Cast me not away, O Holy Virgin!"

Then he fell back on his pillows. He was dead.

VIII

At the same time Cæsar Borgia likewise lay between life and death. Monsignor Gaspare Torella, his episcopal physician, ordered a heroic remedy; the patient was to be plunged into the belly of a newly-slain mule, then into icy water. Whether by virtue of this severe treatment, or of his extraordinary strength of will, Cæsar recovered.

During all those terrible days he had maintained complete calmness and self-possession. He followed the course of events, listened to reports, dictated letters, and issued orders. When news came of the Pope's death, he had himself transported by the secret passage from the Vatican to the Castle of St. Angelo.

Strange stories touching Alexander's death were circulated through the town. Marin Sanuto reported to the Republic of Venice that an ape had come into his room, and when one of the cardinals would have captured it, the Pope cried out:—

"Let it alone! Let it alone! It is the devil!"

"It was also said that he frequently cried out:—

"I will come! I will come! Do but wait a little longer!"

And the explanation ran, that upon the death of Innocent VIII, Rodrigo Borgia had sold himself to the Evil One for the sake of twenty years of the papal power.

Again it was related that at the moment of death, seven demons appeared at his pillow; and he was no sooner dead than the body began to rock and to boil, and steam came from his mouth as from a cauldron; his form swelled till it had lost all human shape, and his face became black as an Ethiopian's.

It was the custom upon the death of a Pope to say funeral masses for nine days at St. Peter's, but such was the terror inspired by this deformed and putrefying corpse, that none could be induced to undertake these extreme offices. There were no lights about the bier, nor incense, nor guards, nor mourners. It was long before any could be found to put him in a coffin. At last six ruffians undertook the task for a bottle of wine. The coffin was too small, but the triple crown having been lifted from the head, the body was rolled in a ragged cloth and forced into the receptacle. It was indeed whispered that he had no coffin, but was dropped into a pit head foremost like a victim of the plague.

But even after its burial this poor corpse was allowed no pardon; the superstitious terrors of the people augmented daily. The very air seemed polluted, and a pervading loathsome stench was added to the epidemic fever. A black dog appeared in St. Peter's, running round and round in ever widening circles. The inhabitants of the Borgo dared not leave their homes after nightfall. Many were convinced that Alexander had not died a natural death, but would reappear on the throne, and the reign of Antichrist would begin.

All these and similar reports did Giovanni Boltraffio hear in the Vicolo Sinibaldi, in the wine-cellar of Yan Khromy, the lame Czech Hussite.

IX

MEANTIME LEONARDO, CARELESS OF POLITICAL events and removed from all his friends, was working on a picture begun sometime ago to the order of the Servite monks of Santa Maria Annunziata at Florence. It represented St. Anne and the Virgin Mary; perfect knowledge and perfect love. St. Anne was like a sibyl, eternally young; on her downcast eyes, on her delicately curved lips, there played a mystery of seduction, full of the wisdom of the serpent, not unlike Leonardo's own smile. Beside her, the face of Mary, childish and simple, breathed the innocence of the dove. She knew because she loved, while Anne loved because she knew. Looking at this picture, Giovanni thought that for the first time he understood the master's saying, "that Great Love is the daughter of Great Knowledge." Leonardo at this time was also designing machines of various kinds and shapes, gigantic cranes, pumps, saws, borers; weaving, fulling, rope-making, and smith's apparatus.

As often before, Giovanni was astonished that he could occupy himself simultaneously in such widely different ways, but the seeming discord was intentional.

"I maintain," he wrote in his *Principles of Mechanics*, "that Force is something spiritual and unseen—spiritual, because the life in it is incorporeal; unseen, because the body in which the force is generated changes neither its weight nor its aspect."

Leonardo's destiny was decided with that of Cæsar Borgia. The latter, though he never lost audacity and calm, felt that fortune had betrayed him. At the time of the Pope's death and Cæsar's own illness, their enemies leagued themselves and seized the Roman Campagna. Prospero Colonna advanced to the city gates, Baglioni on Perugia. Urbino, Camerino, Piombino recovered their independence. The conclave, assembled for the election of the new Pope, demanded the removal of the duke from Rome. The whole order of things was changed; it seemed as if all were lost.

Those who had trembled before "the elect of Heaven," as Machiavelli had called him, now rejoiced at his overthrow, and kicked the dying lion with asses's hoofs. The poets furnished epigrams:—

"Cæsar or nothing! Both we find in thee,
Who Cæsar wast, and soon shalt nothing be."

Leonardo, conversing one day in the Vatican with Antonio Giustiniani the Venetian, turned the conversation on Machiavelli.

"Has he told you of his book on statecraft?"

"Oh yes; he has mentioned it frequently, but no doubt he spoke in jest. That is not a book to give to the world! Who writes such books? Counsel to rulers? Revelation of the secrets of government?—showing that all rule is violence covered by a mask of justice? 'Twere to teach the hens the methods of the fox; to arm the sheep with wolf's teeth! God guard us from such politics!"

"Then you think Messer Niccolò in error, and that he will change his opinions?"

"Nay! my opinion is with him! We do well to act as he counsels; only let us not *speak* it. Yet if he do give his book to the world, I doubt it will harm any but himself. The sheep and the fowls will go on trusting the wolves and the foxes. All will be invariable as before. God is merciful; the world will last our time."

X

In the autumn of 1503 Piero Soderini, Perpetual Gonfaloniere of Florence, invited Leonardo to enter his service, intending to employ him in the construction of military engines for the siege of Pisa. The stay of the artist in Rome was therefore nearing its close.

One evening he wandered on the Palatine Hill, where had stood the palaces of Augustus, Caligula, and Septimius Severus. Now only the wind howled in the ruins, and among the olives and the acanthus was heard the bleating of sheep and the chirrup of the grasshopper. The ground was strewn with marble fragments, and Leonardo knew that statues of rare beauty of the gods and heroes of the ancient world were buried under the ruins, like dead men awaiting the resurrection. The evening was serene and fair; the brick skeletons of arches, vaults, and walls, glowed fiery in the rays of the sinking sun. The autumn foliage was all scarlet and gold, as once had been the chambers of the Roman emperors.

On the northern slope of the hill, not far from the gardens of Capranica, Leonardo knelt to examine a fragment of marble. At this moment a man appeared on the tangled footpath.

"Is it you, Messer Niccolò?" said Leonardo, rising and embracing him.

The Florentine secretary seemed still shabbier than when Leonardo had made his acquaintance on the road to Fano; it was evident that the Signoria still neglected him. He was thin, his shaven cheeks seemed quite blue, his long neck bent wearily, his nose seemed more prominent and beak-like, his eyes more fevered. Leonardo asked him of his whereabouts and his affairs; but when he spoke of Cæsar, Niccolò turned away, shrugging his shoulders and replying with simulated indifference:—

"I have seen strange things in my life; I no longer wonder at anything"; and then he fell to questioning Leonardo as if anxious to change the subject. When he heard that his friend had entered the service of Florence, Machiavelli cried:—

"Be not elated! God only knows which is the worse, the crimes of a hero like Cæsar, or the virtues of our ant-hill of a republic. Oh, I know the beauties of a popular government!" and he smiled bitterly.

Leonardo told him Giustiniani's parable of the hens and the foxes, the sheep and the wolves.

"Truth remains truth," said Niccolò, restored to good humour. "True, I irritate the hens and the foxes too; they are ready to burn me at the stake for being the first to describe what they have all being doing ever since the world began. The tyrants think me an inciter to revolution, the populace believe me in league with the tyrants, the religious call me an infidel, the good call me wicked, and the wicked hate me more than they all because I seem to them more wicked than themselves. Ah, Messer Leonardo, do you recall our conversations? You and I have a common fate. The discovery of new truths is, and has ever been, more dangerous than discovery of new lands. You and I are solitary in a crowd, strangers, superfluous, homeless wanderers, perpetual outcasts. He who is unlike others is alone against all; for the world has been created for the masses, and outside the vulgar no one is anything. Ay, my friend, this is a serious matter, for it means that life is tedious; and the worst misfortune in life is not sickness, nor poverty, nor grief; but tediousness."

In silence they descended the western slope of the Palatine, and by the Via della Consolazione reached the foot of the Capitol, the ruins of the temple of Saturn, the place where in the days of glory had stood the Forum Romanum.

From the Arch of Septimius Severus, as far as to the Flavian amphitheatre, the Via Sacra was flanked by wretched hovels. Their foundations were formed of fragments of statues, of the limbs and torsos of Olympian gods. For centuries the forum had been a quarry. Christian churches languished on the ruins of pagan shrines. Layer upon layer of street rubbish, of dust, of filth, had raised the level of the ground more than ten cubits. Yet still lofty columns soared upwards and carried sculptured architraves—last traces of a vanished art.

Machiavelli showed his companion the site of the Roman Senate, the Curia, where now a cattle-market was held, giving to the whole glorious area the ignoble name of "Campo Vaccino." Huge white bullocks, and the black buffaloes of the Pontine marshes lay on the ground, swine routed in the puddles, liquid mire and every sort of filth befouled the fallen columns, the marble slabs, the half-defaced inscriptions. A feudal tower, once the stronghold of the *Frangipani*, leaned against the Arch of Titus; beside it was a tavern for the peasants who came to the market. Cries of brawling women were heard through the windows, and the refuse of meat and fish was flung out by careless hands. Half-washed rags were dried on a string, and beneath them sat an aged and deformed beggar, bandaging his sore and swollen foot. Behind this squalor rose the arch, white and pure, less shattered than the remaining monuments. Bas-reliefs adorned both sides of the interior; on the right Titus the conqueror, on the left the captive Jews with their altar, shewbread, and seven-branched candlestick, mere trophies for the victor; at the top of the arch a broad-winged eagle bearing the deified Cæsar to Olympus. Machiavelli read the inscription in sonorous tones; "*Senatus Populusque Romanus divo Tito divi Vespasiani filio Vespasiano Augusto*."

The sunlight coming through the arch from the direction of the Capitol lit up the emperor's triumph, the malodorous curls of smoke from the tavern seemed like clouds of incense. Niccolò's heart beat as, turning once more to the Forum, he saw the light on the three exquisite columns before the church of St. Maria Liberatrice; the dreary jangling of the bells sounding the Ave Maria seemed to him a dirge over fallen greatness. They directed their steps to the Coliseum.

"Ay," he said, contemplating the titanic blocks of which the amphitheatre's walls are made, "those who could erect such monuments were more than our equals. 'Tis only here in Rome that one can feel the difference between us and the ancients. We are unable even to figure what men they were."

"I know not," said Leonardo, awaking with an effort from his musing; "we of this age have not less force than the ancients; only 'tis force of another sort."

"Christian humility, I suppose?"

"Ay, humility amongst other things, perhaps."

"It may be so," said Niccolò coldly.

They seated themselves on a broken step of the amphitheatre.

"Men should either accept Christ or reject him," exclaimed Machiavelli in a sudden outburst; "we do neither the one nor the other. We are neither Christian nor heathen. We have fallen away from the one, and have not submitted to the other. We have not the strength for righteousness, we have not the courage for wickedness. We are neither black nor white, but a scurvy grey; neither cold nor hot, but a mawkish lukewarm. We have become so false, so pusillanimous, we have twisted about, and halted so long between Christ and Belial, that now we neither know what we want nor whither we are tending. The ancients at least knew that much, and were logical to the end; did not pretend to turn the right cheek to him who smote the left. But since men began to believe that to earn paradise they should suffer any injustice, any violence on earth, an open door has been set before rascals. Is it not a fact that Christianity has paralysed the world, and made it a prey to villains?"

His voice shook, his eyes flashed with consuming hatred, his face was contorted as if from unendurable pain.

Leonardo made no answer. He gazed at the blue heavens shining through gaps in the Coliseum walls; and he reflected that nowhere did the azure sky seem so radiant and stainless as in the interstices of ruins. Birds were flitting in and out of the holes left where the barbarians had wrenched away the iron bars. Leonardo watched them fluttering to their roosting places; and he thought how the world-swaying Cæsars, who had erected the building, and the northern hordes who had pillaged it, had worked for those of whom it is written; "They sow not, neither do they reap; and God feedeth them."

Everything to Leonardo was joy, to Niccolò all was vexation; honey to one was gall to the other; perfected knowledge had bred love in the one, hatred in the other. But Machiavelli interrupted these musings, as usual anxious to end the conversation with a joke:—

"I perceive, Messer Leonardo, that they who think you impious stand in gross error. In the Judgment, when the angelic trump shall separate the lambs from the wolves, you will be among lambs."

"Well," said the painter, falling in with his humour, "if I get to Paradise, you will come with me."

"I cry you mercy! I have suffered overmuch in this world from tedium! My place I will give to any anxious for it. Hearken, good friend, and I will relate to you a dream. I was taken into an assembly of hungered, unwashen outcasts, monks with yellow faces, old beggars, slaves, cripples, idiots, and taught that these were they of whom it is written: 'Blessed are the poor in spirit, for theirs is the kingdom of Heaven.' Then they had me to another place, where I saw an assembly of men in semblance like Senators. Among them were emperors, and popes, and captains, and lawgivers, and philosophers; Homer, Alexander the Great, Marcus Aurelius. They talked of learning and of statecraft. And to my wonderment I was told this was hell, and these were all sinners cast out by God, because they had loved the world and the wisdom of the world, which is foolishness with the Lord. And I was bidden to choose between hell and heaven, and I cried: 'To hell with me! With the sages and the heroes!'"

"If the reality be as you describe it," said Leonardo, "I also should prefer. . ."

"Nay, it is too late! You have made your choice. You will be rewarded for Christian virtues by a Christian heaven!"

They lingered in the Coliseum till dark. The yellow moon had sailed up from behind the stupendous arches of the Basilica of Constantine, severing with her rays a bed of cloud, transparent and delicately tinted as mother-o'-pearl. The three columns in front of St. Maria Liberatrice shone like phantoms. And the cracked bell sounding the Christian "Angelus" seemed more than ever like a dirge over the trampled and forgotten Romans.

Book XIV

Monna Lisa Gioconda—1503–1506

"The darkness of that subterranean place was too deep, and when I had passed sometime therein, two feelings awoke within me and contended—fear and curiosity; fear of exploring that dark depth; curiosity as to its secret."

—Leonardo Da Vinci

I

Leonardo used to say:—

"For portraits, have a special studio; a court, oblong and rectangular, ten *braccia* in width, twenty in length, the walls painted black, with a projecting roof and canvas curtains for the sun. Or, if you haven't the canvas curtains, paint only in the twilight, or when it is clouded and dull. That is the perfect light."

Just such a court for the painting of portraits he had made for himself in the house of the Florentine citizen who lodged him; a notable personage, commissary of the Signoria, a mathematician, a man of intellect and of amiability, his name Ser Piero di Braccio Martelli. His house was the second in the Via Martelli, on the left as one goes from San Giovanni to the Palazzo Medici.

It was a warm misty afternoon, towards the close of spring, in the year 1505. The sun shone through clouds; there was a dull light, which seemed as if shining under water, throwing delicate liquid shadows—Leonardo's favourite condition of the atmosphere; which, he thought, gave special charm to the face of a woman.

"Will she come?" he asked himself, thinking of her whose portrait he had been painting for nearly three years, with a tenacity and a zeal unwonted.

He arranged the studio for her reception. Boltraffio, watching him, marvelled at his unusual solicitude.

He prepared palette, brushes, and skins of paint, each one coated with a transparent film of gum arabic. He removed the cover from the portrait, which was disposed on a movable three-legged stand called a *leggio*. He set the fountain playing in the middle of the court. It had been constructed for her delight—falling streams striking against glass spheres put them in motion and produced a strange low music. Her favourite flowers had been planted round the fountain—pale irises—the lilies of Florence. Then he crumbled bread in a basket for the tame doe which lived in the court, and which she used to feed with her own hands; lastly, he arranged her chair, of smooth dark oak with carved back and arms; before it placed a soft rug, upon which was already curled and purring a white cat of a rare breed, procured for her pleasure, a dainty foreign beast with varicoloured eyes, the right yellow as a topaz, the left sapphire blue.

Meantime, Andrea Salaino had begun to tune the viol; another musician, one Atalante, whom Leonardo had known at the Milanese court, brought the silver lyre, shaped like a horse's head, which the artist had invented.

The best musicians, singers, story-tellers, and poets, the most witty talkers, were invited by Leonardo to his studio to amuse *her*, and avert the tedium of her sittings. He studied the changeful beauty of *her* expression as reflects of thought and feeling were awakened by talk, music, poetry, in turn.

Now all was ready, but still she delayed her coming.

"Where is she?" he thought; "the light and the shadow today are just her own. Shall I send to seek her? Nay, but she knows how ardently I await her! She will come."

And Giovanni noticed that his impatience grew.

Suddenly a light waft of the breeze swayed the jet of the fountain, the delicate irises shook as the spray fell on them. The keen-eared doe was on the alert, with outstretched neck. Leonardo listened. And Giovanni, though he heard nothing, knew it was *she*.

First, with a humble reverence, came Sister Camilla, a lay-companion who lived with her, and always attended her to the studio, sitting quietly apart studying a prayer-book, and effacing herself, so that in three years Leonardo had hardly heard her voice. The sister was followed by the woman all expected; a woman of thirty, in a plain dark dress, and a dark transparent veil which reached to the centre of her forehead—Monna Lisa Gioconda.

She was a Neapolitan of noble birth; her father, Antonio Gherardini, had lost his wealth in the French invasion of 1495, and had married his daughter to the Florentine, Francesco del Giocondo, who had seen the death of two wives already. Messer Francesco was five years younger than Leonardo; was one of the twelve *Bonuomini*, and was likely later to be made Prior. He was a mediocre personage, of a type to be found in every country and in every age; neither good nor bad; busy in a commonplace way, absorbed in his affairs, content with daily routine. He regarded his young wife as nothing more than an ornament for his house. Her essential charm he understood less than the points of his Sicilian cattle, or the impost upon raw sheepskins. She was said to have married this man solely to please her father, and by her marriage to have driven an earlier lover to a voluntary death. It was also said that she still had a crowd of passionate adorers—persevering, but hopeless. The scandalmongers could find nothing worse than this to insinuate. Calm, gentle, retiring, pious, charitable to the poor, she was a faithful wife, a good housekeeper, a most tender mother to Dianora, her twelve-year-old step-daughter.

Giovanni knew all this of Monna Lisa. Yet she never visited Leonardo's studio without seeming to the pupil a wholly different person from Messer Francesco's wife. She had been coming now for three years, and Giovanni's first impressions had been only confirmed by subsequent observations. He found something mysterious, illusory, phantasmal about her which filled him with awe. Leonardo's portrait seemed more real than she was herself. She and the painter—whom she never saw except when sitting to him, and then never alone—appeared to share some secret; not a love-secret, at least not in the ordinary sense of the term.

Leonardo had once spoken of the tendency felt by every artist to reproduce his own likeness in his pictures of others, the reason of this tendency being that both his own material semblance and his work are the creation and manifestation of his soul. In this case Giovanni found that not merely the portrait, but the woman herself, was growing daily more like the painter. The likeness was less in the features than in the expression of eyes and in the smile. But he had already seen this smile on the lips of Verrocchio's Unbelieving Thomas; of Eve before the Tree of Science, Leonardo's first picture; in the Leda; in the Angel of the *Madonna delle Roccie*; and in a hundred other drawings, executed before ever he had met Monna Lisa: as though, throughout life, he had sought his own reflection, and had found it completely at last.

When Giovanni looked at that smile, he felt perturbed, alarmed, as if in presence of the supernatural; reality seemed a dream, and the dream-world reality; Monna Lisa, not the wife of Giocondo, the very ordinary Florentine citizen, but a phantom evoked by the will of the master, a female semblance of Leonardo himself.

Lisa took her seat, and the white cat jumped on her lap; she stroked it with delicate fingers, and faint cracklings and sparks came from the silky fur. Leonardo began his work; but presently he laid it aside and sat silent, looking into her face with an intentness that no faintest shadow of change in her expression could have escaped.

"Madonna," he said at last, "you are preoccupied—troubled about something today."

Giovanni had observed that today she did not resemble the portrait.

"I am a little troubled," she replied; "Dianora ails, and I have been up with her the whole night."

"Then you are wearied, and the pose will try you. We will defer the sitting to another time."

"Nay, we cannot lose this delightful day! See the misty sunlight and the delicate shadows! It is *my* day!"

There was a short silence. Then she went on; "I knew you expected me. I was ready to come earlier; but I was kept. Madonna Sophonisba—"

"Who? Ah, I know. She with the voice of a fishwife and the scent of a perfumer's shop!"

Monna Lisa smiled quietly. "She had to tell me about the fête at the Palazzo Vecchio, given by Argentina, wife of the *Gonfaloniere*; of the supper, the dresses, the lovers—"

"Ay, 'tis not Dianora's indisposition has disturbed you, but this woman's senseless gossip. Strange case! Have you never noticed, madonna, how sometimes a single absurdity on an indifferent subject from an uninteresting person will throw a gloom over the mind, and afflict us more than our proper cares?"

She bent her head silently; it was clear they understood each other too well for words to be always necessary.

Leonardo again addressed himself to work.

"Tell me something!" she cried.

"What shall I tell you?"

She smiled. "Tell me about *The Realm of Venus*."

The artist had certain favourite stories for La Gioconda; tales of travel, of natural phenomena, of plans for pictures. He knew them by heart, and would recite always in the same simple half-childlike words, accompanied by soft music, in his feminine voice, the old fable, or cradle-tale. Andrea and Atalante took their instruments, and when they had executed the *motif* which invariably preluded *The Realm of Venus*, he began:—

"The seafarers who live on the coasts of Cilicia tell of him who is destined to drown, that for a moment, during the most tremendous storms, he is permitted to behold the island of Cyprus, realm of the Goddess of Love. Around boil whirlwinds and whirlpools, and the voices of the waters; and great in number are the navigators who, attracted by the splendour of that island, have lost ships upon its rocks. Many a gallant bark has there been dashed to pieces, many sunk forever in the deep! Yonder on the coast lie piteous hulks, overgrown with seaweed, half buried by sand. Of one the prow juts exposed; of another the stern; of another the gaping beams of its side, like the blackened ribs of a corpse. So many are they, that there it looks like the Resurrection Day, when the Sea shall give up its dead! But over the isle itself is a curtain of eternal azure, and the sun shines on flowery hills. And the stillness of the air is such, that when the priest swings the censer on the temple steps, the flame ascends to heaven straight, unwavering as the white columns and the giant cypresses mirrored in an untroubled lake lying inland, far from the shore. Only the streams that flow from that lake, and cascades leaping from one porphyry basin to another, trouble the solitude with their pleasant sound. Those drowning far at sea hear for a moment that soft murmur, and see the still lake of sweet waters, and the wind carries to them the perfume of myrtle and rose. Ever the more terrible the outer tempest, the profounder that calm in the island realm of the Cyprian."

He ceased: the strains of lute and viol died away, and that silence followed which is sweeter than any music. As if lulled by the words just spoken, as if caught away from actual life by the long hush, a stranger to all things except the will of the artist, Monna Lisa, like calm and pure and fathomless water, looked into Leonardo's eyes with that mystic smile which was the very counterpart of his own. Giovanni Boltraffio, watching now one, now the other, thought of two mirrors, each reflecting, absorbing the other into infinity.

II

Next morning Leonardo was working in the Palazzo Vecchio at his "Battle of Anghiari."

In 1503, when he had come from Rome, he had received an order from Piero Soderini, then the supreme authority in the republic, to paint some memorable battle on the wall of the new council-chamber. He chose the famous Florentine victory of 1440, over Niccolò Piccinino, the general of Filippo Visconti, Duke of Lombardy.

A portion of the picture was already completed: four horsemen struggling for possession of a standard—little more than a rag fluttering on a staff, its pole snapped and about to be shivered into pieces. Five hands have seized the shaft, and are pulling furiously in contrary directions. Sabres cross in the air; mouths are opened in a horrific yell. The distorted human faces are not less hideous than the jowls of the monstrous creatures on their helmets. The horses have been infected with the fury of their riders, and are rearing and striking each other with their forelegs, their ears laid back, their eyeballs rolling and glaring, as they gnash their teeth and bite like tigers. Below, in a pool of blood, one man is killing another, clutching his hair and dashing his head against the ground, not noticing that in a moment they will both alike be trampled down by the advancing hoofs.

This was war in all its horror, the supreme folly of humanity, the "most bestial of madnesses," according to Leonardo's own expression, "which leaves no footprint unfilled with blood."

This morning the painter had scarcely taken his work in hand when he heard steps upon the brick floor; he recognised them, and frowned without looking up. It was Piero Soderini, the *Gonfaloniere*.

Soderini required a precise account of every *soldo* advanced by the treasury for the purchase of wood, lac, chalk, paints, linseed oil, and other trifles. Never, when in the service of "tyrants," as the *Gonfaloniere* contemptuously called them, at the courts of Ludovico Sforza, or of Cæsar Borgia, had Leonardo been subjected to such petty interferences as here in the service of the free republic, in the region of civil equality.

"For what had you hoped?" asked the painter with a certain curiosity.

"We had hoped that your work would immortalise the warlike renown of the republic, and show the memorable exploits of our heroes; had hoped for something to elevate the soul, to give a noble example of patriotism. I grant you that war is as you have shown it; but, I ask you, Messer Leonardo, why not ennoble and adorn it, and modify its extremes? for the great thing is 'moderation in all things!' I may be mistaken, but to my thinking the painter's true business is to benefit the people by instructing them."

He had now touched on his favourite theme, and with brightened eyes he talked on; his monotonous voice had the ceaseless trickle of water, wearing away a stone. The painter scarcely replied; though, curious to know what this worthy citizen really thought on the subject of art, he listened at intervals with some attention. He felt as if he had gone into a dark and narrow room, crowded with people, and with an absolutely stifling atmosphere.

"Art which has no profit for the people," said Messer Piero, "is merely an amusement for the rich, a distraction for the idle, a luxury for tyrants. You agree, my good sir?"

"Certainly," assented Leonardo, and he continued, sarcastic purpose scarce visible in the twinkle of his eyes. "Permit me, sir, to suggest a practical method of terminating our perennial debate. Let the citizens of the Florentine Republic assemble in this very chamber, and take a vote on the question whether or no my picture be moral—that is, popular. There would be great advantage in this course. The question would be settled with mathematical certainty by counting heads; for the voice of the people is, as you are aware, the voice of God."

Soderini weighed the suggestion. He was so impressed by the virtue of the black and white balls used for voting, that it never occurred to him a mock could be made at the mystery. Presently, however, he understood, and fixing his eyes on the painter, stared in blank astonishment, almost terror. Yet he quickly recovered himself. Artists are known to be persons unreliable and devoid of common sense, and it ill behoved him to take offence at this painter fellow's gibe.

Messer Piero did not pursue the subject; in the tone of a superior addressing a dependent, he mentioned that Michelangelo Buonarroti had received an order to paint the second wall of the council chamber, and curtly took his leave. Leonardo followed him with his eyes. Sleek, grey, with crooked legs and a bent back, he seemed even more closely than usual to resemble a rat.

III

On leaving the Palazzo Vecchio Leonardo paused in the piazza before Michelangelo's "David." It stood as if on guard, a giant of white marble, relieved against the background of dark stone. Young, thin, naked, the veins swollen in his right hand which held the sling, his left arm was raised in front of his breast, the stone within the hand.

His brows were knit, his gaze far away, like one taking aim. The curls upon his low forehead seemed already the garland of victory. Leonardo remembered the description in the Book of Kings; and seeing him stand there where Savonarola had been burned, he thought of the prophet Fra Girolamo had desired in vain, the hero for whom Machiavelli was still waiting.

In this work of his rival's Leonardo recognised the expression of a soul great as his own, but eternally opposed to it; opposed as action is to contemplation, passion to apathy, storm to tranquillity. This alien force attracted him; he felt the inevitable fascination of something new, the desire to come close to it, to study, and understand it.

Two years earlier, among the building stones of Santa Maria del Fiore, lay a huge block of white marble, spoilt by an unskilled sculptor. The best masters had refused it, thinking it no longer good for anything. It had been offered to Leonardo himself, and with his usual slowness he had meditated, measured, calculated, hesitated. Then came another, twenty-three years younger than he, who had undertaken the task without misgiving; with incredible rapidity, working by night as well as by day, he had made this giant in two years and one month. Leonardo had worked for six years at the clay of his Colossus; he dared not think how long he would have required for a marble statue like this David.

The Florentines had proclaimed Michelangelo Leonardo's rival in the art of sculpture, and the young man had not hesitated to accept his challenge. Now it seemed he was about to place himself in competition with the older master as a painter also. He had yet hardly taken a brush in his hand, but with a daring which might seem presumption, he was about to paint the second war-picture in the council chamber.

Leonardo had met his youthful rival with goodwill and every consideration; but Michelangelo hated him with all the fire of his impetuous nature. Leonardo's calm he fancied contempt: he listened to calumnies, he sought pretexts for quarrels, he seized every occasion to damage his rival. When the "David" was finished the best painters and sculptors were invited by the Signoria to discuss where it should be placed. Leonardo agreed with Giuliano da San Gallo, the architect, that the most suitable position would be under the Loggia de' Priori, and not, as others suggested, in front of the Palazzo della Signoria. Michelangelo swore that Leonardo, prompted by envy, wished his rival's work hidden in a corner where no one could properly see it.

Discussions on abstract questions were at this time much the vogue, and on one occasion a company, including the brothers Pollaiuoli, the aged Botticelli, Filippino Lippi, and Lorenzo di Credi, assembled in Leonardo's studio to debate whether sculpture or painting held the higher place among the arts. Leonardo quickly, with a whimsical expression, gave his opinion thus:—

"The further art is removed from a handicraft the nearer it approaches perfection. The major distinction between the two arts lies in the fact that painting demands greater effort of mind, sculpture greater effort of body. The shape, contained like a kernel in the block of marble, is slowly set free by the sculptor's blows of chisel and mallet, needing the exertion of all his bodily powers. Great fatigue ensues, the labourer is drenched with sweat, which mingling with dust becomes a miry crust upon his garments; his face is smeared and covered with white like a baker's, his studio is filled with chips. Whereas the painter, perfectly calm, in elegant habiliments, seated at ease in his chair, plies a light brush and manipulates pleasant paints. His house is clean, and quiet, so that his toil can be sweetened by converse, or music, or reading, undisturbed by hammerings or scrapings."

These words came to the ears of Michelangelo, who imagined them aimed at himself. He took occasion to make venomous reply:—

"Let this Messer da Vinci, a kitchen-wench's bastard, be ashamed of dirty work; I, the heir of an old and honourable house, despise neither sweat nor mire. The dispute is foolish, for all the arts are equal, proceeding from one source, aiming at one goal. He who maintains that painting is nobler than sculpture knows no more of either than my serving-maid."

He set to work with feverish energy on his picture for the council chamber, wishing to overtake his rival—a feat by no means difficult. His subject was an incident in the Pisan campaign: a sudden attack by the enemy while the soldiers were bathing. The men hurry to the bank, scramble out of the pleasant waves, draw on their sweated and dusty clothes, don their cuirasses and helmets, which are burning hot under the fiery sunshine. Michelangelo thus showed war as a contrast to Leonardo's representation: not as "the most bestial of madnesses," but as the performance of hard and manful duty to the denial of ease and pleasure; as the struggle of heroes for the greatness and glory of their country.

The Florentines watched the growth of the two pictures and the rivalry between the artists with all the keenness of spectators at a raree show; and as strife unconnected with politics seemed to them tasteless as broth without salt, they affirmed that Michelangelo was for the republic against the Medici, Leonardo for the Medici against the republic. The artistic duel now became intelligible to everybody; the town was divided into two parties; and men, to whom art was a sealed book, declared themselves the adherents of one or other of the two artists whose works had become the ensigns of hostile camps. Stones were thrown secretly at the "David"; the rich accused the poor of this outrage, the demagogues accused the substantial burghers; the artists, the pupils; and Buonarroti, in the presence of the *Gonfaloniere*, asserted that ruffians had been hired by Leonardo to damage his statue.

One day Leonardo, working at his portrait in the presence of Boltraffio and Salaino, said to Monna Lisa:—

"Could I but come to speech with Messer Michelangelo, face to face, as I speak with you, madonna, all would be explained, and no trace would remain of this stupid quarrel. He would learn that I am not his enemy, and that there is no man living could love him better than I."

Madonna Lisa shook her head.

"Nay, Messer Leonardo, he would not understand you."

"Such a man could not fail to understand. The mischief is that he is diffident and has too little self-confidence. He fears and tortures himself and is jealous, because he does not yet know his own strength. It is folly in him. I would reassure him. What has he to fear in me? I have seen his sketch for the 'Soldiers bathing' and, believe me, madonna, I was astounded, and could scarce believe my own eyes. No one can conceive the value of this young man, nor what he will rise to. Even now he is not only my equal, but stronger than I. Deny it not, madonna, for I speak what I know to be true: he is my superior."

She smiled, reflecting his expression like an image in a mirror.

One day in Santa Maria del Carmine, in the Cappella Brancacci, where were the famous frescoes of Tomaso Masaccio, the school of all the great masters, he saw a lad, scarcely more than a boy, studying and copying as he had done himself in his youth. He wore a paint-stained old black frock, clean but coarse and homespun linen. He was tall and willowy, with a slight neck, very white and long, delicate as a girl's. His face was oval, clear cut, and pale, with a somewhat sensuous beauty, and great dark eyes like those of the Umbrian peasant women from whom Perugino painted his Madonnas, eyes with no depth of thought, deep and void as the sky. Leonardo saw the youth a second time in the Sala del Papa at Santa Maria Novella, where his own cartoon for the "Battle of Anghiari" was exhibited. This the lad was studying and copying with no less care than he had bestowed on Masaccio's frescoes. He evidently knew Leonardo by sight, but did not venture to speak to him.

The Master addressed him; and then hurriedly, excitedly, and with many blushes, half-presumptuous yet childishly artless, the boy confessed that he looked on Leonardo as his master, as the greatest of all Italian masters, whose shoe's-latchet Michelangelo Buonarroti was not worthy to unloose.

Leonardo examined his drawings, and after further converse, on other occasions, became convinced that here was a great master of the future.

Sensitive and responsive as an echo to all voices, submissive to influence as a woman, he at present imitated both Perugino and Pinturicchio (with whom he had recently been working in the library at Siena), and also Leonardo; but under this immaturity the latter found a freshness of feeling in him superior to any he had met. And the lad seemed to have already fathomed by guesswork the deepest mysteries of art and life; had surmounted the greatest obstacles as if involuntarily, lightly, by chance, almost in play. Every gift seemed to have been bestowed on him freely; he knew no searchings of heart, no weary toil, no hesitation, no despairing efforts, no hopeless puzzles, such as had always been to Leonardo an incubus and a curse. And when the Master spoke to him of the need for patient study of nature, and of the laws of painting, the youth fixed on him soft wondering eyes, and, it was evident, listened merely out of reverence for the great man's opinion.

One day he made an observation which surprised Leonardo by its depth:—

"I have noticed," he said, "that while one is painting one should not think. Everything then turns out better."

It seemed as if this youth's whole being was a proof that the perfect harmony of reason and feeling, of love and science, which the Master sought so ardently, did not, nor could not exist. And in face of the modest and careless frankness which shone in those unanxious eyes, Leonardo felt greater doubt of the work of his own whole life, greater doubt of the future destiny of art, than had ever tormented him when confronted by the rivalry and scorn of Michelangelo.

At one of their first meetings Leonardo had asked the lad his name, parentage and native place.

"I come from Urbino," he replied; "my father is Giovanni Sanzio the painter, and my name, Raphael."

IV

THE EVENING BEFORE LEONARDO'S DEPARTURE from Florence to mend a dam which had burst on the river Arno, he was returning from a visit to Machiavelli, who had alarmed him by his admissions with regard to Soderini.

He was crossing the bridge of the Santa Trinità, towards the Via Tornabuoni. The hour was late, and few people were about; after a hot day a shower had freshened the air. From the river came the sharp perfume which water acquires in the warmth of summer; the moon was rising behind the dark hill of San Miniato. On the bank near the Ponte Vecchio a cluster of very ancient houses, with uneven balconies and wooden supports, were reflected in the dull green water. Behind Monte Albano glittered a single star. The outline of Florence was cut against the clear sky like a golden capital letter in some ancient manuscript; an outline unique in the world, familiar to Leonardo as the outline of a human face. To the north rose the ancient belfry of Santa Croce, near it the straight slender stem of the tower of the Palazzo Vecchio; then Giotto's marble campanile, and the red cupola of Santa Maria del Fiore, like the gigantic expanding blossom of the purple lily, the flower of Florence on her standards and escutcheons. All Florence, bathed in moonlight seemed a huge silver flower.

Leonardo noted that every city has its own especial perfume; that of Florence was a mingling of the scent of iris flowers, and the faint odour of dust and damp and old varnish which belongs to ancient pictures.

His thoughts veered to her who was becoming their constant preoccupation—Monna Lisa Gioconda. He knew scarce more of her life than did Giovanni his pupil; it was less an annoyance than a perpetual astonishment to him to reflect that she had a husband—Messer Francesco, so tall and lean, with a wart on his cheek, thick eyebrows; a positive soul; whose talk was of Sicilian cattle and the tax upon sheepskins. There were moments in which Leonardo rejoiced in her ethereal charm, which seemed above common humanity, yet was more real to him than aught belonging to everyday life. There were other moments in which he acutely felt the beauty of the living woman.

Lisa was not one of those celebrated by the poetasters as *dotte eroine* (learned heroines). She never displayed her knowledge of books; only by chance he found out that she read both Latin and Greek. She spoke so simply that many imagined her stupid. But Leonardo found in her what is most rare, especially among women, instinctive wisdom. Sometimes by a chance sentence she would reveal herself so near, so akin to him in spirit, that he felt her his one and eternal friend, the sister of his soul. At these moments he would fain have overpassed the magic circle which divides contemplation from life; but such desires he quenched at once. Was this love which united them? Platonic ravings, languid sighs of ideal lovers, syrupy sonnets in the Petrarchan style, had never excited in him anything but amusement or boredom. Equally alien to his nature was the passion which most men call love. Just as he ate no meat, because it seemed to him repulsive, so he refrained from women, because all material possession—in marriage or outside it—seemed to him coarse. He avoided it as he avoided the shambles, neither blaming nor approving, acknowledging the law of natural struggle for hunger or for love, but refusing to take any part in it himself, and obeying a purer law of chastity and love.

Yet even if he had loved her, what more perfect union with the beloved could he have wished than in this secret and mystic intercourse, in the creation of this immortal image, this new being, born of them both, as a child of its parents, in which he and she were one? Nevertheless he felt that even in this mystic union, stainless as it was, there was danger—it might be greater danger than in the bond of ordinary fleshly love. They walked on the verge of a precipice where none had walked before, resisting the vertigo and the fatal attraction of the abyss. Between them were simple words, vague and uncompleted phrases, through which their secret showed as the sun shines through the morning mist. At times he thought, What if the mist should scatter, and the blinding sun shine out which kills mystery, dissolves all phantoms? What if he or she should prove unequal to the strain, should overstep the magic circle, materialise imagination into fact, contemplation into life? Had he the right to test a human soul, the soul of his life-long friend, his spiritual sister, as he tested the laws of mechanics, the structure of plants, the action of poisons? Would she not revolt, cast him from her with contempt and hatred?

Again at times he fancied he was subjecting her to a slow and a terrible death. Her submissiveness alarmed him; it seemed limitless, like his own eternal search for knowledge, the delicate yet penetrating scrutiny to which he subjected her. Sooner or later he would have to decide what she was to him, a woman or a spirit. He had been hoping that temporary absence would postpone this inevitable decision, and for this reason was glad to be leaving Florence.

But now that the moment had come, that separation was imminent, he realised that he had been mistaken, and that instead of deferring, his departure must hasten the decision.

Absorbed in these thoughts, he did not notice that he had wandered into a lonely blind alley, and on looking about him did not at once recognise where he was. Giotto's campanile appearing above the houses showed he was in the vicinity of the cathedral. One side of the narrow street was lost in blackest shadow, the other was white under the rays of the moon. A distant light glowed red. It came from one of the *loggie* characteristic of Florence, with a balcony and semi-circular arches on slender pillars; a company in masks and cloaks were singing a serenade, to the gentle tinkling of a lute.

It was the old love-song, composed by Lorenzo Il Magnifico, which had once sounded in the carnival procession; a melancholy yet joyous melody, pleasant to Leonardo's ears because he had know it in his youth.

Quanto è bella giovinezza!
Ma sen fugge tuttavia
Chi vuol esser lieto sia
Di doman non v'è certezza.

(Fair-fleeting Youth must snatch at happiness:
He knows not if tomorrow curse or bless.)

The last line lingered sadly in his ears with mournful foreboding.

Already on the threshold of old age, and approaching darkness and solitude, had not Fate sent him at last a living soul, a kindred soul? Must he repulse it? must he deny it? sacrifice life for contemplation, as he had so often done before? renounce the near for the faraway, the real for the ideal? Which was he to choose, the true and living and mortal Gioconda or the immortal, which had no material existence? They were equally dear to him, yet he must choose between them; choose at once, for her sake. But his will was weak. He could arrive at no decision, and wandered on aimlessly through the streets, debating, debating with himself.

Presently he reached the house of Piero Martelli, where he lodged. The doors were shut, the lights extinguished. He raised the hammer hung on a chain, and knocked. The porter did not come. Repeated blows were only answered by echoes from the sounding arches of the stone staircase. Echoes died away and silence succeeded, seeming the more profound for the brightness of the moonlight.

A clock boomed from a neighbouring tower. The heavy measured clanging told of the silent and dreadful flight of time, of the darkness and loneliness of age, of the past which could never return. And long did the last clang vibrate in the moonlit stillness, quivering on the air, now weakening, now strengthening again in ever widening waves of sound, as if repeating—

Di doman non v'è certezza.

V

The next day, at her habitual hour, Monna Lisa came to the studio for the first time unaccompanied. She knew it was their last interview. It was a brilliant morning, and Leonardo lowered the canvas curtain to produce that dim and tender light, transparent as submarine shadows, which gave her face its greatest charm.

They were alone.

He kept working on in silence, calm and absorbed, forgetting his thoughts of the previous night, forgetting the parting, the inevitable choice. Past and Future had alike vanished from his memory; time had come to a standstill; it seemed as if she had always sat, and would ever thus sit before him, with that calm strange smile. What he could not do in life he did by imagination; he blended the two images in one—mingled the reality and its reflection—the living woman and the immortal.

He had now the sense of a great deliverance. He no longer either pitied her or feared her. He knew her submissiveness, that she would accept all, endure all; die, perhaps, but never revolt. And momently he looked at her with that curiosity which had taken him to the execution of the condemned, that he might watch the last shudders of fear on the dying faces.

Suddenly he fancied that a strange shadow, as of an unbidden thought, which he had not evoked, which he wished away, appeared upon her countenance, like the cloud of human breath upon the surface of a mirror. To preserve her, to recall her anew to the Type, within the fatidic circle, to banish from her this human shadow, he related gravely, like a magician pronouncing an incantation, one of his mystic tales.

"Unable to resist the desire of beholding new forms, the secret creations of nature, I at length reached the cavern, and there at the entrance stood still in terror. I stooped, the left hand on the right knee, and shading my eyes with my hand to accustom myself to the darkness, I presently took heart and entered, and moved forward for several steps. Then, frowning, straining my sight to the utmost, I unwittingly changed my course and wandered hither and thither in the darkness, feeling my way and groping after the definite. But the obscurity was overpowering, and when I had passed sometime in it, Fear and Curiosity contended most mightily within me: fear of searching that dark cavern, and curiosity after its secret."

He was silent. The unwonted shadow lay still upon her face.

"Which of the two feelings gained the day?" La Gioconda murmured.

"Curiosity."

"And you learned the stupendous secret?"

"I learned. . . what could be learned."

"And will reveal it to men?"

"I would not, nor could not, reveal all. But I would inspire them also with curiosity strong enough to vanquish fear."

"*And if curiosity be not enough*, Messer Leonardo?" she said slowly, an unwonted fire in her eyes; "if something further, a profounder feeling, were needed to lay bare the cavern's last and greatest treasure?"

And she turned toward him a smile he had never seen before.

"What more is needed?" he asked.

She was silent. Just then a slender blinding ray shone through a rent in the curtain; the dimness vanished; the mystery, the clear shadows, tender as distant music, fled.

"You leave tomorrow?" she said suddenly.

"No. Tonight."

"I, too, am soon departing."

The artist looked at her steadily, attempted speech, and said nothing. He devined her meaning; that she would not stay in Florence without him.

"Messer Francesco," she continued, "goes presently for three months to Calabria. I have asked him to take me with him."

He frowned. This sunshine was not to his mind; the fountain had been ghostly white; now it had taken the rainbow hues of life. Leonardo felt that he was returning to life, timid, weak, pitiable.

"No matter," said Monna Lisa, "draw closer the curtain. It is early yet. I am not tired."

"I have painted enough," he said, throwing down his brush.

"You will not finish my portrait?"

"Why not?" he cried hastily, as if alarmed. "Will you not come to me when you return?"

"I will come. But shall I be the same? You have told me that faces, especially the faces of women, quickly change."

"I long to finish it. But sometimes to me it seems impossible?"

"Impossible?" wondered La Gioconda. "Ay, they tell me you finish nothing because you are always seeking the impossible."

In these words he fancied a tender reproach.

"The moment has come!" he thought.

She rose and said with her usual calm:—

"Farewell, Messer Leonardo. I wish you a good journey." He also had risen, and looking at her he saw again helpless entreaty and reproach on her face. He knew that this moment was irrevocable for both—final and solemn as death. He felt he must break this pregnant silence, yet no words came to him. The more he forced his will to find a solution, the more he was conscious of his own powerlessness and the profundity of the abyss which must divide them. Monna Lisa still smiled her quiet smile; that calmness, that brightness, seemed to him now the smile of the dead. Intolerable pity filled his heart and weakened him still more.

She stretched out her hand; he took it and kissed it for the first time since he had known her. As he did so she bent quickly, and he felt that La Gioconda touched his hair with her lips.

"May God have you in his keeping," she said simply.

When he recovered from his wonder—she was gone. Around him was the dead silence of a summer afternoon, more menacing than midnight. Again he heard the heavy measured clanging of the clock, telling of the irremediable flight of time, of the darkness and loneliness of age, of the past, which can return no more. And as the last vibrations died away the words of the plaintive love song echoed in his ears:—

"Di doman non v'è certezza."
"And count not on the day to come."

VI

Learning that Messer Giocondo was not returning from Calabria till October, Leonardo deferred his return to Florence for ten days that he might not reach the city till Madonna Lisa was there. He counted the hours till that moment should arrive; superstitious dread oppressed his heart when he remembered that accident might easily prolong the separation. He strove not to think; he asked no one for news lest he should hear something disappointing.

At last the day came, and he reached Florence early in the morning. Autumnal, damp and dull, the city yet seemed especially fair. It spoke to him of La Gioconda. It was one of *her* days; misty, transparent, with subdued light, as of sunlight seen through water.

He no longer asked himself how they would meet, what he should say, nor how he must act that they might part no more, that he might keep her forever as his only friend, the sister of his soul.

"Things turn out best when one does not think too much. The great thing is, not to think," he said to himself, quoting the lad Raphael. "I will question her; and she will tell me all which that day we left unsaid; she will explain what more than curiosity is necessary if one is to discover the marvel of the cavern."

Gladness filled his soul as if he were a boy of sixteen with his life before him; yet deep down under this gladness there lingered a half unconscious presentiment of mishap.

In the evening he visited Machiavelli, intending to go to Messer Giocondo's house next day. Impatience, however, overcame him, and he decided to call at once and ask for news from the porter of Madonna Lisa's safe arrival. He went down the Via Tornabuoni towards the Ponte Santa Trinità, the same route, though in the opposite direction, which he had followed the night before his departure. The weather had suddenly changed, as often happens in Florence on autumn evenings. The north wind, piercing as a knife, blew down the valley of the Mugnone, and the crest of the Mugello was whitened with snow. In the town it was raining; but just above the horizon there remained a narrow strip of clear sky, and from it the sun suddenly burst forth, flooding the wet streets and shining roofs and the faces of the passersby with a harsh yellow light. The rain seemed like copper dust, and the glass of distant windows glowed like live coals.

Near the bridge and opposite the church of Santa Trinità, in the angle formed by the river bank and the Via Tornabuoni, rose the imposing Palazzo degli Spini, built of large warm-grey stones, with barred lancet windows and castellated roof like a fortress. Down below was the customary row of stone benches, where the citizens congregated to tell the news, to sun or to shade themselves, to play at dice or draughts. There was a loggia at the other side of the palace, looking out upon the Arno.

As he passed, Leonardo saw in this loggia a group of persons, strangers to him for the most part, disputing so vehemently that they did not notice the storm.

"Messer Leonardo! come hither and resolve our question!" they called to him. He stopped. The dispute was about certain lines in the thirty-fourth canto of Dante's *Inferno*, where Lucifer is described buried breast-high in the ice at the very bottom of the accursed Pit.

The matter was expounded to Leonardo by one of the disputants, a rich old wool merchant. The artist, however, was but half attending, for his eyes were fixed on a man coming along the Lungarno Acciaioli. This person walked heavily, shambling like a bear: he was bent and bony, with a large head, black hair, and ill-shaped beard; his clothes were poor and carelessly thrown on. He had a broad-browed heavy face, with projecting ears and a broken nose. His small eyes dilated and glowed strangely under excitement, and much night-work had reddened his eyelids. Indeed he was said to work preferably in underground darkness, with a small round lamp attached to his forehead, like a new Cyclops. It was Michelangelo.

"Give us your opinion," urged the disputants of Leonardo.

"I have heard," replied the painter, "that Messer Buonarroti is a student of the great Alighieri. Ask him; he will answer your question better than I."

For Leonardo had always hoped that his difference with Michelangelo would die a natural death; and he was anxious for an occasion which would bring them to speech together.

The younger man, hearing his name pronounced, stopped and raised his eyes. He was reserved and shy, even to wildness, dreading the stare of strangers, and fancying that they scorned his ugliness, which he himself was never able to forget. Now he looked suspiciously at the company in the loggia; but when he saw Leonardo's smile, and his piercing glance bent down upon him, for the older man was much the taller of the two, shyness changed into rage. He grew pale and red by turns; words choked him; but at last he blurted out:—

"Explain it yourself, most intelligent of sages, sold to the Lombards! Books are your proper pastime; you who spent sixteen years trying to hatch a clay horse, and when you tried to cast it in bronze threw up the task in despair." He knew he was speaking outrageously; but such was his fury that no words seemed to him sufficiently insulting to hurl at his rival.

Leonardo made no reply; he looked the other full in the face, and the bystanders also were silent, watching the two men.

Before the violence of Buonarroti, Leonardo's calm almost feminine smile, tinged with sadness, suggested weakness. But he himself remembered Monna Lisa's words, that Michelangelo would never pardon him for his gift of that quietness which is mightier than storm.

Michelangelo finding no more words waved his hand, turned quickly, and went on his way, with his shambling gait, his dull unconscious habit of growling, his bent head and bowed shoulders, upon which seemed to rest some superhuman burden. Soon he disappeared as if dissolved into the turbid copper-coloured rain and the wild and threatening sunlight.

Leonardo walked on. On the bridge one of the company in the loggia of the Palazzo Spini overtook him—a little man with the aspect of a Jew, though a pure-blooded Florentine, known to Leonardo as a scandal-monger. The painter crossed the bridge, the other running by his side, talking of Michelangelo, and trying to force Leonardo into some adverse criticism of his rival, which no doubt he intended to repeat at the earliest opportunity. Leonardo, however, refused to be drawn into this trap, and remained silent.

The intruder was not to be shaken off.

"Tell me, Messere," he said, "have you yet finished your portrait of La Gioconda?"

"I have not," answered the painter. "Why are you interested?"

"Nay, I was only considering the matter. For three years you have laboured at one picture, and you say it is still incomplete. But to us ignorant amateurs it seems already perfection, and we can conceive of nothing further to be done."

And he smiled obsequiously. Leonardo would have liked to take the little man by the collar and fling him into the river.

"And what will you do now?" continued the irrepressible one. "But perhaps you have not heard, Messer Leonardo?"

Through his aversion the artist felt a spasm of dread. The other had evidently something on his tongue; his eyes danced, his hands shook. He seemed like some noxious insect.

"Oh, *Santo Iddio benedetto*!" he exclaimed; "forsooth you only returned to Florence this morning, so the news may not have reached you. Poor Messer Giocondo! to be thrice widowed! Conceive what bad luck! 'Tis now a month since Madonna Lisa, by the will of Heaven, expired!"

Darkness fell upon Leonardo's eyes; for a moment it seemed to him he must swoon. But the keen inquisitive gaze of his tormentor helped him to a superhuman effort of self-control; he turned pale, but his face remained inscrutable. The other, disappointed, presently took his leave. Left alone, Leonardo gradually recovered his composure. His first thought was that the busybody had lied; inventing the evil tidings on purpose to see what effect they would produce on the artist whose name had long been whispered as a lover of La Gioconda's. It was incredible that she could really be dead.

Before nightfall, however, he had learned all. Madonna Lisa, victim, said some, of a contagious malady of the throat, had died at the obscure town of Lagonero, on the return journey from Calabria to Florence.

VII

The attempt to divert the Arno from Pisa ended in disaster. Floods destroyed the works, and turned the blooming lowland into a pestilential swamp, where the workmen died of malaria. The labour, the money, the lives had been expended for naught: the Ferrarese engineers threw the blame upon Soderini, Machiavelli, and Leonardo. They were placed under a ban, and their acquaintances turned from them in the streets. Niccolò fell ill of vexation.

Two years before this, Leonardo's father, Ser Piero da Vinci, notary of the palace of the Podestà, had died at the age of eighty.

In the matter of inheritance Ser Piero had frequently expressed an intention of placing Leonardo on an equal footing with his legitimate sons. They refused to execute his will. Leonardo's affairs were at this time much involved, and he was induced to assent to the proposal of one of the Hebrew usurers, from whom he had borrowed on the security of his expectations, that he should sell him his claim on the paternal inheritance. A lawsuit followed which lasted for six years. Taking advantage of Leonardo's unpopularity, his brothers poured oil on the flames, accusing him of sorcery, atheism, high treason during his service with Cæsar Borgia, and violation of tombs by digging up corpses for dissection; they even insulted the memory of his dead mother, Caterina, and revived the twenty-year-old slander, accusing him of vice.

In addition to all these trials was added the failure of the picture in the Council Chamber. Notwithstanding his experience with regard to the *Cenacolo*, he had used oil paints also for the "Battle of Anghiari," though with what he believed an improved method. When the work was half finished he attempted to hasten the fixing of the paint in the plaster by means of a great fire in a brazier before the picture. But the heat acted only on the lower part of the surface; the varnish and paint higher up would not dry.

After many fruitless experiments he realised that the second attempt at wall-painting in oil was unsuccessful as the first, and that the "Battle" would fade away as surely as the "Last Supper."

Once more, in Michelangelo's words, he was obliged to throw up his task in despair.

The picture troubled him more than the Pisan canal or the fraternal lawsuit. Soderini had harassed him with demands for mercantile exactness in the carrying out of the order for the fresco, pressed for completion within a given time, threatened him with penalties, finally accused him openly of having misappropriated public money. Yet when Leonardo, having borrowed from his friends, proposed to restore all he had received from the treasury, Messer Piero refused to accept his offer, and meanwhile was not ashamed to write to the Seigneur Charles d'Amboise, governor of Lombardy, who was negotiating for the transfer of the painter from Florence to Milan:—

"The conduct of Leonardo da Vinci has not been honourable: for having received a large sum for the execution of a great work, he abandoned it when he had completed but a very little, and in this matter had acted as a traitor to the republic."

One winter night Leonardo sat alone in his working room. The wind howled in the chimney, the walls shook, the candle flickered, the stuffed bird, suspended from a wooden bar, swayed as if attempting to fly; above the bookshelf the familiar spider ran in alarm about his web.

Drops of rain battered the window like the knocks of one wishing to enter.

After a day spent in working for his livelihood, Leonardo felt exhausted, as by a night of fever. He tried to employ himself by scientific study, by drawing a caricature, by reading; but everything fell from his hands. He had no inclination to sleep, and the whole night was before him.

He looked at the piles of books, at the crucibles, the retorts, the bottles containing monstrosities preserved in spirit; at the brass quadrants, the globes, the apparatus for the study of mechanics, astronomy, physics, hydraulics, optics, and anatomy. An unwonted repugnance to them all filled his soul. Was not he the fellow of yonder old spider in the dark corner above the mouldy books, the human bones, the limbs of lifeless machines? What was left to him, what lay between him and death, between him and utter oblivion except certain sheets of paper, which he was covering with writing that no one could read? And he remembered his happiness when as a child he had climbed the heights of Monte Albano, had seen the flocks of cranes, had smelt the freshness of spring, had gazed at the fair city of Florence, lying in the sunlight haze like an amethyst, so small that it could be framed between two branches of juniper. Yes, he had been happy; thinking of nothing, knowing nothing.

Was the whole labour of his life a mockery? Was Love, after all, *not* the daughter of Knowledge?

He listened to the howling, the shrieking, the roaring of the storm, and he remembered Machiavelli's words; "The most fearful thing in life is not poverty nor care, sickness nor sorrow, nor death itself. It is weariness of spirit."

And still the inhuman voice of the night wind spoke of things unavoidable yet unintelligible to the mind of man; of the loneliness, the blackness of utter darkness on the bosom of old Chaos, mother of all that is; of the boundless weariness of the spirit of the world. Leonardo rose, took a candle, went into the next room, uncovered a picture standing on an easel and veiled with a heavy drapery like a shroud. It was the portrait of Monna Lisa Gioconda.

He had not looked at it since their parting. Now it seemed that he saw it for the first time; such vigour of life was in it that he trembled before his own creation. He remembered old-world traditions of magic portraits which, if pierced by a needle, caused the death of the living originals. In this case had he not done the contrary, taken life from the living woman to give it to the dead?

It was all vivid and exact, to the last fold of her dress, to the little stars of the delicate embroidery garnishing the opening round her neck. It seemed as if the white bosom heaved, the blood beat warm in the arteries, the expression of the face changed. Yet was she spectral, far off, alien; more antique, in her deathless youth, than the cliffs in the picture background—strange, sky-blue rocks, like stalactites, that seemed visions of a world long extinct. Ah! and the waves of her hair fell from under the dark transparent veil, by the same laws of divine mechanics as fell the waves of water in the cataract! It was only now, when he had lost her, that he knew the charm of Monna Lisa. Hers was the charm which he had sought in nature; the secret of the universe was the secret of this woman, whom he had loved.

And it was no longer he who was putting her to the test, but she who was trying him. What meant the gaze of those eyes, reflecting his own soul? Was she repeating what she had said at their last meeting—telling him that more than curiosity is needed, if the most wondrous secret of the cavern is to be discovered? Or was this the alien smile of perfect knowledge with which the dead look at the living? For the first time he realised that she was truly dead. Could he or could he not have saved her? Never before had he looked into the face of Death so directly, so near. Terror turned his soul to ice. He drew back from the horror: for the first time in his life he did not wish to *know*.

With a hasty and furtive movement he dropped the shroud again over the canvas, and turned away.

IN THE SUCCEEDING SPRING, BY the good offices of Charles d'Amboise, Leonardo was freed from his engagements to the Florentine Republic, and able to return to Milan. Now, as twenty-five years before, he was glad to leave his home, and to see the snowy crests of the Alps rising above the great plain of Lombardy. Now, as then, he was an exile, cast out from his country and his home.

Book XV

The Holy Inquisition—1506–1513

Know all; but be known of none.

—Asil The Gnostic

I

In the year 1507 Leonardo definitely entered the service of Louis XII, established himself at Milan, and went no more to Florence, except for small matters of business.

Four years passed uneventfully.

Towards the close of 1511 Giovanni Boltraffio, who was now a master of repute, was working at a wall-painting in the new Church of San Maurizio. It belonged to the ancient foundation of the Monastero Maggiore, and was built on the ruins of the Roman circus. Beside it, enclosed by a high fence and abutting on the Via Della Vigna, was a neglected garden, and the once splendid but now deserted and ruined palace of the Counts of Carmagnola. The nuns of the Monastero Maggiore had let this house and garden to Messer Galeotto Sacrobosco, the old alchemist, who had lately returned to Milan with Cassandra his niece. Their cottage by the Porta Vercellina having been destroyed at the time of the first French invasion, the pair had wandered for nine years in Greece, the islands of the Archipelago, Asia Minor, and Syria. Strange tales were told of them: Galeotto had found the philosopher's stone; he had appropriated vast sums lent him by the Devâtdâr of Syria for experiments, and had fled for his life. Monna Cassandra, by the help of the devil, had found treasure on the site of an ancient Phoenician temple; she had bewitched, drugged, and plundered a wealthy merchant at Constantinople; at any rate the pair had left Milan beggars, and had returned rich—that much was certain. Pupil of Demetrius Chalcondylas, and also of Sidonia the witch, Cassandra appeared now a devout daughter of the Church. She observed all fasts and ceremonies, she attended the holy offices, and by her charities had acquired the favour not only of the sisters of the Monastero Maggiore, but that of the archbishop himself. Evil tongues, however, declared that her religion was a pretence, that she was still a pagan, that she and her uncle had only escaped the Inquisition by flight from Rome, and that sooner or later she was certain to be burned at the stake. Messer Galeotto still reverenced Leonardo, and considered him his master in the occult wisdom of Hermes Trismegistus. The alchemist had collected many rare books in the course of his travels; for the most part those of Alexandrian scholars of Ptolemaic times. Leonardo borrowed these sometimes, and generally sent Giovanni to fetch them, since he was working close to the alchemist's house. As had happened before, Giovanni fell under the spell of Cassandra, and his visits became more frequent. At first she spoke to him guardedly, acting up to her part of repentant sinner, and expressing a desire to take the veil. Little by little she dismissed her fears, and became confidential. They recalled their meetings of ten years ago, when they had both been little more than children—the lonely terrace above the quiet Cantarana, the walls of the Convent of St. Radegonda; especially that sultry evening when she had spoken to him of the Resurrection of the Gods, and had invited him to the Witches' Sabbath. Now she lived as a recluse; was ill, or pretended to be so; and when she was not at church she hid herself in a remote secluded dark chamber, where the windows looked out on the neglected garden, densely shadowed by cypress trees. The room was furnished like a library or a museum. Here were the antiquities she had brought from the East; fragments of statues, dog-headed gods of black syenite from Egypt, mysterious stones upon which was incised the magic word *Abraxas*, signifying the three hundred and sixty-five celestial spheres of the Gnostics; precious Byzantine parchments, which time had rendered hard as ivory; fragments from Greek manuscripts, hopelessly lost; earthen shards, with cuneiform Assyrian inscriptions; books of the Persian magi, clasped with iron; Memphian papyri, transparent and thin as the petals of a flower.

Cassandra told Giovanni of the wonders she had seen; of the desolate grandeur of marble temples standing on sea-worn cliffs, at their feet the blue Ionian waves, their columns bedewed with the brine, like the naked body of the foam-born goddess long ago. She told of her incredible exertions, dangers, accidents. He asked her what she had sought, why she had collected these things at the cost of so much toil, and she answered in the words of Luigi her father:—

"To bring the dead to life."

And her eyes glowed with the fire that had belonged to Cassandra, the witch of days gone by.

In appearance she was little changed; she had the same face, untouched by grief or joy—impassive as the faces of the ancient statues; the same broad low forehead, straight fine eyebrows, firm unsmiling lips, and amber eyes. Yet now her face, refined by illness, or perhaps by the over-insistence of a single thought, had taken an expression calmer and more austere than it had worn in her girlhood. Her dark hair, twined and wreathed like Medusa's snakes, still gave the impression of having a life of its own, still formed a frame for her pale face, and enhanced the brilliance of her eyes, the scarlet of her lips. The charm of the girl attracted Giovanni irresistibly as of old, and renewed in his soul the old feelings of curiosity, compassion, and fear.

In her journey across the land of Hellas she had visited her mother's native place, the lonely little town of Mistra, near the ruins of Sparta, among the bare hills where, half a century before, had died Gemistus Pletho, last teacher of the Hellenic philosophy. Telling Giovanni of her visit to his grave, she repeated Pletho's prophecy that after a few years the world would return to a single faith, not differing from the ancient paganism.

"The prophecy is not fulfilled," said Giovanni, "though more than fifty years have passed. Have you still faith in him, Monna Cassandra?"

"There was not perfect truth in Pletho," she replied calmly, "for there was much he did not know."

"What?" asked Giovanni; and under the intentness of her glance he felt his heart sink.

She took a parchment from the shelf, and read to him certain lines from the *Prometheus*, in which the Titan, having enumerated his gifts to men, more especially that fire which he had stolen from heaven, and which would make them equal with the gods, goes on to prophesy the fall of Zeus.

"Giovanni, have you never heard of the man who, ten centuries ago, dreamed, like Pletho, of reviving the dead gods—the Emperor Flavius Claudius Julian?"

"Julian the Apostate?"

"Ay, so they called him."

"He gave his life in vain for the Olympians." She hesitated, then continued in a lower voice; "If I were to tell you all, Giovanni! But for today I will say only this. Among the Olympians is a god nearer than all others to his brethren below; a god both bright and dark; fair as the dawn, yet pitiless as death; who came to earth and gave to mortals—as Prometheus had done—the forgetting of death and the boon of fire—new fire—in his own blood, in the intoxicating juice of the vine; and, my brother, who is there among men who will understand? who will go boldly forth and say to the world, 'The love of him who is crowned with the vine is like the love of Him who is crowned with thorns (who said, "I am the true vine"); of Him who, no less than Dionysus, makes the world drunk with his blood?' Have you understood, Giovanni, of whom I speak? If not, ask me nothing, for here is a secret which we may not, as yet, reveal."

Of late a great audacity of thought had come to Giovanni. He feared nothing, because he had nothing to lose. He had convinced himself that neither in the faith of Fra Benedetto, nor in the knowledge of Leonardo, would he find peace. Cassandra's prophecies gave him a glimpse of a new idea, so startling as to be terrible. Instead of turning away he approached it with the courage of despair. Day by day their souls came closer to each other.

Once he asked her why she hid what she believed to be the truth, why she even dissembled?

"All things are not for all men," she answered. "Martyrdoms, wonders, and signs are necessary for the crowd. Only those whose faith is imperfect die for their faith, that they may convince others, and themselves. But perfect faith is the same thing as perfect knowledge. Did the truths of geometry discovered by Pythagoras require that he should die in proof of them? Perfect faith is silent; and its secret is above profession, for the master said, 'Ye know all, but be ye known of none.'"

"What master?" asked Giovanni, thinking of Leonardo.

"Basil, the Egyptian Gnostic," she replied; and explained that the great teachers of the early Christian ages, to whom faith and knowledge had been one, had called themselves Gnostics, or Knowers; and she went on to repeat to him many of their sayings, often strange and monstrous, like the visions of the delirious.

He was especially impressed by a legend as to the creation of the world and of man, put forth by the Alexandrine Ophites, or snake worshippers.

"'Above all the heavens is boundless Darkness, immovable, fairer than any light; the Unknown Father, the Abyss, the Silence.' His only-begotten daughter, the Wisdom of God, separating from the

Father, knew life, and sorrow, and darkened her splendour. The son of her travail was Jaldavaoth, the creating God. Falling away from his mother he plunged yet more deeply into existence, and created the world of the body, a distorted image of the spiritual world. In it was Man, formed to reflect the greatness of his creator, and to bear witness to his power. The elemental spirits, the ministers of Jaldavaoth, brought the senseless mass of flesh to Jaldavaoth to be endowed with life; but the Wisdom of God inspired it also with a breath of the divine wisdom, received by her from the Unknown Father. And then this mean creature, formed of earth and dust, became greater than Jaldavaoth its creator, and grew into the shape and the likeness not of him but of the true God, the Unknown Father. Four-footed Man raised his face from the earth, and Jaldavaoth, at the sight of the being which had slipped from his power, was filled with anger and alarm. He formed another creature, the Angel of Darkness, the serpent-like Satan, the wisdom accursed. And by the help of the serpent Jaldavaoth formed the three kingdoms of Nature; and set Man therein, and gave him a law. 'Do this; do not that: if thou breakest the law, thou shalt die.' For he hoped by the yoke of the law, and by the fear of death to recover his power over man. But the Wisdom of God still protected Man, and sent him a comforter, the Spirit of Knowledge—snake-like also, but winged like the morning star, the Angel of the Dawn, him to whom allusion is made in the saying, 'Be ye wise as the serpent.' And the Spirit of Knowledge went down to men and said, 'Taste and know, and your eyes shall be opened, and ye shall be as gods.'"

"Hearken, Giovanni," concluded Cassandra; "the men of the crowd, the children of this world, are the slaves of Jaldavaoth and of the serpent Satan, living under the fear of death, bound by the yoke of the law. But the children of light, those who *know*, the chosen of Sophia, the Wisdom of God, transcend all laws, overstep all bounds, are free as gods, are furnished with wings, remain pure in the midst of evil, even as gold glitters in the mire. And the Spirit of Knowledge, the Angel of the Dawn, leads them through life and death, through evil and through good, through all the curses and the terrors of the world of Jaldavaoth, to the great mother, Sophia, the Wisdom of God; and she bringeth them to the bosom of the great Darkness, which reigns above the heavens, which is immovable and fairer than any light; to the bosom of the Father of all things."

And hearing this legend of the Ophites, Giovanni could not help inwardly comparing Jaldavaoth to the son of Kronos; the breath of Divine Wisdom to the fire of Prometheus; the Beneficent Serpent the Angel of the Dawn, Lucifer, Son of the Morning, to Prometheus the Titan. In all ages and nations, in the tragedies of Æschylus, in the legend of the Gnostics, in the history of Julian the Apostate, in the teaching of Pletho the philosopher, Giovanni found the echoes of the great discord, the same great struggle, which darkened his own spirit. Ten centuries ago men were suffering as he suffered now, were contending with the same double thoughts, were the victims of the same contradictions, the same temptations. The knowledge that this was so solaced him, yet it deepened his anguish. Sometimes he felt overwhelmed by all these thoughts as by drunkenness or delirium. And then it seemed to him that Cassandra only pretended to be strong and inspired and initiated into the mystery of truth, while in reality she was no less ignorant, no less astray than he was himself; and that the two of them were as helpless and lost as they had been twelve years before; and this new sabbath of half divine, half satanic lore was even more senseless than the Witches' Sabbath to which she had once invited him, and which she now despised as childishness. Giovanni became alarmed and wished to flee, but it was too late; curiosity drew him like a spell, and he felt he would not leave her till he knew all to the end; till he had found salvation and had perished with her.

Now about this time there came to Milan a famous inquisitor and doctor of theology, Fra Giorgio de Casale.

The Pope, Julius II, alarmed by the spread of sorcery in Lombardy, had sent him with bulls and powers of committal and of extraordinary punishments. Monna Cassandra stood in grave peril; and was warned both by the nuns of the Monastero Maggiore and by the archbishop. She and Messer Galeotto had already fled from Rome to escape this same Fra Giorgio; they knew that once fallen into his hands they would find no escape, and determined to take refuge in France, perhaps in England or even Scotland.

Two days before their setting forth, Giovanni was with Cassandra in her lonely room of the Palazzo Carmagnole. The sunshine, veiled by the thick cypress branches, was scarce brighter than moonlight; the girl seemed even fairer and calmer than was her wont. Now that parting was at hand, Giovanni realised how dear she was to him.

"Shall I not see you yet once more?" he asked her. "Will you not reveal to me that mystery of which you have spoken?"

Cassandra looked fixedly at him; then drew from a casket a flat four-cornered stone of transparent green. It was the famous "Tabula Smaragdina," the emerald tablet said to have been found in a cave near Memphis in the hands of the mummy of a certain priest, who was an incarnation of Hermes Trismegistus, the Egyptian Horus, the god of boundaries, the guide of the dead to the underworld. It was engraved both in Coptic and in Greek with these verses.

(Greek: Ourano anô ourano katô
Astera anô astera katô
Pan anô pan touto katô
Tauta labe kai eutyche.)

(Heaven above, heaven below;
Stars above, stars below;
All that is over, under shall show.
Happy thou who the riddle readest.)

"Come to me this night," she said gravely and softly, "and I will tell you all that I know myself—do you hear?—all, to the very end. And now before we part, let us drink together the cup of friendship."

She fetched a small pottery vessel, sealed with wax as in the far East, poured out wine, thick as oil, golden-ruddy, and with a strange perfume, into an ancient goblet of chrysolite, with a relief of Dionysus and the Bacchantes. Going to the window she raised the cup as if about to pour a libation; the rosy wine, like warm blood, gave life to the figures of the naked Mænads on the transparent cup.

"There was a time, Giovanni," she said, "when I fancied that your Master Leonardo possessed the great secret, for his face is as that of an Olympian god, blended with a Titan. But now I see he aims, but he does not attain; seeks and finds not; knows, but understands not. *He is the precursor of him who shall come after him, who is greater than he.* Let us drink together, O my brother, this farewell goblet to the Unknown whom we both invoke; to the supreme Reconciler."

Devoutly, as if performing a religious rite, she drank half the cup and handed it to Giovanni.

"Fear not!" she said, "this is no poisoned philtre; this wine is from grapes of Nazareth; 'tis the purest blood of *Dionysus, the Galilæan*!"

When he had drunk, she laid her hands on his shoulders, and whispered rapidly and solemnly—

"If you would know all, Come! Come, and I will tell you the secret, which never yet have I uttered to anyone. I will reveal the extreme joy, the extreme sorrow which shall unite us forever, as brother and sister, as bridegroom and bride."

In the sun's rays, veiled by the thick cypresses, and pale as moonlight, just as once before by the Cantarana water in the whiteness of the summer lightning, she put her face close to his, her face white as marble, framed by its Medusa locks, with its scarlet lips, its amber eyes.

The chill of a familiar terror froze Giovanni's heart, and he said to himself:—

"*La Diavolessa bianca!*"

That night at the appointed hour Giovanni stood at the door of the Palazzo Carmagnole. He knocked long, but none opened to him. At last he went to the Monastero Maggiore, and there he learned the terrible news. Fra Giorgio da Casale had appeared suddenly, and had given orders at once to apprehend Galeotto Sacrobosco and his niece Cassandra on a charge of black magic.

Messer Galeotto had succeeded in escaping, but Cassandra was already in the clutch of the Holy Inquisition.

II

NEXT DAY BOLTRAFFIO DID NOT leave his bed. He was indisposed, and his head ached; he was half unconscious, and cared for nothing.

At nightfall there was an unwonted pealing of bells, and through his room spread a faint but repulsive odour. His headache increased, he felt sick, and he went out into the air. The day was warm and damp, a day of *scirocco*, frequent at Milan in the early autumn. There was no rain, but the roofs and the trees dripped, and the brick pavement was shining and slippery. Yet in the open air Giovanni found the noisome odour still stronger than in his room.

The streets were thronged, the people all coming from the Piazza del Broletto; as Giovanni looked in their faces he fancied them in the same state of semi-unconsciousness as himself. Presently chance words from a passerby explained to him the noisome odour which pursued him; it was the appalling stench of burned human bodies. They were burning witches, sorceresses. Perhaps—O God!—burning Cassandra!

He began to run, not knowing whither, jostling people, staggering like a drunken man, trembling with ague, feeling the foul savour in the greasy and yellow mist, feeling it follow him, catch him by the throat, stifle his lungs, bind his temples with a dull and gnawing pain.

He never remembered how he made his way to the Monastery of San Francisco and to Fra Benedetto's cell. It was empty, for Benedetto was at Bergamo. Giovanni shut the door, lit a candle, and sank exhausted on the pallet-bed.

In this familiar and peaceful retreat all breathed of holiness and peace. The stench had dissipated, he smelt only incense, fast-day olives, old books, and the varnish for Benedetto's simple paintings. On the wall hung a crucifix and an ancient gift of Giovanni's, a withered garland of flowers gathered on the heights of Fiesole in those days when he sat at the feet of Savonarola.

He raised his eyes to the Crucified. The Saviour still extended his nailed hand as if calling the world to his embrace; "Come unto me all ye that are weary and heavy-laden." Was not that the one, the perfect truth?

But the prayer died on his lips. Not though eternal damnation threatened him could he cease to know what he did know, could he drive out or reconcile the two truths which were contending in him. In his old calm despair he turned away from the Crucified, and at the same moment he fancied that the noisome mist, the terrible stench of the burning had reached him even here in this last refuge.

And there rose before him a vision which he had seen often of late, so distinct he scarce knew if it were reality or dream; the vision of Cassandra in the glow of the scarlet flame, among the instruments of torture and stains of blood; she white, virginal, firm as the marble of a statue, preserved by the power of the Beneficent Serpent, the Reconciler, the Deliverer, insensible to the iron and the flame and the gaze of her tormentors.

Coming to himself, he knew by the dying candle, by the strokes of the convent clock, that hours had passed in oblivion, and that it was now past midnight. It was very still, and the air was hot. Through the window were seen pale blue flashes of lightning, as on that memorable night long ago by the Cantarana. The dull roar of distant thunder seemed to come from below the earth. His head ached, his mouth was parched, thirst tortured him; he remembered having seen a pitcher of water in the corner. He rose, dragging himself along by the wall, found it, drank, and was returning to his couch when he became conscious that someone was with him in the cell. Seated on the couch was a figure in the long dark habit of a monk, a hood covering the face. He was astonished, for the door was locked, yet he felt relieved rather than alarmed. His head ceased to ache, his senses were quickened. He approached the seated figure. It rose, and the cowl fell back; Giovanni saw the face, marble white, passionless, the lips red as blood, the amber eyes, the halo of black hair like Medusa's snakes.

Solemnly, slowly, as if for an incantation, Cassandra rose, her arms extended. The black robe fell back. He saw the glowing warmth and beauty of her neck. Was she alive? My God! was she alive?

For the last time Giovanni murmured, "The white sorceress!" It seemed as if the veil of life were rent before him. He was face to face with the mystery of the supreme union. She knelt before him. . . She folded him in her arms. . . Ah! the inexpressible sweetness! the inexpressible fear! . . . Delirium! delirium!

III

Zoroastro da Peretola had not died, neither had he recovered from his fall. He was a cripple, and able to mutter only fragmentary words intelligible to none but the Master. Sometimes he roamed about the house, clattering on his crutches; sometimes he listened to conversation as if trying to understand it; or he would sit in a corner winding strips of linen, or planing wooden staves, whittling sticks or carving tops, for his workman's hands had not lost their need of movement, nor entirely their skill. But often he would rock himself for hours together, a smile on his face, and his arms waving as if they were wings, while he crooned an unending ditty:—

"Cucurlu! Curlu!
Cranes and eagles
Up they flew!
Up they flew,
Cranes and eagles,—
Cucurlu!"

And then, looking at the Master, he would weep—a sight too painful for Leonardo to bear. He never deserted the broken creature, but cared for him, gave him money, and whenever possible kept him in his house.

Years passed, and the cripple remained a living reproof, a mockery of his life-long effort, his fashioning of wings for men.

Scarce less distressed was Leonardo by the attitude of Cesare da Sesto, that one of his pupils who was perhaps nearest to his heart. Like Astro and Giovanni he was mentally crippled, anxious to stand alone, but overwhelmed by the Master's influence, and reduced to nullity. Not content to be an imitator, not strong enough to be independent, he wore himself out with fruitless fretting and impotent rage, incompetent either to save himself or to perish. He was one of those upon whom Leonardo was accused of having cast the Evil Eye.

Cesare was said to be in secret correspondence with Raphael, who was working at the frescoes of the Vatican Stanze, and Leonardo sometimes thought treachery was meditated. But worse than the treachery of enemies was the so-called fidelity of friends. Under the name of the *Accademia di Leonardo*, a school of young painters had grown up in Milan, a few of them his pupils, the greater number newcomers, who clung to him like parasites, and persuaded themselves and others that they were following in his steps. He stood aloof, and watched them. At times disgust overwhelmed him when he saw how all that he had reverenced as great and sacred had become the property of the common herd; how the Lord's face in the *Cenacolo* was copied till it was mere ecclesiastical commonplace; how the smile of La Gioconda was imitated, exaggerated, vulgarised, till it became stupid, if not sensual.

One winter's night Leonardo was sitting alone, listening to the shriek and roar of the storm; it was just such a night as that in which he had heard of Monna Lisa's death; he was thinking of her, and thinking of Death itself, of the last dread solitude in the bosom of ancient Chaos, of the infinite weariness of the world. There was a knock; he rose and opened the door. A young man entered, a lad of nineteen, with bright eyes, fresh cheeks reddened by the cold, melting snowflakes in his chestnut curls.

"Oh Messer Leonardo!" he exclaimed, "do you not know me?"

Leonardo looked and recognised his little friend, the child with whom he had roamed the woods of Vaprio, Francesco Melzi. He embraced him with fatherly tenderness. The youth related how, after the French invasion of 1500, his father had taken his family to Bologna, and there had fallen sick of a malady which had lasted for long years. Now he was dead, and the son had hastened to Leonardo, remembering his promise.

"But what promise?" asked the painter, bewildered.

"Ah! you have forgotten! And I, poor simpleton, have been counting on it! Nay, then! do you not remember? You were carrying me in the mine at the foot of Monte Campione, and you told me how you were to serve Cæsar Borgia in Romagna. And I wept, and prayed you to take me with you, and you promised that after ten years' time, when I should be grown—"

"Ay! I recall it!" said Leonardo warmly.

"You see? Ah, Messer Leonardo, I know you have no need of me. But I will be no burden to you, I will not disturb you. Pr'ythee drive me not hence! If you drive me hence, I will not go! I will never leave you again!" cried the lad.

"My dear, dear boy!" said the Master, and his voice shook.

He embraced him again, and Francesco clung to his breast as he had done years ago when Leonardo had carried him into the subterranean darkness of the forgotten pit.

IV

Since Leonardo had left Florence in 1507, he had been enrolled as court painter in the service of the French King, Louis XII. He had no fixed salary, but relied on the royal bounty. The treasurers frequently forgot him altogether, nor was he able to call opportune attention to himself by his productions, for as years increased upon him he worked less and less. He was consequently, as of old, in continual straits and entanglements; he borrowed wherever he could, and contracted new debts before he had paid off the old. He wrote the same timid, clumsy petitions to the French Viceroy and Treasurer as formerly to the officials of Ludovico Il Moro.

"Not wishing to fatigue your Excellency's generosity, I permit myself to request that I may receive a regular salary. More than once have I addressed your lordship on this subject, but hitherto have been vouchsafed no reply."

In the ante-chambers of his patrons he quietly waited his turn among other suppliants, though with advancing years he increasingly knew—

"How salt another's bread is, and the toil
Of going up and down another's stairs."

The service of princes was as bitter to him as had been the service of the republic; everywhere and always he felt himself a stranger. Raphael had become rich and splendid as a Roman patrician; Michelangelo was hoarding money against the evil days; Leonardo was still a homeless wanderer, not knowing where he could lay his head when he came to die.

Wars, victories, the defeat of his friends, changes in governments and laws, the enslaving of peoples, the chasing forth of tyrants—all that to the generality seems important, was to him as a whirl of dust to a wayfarer on a high road. With equal indifference he fortified the Castle of Milan for the French king against the Lombards, as once he had fortified it for the Duke of Lombardy against the French.

Trivulzio, the ambitious general, was intriguing against Massimiliano, and Leonardo saw the fate of the father, Il Moro, threatening Il Moretto. Wearied by these monotonous and arbitrary political changes, sickened by the manufacture of triumphal arches and the mending of the wings of the trumpery angels, he determined to leave Milan and pass into the service of the Medici.

In Rome, however—for Giovanni de Medici, having become pope, with the style of Leo X, had nominated his brother Giuliano as Gonfaloniere of the Holy Church. He had already gone to Rome, and it was arranged that Leonardo should join him in the autumn. He was to be both painter and "alchemist" in Giuliano's service.

On the morrow of the day when the hundred and thirty-nine witches had been burned in the Piazza del Broletto, the monks of San Francesco had found Giovanni Boltraffio stretched senseless on the floor of Fra Benedetto's cell. Clearly he was suffering, as he had suffered fifteen years earlier, after having heard the tale of Savonarola's martyrdom. On this second occasion his recovery was rapid; nevertheless there were times when his unspeculative eye, his strangely impassive face inspired Leonardo with greater fear than during his long illness of years ago.

However that might be, on the 23rd of September 1513 Leonardo rode out of Milan for Rome to join his new patron Giuliano, with Francesco Melzi, Salaino, Cesare, Astro, and Giovanni.

Book XVI

Leonardo, Michelangelo, and Raphael—1513–1515

La pazienza fa contra alle ingiurie non altrimenti che si faccino i panni contra del freddo; imperò che, se ti multiplicherai di panni secondo la multiplicazione del freddo, esso freddo nocere non ti potrà; similmente alle grandi ingiurie cresci la pazienza, essa ingiurie offendere non ti potranno la tua mente.

—Leonardo Da Vinci

(Patience acts against insults as garments act against cold. With the doubling of your misfortunes, put on a double cloak of endurance.)

I

Pope Leo X, true to the traditions of the house of the Medici, posed as patron of art and learning. When he heard of his own election he said to his brother:—

"Let us *enjoy* the papal power, since God has conceded it to us!"

And Fra Mariano, his favourite jester added:—

"Seek your own pleasure, Holy Father! All else is folly."

The pope surrounded himself with poets, musicians, painters, and scholars. A golden age had dawned for imitative men of letters, who had one unassailable article of faith, the perfection of Cicero's prose and of Virgil's poetry.

The shepherds of Christ's flock avoided the mention of His name, because it was a word unknown to Cicero's *Orations*. They called nuns, vestals; the Holy Ghost, the Inspiration of the Supreme Jove; and they requested the Pope to include Plato in the roll of saints. Bembo, a future cardinal, owned that he did not read the Epistles of Paul (he called them *Epistolaccie*) lest he should spoil his style. When Francis I asked for the Laocoön, Leo X replied that he would sooner give him the head of Peter the Apostle.

The pope loved his scholars and artists, his poets and pedants; but above all he loved his jesters. He solemnly crowned Cuerno, the celebrated rhymster and drunkard, and was no less liberal to him than to Raphael. He spent huge sums on feasts, though he ate sparingly himself, being afflicted with a weak digestion, and an incurable purulent disease; and his soul was no less sick than his body, for he suffered from continual *ennui*.

When Leonardo first presented himself at the Vatican he was told that his only hope of obtaining audience of His Holiness was to declare himself a buffoon. He did not follow this good advice, and failed of admission time and again. Of late he had experienced strange forebodings which he tried to put from him as senseless and absurd. It was not anxiety as to his affairs which oppressed him; nor was it his failure to gain adequate recognition from Leo X or Giuliano de' Medici. He had been too long used to annoyances of this kind. But his vague disquiet, his ominous apprehension, continually increased; till one radiant autumn evening, as he was returning from the Vatican, his heart sank, under the pressure of imminent catastrophe.

He was living in the same house where he had lived during his former visit to Rome; one of the small detached buildings behind St. Peter's, which had belonged to the Papal Mint. It was old and gloomy, and having been unoccupied for several years was exceedingly damp. He entered a large vaulted apartment with cracks on walls and ceiling, and windows overshadowed by the wall of the adjoining house.

In the corner sat Astro the imbecile, his feet drawn up under him, his hands busy whittling sticks, while he purred his monotonous lullaby—

Cucurlu, curlu!
Eagles and cranes
Up they flew!

Leonardo's anxiety perceptibly increased.

"What's the matter, Astro?" he asked kindly, laying his hand on the cripple's head.

"Nothing," said Astro, with a curious look of intelligence, "nothing with me. It's Giovanni. But it's all the better for him. He has flown away."

"Giovanni? Where is Giovanni?" cried Leonardo, suddenly realising that his forebodings had centred on this unhappy disciple. "Astro! I implore you, my friend, try to remember! Where is Giovanni? I must see him at once. Where is he? What has happened?"

"Don't you understand?" muttered Astro, vainly seeking for the right words. "He is up there—he has escaped—flown away. You don't understand? I will show you then. It is better for him to have flown away."

He rolled himself to his feet and shuffled along on his crutches, leading his master up the creaking stair to the attic, where the sun burned hot on the tiled roof, and the sunset rays shone upon the dormer-window. As they entered, startled pigeons fluttered their wings noisily and flew away.

"There he is," said Astro, simply, and pointed to a dark corner. Leonardo saw the figure of Giovanni, apparently standing, very erect and quite motionless, his widely opened eyes staring fixedly straight before him. "Giovanni!" cried Leonardo, with shaking voice, a cold sweat bursting out on his forehead.

He drew nearer; saw that the face was strangely distorted; touched the nerveless hand, and felt it cold. The body oscillated heavily to and fro. Giovanni had hanged himself from an iron hook lately inserted for mechanical purposes into the cross beam; and by means of a strong silken cord, one of the attachments of the flying machine.

Astro had fallen back into his torpor, and was looking serenely out of the window. The house stood high, and commanded a view of the tiled roofs, the domes and towers of Rome, of the Campagna spreading like a sea, traversed by long lines of ruined aqueducts, of the hills of Albano and Frascati, of the clear sky where the swallows swooped and circled. Astro watched them, and smiled, and waved his arms joyously as if imitating their flight.

Cucurlu!
Up they flew!
Curlu!

he crooned contentedly.

Leonardo stood, still as a stone, between his two disciples, the imbecile and the suicide.

A FEW DAYS LATER HE found Giovanni's diary and read it attentively.

"The white witch!" always and everywhere! May she be accursed. The last mystery: two shall be in one. Christ and Antichrist are one. The heaven above—the heaven below!

"No! No! This shall not, must not be! Rather, death!"

"Into thy hands I commit my spirit, O God! Be thou my Judge!"

There came an abrupt end to the entries. Leonardo understood that these words had been penned on the day of the writer's suicide.

II

After the death of Giovanni, Leonardo wearied of his life in Rome. Uncertainty, waiting, forced inaction enervated him. His usual occupations, his books, machines, experiments, paintings failed in interest.

Leo X had not yet found time to receive him, nor to give him the order for a painting. However, he set the artist to the mechanical task of perfecting the coining mill for the Papal Mint. Leonardo despised no work, however humble; he did what was required, and devised new machinery, by means of which the coins, uneven and jagged before, were cut perfectly true. The artist was at this time overwhelmed with debts, and the greater part of his salary went in the payment of the interest on his borrowings. But for the generosity of Francesco Melzi, who had inherited property from his father, he would have been in extreme want.

In the summer of 1514 he was attacked by the malaria. It was his first serious illness. He refused doctors and medicines, but allowed Francesco to wait upon him. Everyday he became more attached to this lad, and felt that God had sent him a guardian angel, a prop for his old age. Men seemed to be forgetting him, but from time to time he made attempts to remind them of his existence. From his sick-bed he wrote to Giuliano de' Medici with striving after the fashionable compliments which did not come easily to his lips or pen.

III

After much rain the end of November brought sunny days, never so beautiful as in Rome, where the decaying splendour of autumn harmonises well with the ruined glories of the Eternal City.

One morning Leonardo went with Francesco to see the Sistine Chapel and the frescoes of Michelangelo; a visit long purposed, but deferred as if from a secret sense of fear.

The chapel is a long, narrow, very lofty building, with plain walls and

Gothic windows. Buonarroti had covered the ceiling and arches with biblical scenes. Leonardo looked, and staggered, as if faint; whatever his secret expectation, he had never thought to behold such potency of art.

In face of the colossal figures, sublime as the visions of delirium—the God of Sabaoth dividing light from darkness in the bosom of Chaos, blessing the waters and plants, creating Adam from the earth, and Eve from Adam's rib—in face of the representations of the Fall, the Redemption and all the incidents of Scripture history; in face of the beautiful nude youths, spirits of the elements accompanying the tragedy of the Universe, the conflict of God and Man, with eternal dancing and song; prophets and sibyls, terrible giants that seemed weighed down with more than human wisdom and with more than human woe; the ancestors of the Messiah, a long file of obscure patriarchs passing on from one to the other the purposeless burden of life, awaiting in darkness the coming of the unknown Redeemer;—in face of these stupendous creations of his rival Leonardo did not measure, nor compare nor judge; he felt himself and his work annihilated.

He enumerated his own productions; the *Cenacolo*, which was perishing, the Colossus, which had been destroyed, the "Battle of Anghiari," and an endless number of other unfinished paintings; a succession of vain endeavours, ridiculous failures, inglorious defeats. He had spent his life in beginning, intending, making ready; he had achieved nothing. Why deceive himself? It was too late now; he would never accomplish anything. His life had been expended in incredible labour; yet now at its close he felt like the slothful servant in the parable who had buried his talent in the earth.

Yet he was conscious that he had aimed at something higher than this other man; to Michelangelo all was turmoil, chaos; Leonardo had seen, and had tried to show, the eternal harmony. He remembered Monna Lisa's parable of the mighty wind, and of the still small voice where the Lord was; he felt that she had discerned a truth, that sooner or later the human mind would return to the path he had shown, the path from discord to harmony, from division to unity, from storm to quietness. The consciousness of how entirely right he had been in theory made still more painful to him, the consciousness of impotence in action.

They left the chapel in silence. Francesco ventured no questions; but he fancied that the Master had suddenly aged, had become feeble and broken. Years had apparently passed since they had entered the chapel.

Crossing the Piazza of St. Peter's, they went by the Borgo Nuovo towards the bridge of St. Angelo. Leonardo was thinking of another rival whom he had perhaps no less reason to fear, Raphael Sanzio. He had seen the young painter's newly finished frescoes in the Stanze of the Vatican, and had felt unable to decide whether the greatness of the execution were not equalled by the poverty of the conception, the perfection of eye and hand by the servile flattery of the princes of this world. Julius II had dreamed of expelling the French from Italy; therefore Raphael had shown him watching the expulsion of Heliogabalus from the profaned temple of the most high God. Leo X posed as a great orator; therefore Raphael celebrated him in the person of Leo the Great, warning Attila to retreat from Rome. He had been taken prisoner by the French and had escaped; Raphael represented this by the miraculous deliverance of St. Peter. Thus he degraded his art into the nauseous incense of a courtier's flattery.

This stranger from Urbino, this dreamy youth with the face of a sinless angel, had managed his mundane affairs to the best advantage. He painted the stables of Chigi the banker; made designs for the table-service of gold which, after the entertaining of the Holy Father, the banker threw into the Tiber, that it might never be used by anyone less illustrious. The "fortunate boy," as Francia called the young painter, acquired fame and wealth as if by play. He disarmed his worst enemies by kindliness; he was what he appeared to be, the friend of all. In everything he succeeded. The gifts of Fortune dropped unsought into his hands. He replaced Bramante on the architectural conclave for the building of the new cathedral; Cardinal Bibbiena offered him his niece in marriage; it was said he had been promised a cardinal's hat. He built a dainty mansion in the Borgo, and furnished it with regal splendour. His ante-chamber was crowded with official personages, and with envoys from abroad, who either wanted their portraits painted, or desired to take home some specimen of the great man's art. He was overwhelmed with patrons and refused new ones. They insisted. Time was wanting to execute his innumerable orders, and many of his pictures were chiefly painted by his pupils. His studio became a factory where such skilful workmen as Giulio Romano turned canvas and paint into ready-money with amazing facility. He himself apparently desisted from the search after perfection, and was content with popularity. He served the people, and they accepted him enthusiastically as their chosen, their beloved, bone of their bone, flesh of their flesh, the incarnation of their own spirit.

The worst of it was, that in his fall he was still great; a seduction not only to the vulgar herd, but also to the elect. He seemed unspoiled by the glittering baubles showered on him by Fortune. He remained innocent and pure. The *fortunato garzone* had no consciousness of the danger for himself and for art. For in this superficial harmony, in this pseudo-reconciliation of discordant elements, there was greater danger for the future than in the chaos and contradictions and wars introduced by Michelangelo. Leonardo could see nothing beyond the work of these two painters; after them, all seemed abysmal and void. He felt how much both owed to himself. From him they had had their science of light and shade, their anatomy, their perspective, their knowledge of Nature and of man. Yes, they had grown out of him; and now the two of them, they had destroyed him! Leonardo walked silently beside his young companion, his eyes downcast, his head bent, his face intensely sorrowful and *old*: he seemed in a trance.

As they approached the bridge, they had to draw aside to give room to a cavalcade—some great man, a cardinal, perhaps, or an ambassador, escorted by sixteen horsemen richly attired. The personage proved a young man, sumptuously clad, riding a grey Arab with gilded and jewelled trappings. His face seemed familiar; and suddenly Leonardo remembered the pale shy youth in the girlish frock, daubed with paint and worn into holes at the elbow, who eight years before had said, "Michelangelo is not worthy to tie the latchet of your shoe!"

Now this boy was the rival both of Leonardo and Michelangelo, and was called "the God of Painting"!

His face, though still boyish, innocent, and unseared by emotion, was somewhat less of a seraph's. He was a man of the great world now; riding from his villa in the Borgo to an interview with the pope, he was accompanied by a troop of pupils, admirers, and friends. Indeed he never went out with an escort of less than fifteen. His every ride seemed a triumphal procession.

He recognised Leonardo; flushed slightly, and with quick, even exaggerated respect, doffed his cap and bowed. His younger pupils looked wonderingly at the old man to whom the "Divine One" showed so much respect; the quiet shabby old man, hugging the wall to let the cavalcade dash by.

Leonardo's attention was caught by the man riding at Raphael's side, apparently the most favoured of his pupils. It was Cesare da Sesto. Leonardo gazed in amazement, scarce able to believe his eyes. Now he understood Cesare's long absence, Francesco's clumsy explanation. The last of his disciples, he whom he had trusted to follow in his footsteps and carry on his method, had deserted and betrayed him. Cesare braved his gaze without flinching; nay, it was Leonardo whose eyes fell in confusion, as if guilty before the other of some unintended crime.

The cavalcade passed on, and the old man, leaning upon Francesco, went his way. They crossed Hadrian's bridge, and went by the Via dei Coronari to the Piazza Navona, where was the bird fair. Leonardo bought magpies, finches, thrushes, pigeons, a falcon, and a young wild swan. He spent all the money he had with him, and borrowed also of Francesco. Slung from head to foot with cages, the quaint pair attracted general attention. The passersby stared curiously, the little boys ran after them. They walked past the Pantheon and Trajan's Forum, crossed the Esquiline, and left the town by the Porta Maggiore, following the ancient Roman road called the Via Labicana. Presently they turned into a narrow footpath leading into the solitude of the wild country.

Before them spread the boundless, the silent, the monotonous Campagna; through the arches of the Claudian Aqueduct, low hills were seen, uniform grey-green, like sea waves in the light of evening; here and there was a solitary tower, the deserted nest of robber knights; misty blue mountains surrounded the great plain, like the tiers of a colossal amphitheatre.

Over the city brooded the great peace of autumn twilight. The last rays of the sun, streaming from between heavy clouds, lay across the landscape in broad zones of brilliance, and shone on a herd of white cattle, which scarce turned their heads at the sound of footsteps. The chirp of the grasshopper, the rustle of the breeze in the stalks of the withered summer flowers, the dull sound of the distant bells, but enforced the stillness; it seemed that here in this immense plain, so desolate so solemn, had already been fulfilled the prophecy of the angel who swore by him that liveth forever and ever, there should be time no longer. They chose a convenient hillock, and relieved themselves of the cages; then Leonardo set the birds free.

As they flew away, with the joyous flutter and rustle of their wings, he followed them with loving eyes. He smiled, he forgot his griefs, and was happy as in his childhood. Only the falcon and the swan were still in their cages; their emancipation was reserved for a later hour.

Now he and Francesco ate a frugal supper of bread, chestnuts, dried cherries, cheese, a flask of the golden Orvieto wine. They were still silent. Francesco glanced at his master from time to time. Leonardo's hair was silvered and thin, his forehead lined, his deep-set eyes were still luminous and thoughtful, but weary. Age had set its effacing finger on the beauty of every feature. It was the face of an enfeebled, patient Titan.

Francesco pitied him, as he pitied all persons who were lonely and sorrowful. The Master, whom of all men he admired and loved, whom he set above the Michelangelo and the Raphael of the people's applause, was but a lonely and poor and despised old man, sitting on the grass among empty bird-cages, cutting his cheese with an old broken clasp-knife, chewing his bread with an effort because his jaws were weakened by age, his appetite lost by recent illness. A lump rose in Francesco's throat, and he would gladly have knelt and assured his friend of his devotion, but he did not do so—he lacked the courage. At all times, even to those who loved him the best, Leonardo showed something alien and unapproachable.

The modest supper ended, Leonardo rose, let loose the hawk, then opened the last and largest cage, that one containing the wild swan. The great white bird came out noisily, stood dazzled for a minute flapping its wings, then flew straight towards the sun. Leonardo watched it with eyes full of unspoken grief. It was grief for the idle dream of his whole life, for the human wings, for the "Great Bird" of which he had written in his diary; "Man shall fly like a mighty swan."

IV

At last the Pope, yielding to the persuasions of his brother Giuliano, ordered a small picture from Leonardo. As usual he hesitated, put off beginning from day today, spent his time in preliminary attempts, in perfecting his paints, in the invention of a new varnish.

His Holiness exclaimed in mock despair—

"Alack! this dull fellow will never perform anything; he studies the end before he has mastered the beginning."

The saying was repeated by the courtiers, and all over the town, and it sealed the fate of the painter. Leo, the supreme judge in matters of art, had pronounced sentence. Henceforward Raphael, Buonarroti, Bembo the pedant, and Baraballo the buffoon, need fear no rivalry; the pope had jested, and the painter's reputation was crushed. The world forgot him, as it forgets the dead. When someone repeated Leo's witticism for his entertainment, he smiled indifferently, as if mockery were no worse than he had expected. That night however, he wrote in his diary:—

"Patience is to the injured what clothes are to the frozen. With keener cold, augment your clothing and it shall not hurt you; with the increase of humiliation, double your cloak of patience."

Louis XII, King of France, died in 1515. Having no son, his crown passed to his nearest relative, Francis of Valois, Duke of Angoulême, who assumed the title of Francis I.

The young king at once took the field for the reconquest of Lombardy. He crossed the Alps, appeared suddenly in Italy, gained a victory at Marignano, deposed Il Moretto, and entered Milan in triumph. About the same time Giuliano de' Medici left Rome for Savoy, and Leonardo, out of favour with the Pope, determined to try his fortune with the new sovereign. In the autumn he went to Pavia to the court of Francis. Here the conquered were celebrating the conquest and the glory of the conqueror, and Leonardo was at once invited to arrange the festival, his reputation as mechanician in the time of Il Moro being remembered. He agreed; and amongst other things constructed a lion which ran automatically across the hall, stood rampant before the king, and opened his breast, from which fell a shower of the white *fleurs de lys*. This toy made Leonardo more famous than all his great works, inventions, and discoveries. Francis was anxious to see Italian scholars and artists at his court, but the pope refused to spare either Michelangelo or Raphael, so Leonardo was offered a salary of seven hundred crowns and the little château of Cloux, in Touraine, near the town of Amboise, between Tours and Blois.

The artist accepted the offer; and in the sixty-fourth year of his life began once more his endless wandering; left his country without hope of return, and settled in the foreign land. He was accompanied by Francesco Melzi, Zoroastro, and his old servants, Battista de Villanis and the fat cook Maturina.

V

The road, especially in winter, was difficult; it led through the passes of Piedmont and Mont Cenis. Early, while it was still dark, they left Bardonecchia, so as to cross the Alps before nightfall. The mules clattered their hoofs and jangled their bells as they clambered along a narrow path skirting the ravine. Spring had descended upon the southern valleys, but up here winter reigned supreme. The morning was just breaking; against the faintly tinted sky the Alps shone as if lighted by internal fire. Leonardo, wishing to see more of the mountains, left his beast, and with Francesco followed a steeper path at a little distance from the mule track. Perfect stillness surrounded them, only interrupted by the distant long-drawn roar of an avalanche. They scrambled higher, Leonardo leaning on the young man's arm. Francesco remembered the descent of the iron-mine when the Master had carried him, now it was he who supported the Master.

"Oh, Messer Leonardo!" he cried suddenly, pointing to the ravine below, "look at the valley of the Dora! We see it for the last time! We are almost at the summit, and we shall not see it again! Yon lies all Lombardy! Italy!" he cried, his eyes wet with conflicting emotions; and he repeated, "Lombardy! Italy! For the last time!"

The Master's face remained unmoved. He looked, then turned silently and pressed onward towards the snows. Forgetting his weariness, he now walked so quickly that Francesco, who had lingered bidding farewell, was left behind.

"Nay, Master, whither go you?" he cried. "There is no path there; you can ascend no higher. I pray you take heed!"

But Leonardo went on, higher and higher, his step firm and light, as if his feet were winged.

Against the pale sky the icy masses towered one above the other; a stupendous wall raised by God between two worlds. They beckoned to Leonardo and drew him up and onwards. It seemed as if behind them rose the last secret,—which alone could satisfy his soul. Divided from him by impassable gulfs, they appeared near, almost within touch. They looked at him as the dead look at the living; they smiled at him with the smile of Monna Lisa.

His pale face lighted with the same glow that was shining upon the mountains and the ice. To him the thoughts of death and of Monna Lisa were now but one.

Book XVII

Death—The Winged Precursor—1516–1519

(Greek: Phereis pterugas hôs isôtheis angelois.)

Inscription on the figure of St. John the Baptist.

(Thou hast wings, like unto the angels.)

Spunteranno le ali.

—Leonardo Da Vinci

(There shall be wings.)

I

In the heart of France, overhanging the Loire, stood the royal castle of Amboise. It was built of stone, mellow in colour as the bloom on a golden plum, which in the pale blues and greens of the fading sunset gleamed soft as a floating cloud. From the square tower the view extended over a forest of primeval oak, beyond the broad meadows flanking the river. In the early summer they were brilliant with poppies invading the azure lines of the flax. Damp mists hung over the valley, dark poplars and silvery willows stood in long rows. It resembled the plain of Lombardy: only the rivers were unlike each other:—the Adda, a torrent, passionate, storm-tossed, young; the Loire, quiet and slow, gliding gently over shallows, wearied and very old.

At the foot of the castle clustered the peaked roofs of the town, slated, black, smooth and shining in the sun, and among them massive brick chimneys. The streets, narrow, winding, and sunless, belonged to the Middle Ages. Everywhere, under all cornices and along all water-pipes, at the angles of the windows, door-frames, lintels, were small stone figures—jolly friars with flagons, rosaries and wooden sandals, grave doctors of theology, thrifty citizens with fat purses hugged to their breasts. The same types were to be seen today walking the city streets; all here was *bourgeois*, prosperous, conventional, pious, and cold.

When the king came to Amboise for the hunting, the little town changed its aspect. The streets grew noisy with the baying of dogs, the champing of horses, the blare of trumpets. Music resounded nightly from the palace, and its walls shone red with the flaring of torches. The king gone, silence descended again upon the streets, the palace was like an abode of the dead; no human step nor voice, save at mass-time on Sundays, and in the spring evenings when the children sang the old song of St. Denis under apple-trees which showered rosy petals on their heads. Night fell, the song was hushed, the children went away, and again there was silence; such silence as made audible the measured beat of the clock over the gate of the Horloge Tower, and the cry of the wild swans far away on the sand-banks of the Loire.

Half a league from the castle, on the road to the Mill of St. Thomas, was a small château called Cloux, once the residence of the royal armourer. It was surrounded partly by a high wall, partly by a stream; in front of the house was a meadow, and a tangle of willows, alders, and hazel bushes descending to the river. The pink walls of the château were sharply defined against a background of chestnuts and elms; the windows and doors ornamented by a dog-tooth moulding in yellow Touraine stone. It was a small building with a high-pitched slatted roof; a tiny chapel on the right of the main entrance, and an octagonal tower, in which was a winding-stair, made it resemble a villa. Rebuilt forty years earlier, the outside was still new, cheerful, and inviting.

This little château Francis I assigned as lodging to Leonardo da Vinci.

II

The king received the artist with cordiality, and talked long with him of his works, past and future, respectfully saluting him as "father" and "teacher."

Leonardo proposed to remodel the castle of Amboise, also to construct an immense canal, which, converting the barren marshes into a luxuriant garden, should connect the Loire and the Saône at Macon, and thus open a new route from Northern Europe to the Mediterranean. In this wise he thought to benefit a foreign country by those gifts of knowledge which his fatherland had contemned. The king was pleased by the project, and at once Leonardo set out to explore the locality, studying the soil of the Sologne near Romorantin, the tributaries of the Loire and the Cher, the level of the waters, the topography of the whole district.

One day he visited Loches, a small town to the south of Amboise, where was the castle in which Ludovico Il Moro, Duke of Lombardy, had been incarcerated for eight years. The old warden told Leonardo how Il Moro had once made his escape, by hiding in a cart loaded with straw; not knowing the roads, however, he had lost his way in the forest, and next day had been easily recaptured. His last years had been spent in pious meditation, in prayer, and in the study of Dante's *Commedia*, the only book he had been allowed to bring out of Italy. At fifty he was a feeble wrinkled old man; only at rare intervals did his eyes flash, when rumours reached him of grave political changes. He died in May 1508 after a short illness.

The warden told further how Ludovico had, a few months before his death, devised a pastime for himself; had begged for brushes and paints and had decorated the walls and arches of his prison. Leonardo found traces of his work on the damp and mouldy plaster; involved patterns, stripes and bars; stars and crosses; red on a white, yellow on a blue ground; in the middle, the helmeted head of a warrior, probably himself, thus inscribed in broken French, "*Je porte en prison pour ma devise que je m'arme de pacience par force de peines que l'on me fait porter.*"

Another sentence ran all round the ceiling; it began with huge letters; "*Celui qui*," then, space failing, continued in characters small and cramped, "*net pas contan*." Reading these piteous inscriptions and looking at the clumsy drawings, Leonardo remembered how Il Moro had smiled admiringly on the swans in the moat of the fortress at Milan. "Perhaps," thought he, "the love of beauty which is certainly in his soul will justify him before the tribunal of the Most High."

Meditating on the fall of the hapless duke, he remembered also what he had been told of the fate of another of his patrons, Cæsar Borgia. Julius II had treacherously handed Cæsar over to his enemies, who had carried him to Spain and confined him in the tower of Medina del Campo. Daring and ingenious, he escaped by means of a rope let down from his prison window. The jailers had time to sever the rope; he fell and was seriously hurt, but none the less crawled to the horse provided by an accomplice, and rode away. He went to Pampeluna to the court of his brother-in-law, the King of Navarre, where he took service as a condottiere.

Consternation spread through Italy; the pope trembled; and ten thousand ducats were set upon the head of the fugitive. On a wintry night of 1507 in an encounter with the French mercenaries under

Beaumont, Cæsar was deserted by his followers, and driven into the dry bed of a river, where, like an animal at bay, he defended himself with desperate courage. At last he fell, pierced by twenty wounds. The mercenaries tore the splendid trappings from the dead warrior, and left him naked where he had fallen. Later, when the Navarrese came to seek him they knew him not; only Juanito, his little page, recognised his lord by reason of his great love for him; and flinging himself on the corpse he embraced it sobbing. Beautiful was the dead face, upturned to the heavens; and it seemed he had died even as he had lived, fearless, and without knowledge of remorse. Madonna Lucrezia, Duchess of Ferrara, wept ever for her brother; and when she died they found a hair shirt chafing her tender body. And Cæsar's youthful widow, Charlotte d'Albret, who in the few days she had been with him had come to love him as a very Griselda, having learned of his death, retired to perpetual seclusion in the castle of La Motte Feuillée, buried in the heart of a forest, where only winds rustled the dry leaves; nor used to leave her chamber, hung with perpetual mourning, save to distribute alms, imploring pensioners to pray for the soul of Cæsar.

And likewise the duke's subjects in Romagna, husbandmen and half-savage shepherds from the valleys of the Apennine, kept most grateful memory of him. Long they refused to believe him dead, but waited for him as a god who should some day return and establish justice in the land, cast down the tyrants, and defend the poor. Beggars who wandered from village to village chanted "the woeful lament for the Duca Valentino," in which was the line—

"Fe' cose estreme, ma senza misura."

Thus Leonardo mused on these two men, Ludovico and Cesare, whose lives had been signalled by great events, yet had passed away like shadows, leaving no trace. And he felt, after all, that his own life, spent in lofty contemplation, had been at least as fruitful.

Thus thinking, he ceased to murmur at the untowardness of Fate.

III

Like the majority of Leonardo's projects, the making of the Sologne canal ended in nothing. Timorous counsellors persuaded Francis of the impracticability of the enterprise. His Majesty grew cold, was disenchanted, and soon forgot all about it; Leonardo found that the King of France was no more to be relied upon than Il Moro, Soderini, or Leo X. He resolved to abandon all hope of enriching mankind by the treasures of his knowledge, and to retire for the rest of his life into solitude.

In the spring of 1517 he returned to Cloux, sick of fever contracted in the marshes of the Sologne. He recovered partially, and by the summer season had strength sufficient to leave his room, and leaning on Francesco's arm to walk daily as far as to the woods. Here he would sit in the shadow of the trees, his pupil at his feet. Sometimes Francesco read to him; sometimes he was content merely to enjoy the sights and sounds of peaceful nature, gazing at the sky, the leaves, the stones, the grasses, the golden moss on the huge tree-trunks, as if bidding them all a last farewell. A sorrowful presentiment, a great pity for the Master oppressed Francesco's heart. Silently he would touch Leonardo's hand with his lips; and then feel that trembling hand laid upon his head in a mournful caress, which deepened his sense of a coming doom.

At this time the Master began a strange picture.

Sheltered by overhanging rocks, in a cool shadow among flowering grasses, sat a god; he was long-haired and fair as a woman, but languid and pale; his head crowned with vine-leaves, a spotted skin round his loins, a thyrsus in his hand. He sat with legs crossed and seemed to be listening, a hinting smile on his lips, his finger pointed in the direction whence came the sound, perhaps the song of Mænads, perhaps the voice of great Pan, that thrilling sound from which all living things must flee.

In Boltraffio's casket Leonardo had found an amethyst gem, doubtless a gift from Monna Cassandra, with an engraving of Dionysus. There were also stray leaves from Euripides' tragedy, the *Bacchæ*, translated from the Greek and copied out by Giovanni. Many times had Leonardo read these fragments; amongst them the address of Pentheus to the unknown god.

"Ha! of thy form thou art not ill-favoured, stranger,
For woman's tempting!
No wrestler thou, as show thy flowing locks
Down thy cheek floating, fraught with all desire;
And white from heedful tendance is thy skin,
Smit by no sunshafts, but made wan by shade,
While thou dost hunt desire with beauty's lure."

And the chorus of Bacchantes, answering the impious king, extol Dionysus as "the most terrible, the most beneficent of gods, who giveth to mortals the drunkenness of ecstasy."

On the same page, side by side with the verses from Euripides, Giovanni had copied verses from the Bible.

Leaving his Bacchus unfinished, Leonardo began another picture, still more strange, of St. John the Baptist. He worked at it more continuously and more rapidly than was his wont, as if feeling that his days were numbered, that his strength was everyday declining, and that now or never he must give expression to that mystery which all his life he had hidden from men,—even from himself.

Soon the picture was sufficiently advanced for the conception to be clear. The background was dark, recalling the gloom of that cavern he had once described to Monna Lisa as the occasion both of curiosity and of fear. Yet the dimness was not impenetrable, but blent with light, melting into it as smoke dissolves into sunlight, as distant music vibrates away into silence. And between the darkness and the perfect light appeared what at first seemed a phantom, but presently snowed more distinct than life itself; the face and figure of a naked youth, womanish, seductively beautiful, recalling the words of Pentheus.

But instead of the leopard's skin he wore a garment of camel's hair; instead of the thrysus he carried a cross. Smiling, with bent head, as if listening, all expectation, all curiosity, yet half afraid, he pointed with one hand to the cross, with the other to himself, and on his lips the words seemed to tremble:—

"There cometh one after me whose shoe's-latchet I am not worthy to unloose."

IV

After a tedious morning spent in touching for the king's evil, Francis I felt a desire for something beautiful to divert his mind from the spectacle of deformity and sickness. He resolved to visit Leonardo's studio. Accordingly, with a few attendants, he presented himself at Cloux.

All day the painter had worked at his Baptist. His room was large and cold, with a brick floor and a high-raftered ceiling. The last slanting rays of the sun streamed in through the narrow window; and Leonardo was hastening to finish his day's task before the coming on of twilight. When he heard voices and footsteps under the window, he said to Melzi:—

"I admit no one. Say I am ill."

Francesco went out obediently to stop the intruders; but seeing the king he bowed respectfully and threw open the doors. Leonardo had barely time to cover the portrait of La Gioconda; this he always did if he expected strangers.

Francis entered; he was richly but gaudily dressed, with excess of jewellery and gold trimmings. He was twenty-four years of age, well built, tall and strong, majestic, and of agreeable manners. Yet there was something displeasing in his face, something at once sensual and sly, suggestive of a satyr.

He refused to allow Leonardo to kneel, bowed respectfully himself, and even embraced the aged painter.

"It is long since we saw each other, Maître Léonard," he said. "How is your health? Do you paint much? Have you done many new pictures? What is that one?" and he pointed to the curtained Monna Lisa.

"An old portrait, sire, which your Majesty has already seen."

"Let me see it again. The oftener one sees your pictures the more one admires them."

The painter hesitated, but to his annoyance a courtier removed the veil, and La Gioconda was revealed.

The king, throwing himself on a chair, gazed long without a word. "Marvellous!" he exclaimed at last. "That is the fairest woman I ever saw! Who is she?"

"Madonna Lisa, wife of a Florentine citizen."

"Did you paint it lately?"

"Ten years ago."

"Is she still beautiful?"

"Sire, she is dead."

"Maître Léonard da Vinci," said Saint Gelais, the court poet, "worked five years at yon portrait, and has left it unfinished—so at least he avers."

"Unfinished?" cried the king. "I pray you, what does it lack? She seems alive—on the point to speak. You are enviable, Maître Léonard! Five years with that woman! Had she not died, I trow, you would not have finished it yet." He laughed, and the resemblance to a satyr increased. It never occurred to him that Monna Lisa might have been a faithful wife.

"I see, sir, you have a pretty taste in women," resumed His Majesty gaily. "What shoulders! what a bosom! And one may guess at further beauties!"

Leonardo remained silent; he grew pale, and his eyes were fixed on the ground.

"To paint such a likeness," continued the king, "'tis not enough to be an artist; you must fathom all the secrets of a woman's heart, that labyrinth, that tangle, impossible to the devil himself. Yon lady seems modest; she folds her hands like a nun; but wait a bit; guess what is in her heart."

"Souvent femme varie
Bien fol qui s'y fie!"

Leonard stepped aside, as if to move another picture to the light, and Saint Gelais whispered scandal to his master concerning Leonardo's supposed tastes in matters of the heart.

Francis seemed surprised, but shrugged his shoulders indulgently, and turned to an unfinished cartoon on an easel near the portrait.

"What is this?"

"Bacchus, methinks," said the poet, pointing to the thyrsus.

"And this?"

"It would seem, Bacchus again," said Saint Gelais.

"The hair and the breast are like a girl," said the king; "it has the same smile as La Gioconda."

"A hermaphrodite then," returned the poet; and repeated Plato's fable of the original men-women, and the origin of the passion of Love. "Maître Léonard would fain restore the primitive type," he concluded mockingly.

Francis turned to the painter.

"Resolve our doubts, Master," he said; "is it Bacchus or a hermaphrodite?"

"Sire," said Leonardo, reddening, "it is St. John the Baptist."

The king shook his head in bewilderment. This mixture of the sacred and the profane seemed blasphemous to him, yet rather attractive. Not that the blasphemy mattered; everyone knows that painters have queer fancies!

"I will buy both pictures," he said; "the Bacchus—I mean the Baptist, and Lisa la Gioconda. What is the price?"

"Your Majesty," began the painter, embarrassed, "they are not yet finished."

"Tut, man! St. John you can finish at once, and as for Lisa, I will not have her touched. I want her with me at once, hear you? Tell me the price, and fear not. I will not try to cheapen her."

What was Leonardo to say to this frivolous coarse man? How explain what the portrait was to its painter, and why no price could induce him to give it up?

"You will not speak? Then I will name a price myself. Three thousand crowns? How say you? 'Tis not enough? Three and a half?"

"Sire," implored the artist, his voice shaking; "I can assure you—"

"Well! well! Maître Léonard, four thousand?"

A murmur of astonishment came from the courtiers. Not Lorenzo de' Medici himself had ever set such a price upon a picture. Leonardo raised his eyes in unutterable confusion. He was ready to fall on his knees, to beg as men beg for their lives, that he might not be robbed of La Gioconda. Francis took his embarrassment for gratitude, rose to leave, and as a farewell, again embraced the painter.

"Then that's settled. Four thousand crowns, and the money is ready for you when you choose. Tomorrow I shall send for her. Make yourself easy. I will hang her with such honour as shall content you. I know her value! I will preserve her for posterity!"

When the king had gone, Leonardo sank into a chair, looking at his picture, scarce believing what had happened. Absurd, childish devices suggested themselves to him: he would hide the portrait; he would refuse to give it up, though threatened with capital punishment. He would send Melzi to Italy with it—nay, he would flee himself.

Night fell. Francesco looked several times into the room, but did not venture to speak. Leonardo still sat before Monna Lisa, his face pale and rigid as that of a corpse. At midnight he went into Francesco's room.

"Get up. We must go to the castle. I have to see the king."

"Master, it is late. You are weary. You have not the strength. Let us wait for the morrow."

"No, it must be now. Light me the lantern, and come with me. If you will not, I will go alone."

Francesco rose and dressed himself, and they went together to the castle.

V

The walk took a quarter of an hour; the path was steep and badly paved. Leonardo moved slowly, leaning on the young man's arm. It was a warm and starless night, black as the pit. The boughs of the trees swayed painfully under the gusts of wind. There were lights in the castle windows, and music made itself heard. The king was supping late with a small company, and amusing himself by making the young ladies of the court drink from a silver cup chased with obscene figures. Among these ladies was his sister Marguerite, called "The Pearl of Pearls," and celebrated for her beauty and erudition. "The art of pleasing was more important to her than daily bread," so said her admirers. At heart, however, she was indifferent to all except her brother, to whom she was devotedly attached. His weaknesses seemed to her charms, his vices strength, his faun's mask the countenance of Apollo. For him she declared herself ready not merely to scatter the ashes of her body to the wind, but to sell her immortal soul. Francis abused her affection, for he made use of her not only in difficulties and dangers, but also in his amorous adventures.

Leonardo's coming was announced; and Francis, having sent for him to the supper-room, advanced with his sister to greet him. The cavaliers and court-ladies watched the artist's entry with glances half respectful, half contemptuous. The tall old man, with the long hair, the melancholy face, the nervous manner, seemed to have dropped from an alien sphere, and sent a chill through the company as if he had come out of a snowstorm.

"Ah! Maître Léonard!" cried the king with his customary cordiality, "you are a rare guest. What shall we offer you? You eat no flesh, I know; but you will partake of sweetmeats and fruit?"

"I thank your Majesty. Sire, you will excuse me; I am fain to speak a few words with your Majesty."

Francis led him aside, and asked if Marguerite might be present.

"I venture to hope that her Highness will intercede for me," said Leonardo with a bow. Then he spread out his hands to the sovereign. "I come, sire, about my picture, which your Majesty has desired to buy—the portrait of Monna Lisa."

"Had we not agreed upon the price?" asked the king.

"I come not about money," said Leonardo.

"Then what is the matter?"

The painter felt again that to speak of La Gioconda to this indifferent affable young monarch was impossible. Nevertheless he forced himself to say:—

"Sire, be merciful to me. Do not take this portrait from me. It shall be yours; I ask no money for it. Only leave it with me till—my death."

He paused, looking entreatingly at Marguerite.

The king shrugged his shoulders and frowned.

"Sire!" said the young lady, "grant the prayer of Maître Léonard. He deserves it! Be compassionate!"

"What, Madame Marguerite, are you on his side? A plot, I declare, a plot! a plot!"

Laying her hand on her brother's shoulder, she whispered:—"Do you not see? He still loves her!"

"But she is dead!"

"Do men never love the dead? You said yourself she lived in her portrait! Leave him his memorial of her. Do not afflict the old man!"

Francis had a dim recollection of having somewhere heard of eternal unions of soul, of fidelity, of love that had no grossness in it. He felt inspired by magnanimity.

"You have a sweet intercessor, Maître Léonard. Be of good cheer. I will do as you ask; only remember the picture belongs to me, and you shall receive the money at once."

Something wistful and plaintive in Leonardo's eyes touched the king, and he tapped him good-naturedly.

"Fear not! I give you my word! None shall part you from your Lisa!"

Marguerite smiled and her eyes shone. She gave her hand to the painter, who kissed it fervently and in silence.

The band struck up and dancing began. No one thought anymore of the uncourtly guest, who had come in like a shadow and vanished again into the starless night.

VI

As soon as the king went away the usual quiet settled upon Amboise. Leonardo worked on at his St. John, but as the picture advanced it became more difficult, and his progress was less rapid. Sometimes in the twilight he would lift the veil from the portrait of Monna Lisa, gaze long at it, and then at St. John, which stood beside it. Apparently he was comparing the two pictures. Francesco, watching breathlessly, fancied at those times that the expression of the two faces, the woman's and the youth's, mysteriously changed; they stood out from the canvas like apparitions, and under the fixed gaze of the painter lived with a supernatural life. St. John grew like Monna Lisa, and like Leonardo himself, even as a son resembles his parents.

Meantime the Master's health was declining. Melzi begged him to rest and leave his work, but this he resolutely refused to do. One day, in the autumn of 1518, he was greatly indisposed. He desisted earlier than usual from his work, and asked Francesco to help him to his bedroom. The winding stair was steep, and often of late he had been unable to ascend it without assistance. So Francesco supported him, and he went up slowly, halting frequently to recover his breath. Suddenly he staggered and fell into the young man's arms. Francesco called the old servant Battista Villanis. Together they lifted the Master and carried him to his bedroom.

He lay six weeks in bed, refusing all medical advice according to his wont. His right side was paralysed, his right arm useless. The winter found him better, but his recovery was slow. He was ambidextrous, but required both hands at once for his work. With the left he drew, with the right he painted; and he maintained that it was this division of labour which had given him superiority over other painters. He feared now that painting had become impossible to him. In the early days of December he rose from his bed, and before long came downstairs to his painting-room, but did not resume his work.

One day at the hour of siesta, Francesco, not finding him in the upper rooms, cautiously opened the studio door and looked in. Of late Leonardo had been increasingly disinclined to society; he spent many hours alone, and would allow no one to enter unbidden. Francesco, peeping now through the half-opened door, saw him standing before the picture of St. John, and trying to paint with his disabled hand. His face was distorted by the anguish of effort, the corners of his mouth drooped, the brows were contracted, and the strands of grey hair, falling over his forehead, were bathed in sweat. His fingers would not obey him, and the brush shook in the hands of the great Master as in the hand of a clumsy beginner. With bated breath Francesco watched this last struggle between the living spirit and the dying body.

VII

THAT YEAR THE WINTER WAS very severe. Drifting ice broke the bridges of the Loire, people were frozen on the roads, wolves came into the suburbs of the town, and prowled even under the windows of the château. One morning Francesco found a half-frozen swallow on the verandah and carried it to Leonardo, who revived it with the warmth of his breath, and established it in a cage near the fire, meaning to restore it to liberty in the spring. The Master no longer attempted to paint, and had hidden the unfinished picture with his brushes and paints in the darkest corner of the studio. The days went by in idleness. Sometimes the notary visited them and talked of the harvests, the salt tax, and the comparative merits of Languedoc and Limousin sheep. Sometimes Francesco's confessor came, Fra Guglielmo, an Italian by birth, but long settled at Amboise, a simple pleasant old man, who could tell stories about the Florence of his youth which made Leonardo laugh.

The early twilight came on, and the visitors took their departure. Then for hours at a time Leonardo would pace up and down the room, occasionally glancing at Astro. Now more than ever the cripple seemed to him a living reproach, the mockery of the one great aim of his life, the making of wings for men. Astro sat in a corner, his feet drawn up under him, winding long strips of linen on a stick, whittling sticks, carving tops, or with his eyes blinking he would rock himself slowly and, smiling, sing his unchanging song:—

"Cucurlu! Curlu!
Eagles and cranes,
Up they flew!"

At last it became quite dark, and silence descended upon the house. Out of doors the boughs of the old trees creaked and roared in the storm, and the roar was like the voice of malignant giants. The eerie howling of wolves was heard in the outskirts of the forest. Francesco piled logs on the fire, and Leonardo sat down beside it. The young man played on the lute and could sing very pleasantly. He tried to dispel the Master's melancholy by his music; once he sang him an old song composed by Lorenzo Il Magnifico for the "Mask of Bacchus and Ariadne," a favourite with Leonardo, who had known it in his youth:—

"Quant' è bella giovinezza
Ma sen fugge tuttavia?
Chi vuol esser lieto, sia;
Di doman non v'è certezza."

The Master listened, greatly moved; he remembered the summer night, the dark shadows, the brilliant moonlight in the lonely street, the sounds of the lute from the marble loggia, the same tender love-song. And he remembered, too, his thoughts of La Gioconda. Francesco, sitting at the old man's feet, looked up and saw that tears were falling from the fading eyes.

Sometimes Leonardo would read over his old diaries, and occasionally he still wrote in them, but of the subject which now chiefly occupied his thoughts—Death.

"Thou see'st that thy hope and thy desire to return to thy native land, and to thy old life, is like the desire of the moth for the flame, and that Man (who, ceaseless in desire, joyous in impatience, ever awaits a new spring, and thinketh that his desire is slow in its fulfilment) does not know that he expecteth but his own destruction and his end. But this expectation is the quintessence of nature, the soul of the elements, and finding itself in the soul of man, it is the desire to return from the body unto Him who made it."

"In nature nothing exists but Force and Movement; and force is the volition of happiness, the eternal striving of the universe after final equilibrium and the Prime Mover."

"Every part desires to be united with its whole that it may escape imperfection."

"As the day well spent gives pleasant dreams, life well lived shall give a happy death."

"Every evil leaves bitterness in the memory, except the greatest evil, which is death, for it destroys the memory together with the life."

"When I thought I was learning to live, I was but learning how to die."

"The outward necessity of nature corresponds with the outward necessity of reason: everything is reasonable, all is good, because all is necessary."

Thus his reason justified death, the will of the Prime Mover; yet in the depth of his heart something rebelled.

Once he dreamed that he awoke in a coffin buried alive under the earth, and with desperate resolution and panting for breath he strove to raise the lid of his prison.

Next morning he told Francesco of his desire that he should lie unburied till the first signs of decomposition should show themselves. He still loved life with a blind unreasoning love, still clung to it and dreaded death as a black pit into which that day or the next he would fall with a cry of the utmost terror. All the consolations of reason, all he had said of divine necessity and the will of the Prime Mover, vanished like smoke before this shrinking of the flesh. He would have relinquished his immortality for one ray of earthly sunshine, one waft of the spring, for the perfume of expanding leaves, for a bunch of yellow flowers from the Monte Albano, where he had been a happy child.

At night, when he could not sleep, Francesco would read to him from the Gospels. Never had they seemed to him so new, so rare in excellence, so little understood of men. Some sayings, as he thought out their meaning, deepened for him like wells.

"Thou shalt not tempt the Lord thy God." Was this indeed the answer to the question of his whole life, "Shall not men have wings?"

"And having ended all his temptation, the devil departed from him *for a season*." What did that mean? When did the devil return to him again?

Words which might have seemed to him full of the greatest error, contrary to experience and natural law, still did not repel him.

"If ye have faith as a grain of mustard-seed, ye shall say unto this mountain, Remove hence to yonder place, and it shall remove."

He had always thought that the final knowledge and the final faith would lead by different paths to the same goal, the blending of outward and inward necessity, the will of man and the will of God. Yet was not the sting of the words in the fact that *to have faith*, even as a grain of mustard-seed, was more difficult than to see the mountain remove unto yonder place?

But there was a saying of Christ's still more enigmatical: "I thank thee, Father, that thou hast hid these things from the wise and prudent, and hast revealed them unto babes." How reconcile this with the injunction, "Be ye wise as serpents"?

And, again, "Consider the lilies of the field, they toil not neither do they spin. Take no thought saying what shall we eat or what shall we drink, for after all these things do the Gentiles seek, and your heavenly Father knoweth that ye have need of all these things."

Leonardo recalled his discoveries and inventions, the machines for giving men power over nature, and asked himself:—

"Is all this care for the body—what shall we eat and what shall we drink, and the like—is it mammon worship? Is there nothing in human toil, in knowledge, but the mere profit? Is knowledge like Martha, who is careful and troubled about many things, but not about the one thing needful? Is love like Mary, who has chosen the good part and sitteth at the Master's feet?"

He knew by experience the temptations inseparable from knowledge.

It seemed to the dying man that he was already face to face with the black, the dreadful pit, into which, if not today then tomorrow, he too must fall with a last despairing cry:—

"My God, my God, why hast thou forsaken me?"

VIII

Sometimes of a morning, when he looked through the frosted windows at the deep snow, the grey sky, the frozen water, he thought the winter would never end. But in February there came a breath of warmth. Drops trickled noisily from the icicles at the sunny side of the houses, the sparrows twittered, and the trees were girt with dark circles where the snow had melted, the buds swelled, and patches of blue sky were seen among the clouds. Francesco placed his master's chair in a sunny window, and for hours the old man would sit quite still with bent head, his wasted hands resting upon his knees. The swallow which had been rescued from the first frost now flew and circled about the room, perched on Leonardo's shoulder, and allowed herself to be handled and kissed on the head. Suddenly she would start up and again fly round the ceiling with impatient cries as if scenting the spring. He followed every turn of her lithe body, every movement of her pinions. The old idea of wings for men stirred within him.

One day he opened a large chest which contained his manuscript-books, stray drawings and sketches, chiefly mechanical, jottings from his two hundred "Books of Nature." All his life he had been meaning to bring order into this chaos, to sort the fragments and unite them in one whole, one great "Book of the Universe." He knew that among them were ideas and discoveries which could materially shorten the labours of those men who were to come after him. He knew also that he had delayed too long, that it was now too late, that all his sowing would fail of fruit, that all his scientific material would perish like the *Cenacolo*, the Colossus, the "Battle of Anghiari." And this, because in science as in art he had only desired with a wingless desire, had begun and not finished, had accomplished nothing. He foresaw that men would seek what he had found, would discover what he had already discovered, would walk in his paths, in his very steps; but would pass him by, would forget him as though he had never lived. In the chest he found a small manuscript-book, yellow with age, and entitled "Birds." Of late years he had scarcely occupied himself with the flying-machine, though he still often thought of it. Today, watching the flight of his tame swallow, a new idea had come to him, a new design had perfected itself in his mind, and he determined to make a last attempt, indulging the last vain hope that by the finally successful making of wings for men the whole labour of his life would be justified.

He entered on this new task with the same resolution, with the same feverish haste which he had expended on the St. John. Ceasing to brood over death, conquering his weakness, forgetting his food and his sleep, he sat for whole days and nights over his calculations and his drawings. Francesco watching him sometimes feared this was not work but the delirium of a sick mind. With increasing alarm he noticed how the Master's face became distorted under the desperate effort of will, under the violent desire for the impossible—which men may not seek with impunity.

The week went by and Francesco never left him, not even to sleep. But a night came when deadly weariness overcame the youth; he threw himself on a chair by the fire and dozed. The morning came grey through the window, the swallow wakened and chirruped. Leonardo was still sitting at his work-table, a pen in his hand; he was greatly bent, his head almost touching the paper. Suddenly he trembled strangely, the pen dropped and his head fell. He made an effort to rise, tried to call Francesco, but could make no sound. Heavily and helplessly he rolled with his whole weight upon the table and overturned it. Melzi, awakened by the crash, sprang to his feet, to find the Master lying on the floor, his candle extinguished, his papers scattered, the terrified swallow flapping her wings against the rafters overhead. He realised that this was a second stroke.

For some days Leonardo lay unconscious, making occasional

mutterings, always of mathematics. When he came to himself he at once asked for his sketches of the flying-machine.

"Nay, Master. Ask of me anything else, but I cannot let you work till you have mended somewhat," replied Francesco.

"Where have you put my sketches?" he demanded, angrily.

"I have locked them in the attic."

"Give me the key."

"Nay, Master, what can you do with the key?"

"Give it me this instant."

Francesco hesitated; the invalid's eyes flashed with wrath. Not to excite him, the young man gave the key. Leonardo hid it under his pillow and seemed satisfied. His recovery after this was more rapid than could have been hoped. In the beginning of April he was able again to play chess with Fra Guglielmo.

One night Francesco, sleeping on his customary bench by the Master's side, started up in alarm, for he could not hear Leonardo's usually heavy breathing. The night-light had been extinguished; he relit it hastily, and found the invalid's bed empty; he waked Villanis and they visited all the rooms on that floor, but Leonardo was not there. Francesco was going downstairs, when he remembered the sketches hidden in the attic. He hastened thither and found the door unlocked. Leonardo, half-dressed, was seated on the floor before an old box, which he was using as a table. By the light of a tallow candle he was writing, while he muttered rapidly as if delirious. His glowing eyes, his matted hair, his brows violently contracted, his sunken helpless mouth, his whole appearance was so strange and alarming to Francesco that for a few minutes he dared not enter.

Suddenly Leonardo snatched up a pencil and drew it across a page of figures so violently that it broke. Then he looked round, saw his pupil, rose and tottered towards him.

"I told you, Francesco," he said quickly and bitterly, "that I should soon make an end. Now I have finished. So have no fear, I shall not work anymore. 'Tis enough. I have grown old and dull; more dull than Astro. I know nothing at all. What I have known I forget. Is it for me to think of wings? To the devil even with the wings!"

And seizing his papers furiously he tore and trampled them.

From that day his health grew worse. He returned to his bed, and Melzi foresaw that he would not again rise from it. Sometimes for whole days he lay in a trance.

Francesco was devout, and whatever the Church taught he believed without question. Alone of Leonardo's pupils he had not fallen under the influence of those "fatal spells"; that "evil eye" attributed to the Master. Though Leonardo did not observe the Church ceremonials, his young companion divined by the instinct of love that he was not impious. The lad did not try to penetrate further into the great man's opinions. Now, however, the thought that he might die unabsolved from errors, perhaps from heresies, was torture to the pious youth. He was afraid to address the Master on the subject, but he would have given his life to save him.

One evening Leonardo, seeing his anxious face, asked him what were his thoughts. Francesco answered with some embarrassment.

"Fra Guglielmo came this morning and wanted to see you. I told him it was impossible—"

The Master looked at his young attendant and saw alarm, entreaty, hope on his face.

"Francesco, this was not what you were thinking. Why will you not tell me?"

The pupil was silent, his eyes downcast. Leonardo understood; he turned away and frowned. He had always wished to die as he had lived, in complete liberty; in the truth, so far as he knew it. But he had compassion on Francesco. Could he, in these last hours of his life, embitter a simple heart, bring offences once more upon one of these "little ones"?

He looked again at his pupil; laid his wasted hand on the lad's hand and said with a quiet smile:—

"My son, send to Fra Guglielmo and bid him come tomorrow. I wish to confess and to communicate. Send also for Maître Guillaume."

Francesco did not answer—he kissed Leonardo's hand in passionate gratitude.

IX

The next morning, Saturday in Passion Week, April 23rd, Maître Guillaume the notary came, and Leonardo imparted to him his last wishes. He bequeathed four hundred florins to his brothers in token of reconciliation; to Francesco Melzi he left his books, scientific apparatus, machines, manuscripts, and the remainder of the salary due to him from the royal treasury; to Battista Villanis, his household furniture, and the half of the vineyard outside the walls of Milan; the other half he left to his pupil Andrea Salaino. Maturina was to have a dress of good black cloth, a cloth cap trimmed with fur, and two ducats. Melzi was named executor, and the ordering of the funeral was entrusted to him. Francesco was solicitous that all should be arranged in a manner to contradict popular slanders, and make it clear that the Master had died a true son of the Catholic Church. Leonardo assented to all he proposed.

Presently Fra Guglielmo came with the Holy Viaticum, and Leonardo made his confession and received the Sacrament "according to the rites of the Church"; "in all humility and submission to the will of God," as the monk afterwards told Francesco; adding that whatever might be said against the Master he would be justified by the words of the Lord, "Blessed are the pure in heart for they shall see God." All day he suffered from breathlessness, but he survived the night, and on the morning of Easter Sunday seemed a little easier.

Francesco opened the window. Pigeons were flying in the blue air, and the rustle of their flight mingled with the chime of the Easter bells.

The dying man no longer heard nor saw what was passing around him. He imagined great weights falling and rolling on him and crushing him. With an effort he freed himself and was flying upward on gigantic wings. Again the weights fell, again he conquered them, and so on, again and again. And each time the weight was heavier, the struggle to overcome it more desperate; till at last he gave up the attempt, crying aloud a despairing cry.

He resigned himself to defeat. And then immediately he realised that the weights and the wings, the falling and the flight were all one; "above" and "below" were the same, and he was borne along on the waves of eternal motion gently as in a mother's arms.

For some days longer his body lived, but he never recovered consciousness. On the morning of May 2nd Francesco and Fra Guglielmo noticed that his breathing had grown feebler. The monk read the prayers for the dying; a little later, and the young man had closed his eyes.

The face of the dead man changed but little; it wore the expression, so frequent in his lifetime, of profound and quiet attention.

The windows were widely opened, and Francesco and the two old servants were performing the last offices for the corpse. Suddenly the tame swallow, which of late had been forgotten, flew into the room, circled over the dead man, and settled at last upon his folded hands.

He was buried at the monastery of St. Florentine, but the exact site of his grave is unknown.

Writing to Florence to the Master's brothers Francesco thus expressed himself:—

"I cannot tell the grief occasioned to me by the death of him who was more to me than a father. Long as I live I shall mourn him. He loved me with a great and tender love. The whole world will grieve for the loss of a man whose like Nature herself will not create again."

"May the Almighty God grant him everlasting peace!"

Epilogue

Now it so happened that just at the time when Leonardo da Vinci died, a certain young Russian courtier named Eutychius came a second time to Amboise in the train of Karachiarov, the Russian ambassador. On his journey this young courtier, who brought a gift of gold and of priceless Persian falcons for King Francis, visited Florence, and had seen the bas-relief on the Campanile, which represented Dædalus experimenting with waxen wings. It had given Leonardo in his boyhood the first idea of Wings for Man; and now it was of interest to the young Russian, who in his spare time, for pleasure, was painting an ecclesiastical icon of "The Winged Precursor." With vague and half-prophetic awe he contemplated the contrast between the material wings constructed by Dædalus, who was perhaps assisted by demons, and the spiritual wings—"upon which pure souls rise to God"—of the "Incarnate Angel," the Precursor, St. John the Baptist.

While at Amboise, Eutychius one day obtained leave to visit the château of Cloux, where the deceased Master, Leonardo da Vinci, had lived. The party was received by Francesco Melzi, who showed them the studio and all it contained. They inspected the strange instruments, the apparatus for the study of the laws of sound, the great crystal eye for experiments on sight, the diving-bell, the anatomical drawings, the designs for engines of war. All this was interesting; but for Eutychius the supreme attraction was the broken frame of a wing resembling the pinion of a great swallow. He learned from Melzi of its history and its purpose; and strange thoughts rose in his breast as he remembered Dædalus on the marble tower of Santa Maria del Fiore.

Presently he stood in bewilderment before the dead Leonardo's picture of St. John the Baptist. The appearance of the Forerunner was almost that of a woman; yet he carried the reed cross, and was clothed with camel's hair. He was not like the Winged Precursor familiar to the painter of icons; but his charm was irresistible. What was the significance of the subtle smile with which he pointed to the cross of Golgotha?

Eutychius stood spell-bound, scarce listening to the animadversions of his fellows. "What? this beardless, naked, effeminate youth, the Precursor? Not of Christ, then, but of Antichrist—accursed forever!"

Eutychius heard without heeding; and when he came away the mysterious figure of the wingless one, fair as a woman, with flowing locks like Dionysus, pointing to the cross—haunted him like a vision.

The young Russian painter was lodged in an attic beside the dovecot; and had arranged his working place in the recess of the dormer-window.

He busied himself with the painting of the icon, already nearly completed, of St. John the Baptist. The saint stood on a sunburnt hill, round, like the edge of a globe. It was bordered by the purple sea, and canopied by the blue vault of heaven. The figure carried in its hand a head, which was the duplicate of his own, but seemed that of a corpse. Thus Eutychius had tried to show that the man who has slain in himself all that is human may attain to a more than human flight. His face was terrible and strange; his gaze like the gaze of an eagle, fixed upon the sun. His hair and beard floated on the blast, his raiment was like the plumage of a bird. His limbs were long and gave an impression of singular lightness. On his shoulder were set great swan-like wings, extended over the tawny earth and the purple sea.

Tonight Eutychius had little more to do than to touch the inner side of the plumes with gold. But his attention wandered, he thought of Dædalus and of Leonardo; he remembered the face of the wingless youth in the Master's last picture, and found it eclipsing that of the winged one which he had drawn himself. His hand grew heavy and uncertain; the brush fell; his strength failed. He left his room and wandered for hours along the banks of the silent river.

The sun had set; the pale green sky, the evening stars were reflected in the water, but in the east clouds were rising, and summer lightning quivered in the air as if waving fiery wings.

Returning, he lit the lamp before the icon of the Virgin, and threw himself on his bed. He could not sleep, but lay tossing and shivering feverishly for hour after hour, fancying weird rustlings and whispers in the stillness, and remembering all the eerie tales of the Russian folklore.

Wearied and wakeful, Eutychius tried to read. He selected an old book at random, and the familiar Russian legend of the "Crown of the Kingdom of Babylon," and of the world-wide sovereignty destined by God for the land of Russia. Then Eutychius turned a page and read another legend, that of "The White Hood."

In days of yore Constantine the emperor, having accepted the

Christian faith and received absolution for his sins from Sylvester the pope, desired to give the pontiff a kingly crown. But an angel, appearing unto him, bade him give a crown not of earthly but of spiritual supremacy—a White Hood like unto a monkish cowl. Nevertheless the Roman Church laid claim to temporal no less than to spiritual power; wherefore the angel appeared to the pope and commanded him to send the Hood to Philotheus, the Patriarch of Constantinople; and when he would have retained it, there appeared unto the Patriarch another vision: Constantine the emperor and Sylvester the pope, bidding him send on the Hood yet further, into the country of Russia, to Novgorod the Great.

"For," said Sylvester in this dream, "the first Rome has fallen by her pride and self-will; and Constantinople, the second Rome, is like to perish by the fury of the infidel; but in the third Rome, which shall be in the land of Russia, the light of the Holy Ghost is already shining, and at the last all Christian nations shall be united in the Russian dominion under the shadow of the Orthodox faith."

Each time Eutychius read these tales, a vague and boundless hope filled his soul. His heart beat and his breath caught, as though he were standing on the edge of a precipice. For it seemed that the legend of the Babylonian kingdom was prophetic of earthly greatness; that of the White Hood, of heavenly glory for his native land. However poor, however wretched she might be now in comparison with other countries, still she was to be the third Rome, the new Zion; and the rays of the rising sun were destined to shine on the seventeen golden domes of the Russian church of St. Sophia, the Wisdom of God. And yet, he asked himself, how should it be that the White Hood, the third, the holiest Rome, should unite itself with the hateful crown of Nebuchadnezzar, who had been cursed of God, whose city was Babylon, and accursed in the Book of Revelation. The young painter's effort to solve the riddle brought fantastic vision to his hot brain.

He fell asleep, and he too dreamed a dream:

He saw a Woman in shining garments, with flaming countenance and fiery wings, standing among fleeting clouds, her feet on the crescent moon; over her was a seven-pillared tabernacle, with the inscription:—

"Wisdom hath builded her an house."

Prophets and patriarchs surrounded her, saints and angels, thrones and dominions and powers, and all the company of Heaven. And among the prophets at Wisdom's very foot stood John the Precursor with his white plumes as on the icon, *but wearing the face of Leonardo da Vinci*, who had dreamed of wings for men. And behind the Woman, golden cupolas and pinnacles of churches innumerable glowed like fire in the azure sky; and beyond them stretched a gloriously boundless expanse, which Eutychius recognised as the land of Russia.

Belfries shook with a triumphant peal; angels sang victorious Alleluia; the seven archangels smote their wings, and the seven thunders spoke. And above the fire-clothed Woman, Hagia Sophia, the Wisdom of God, the heavens opened, and bright as the sun—terrible—shone the White Hood, the heavenly head-dress, over the land of Russia.

EUTYCHIUS AWOKE. HE OPENED THE windows, and to him was wafted the fragrance of leaves and grasses washed by rain. The sun had not yet risen, but gold and purple decked the place of his coming—the skyey verge above the woods, and the river, and the fields. The town still slept in twilight; only the belfry of St. Hubert glistened with a pale green light. The hush was full of great expectation. Far away on the sand-banks of the Loire the white swans were calling.

Suddenly, like a live coal, the sun shone out behind the forest. Something like music passed across the earth and the heaven. Pigeons shook their wings and rose in circles. Day, entering the window, fell full on the icon of the Forerunner; the wings, extended over lands and seas, flashed and sparkled in the morning radiance, as if informed with supernatural life.

Eutychius, dipping his brush into crimson, wrote these words on the scroll upon the icon, under the Winged Precursor:—

"Behold I will send my messenger before my face, and he shall prepare my way before me."

THE END

A Note About the Author

Dmitry Merezhkovsky (1866–1941) was a Russian novelist and poet. Born in Saint Petersburg, Merezhkovsky was raised in a prominent political family. At thirteen, while a student at the St. Petersburg Third Classic Gymnasium, Dmitry began writing poetry. Soon, he earned a reputation as a promising young writer and enrolled at the University of Saint Petersburg, where he completed his PhD with a study on Montaigne. In 1892, he published *Symbols. Poems and Songs*, a work inspired by Poe and Baudelaire in which Merezhkovsky explores his increasingly personal religious ideas. In 1895, he published *The Death of the Gods*, the first novel in his groundbreaking *Christ and Antichrist Trilogy*. With these novels, Merezhkovsky was recognized as a cofounder of the Russian Symbolist movement. In 1905, his apocalyptic Christian worldview seemed to come to fruition in the First Russian Revolution, which he supported through poetry and organizing groups of students and artists. Formerly a supporter of the Tsar, Merezhkovsky was involved in leftist politics by 1910, but soon became disillusioned with the rise of the radical Bolsheviks. In the aftermath of the October Revolution, Merezhkovsky and his wife, the poet Zinaida Gippius, were forced to flee Russia. Over the years, they would find safe harbor in Warsaw and Paris, where Merezhkovsky continued to write works of nonfiction while advocating for the Russian people. Toward the end of his life, he came to see through such leaders as Benito Mussolini, Francisco Franco, and Adolf Hitler a means of defeating Communism in Russia. Though scholars debate his level of commitment to fascist and nationalist ideologies, this nevertheless marked a sinister turn in an otherwise brilliant literary career. Nominated for the Nobel Prize in literature nine times without winning, Merezhkovsky is recognized as an important figure of the Silver Age of Russian art.

A Note from the Publisher

Spanning many genres, from non-fiction essays to literature classics to children's books and lyric poetry, Mint Edition books showcase the master works of our time in a modern new package. The text is freshly typeset, is clean and easy to read, and features a new note about the author in each volume. Many books also include exclusive new introductory material. Every book boasts a striking new cover, which makes it as appropriate for collecting as it is for gift giving. Mint Edition books are only printed when a reader orders them, so natural resources are not wasted. We're proud that our books are never manufactured in excess and exist only in the exact quantity they need to be read and enjoyed.

Printed in the USA
CPSIA information can be obtained
at www.ICGtesting.com
JSHW022203140824
68134JS00018B/838